An Obese White Gentleman
in No Apparent Distress

Also available

Aikido in Everyday Life: Giving In to Get Your Way
    by Terry Dobson and Victor Miller

It's a Lot Like Dancing: An Aikido Journey
    by Terry Dobson, edited by Riki Moss,
    with photographs by Jan E. Watson

An Obese White Gentleman in No Apparent Distress

A NOVEL BY

Riki Moss

with Terry Dobson

BLUE SNAKE BOOKS
Berkeley, California

Published by Blue Snake Books

Blue Snake Books' publications are distributed by
North Atlantic Books
P.O. Box 12327
Berkeley, California 94712

Cover and book design by Brad Greene
"The Hermit" by Robert Bly used with permission of the author.
Printed in the United States of America

An Obese White Gentleman in No Apparent Distress is sponsored by the Society for the Study of Native Arts and Sciences, a nonprofit educational corporation whose goals are to develop an educational and cross-cultural perspective linking various scientific, social, and artistic fields; to nurture a holistic view of arts, sciences, humanities, and healing; and to publish and distribute literature on the relationship of mind, body, and nature.

North Atlantic Books' publications are available through most bookstores. For further information, call 800-733-3000 or visit our Web sites at www.northatlanticbooks.com and www.bluesnakebooks.com.

Library of Congress Cataloging-in-Publication Data

Moss, Riki.
    An obese white gentleman in no apparent distress / a novel by Riki Moss with Terry Dobson.
        p.   cm.
    Summary: A novel based on the writings and recordings of Terry Dobson.
    ISBN 978-1-58394-270-3 (trade pbk.)
    1. Dobson, Terry—Fiction. 2. Martial artists—Fiction. 3. Martial arts—Fiction. 4. Aikido—Fiction. 5. Artists—Fiction. 6. Man-woman relationships—Fiction. I. Dobson, Terry. II. Title.
    PS3613.O78O24 2009
    813'.6—dc22
                                                                    2008042688

1 2 3 4 5 6 7 8 9 SHERIDAN 15 14 13 12 11 10 09

For RWO

A Note to the Reader

This is a novel based on a fictionalized/mythologized autobiography by a real person, arranged in a timeline by another real person. Another description: this is an autobiography embedded in a novel. You can open up a dialogue here about what is reality and what is truth, and which is best contained in biography or fiction—go for it, as Terry Dobson would say.

Terry told marvelous stories of his life and his teacher, Morihei Oeshiba, known as *O-sensei* ("The Grand Teacher"), incorporating the people he met and grokked (*grok:* "to understand and empathize with something or someone to the extent that the object or person becomes part of one's sense of self"—*The Urban Dictionary*) along the way. Are they true stories? Sure, in the sense that all real fiction is true, going down to the kernels, the bones of real lives.

I came to think of Terry as a man trained to mythologize himself, to live within the framework of story. It was part of his genius, I think, to convey himself thusly without betraying (aggrandizing) his own humble self as a contemporary man trying to figure things out in a complex world.

One thing he never did was write his stories down. So I did. Then I made up an audience for him out of real and imaginary friends, students, and dogs and put the two timelines together.

The one thing this book *isn't,* is a memoir.

Riki Moss
Grand Isle, Vermont
Autumn 2008

Darkness is falling through darkness,
Falling from ledge
To ledge.
There is a man whose body is perfectly whole.
He stands, the storm behind him
And the grass blades are leaping in the wind.
Darkness is gathered in folds
About his feet.
He is no one.
When we see
Him we grow calm
And sail on into the tunnels of joyful death.

   —Robert Bly, "The Hermit"

You got to have smelt a lot of mule manure
before you can sing like a hillbilly.

　—Hank Williams

Max says:

I had a terrible childhood. I was a fat miserable bully in a Park Avenue apartment. My mother was a rich divorcee with a big social life. Alone at night, I waited up for her reading in the library, devouring her books—mostly military history. Lining the entry were museum cases displaying the military uniforms of my famous ancestor, the second recipient of the Purple Heart. His name was Daniel and he was a friend of Daniel Boone and Mother worshiped them both. On the wall were portraits of these two Daniels. I used to lie on the divan between them dreaming about becoming a hero just like them.

I knew that Daniel Boone took off at the age of ten to live in the woods alone until his family tracked him down two years later. I wondered, *How did he ever do such a thing?* I was dying to know, for I thought that if I was as brave a boy, my mother might like me as much as she liked old Daniel Boone.

We had a summer place on an island in Lake Champlain in Vermont called North Hero. Here I'd practice the skills that I might need to live on my own: patience and fortitude, hardening my body to withstand pain and deprivation. If the day were cloudy, I'd drive everyone nuts asking if they thought it might rain—it was important to me that they notice I was unfazed by harsh conditions. And if it did rain, I'd slide out of the house and go down to the lake, where I would remove my clothes and walk into the freezing water up to my chin. I would remain immersed as long as I could, imagining that I was waiting for an enemy to show up so I could conquer him.

Someday, I was sure, I would be called to lie out in the rain on a freezing night and not move. I had no idea why, only that I must be prepared. I always thought of my life as training, you see. I would give the enemy until suppertime to show his evil and ugly face.

For this, I needed weapons, and my mother was happy to buy them for me. By the time I was nine, I could sink a tomahawk in a sapling at eight paces at a dead run. No erector sets for this kid; I had a bull-whip, a machete, a Bowie knife, bolas from the Argentine pampas, handcuffs for possible prisoners, a signal mirror for calling in artillery or reinforcements, piano wire for garroting sentries camouflaged as fence posts, and a .22 rifle with which to terrorize the small animals in the woods.

When I was eleven, I would sometimes wake up on stormy nights; tiptoeing past my sleeping brother and stepbrothers, I would steal out into the forest to stand watch. Beneath the lashing trees, I would slither through the underbrush to spy on a trail, fantasizing Iroquois, Malaccan pirates, or graceful Masai warriors armed with lion-spears. Finally, soaked and shivering beyond control, I'd slip back into the house to make my silent report to the portraits of the Daniels, imagining them on the walls of our library in New York.

They never failed to listen attentively, those two "long hunters," warriors who lived in a time when panthers roamed the outskirts of Philadelphia, when a family's life might hinge on a baby's cough, when "captured by the enemy" meant that before the Shawnee women roasted you alive, they first tore out your fingernails with their teeth.

The Daniels presided in noble silence at the telepathic debriefing of their tired descendant-at-arms. "Well done, Scout," I would hear them reply, and I would creep back to bed confirmed in valor.

North Hero, Vermont; an ice storm

Max lies in bed listening to a radio commentator jubilantly declare the end of the year 1984. The usually reasonable voice is celebratory, edged with hysteria, as if we'd magically avoided George Orwell's prophecy of a totalitarian state in 1984, but only by the skin of our teeth. No, Max begs to differ, it's been 1984 in America since McCarthy, and anyway there's still a few days left.

His bed is a platform built over the kitchen woodstove, now cold. He's sleeping in the kitchen because it's winter and the rest of the house, being a summer place built around the turn of the century, is uninsulated, half of the windows broken out, one of them with a tree branch protruding partway across the room to the crumbling chimney.

He'd built his bed too close to the ceiling to sit upright; he has to squirm out like a screw, kicking through the bedclothes tangled at his feet, taking care not to fall down the steep ladder. Shivering in the freezing kitchen, he feels washed through with a terrible loneliness, a beached sea creature noticing that feet will be needed for the next part of its life. He pulls on his clothing from the pile on the nearest chair, sits down, and sticks his feet in his boots.

The commentator has switched to the weather. A major ice storm is heading for the islands out of Canada. Thousands of animals have been killed, woodlands decimated, highways closed, power lines down, Montreal in a panic. It's suggested that anyone left on the islands evacuate immediately; after that the National Guard will close off access.

A message from a humorless God, Max tells himself; don't argue. He begins throwing clothes in his duffel. He'll save himself and leave his home to the wildlife—from the sounds in the walls, they've already settled in—for safekeeping. A good meal, some conversation, a date even would do him good. He'll hole up in town and call a friend. There must be some woman who remembers him fondly; he has an address book filled with names coded by state, it's probably still in his duffel bag, unpacked from California. He'll get a hot bath, read the *New York Times*, eat brunch at the Zone Out, and take in a movie: that *Rambo* rerun at the Nickelodeon.

After the storm subsides, he can come back, if there's anything left. Or not.

The lights flicker twice. He grabs his jacket, a carton of cigarettes. Coughing, he goes out the door, locking it carefully behind him, and hurries to his truck.

Then he drives down the ice-coated route toward the highway, takes a wrong turn, and hits a cow.

Ten miles south on the next island down the chain, called, reasonably enough, South Hero, Lena Zinelli is working in her studio when her husband walks into the kitchen and starts pulling groceries out of plastic bags. He has just turned up after a three-day unscheduled disappearance. Lena doesn't get up. She carefully removes the bowl she's been throwing off the potter's wheel and slaps down another lump of clay. Ordinarily, when he shows up after one of his disappearances and cooks dinner, he's signaling the end of a fling, nothing that couldn't be talked away over a good meal, a bottle of wine. By the time he'd brought out the Rémy Martin, his romantic interlude would have been reduced to a bad patch in their otherwise flawless existence, at least when compared to the real crap other couples dealt with, like heroin addiction or transgendering or pedophilia. And really, he always felt cleansed when he came back, more in love with her than ever, as if he'd undergone a purification ritual like fasting— only more like bulimia.

Only this time, it's different. Lena knows what her husband, Julian Moon, has no idea she knows: that he thinks he's in love. Her friend Marianne had set her straight on the phone last night. Julian's been fucking a French transfer student young enough to be his sugar baby who calls herself Countess something-or-other for at least six months. She's back in Paris for *La Xmas,* and that's why Julian's shown up. It has nothing to do with reconciliation, he's just lonely. After Marianne's announcement Lena had torn through Julian's office looking for proof, which she'd found in their shared Visa statements piled on his desk. Really, she'd thought, as she'd flipped through, what kind of an asshole charges three hundred bucks every other weekend at the Plaza in Manhattan—plane tickets for two, room service, taxis, theater tickets—on their joint credit card instead of his personal business Amex. The weekly 1-800-FLOWERS was the guilt gift for her. She'd felt reasonably calm, and giddily triumphant, as if this crisis had precipitated something she wanted but didn't have the courage to demand: the end of her marriage. She'd grabbed a bottle of his best wine from his closet stash, dropped her clothes on his office floor, and continued outside to the deck. Holding the bottle aloft, she'd slid into her hot tub. She'd raised her face into the onyx night and wished the northern lights to bathe her with unequivocal affirmation.

Now here he is, calling her name from the other side of the door. "Lena," he calls, "honey, how about I bring you a glass of wine?" No way she'll let him stay here. If she isn't careful, in the morning he'll be on the sofa watching TV tennis in his underwear with a glass in his hand, sneaking the mobile out to the deck to make phone calls to France. What if he weasels his way into her bed? By New Year's Eve she'll have turned into his mother. But what is she to do? There's nothing the man won't try to lie his way out of.

The door opens. He shoulders his way into the room, hands filled with glasses and trays. She picks up the wad of clay in front of her and aims. Off it goes. It's a near miss, but effective, splattering inches over his head. Astonished, he backs away, spilling wine on the kitchen tiles. On the stove, burned mustard seeds pop out of the pan.

Max drives the 1957 cherry-red GMC pickup that once belonged to the caretaker of the estate in its heyday. When his mother had suffered a stroke in New York in the late seventies, the truck had been put on blocks in the stable and had not been driven until this spring, when he'd flown from California because Mother seemed finally to be dying. She hadn't died, not yet, so Max had stayed on. All it had taken to get the old beauty roadworthy was spark plugs and tires.

It turns over smoothly and he throws it a kiss, puts it in gear, testing the brakes as he rolls along the icy lane to the main road. His windshield wipers struggle to keep up with the accumulation of slush, leaving but a slit for him to see through. Visibility is almost zilch, dreamlike, creating a feeling of sailing into destiny, a liability when you really need to focus on the road.

He reaches the end of his lane just as the salt truck appears, crawling behind it to the drawbridge where the truck turns back, leaving him face-to-face with total blackness. He can't see the water when he crosses the bridge. He has to drive on faith, letting the road steer him, trusting it knows where it's going, turning him left, then straightening him out, tolerating him on its back.

Over the bridge, on the next island, the road has been salted, so he increases his speed to maybe twenty, thirty miles per hour—he can only guess, as there are no lights in the cab. As he glides along, the glow in the windows of houses and barns on either side of the road extinguish sequentially, *pop pop pop*. At one point, he sees a power line whipping through the broken bushes spitting sparks. From the black sky now pours a curtain of impenetrable rain. He shifts into second gear, slides between the shadows he trusts mark both sides of the road. He drives and drives, not noticing when he mistakenly veers left at a fork on a dirt road. It's only by the change in the quality of the light that he realizes he's no longer paralleling the lake; instead, he's headed west toward it. By then it's too late: he's on a slight downward turn, the brakes shuddering with the strain.

Lena stands at the window numbly watching her husband drive out of her life. Her reflection laughs back in her face. She swipes a half circle through the frost with her shirt, peers through and sees her dog, Zia, coming down the road in the rain. She must have slipped out with Julian.

Zia isn't supposed to be outside without supervision. She'd been caught several times on the road from the neighboring farm with a dazed but unharmed chicken in her mouth. The last time, the sheriff threatened to shoot her. Lena started driving the chickens back to the farm hoping to get Zia off the hook—at least, she'd told the sheriff, until things settled down at home and the dog stopped acting out.

At which point the sheriff said he had a mind to shoot them both, prompting Lena to send a large check to the Retired Officers' League and to promise to install an electric fence, which she hadn't done, feeling unequal to the challenge of zapping her dog.

She knows better than to call Zia in; begging begins the game of chase. The dog thinks her purpose in life is to protect the herd, even when the herd's but a cellular memory fragment, by settling it in a safe spot so she can race around the perimeter eating coyotes and—yes, it has been said—lions if necessary, and for this she needs her freedom. Try arguing with your dog about its purpose. She'll only come in on her own volition, so all Lena can do is prop the door open and hold her breath.

Today, it works. Throwing her mistress an indifferent glance, her eyes glittering under their hooded lashes, Zia slowly heads into the kitchen. Her big pointed feet slap the tiles. Her thick white fur glistens with ice; little icicles sprout in her ears. She settles down on the floor at Lena's feet and looks away as Lena reaches over her to turn off the stove burner. As she sweeps the burned pan into the sink, the lights flicker once, then twice, then die.

On the floor with her dog, Lena realizes she's been so absorbed, first with trying to figure out what was going on and later imagining what it would be like living alone, that she hasn't prepared for the storm. She'd known it was coming, for its progress has been tracked all week; there'd been talk of evacuating the island, until the drawbridge had lifted inexplicably and froze in the air with a two-foot gap. But what harm could come to her here in her snuggly rural house? The worst would be bedding down in front of the wood stove, snuggling under quilts with a dog.

She should at least bring in some wood.

And after that, she should get in the tub before the power crashes.

Ten minutes later, helping her nose to a couple of sniffs from the plastic snorter she keeps in an Aunt Jemima cookie jar—a birthday present from Marianne—she works her way naked along the slippery deck. Behind her, four-foot-long icicles with ends like knitting needles crash from the eaves. The rain is on its way to ice now, feeling like cat's claws on her back. Her hair freezes to her scalp as she struggles with the heavy hot tub cover, opening up a slit wide enough to slide into the jasmine-scented scum. The coke she's snorted shoots straight into her brain like a startled animal. She lies against the sharp jets feeling like a blind person in a big hot pot and listens to the noise of her little universe demolishing about her. Branches crash, trees decapitate. An icicle hits the water, bouncing against her ribs. The sensation is immediate and startling, ice on hot skin, so extreme as to be blissfully painful, the ecstasy of contradictions.

Lena lies back, feeling her old life boiling away, and soon she's laughing and crying and thrashing about, and then another icicle comes crashing down, this time much closer, so loud that it startles the dog, who gets up and trots though the door where she lowers her nose to the drafty sill.

The delicious outdoors drifts up through an inch-thick slit between the door and the jamb. Zia sticks her nose in the slot. The door moves. After working it a few more inches, she squeezes through and lopes past the hot tub to the stairs leading down to the driveway, throwing a look at her blissed-out mistress as she passes. Lena catches the movement in the corner of her eye and sits up with a groan, but it's too late, for her dog has hit the road and headed for the neighboring farm, vanishing into the forbidden, chaotic, and dangerous night that carries on its wet wind the irresistible scent of chicken.

Zia races down the driveway. She turns left toward the lake, angling behind the big cornfield for the barn where cows sway by the half-open door staring through the rain. Maneuvering between their skinny legs to the coop attached to the back of the last stall, she plucks a dozing hen from its roost and leaves. Three cows detach from the shadows and follow. Down the dark, dirty road they go, under the bowed power lines; lumbering cows trailing the dog with a chicken in her jaws. Zia turns in at her driveway. The cows stop uncertainly in the shadows of the tree line as the dog continues to the deck.

Zia climbs up the steps, eases her chicken down on the strip of dry decking under the eaves, then heads back down for a second run. The cows all follow her back to the dirt road; two of them cross it and continue behind the dog to the barn.

But the third cow hears something and slows down, a vibration in the road buzzing through her hooves and bones to the velvety recesses of her twitching ears. She stands still and turns around, clueless.

The truck tires spin at the top of the incline as Max loses control on the down slope. He peers over the steering wheel through the tiny, dirty paths made by his wipers. All he can see is blackness. He senses something ahead, in the form of a thickening void, if there is such a thing. Time slows; there's time enough to think about all this, about how the cliché of time slowing is actually true, and to wonder if his life would pass before his eyes. It doesn't. He drives into the turbid dark, feeling as though he's entering another space where, once inside, he will be different. You move through a doorway, you come out changed. He has no idea what's waiting for him there, only that his life will never be quite the same.

What's waiting for him is the cow. It expands before his eyes, its blunt face turned slightly away so that its beautiful, uncurious eye meets his gaze, drawing him on. He's about to drive right into that eye. Does it see him? He wonders about that. Marvels at the ice hardening on its matted pelt fur, the green snot-threads hanging off the thin hairs in its nostrils. He takes his foot off the brake, all the better to ponder the incoming sound of his two tons of metal plowing into all that flesh.

The impact pops the truck off the road at a forty-five degree angle to a new trajectory through the cornfield that ends at a large apple tree. The cow rises with it, hoisted on its hood.

Chasing Zia, Lena gropes along her driveway to the intersection with Yellow Barn Road, clinging to the hanging branches. She's a city girl; finding herself alone on a road without vapor lamps is right up there with *The Texas Chain Saw Massacre*. When she hears the sound of the crash, she's sure that Zia's been hit. She races across the road into the cornfield, slipping over piles of broken stalks and cow pies, until she comes upon the red truck folded up against an apple tree next to a fallen cow.

She sees a person struggle out the driver's side, and then his hazy figure heading across the field toward the flat rock in the middle of the clearing. Zia appears behind him, matching her pace to his, watching as he lowers himself carefully on the rock.

Dizzy with relief at finding her dog unhurt, Lena snaps on the leash.

Zia sits down dutifully. Lena pats her. She then calls out, "Are you all right? Hey, you, can I help you?"

The man nods weakly but remains silent, looking over her shoulder at the cow. Lena follows his gaze, turns and squats down, placing her fingers on the animal's heaving chest. She stares into the big brown eye and watches the fading of its light. She strokes the freezing flank, letting her mind drift up and away, and finally rests her head against the animal's faint heartbeat. In a moment, she feels Zia press against her, as if in a kind of embrace, and then the weight of a hand on her shoulder, its surprising warmth tracking down through the fleece of her jacket.

Lena looks up and squints through the gloom. She sees the man, still sitting on the rock, exactly as before, skinned over in ice. In a moment, they'll be frozen together, along with the dog and the dying cow. Her impression is vague, a big bearded man looking at her calmly, and—she senses this—with kindness. Ice melts on his forehead, pools down his cheeks. Tiny icicles stick on his beard. His nose is red, and his eyes filled with—what? Is it mirth? He's looking at her as if they've known each other forever, and will share the very last joke before the universe dissolves.

Someone has apparently heard the crash, for an ambulance has pulled up at the side of the road. Doors slam, men call out noisily. Lena makes an effort to unglue herself from the tableau. As she struggles to her feet, the big guy finally has something to say. He tugs off the white scarf hanging around his neck and drops it. He puts both his hands, one over the other, on her head, and says in a hoarse voice, "Born in the year of the Ox, am I thus to be cowed?" Then he allows himself to be carefully lowered on the waiting gurney and carried away.

Two days later Lena's house jumps back to mechanical life—radio clacking, water dripping, throbbing appliance motors—it's as disorienting as a herd of donkeys exploding out of the dishwasher. When the phone rings, Lena stares at it, wondering what it might want. It takes a moment for her to pick up the receiver.

"Hey, are you still alive? Did I interrupt something?" It's Marianne, calling from the Zone Out, throwing out questions without waiting for answers. "Can I still get up there? Your little island's national news, honey, you're on TV, they say the military's heading your way up the interstate, and that no one can get on or off, but really, does that mean me? Lena?"

"It's the National Guard, not the Roman Army. And no, you can't get through. No one can. Are you at the club? Rehearsing?"

"It's a disaster here, a real mess; and don't be so sanguine, it could be an invasion. It's still 1984, we're at war, or not, who knows." Marianne's been obsessed by 1984 the entire year. She's been using the dystopian theme, the idea of totalitarianism and social destruction, in her conceptual art classes to create a performance piece to send off the onerous year. Good riddance, 1984. The Arts Council has funded the project, including a stipend for Lena to make a series of masks out of papier-mâché. She made the models months ago and planned to cast the masks this week. Which is why Marianne's concerned about getting to the island; she wants to check them out. "Everyone's shown up for this rehearsal; it's kind of a hoot. Half the homeless population and all my students, they have no choice. One of them asked if Big Brother was a gang leader in the Bronx." Marianne fears her art piece could disintegrate into a toga party. She's not in a good mood. Nor is she willing to let a mere convoy of armed guys thwart her desires.

She's half listening to Lena, who's been talking about some accident across from her house. "In the cornfield, actually," Lena says. "I was out there, chasing down the fucking dog, and there was this guy sitting on a rock. He'd hit a cow. It was, I don't know, surrealistic. I felt like I'd walked into a dream. Look, I'll finish up the masks; I'll cast them and bring them down."

"You can do that by the end of the week?"

"Sure. I just won't be able to paint them."

"So what? They'll be more powerful that way. So what have we got? The Richard Nixons, the pigs. What else?"

"Iconic. Without features, they'll be iconic, right?"

"Good. OK. Hey, I can't thank you enough."

"So, the cow he hit?" Lena goes back to the accident. She's been thinking about it, off and on, about the cow and the man who seemed so OK with it all, as if finding himself with a dead cow in a frozen field talking with a strange woman had been his idea all along. "That cow, or one like her, was always wandering along that road. I told that farmer there's going to be an accident, and now there's a dead cow, and that old antique truck just totaled."

Marianne perks up at this. She has an old friend living in the islands who drives a beat-up fifty-something red pickup, she's been wanting to get in touch with this guy, she feels he could help her with this piece of crap she's involved in. Not only conceptually—he's got a great big brain—but as emotional support.

"So who was driving?" she asks.

"Some guy. He'd just killed a cow, and you'd think he'd be hysterical . . . but he was the one calming me down."

"A big guy? Maybe forty-five? Fifty?"

"What, you think you know him?"

"Not really," says Marianne, positioning her thumb to disconnect.

"Well then," Lena says, "I'll see you at the end of fucking 1984. If the roads open up."

Marianne has no problem finding Max. He's still in the hospital two days after the accident, and Burlington's a one-hospital town. After an hour in the ER enduring the misery of windshield glass tweezed from his cheeks, he would have been released, had there been anywhere for him to go, had he not seemed disoriented. So he was taken upstairs for observation, where Marianne finds him lying on top of the blankets in his hospital Johnny reading the latest *New Yorker*.

"Hi," she says. "Remember me?" She sits down on the bed and tosses him a box of chocolates from the hospital gift shop.

Max lowers the magazine and squints over his glasses. "Ms. Marianne, you little vamp." He remembers her, of course he does. She'd been the worst aikido student he'd ever had, and that was saying quite a bit.

"Yes, and how are you?"

"You look like a beautiful silver fairy in that arctic gear. You know, I've been trying to get hold of you, but you're never around." Although in truth he'd been more *thinking* of calling her, rather than *trying*.

"But my answering machine has been around, Max," Marianne says, inspecting her fingernails.

"I hate those things."

"When my friend Lena told me about running into some guy in an ice storm who'd just totaled his truck, I thought, how many fat guys in Northern Vermont could there be who manage to run over a cow just as a beautiful woman comes by walking her dog?" She flashes her big red lips like a streetlight and stares straight at him.

"Believe me, I'm sorry about not getting in touch. I didn't call anyone. But please, can't you get out of that silver thing? It's dripping on my thigh."

"Sorry. I never take it off before April. Can we unplug you?"

"Marianne, please. Nutrients are being dripped into my body as we speak."

"Hey, dork, wake up. I'm offering to take you home. Are you hurt?"

"Really? I'm feeling odd, is all. As if the impact pushed my life off a fraction to the left, know what I'm saying?"

"I normally feel that way," she says, and they both laugh.

"They put me through some tests, but came up with nothing, except a bit of idiopathic heart flutter, a little fib, nothing to worry about."

"What, are you sick or something?"

"Other than being old and tired and half frozen to death? I can't go back to North Hero. The pipes surely have burst and the mice eaten all of my cornflakes."

"So, get out of that paper sack, and I'll go find someone in charge."

"Hey, Marianne, really. Thanks. It'll only be for a few weeks. I have a gig in California, in that other life, that is, the one I'm supposed to be leading; I'll be out there until June. And then back, maybe for good."

Marianne stands up, makes a stab at organizing the multiple layers underneath her parka, and goes off to arrange for a discharge.

"I still can't believe you hit a cow," she says, as they step outside into the wrecked, dripping world and join the pedestrians filing gingerly around fallen lines, dripping branches, patches of ice on the pavement. It's eerily warm, the sun a wan glow in the low clouds.

"I don't know why everyone thinks hitting a cow is funny." He takes her arm. "Black night, black ice, black cow. You try it, missy. It's a bitch."

The studio of my dreams, Lena thinks, as she walks in from the kitchen holding a cup of tea. She gazes at the shelves stacked with unfinished work, the electric kilns waiting to be unloaded, the cart with ware for the big gas kiln in the shed. She should be in love with it, but she's not. In fact, she's having trouble working. Too much production work with no time to think or dream, and without Julian to add his support, she's going to have to churn out even more crap for the trade. She sits down on the sofa in front of the blazing wood stove, sticking her feet up on the sleeping dog. She and Julian had converted the garage together to make this beautiful space. The problem was, they weren't operating under the same premises. She wanted to make sculpture; he wanted her to make money.

She sips her tea and tells herself to concentrate on George Orwell. The last of the masks were finished, all of them released from the molds, and now were strewn about the floor drying; chalk-white featureless Proles, blocky-jawed cops, Winstons modeled after one of the Zone Out bartenders, and a bunch of stressed-out pigs, with boils and nose hair, and the prototypical skinhead for Big Brother. She hoped the faces were strong enough to be read as iconic, illustrating the isolation of a destroyed society.

She is curious about why Marianne had invited herself up to the studio. For all the projects they've collaborated on these many years, never once had Marianne volunteered to do the actual physical work on an art piece. She hires out, she lives on take-out and has a personal trainer and pays people to actualize her ideas. Could it be that Marianne had a romantic interest in Lena's assistant, Jocelyn, even though she knew he and Lena were involved? Or was it someone else?

The next morning, Lena packs the car with cartons of masks and helps the dog settle in the hatchback. It's the first time she's been able to drive out since the storm, for until today soldiers stationed at the intersections had waved everyone back to their homes. They're gone now and it's a different world, the sun has barged through the lingering clouds and melted the ice down the trunks of the few standing trees, liberating the remaining branches with startling noises like sprung whips.

The car bottoms out on the deeply rutted road. When she reaches the end of the driveway she stops to look at the cornfield, which has been blown up in her mind as a stage set weird enough to accommodate a Shakespearean tragedy—the joke-cracking ghost, dripping moisture, portentous mist—and she's disappointed to see that in the light of day, it just looks like a beat-up junkyard, strewn with dead branches, rocks, broken bottles, and plastic bags.

Along Route 2 the traffic squeezes into one narrow lane past military trucks, town work vehicles, cherry-pickers, and earthmovers lining both sides of the road. The remaining soldiers stand around, their jackets open, cutting up branches with chain saws and feeding them to the mulching machines bouncing away on the back of trucks.

Marianne's kitchen door is open. Lena comes through the pantry with Zia trailing her leash behind. A man with long gray hair, wearing a black beret, sits at the table with his back to her, looking over an open newspaper at the television perched on the kitchen counter. The volume's up: perhaps he didn't hear her, and she doesn't want to startle him, so she knocks on the wall and calls out hello.

"Hello," he says, wiggling his fingers without looking around. "We're going to get ourselves into this war, you'll see. My sweet ass we're neutral. We're too stupid to play one side against the other without getting drawn in."

"Have we met?" Lena says, pulling up a chair. He looks familiar. Perhaps just as a scruffy, friendly sort of type. He's wearing an old bathrobe open over his bare chest, jeans, and heavy gray socks. Marianne's kind of guy, she guesses, the type to tie her to the bedpost while quoting Yeats. But wouldn't Marianne have mentioned him? She unwinds the scarf around her neck and opens her jacket.

He turns around now and looks at her carefully. *As if I'm a present,* she thinks, feeling a blush on her cheeks and an urge to go stamping out the door. Instead, she stays put and stares back.

"I don't know. Have we?" he says. He fumbles through his pocket and pulls out a small silver case, which he flicks open with his thumb to reveal a dozen expertly hand-rolled joints.

"I don't smoke," she says, mistaking them for cigarettes.

"You smoke these." Grinning, he removes two, puts both between his lips, and lights them with a Bic and hands one to her. She inhales tentatively, finds it mild and smooth, and proceeds to suck the smoke down deep.

"Umm, nice," she says, on the exhale, looking around. "Marianne's kitchen is nice, isn't it? No fifties detail untouched. Totally iconic. Did you grow up with avocado appliances?"

"I gave her the Fiestaware, from our summer house in North Hero. Hello, I'm Max."

"Oh, I get it," she leans back, pointing the joint at him. "You're the guy who hit the cow. I wonder why Marianne never told me about you."

"And you are—"

"Lena Zinelli. I live across the road. From the field."

"My lady of the cornfield!" He throws his head back, laughs, and grips her wrist. "Have you had breakfast? Would you care for an egg?" He points to a bowl—Fiestaware, brilliant red—filled with shelled hard-boiled eggs.

At that, Zia, who has been sitting quietly against the kitchen cabinets, comes over and puts her head in his lap. "Well, hello, magic doggie," he says, lifting an egg from the bowl and bending down to rub her ears. Zia opens her mouth, wrests the egg daintily from his hands, and swallows it whole. "Goodness, what big jaws you have. Is she always so polite? I didn't even notice her sitting here. In the Village years ago I used to go to the Figaro, and often I'd see a woman playing chess there with two Great Danes sitting right under the NO DOGS ALLOWED sign. Your dog has that quality; I think of it as tact."

"Maybe we met there. I used to waitress at the Feenjon."

"That's right," says Max. "Manny Dworman's place. But I was in Japan then. I basically missed the sixties."

"But the sixties found you, didn't they?" she says, twisting around for a look at the wall clock. It's almost noon. She hands him her sodden joint and gets to her feet. "Sorry, two tokes and I'm brain dead. I've got some stuff to bring over to the club. I'm parking Zia here for the party; hang on to her until Marianne gets back, will you?"

Max nods, *yes, of course.* "We can get into bed and read *Moby-Dick*."

"You don't want to go?"

"Like I want to walk on coals. It sounds like a terrible idea, badly conceived. I'd get up, but your humongous dog's sitting on my toes. I used to do something similar with my aikido students. Stand on their feet while egging them on to attack me."

Lena shakes her head. She hears "aikita," and thinks *big white dog.*

"Aikido. The softest martial art next to t'ai chi. I brought it to America."

"Did you?" Lena sounds doubtful. She stands up and puts on her coat.

"To New York, at least. Don't get me started."

"I won't," she says, handing him a leash. "Be good to this gentleman," she says to her dog, and leaves.

Max is in the shower when Marianne charges in later that afternoon carrying an armload of folded clothes. "Do not shed," she warns Zia, who's stretched out on the bed, unmoving as Marianne dumps the clothing around her. Max emerges, clad in a towel. He flops down next to Zia and turns up the TV. "Don't even think about trying to get out of coming with me," Marianne tells him pointedly. "You are the designated date." Then she darts into the bathroom.

When she returns fifteen minutes later, fully dressed, he's still in his towel and is watching the news, smoking. "Come on, we're going to be late," she says, grabbing the cigarette.

"What they're not saying is, we're arming the Ayatollah. Such a nice guy." On the screen, a lieutenant stands in front of a podium while in the background runs footage of an airplane screaming through the clouds.

"I thought it was all about oil. You're not supposed to smoke."

"On a deeper level, it about fucking up the entire region so we can grab it for ourselves."

"*Moby-Dick* was all about oil. How much deeper does it get than that?" She steps in front of the TV blocking the screen. "So how do I look?" She pokes his shoulder.

Max sighs, flips off the remote. "You are fantastic. Where did you get that amazing fedora?" He suspects it's the very same hat he used to wear in publicity shots when he did that sort of thing years back, she appropriated it without his knowing it, probably lifting it right off his head, and now it frames the bright black hair falling dramatically over her face. She's wearing a form-fitting man's suit, wide maroon tie, and wrinkled white shirt, and her eyes glisten under four pairs of fake lashes, and her wide mouth beckons even more brilliantly, defiantly red than usual. "Keep it, darling, it looks great on you," he says, putting his arms around her thighs.

She drops her chin on his head, but carefully, so as not to disturb her complicated do, and says, "I want to throw up."

"Don't start feeling like a schmuck until the night is over and we do our critical analysis and tear you apart."

"I feel really stupid. I'm going to humiliate myself. I'm trying to be Laurie Anderson, but I'm feeling like Miss Piggy."

"Nobody here knows from Laurie Anderson. Think of this as exploring your Inner Trite. Go have fun. Learn what you're supposed to learn, and stop this intellectual angst."

"This is why I need you to come with me."

"I have nothing to wear. Pity."

"Untrue." She slips out of his grasp, picks up the pile of clothing—

a well-worn über-sized jacket and pair of faintly striped gray pants and thrusts it at him. The dog doesn't move.

He picks it up reluctantly, holds the jacket against his shoulders, stroking the material. It's a fine worsted, and he's obviously appreciative. "By God, this could have been made for me," he says.

"Probably it was the same suit you pawned when you split this scene. Get dressed, come on, hurry."

"The dog—" he says.

"The dog sleeps. Come on, big boy, think of your obligation to society."

"This better work off my debt up until the millennium."

Marianne might be feeling nervous about this project, but really, how clever she is! Max gets it immediately as he follows her bobbing head through the moving mass of grayish tonalities, everyone in the same iconic suit wearing his splendidly wide-brimmed, right-out-of-*Casablanca* fedora; may the Arts Council never learn how she'd spent their money.

"Art students," she shouts over her shoulder, but there are also skinheads, bankers, and could that be his former lesbian dentist under the bone-white pig mask with a dick for a nose? Could some of these people be his former students? A large woman shooting video backs into him, pushing him into the bar.

He grabs at a post to keep from being swept back by the crowd and sees Lena Zinelli against the wall facing a tall man in a Panama hat wearing a real Armani. Through her mess of red hair, he can see her features morphing through myriad emotions, a dramatic range of misery, fury, grief, and arrogance as she argues with this guy. The husband, he'd bet.

A blast of metallic hatred rocks the room, as the crowd breaks out in a rendition of "The Star-Spangled Banner" capable of buckling steel. Marianne pulls on his sleeve and shouts something. Distracted, he turns away, and when he looks back at the bar, Lena Zinelli is nowhere in sight, and a kid wearing Mickey Mouse ears has planted herself in the Armani man's lap.

Marianne leads him up a spiral staircase to a narrow balcony where it's much quieter. Directly below them is the edge of the dance floor, and to their right the back of the bar. Spotlights anchored to the underside of the balcony wash over the hundreds of thrusting fedoras bobbing above the gray flannel wave. Images projected from surveillance cameras hidden in the unisex bathrooms strobe on the ceiling, one quickly replaced by another, creating a startling impression of invaded privacy without revealing identities or the nature of their acts.

Max goes to the railing and scans the crowd, eventually catching sight of Lena dancing directly below him, her mask sitting on her head, the elastic holding her hair off her face, the holes for eyes staring straight at him. All he can see of the man she's undulating against is the top of a tiny fedora worn over bulbous dreadlocks. This must be Lena's gorgeous young Caribbean assistant. He leans over, waving to get her attention. Then the lanky Jamaican grabs Lena around the waist and he forces himself to sit down as they fight their way to the exit.

The next morning, Max gets up early, dresses in a blue shirt and new jeans, and drinks three cups of coffee. He walks Zia around the block so many times she now hides from him under the stairs. In between walks, he reads the *Times*, then the *Boston Globe*, then he starts on the year's worth of weekly *Vermont Vanguards* piled up in the bathroom, all the while Marianne sleeps in her room, sedated, and the phone rings and rings. He'd like to go out to the coffee shop for breakfast but doesn't want to miss Lena when she shows up for her dog. When she finally walks in with the Jamaican she'd left the party with, Max grabs her by the arm and says, "Hello, let's go."

The Jamaican—Jocelyn Wales—throws him an exhausted smile and drops his overcoat on the floor and heads to the big brown sofa in the living room, mumbling "See you later, baby."

"Let's go *where?*" whispers Lena, looking dazed.

"Wherever, let's go *now*," Max whispers back, for he hears Marianne starting down the stairs very, very slowly.

They settle in a pretty little pink hovel of a Thai restaurant with frilly lamps, curtains, and gilt masks of the elephant god Ganesha on the walls. "Wrong deity," Max says, steering Lena to a back table, "but the food's authentic." When the waitress arrives and greets him warmly—he's obviously a regular—he waves away the menu and orders, *"laab, kow moo dang, tom yum goong."* "You'll love this shit," he tells Lena.

"Tea for me," she says to the waitress, wincing. "Jasmine tea. Pots of it."

"Big night?"

Lena ignores the innuendo. "Did you read the paper this morning? Marianne's the trash queen of the day. And I feel for her, it just did not work out."

The waitress brings a tray with tea things and a plate of spring rolls. Lena picks up the pot, puts it down. She leans forward and pulls at her hair and waits.

He says, "Listen, I want to talk to you about that night in the corn-field. I need your help. The thing is, I don't remember anything, and I think I'm suffering some kind of shock because of that. I want you to prod my memory." *All this blather,* he thinks, leading up to what's really on his mind: *getting together with her.*

"So what do you remember?" Lena settles back and smiles. She'll go with the game.

"You. I remember you and thinking you were an angel. I thought, *Oh, Lord, this is the face of the angel who came to me at that difficult time in my life.* Are you laughing at me? Stop that immediately. I did actually think that."

"Really."

"I had just murdered a great big sentient being and couldn't han-dle it. I knew it was there, but I couldn't look at it. Then you came along and you put your face right on her pelt without a second thought. I thought, *What a beautiful person.* I thought, *I really know this person.* You know, many people come your way, but it's rare that one really *sees* that other person."

"I don't know what to say."

"Neither do I. If the food doesn't get here within the next nanosec-ond I am going to ask you to marry me. There it is. Thank God, just in time." He motions the waitress to leave the dishes in the center of the table and please go away.

"I'm not laughing at you," Lena says, looking at her hands. "It was profound. I kept thinking you were a mirage and would disintegrate into the mist at any moment." She looks at the food and at their empty plates, picks up the teapot and pours their tea. "I don't mean to mystify it: I was surprised, that's all." Of course she wants to mystify the

experience. Not to do so would make him just a guy in a field. Someone she wanted to know, and she doesn't need any complications in
her life right at this moment. She doesn't mention Julian.

"Thank you," he says, handing her a shrimp. "It's all coming back,
as vivid as when it happened. It'll take some time for me to assimi-
late all that. Being on the road that night was stupid. I thought, oh
well, that was destiny. I was born to hit that animal. I have dreams
about metal striking flesh. I have dreams sometimes that there's a cow
in me."

At that moment, there's commotion at the door, the sounds of people yelling and a barking dog. "Zia, what's she doing here?" mutters
Lena, handing back the shrimp, pushing away from the table. "Sorry."
She walks quickly to the door where the waitress and the restaurant
manager now stand speaking Thai. Outside, she finds Jocelyn hanging
on to Zia's leash with two hands. At the other end, growling, barking, in a low crouch, the dog has one of Burlington's homeless pinned
to a van. Behind him, Marianne hops up and down.

"I will never forgive you for this," the homeless guy screams at Zia.
The waitress yells, "Mi dee, ma! Mi dee, ma!"

Lena grabs the leash from Jocelyn and ropes the dog in with both
hands.

Max drops a handful of bills on the table by the uneaten food and
joins the crowd at the door. He puts a bill in the homeless man's shirt
pocket and suggests that he go get himself something to eat. The
restaurant staff shuts the door, leaving the four of them standing on the
otherwise empty street.

It's warmed up quite a bit, everywhere the sound of water dripping
as the ice melts and drains down the gutters and along the sidewalk.

"Well, Happy New Year," says Lena, looking uncomfortable. She and Jocelyn haven't really talked much about what they're doing, or if they're doing anything at all. Last night was a drunken hoot, and she'd like to leave it at that. She just assumes it's the same for him.

"Greetings," says Jocelyn.

"How you doing, man," says Max.

"Max is a famous martial artist," says Marianne.

"That and a quarter will get you into the subway," says Max. "Aikido, you probably never heard of it."

"Oh, for sure. It be hot down in Jamaica. Like bobsledding," he teases. "You come to Jamaica, Mon!"

Surprised at the sudden patois, Lena pokes Jocelyn with her elbow.

"Yeah," says Max, "Fuck United Fruit. Come up to North Hero when I get back to the East Coast."

Marianne moves over to Lena and whispers in her ear, "Oh, lucky girl, they're vying for you."

Ignoring her, Lena asks Max where he's getting back from.

"California," he says, crossing his hands over his chest.

"On that note," says Marianne, "I'm done. Jocelyn, why don't you take me home."

"Cannah. I'm going up to the islands with Miss Lena. We driving a truck to Balt-i-more tomorrow for a trade show."

"Lena," says Max, taking her arm, "can we talk for a moment?"

They move back into the restaurant doorway.

"Does he always talk like that?"

"Like what?" Lena puts her hand on Zia's head. The dog sits down on her feet.

"Have dinner with me tonight."

"Canna do," says Lena, cocking her head. "You heard my clay brother; we have a gig tomorrow. Sorry. When I get back, maybe."

"You two lie in bed exchanging glaze recipes?" Max reaches over to scratch the dog's ears.

"Copper Reds. They're very elusive."

"Come on, guys," yells Marianne. "I'm freezing out here."

"OK," says Lena, looking at Max, shrugging. "Gotta go." She walks away, then runs back to kiss him lightly on the cheek.

2

*I saw my mother moving slowly and silently past me,
blue murder in her eyes…*

—John Gardner, *Grendel*

Max says:

Look at this photo of me. It was taken in 1947, at our summer home, on Lake Champlain. North Hero was the name of our town and for a long time I thought we lived there because we were heroes. Why not? I'm a huge glowering twelve-year-old in a baggy sweatshirt, chino pants straining at the thighs, and a plaid hat with the brim smashed down to my nose. I'm clutching a tomahawk and a crossbow in my left hand. A bullwhip and powder horn dangle from my neck. My right hand holds a stone axe head on a stick. I have a hunting knife in my belt, a revolver in a holster, and a rifle on the ground pointing to my jaw. Concealed are the toy grenade in one pocket, ammo in another, a Bowie knife in my socks, and a vial of poison made in my mother's kitchen tucked into my shorts.

It's a pretty weird photo, but what's really weird is that Mother took the shot.

She was hosting one of her croquet luncheons down by the lake for cousins and friends. On the lawn, people in white shirts and knickers sat in wicker chairs around the bar cart. Peals of laughter. Do I remember all this? Of course not. I remember the mood. It was a Gatsby summer day, but I was in a Grendel kind of mood, hanging out by myself around the icehouse. Here's where my weapons were stored. Now let me be clear here: these weapons were not to harm these beautiful people. They were meant to protect them. Should our property be somehow invaded, I would save their lives.

At some point I heard Mother calling for me: "Oh, do get Max in here at once to show us his weapons." The next thing I knew, I was propped up against this wall facing her Brownie.

When I tell you Mother was trained to shoot by Annie Oakley, you'll see the scene makes a certain sense. She liked weapons. Most of mine were borrowed from her private collection. Whenever her blood reached a certain alcohol level, she'd call me out and show me off. It was a form of humiliation, but also a point of pride.

This picture is embarrassing, but I always show it to my students. This is a truthful picture. And extremely provocative: If a misfit like me grows up to teach peace and nonviolence, then there's hope for any one of us, right?

Now, take a look at this other photo. It shows another side of Mother, a different take on her plans for my future. Here's my baby brother, Evans, and me all dressed up in our worsted suits with the short pants and with ironed white hankies sticking out from our breast pockets. My arm is around him. Note my stance, one leg in front of the other, hands in my pockets. This is a power pose. I see myself already, at the age of seven, as a protector of the Democracy. This photo was taken in our New York apartment, probably at a Red Cross fundraiser. "Here they come, my little men," Mother would call out from the couch. This was her signal for Cook to send us through the swinging doors like two bumper cars, each of us holding a tray of hors d'œuvres—cheese whip on Triscuits, pigs-in-blankets, grilled shrimp—while a hired photographer took our picture. My poor little brother, trying so hard not to drool in the dip, would inevitably dump his tray in some relative's lap, and then we'd be whisked away like dust motes. To this day I remember how the sweat gathered under the itchy wool, streamed down my legs to the backs of my white leather shoes.

One Thanksgiving, we were on the island when some guys appeared. They looked about fifteen—my age—and they were hunters. They surrounded a big bush, trying to rouse out a deer, and started shooting at each other's feet.

I was hiding on top of a hill watching. I saw my mother come out of the house shooting rounds in the air with her rifle as she walked toward the bush, and when she reached the boys, who were now frozen in place, she said, "Get off of my goddamn land or I will shoot out your eyes," or something to that effect. In my eyes she looked stunning with her flared gabardine skirt ruffled by the wind, holding a .30-06 out like a champagne flute, and I was howling with laughter. But in my heart, I knew without a doubt that my mother would have shot their lights out, had she had a mind to, which meant that none of us was safe, especially me.

She divorced Dad right after my little brother was born, and shortly after remarried a man with two kids whose mother had died while he was in the war. The kids and I hated each other on sight, starting in fighting right at the station. I was a fat, dreamy kid, used to being Little Master. Being older, they beat me up every day until I was at the bottom of our new pecking order.

In boarding school, I found the sport where my particular combination of brilliance and violence would be rewarded: football. Once in a tight game I told my opposite number to lie down or I'd kill him, and to encourage him I gave him a shot with my forearm right in the mouth. Two of his teeth were stuck in my arm, I broke his nose and his cheekbone, and we won the game. Afterward, walking to the locker room, everyone congratulated me. But I felt miserable. For the first time in my life, inflicting pain had brought me no pleasure.

Now I was beginning to believe there was some sort of demonic spirit, old and mean, living inside of me, who hated me, thought I was an asshole, and was bent upon using me as an outlet for his violence. I realized then that when my teammates applauded me for knocking out that kid's teeth in the game, they were applauding this old one inside of me. This was very alarming, for I had no idea when this entity would jump out.

It was about then I began thinking about what it is to have power, and that how you use power matters in life. It is to weep. I just feel so miserable when I think about that kid. I'm a Little Lord Serial-Killer-in-Waiting. What saved me was what saves all martial men: love. Martial men are filled with love.

There's a wonderful line by Chandler: "Down these mean streets a man must go who is not himself mean, who is neither tarnished nor afraid." I'm not that man yet, maybe I will be someday. I'm no longer a little fat kid: I'm a big fat guy. I have this power. I know how to hit, and I know how to receive.

And so do you.

So what are we supposed to do about it?

Oakland, California, 1985

The way Max tells it, he lands on a sunny March afternoon in Oakland to find two senior teachers from the Marin aikido dojo, Kevin and Bill, waiting with flowers and a key to a houseboat in Sausalito. His contract with them is for a two-month-long paid gig—not *well*-paid, but at least it was in the coin of the realm. After that, he would participate in workshops in New Age conference centers from Seattle down to Long Beach, and teach in various dojos.

That night in Marianne's kitchen, when he'd told Lena about bringing aikido to America, he hadn't been hyperbolic; he truly believed that O-sensei, his teacher and the founder of the art, had entrusted him on his deathbed with the mission of spreading the art through the West, lest it suffocate at the hands of its own tradition on its native island. The problem was, by the time Max left Japan for home, the East Coast had already been divided up among O-sensei's Japanese students. Vermont, however, was still open—so he'd formed a little dojo in Burlington, and later, as his reputation grew, he attracted students to a new dojo in the Bowery. Even so, he kept traveling, for he was sure O-sensei never wanted him to have his own dojo. He was meant to be a road man.

The road this afternoon leads past the slums of Oakland and across the Bay Bridge into San Francisco, then over the Golden Gate Bridge and into Marin in a silver Audi convertible, Kevin driving with Bill folded gracefully in the back seat with the luggage and Max sideways in the passenger seat. They take off from the airport with the top down and head up the Nimitz toward the Golden Gate.

Bill, a small wiry man in his forties, had taken Max as his teacher back in the Bowery days. He'd moved out to Mill Valley, started studying at Marin, and lobbied hard for Max to leave the filthy, impossible city and relocate to California where everything Japanese was a hot item for the lifestyle: food, clothing, sleeping on mats, the language, aikido. Aikido people, serious people hopeful of a better world—which meant a gentler America—were writing books, consulting with corporations, lecturing at universities, joining conferences. There was aikido excitement in the air. Max had the clout of having studied in Japan with the founder, as well as being a gifted teacher. In fact, Bill swore, it was essential that he come out, if he didn't want to fall out of aikido history.

Well, Max wasn't so sure about that, but he was fed up with New

York and hot to hit the road. This was five years ago. He drove out with a love-of-his-life, and a bed and a cook stove in the back of his red truck.

Everything Bill had said was true. There were all these new philosophers and systems people, educators and mental health workers, hot to parley their spiritual work into best-sellers, into the corporate culture or college curriculum. They had listened to his ideas, pressed upon him their business cards, promised to call, patted him on the shoulder, and taken his leave with "Let's take lunch." The Aquarian Age—which New Yorkers thought was a joke—was moving right along with copious funding. Conflict resolution was the way to go.

For a while his dance card was full. The love-of-his-life wore designer clothes and wrote articles on San Francisco style. They went to all the parties and talked up the two books he'd coauthored, borrowing aikido principles for the self-help industry.

And his classes were packed.

But then—it's hard to say what happened, maybe his fifteen minutes of fame were over, maybe another guru of the day had flown in—people stopped returning his phone calls. Before he'd had a chance to figure out what was happening, his mother had had a stroke, his girlfriend had orchestrated a humiliating breakup, and he had broken his contract and flown back to Vermont.

But Bill kept calling, lobbying for the West Coast, insisting that all he needed to do was give it more time, and finally coming up with this lucrative teaching gig .

Kevin seems to be the designated cheerleader. He drives fast with one hand on the wheel leaving the other free to graze his own thigh, back and forth, a gesture Max finds fascinating. "John Denver practiced for a week during a gig out here," Kevin yells over the wind. "Joan Baez, you know about her? She's training with us, really anxious to meet you."

"We've met," says Max, "Joanie. In a hot tub somewhere."

All this yelling over the wind is headache-producing; one has been brewing since somewhere over Philadelphia and the aspirin's in his suitcase. He twists around to ask Bill if he's got anything for it. Bill says "Sorry" and starts talking about a gig at Esalen they've lined up, adding that Ram Dass will be there at the same time, speaking about compassion. "Always, he tells that story of yours, the one on the train in the Japanese Alps. He says it's the best illustration of real compassion he's ever read. It's a brilliant story, by the way. I hope you're writing more."

"Ram Dass, that's nice." Max nods, grits his teeth and sets his gaze on the racing landscape. "Yeah," he lies, "I'm writing. Always writing." They're over the bridge now, heading into Marin. Well, he thinks, this could be Vermont, except for the movie people screening aikido action films in mansions dangling over cliffs in mud slide zones. And he conjures up a vision of himself by the lake, his old red Selectric typewriter on the picnic table, marshmallow clouds in the celadon sky, checkerboard loons bobbing on neat little waves.

Bill brings him to a party in a steel and glass house on the west rim of Mount Tamalpais to meet an entire new set of wheelers and dealers who've evolved in the eight months Max has been away. Like before, he shakes hands, smiles, cracks jokes, drops names, gallivants nimbly; but soon the night begins to slump. The problem he's having? He finds that he has nothing new to tell these people because they have

already co-opted his *stuff* for their own. He understands about zeit-
geist, that ideas float around, up for grabs, and that he and O-sensei do
not have monopolies on how to peacefully resolve conflict. O-sensei
used to say that everything is aikido: the principles of aikido are universal. And everyone but him seems to have figured out how to exploit
that concept.

As Bill keeps telling him, it's OK to make a living. In fact, it's essential. The next week, Bill arranges for a presentation to a management
team at a brokerage house for a fee exceeding the whole of Max's previous year's income. They'll need to create a slide show, illustrating
how aikido principles will solve employee-employer conflicts without
jeopardizing production. Getting this together will take a huge amount
of work and expense—making graphs, finding quotes and photos, hiring a graphic designer, and copying color brochures—but Bill thinks
the result will be useful for the future, as a template for other lectures
to other audiences, like United Nations peacekeepers or prison reform-
ers or teachers of ballet. *Brilliant*, thinks Max. *Why not.*

But he's also thinking, *You've got to be kidding.* He's done this all
before: he spent so much time hustling the business world in Japan he
was too exhausted to practice aikido. O-sensei knew it; everyone knew
it. It was compromise then, and it's the same now, and you can't do
both, you can't hustle without contaminating your spirit: if greed leads
you to the enemy's table, don't be surprised to find yourself poisoned.

Still, he dresses in his suit and brown shoes, and rides with Bill to
the twentieth floor of a glass tower on Market Street. They sit in a
conference room where a young man asks questions and takes notes on
a pad while Bill sets up their carousel in the projector. His name is
on a placard. A giant pad of paper sits on an easel with colored felt

pens. Twenty people group around a big oval table, pens and paper-clips lying next to notebooks like tableware.

The young man walks to the lectern. He introduces Max as the famous sensei in the Japanese martial art aikido. He tells them that Japanese companies run with similar hierarchical structures as over here, but over there, everyone has great team spirit. They've found ways to resolve conflicts between management and workers, and Max means to help us brainstorm better management techniques without hurting profits. Max shakes his hand and takes his place and opens his book of notes. The lights dim and the first slide lights up on the screen.

He looks at the audience. They look up at him, crossing and uncrossing their legs as the moments pass. He gazes from one face to the next, moving slowly. When he's looked all twenty people in the eye, he closes his book and says, "I'm sorry, but I find that I have nothing to say to you. I mean, this slide thing is garbage: you know that, I know that. I would, however, like to tell you a story." The one that comes to mind is the train story that Ram Dass has been telling his audience for so many years. It has nothing and everything to do with Japanese hierarchies or maximizing profits.

He puts his fingers together and begins.

"A train clanks and rattles through the suburbs of Tokyo on a drowsy spring afternoon. My car is comparatively empty—a few house-wives with their kids in tow, some old folks going shopping. I gaze absently at the drab houses and dusty hedgerows.

"At one station the doors open, and suddenly the afternoon quiet is shattered by a man bellowing violent, incomprehensible curses. The man staggers into my car. He's wearing laborer's clothing, and he's big, drunk, and dirty. Screaming, he swings at a woman holding a baby. The blow sends her spinning into the laps of an elderly couple. It is a miracle that she's unharmed.

"Terrified, the couple jump up and scramble toward the other end of the car. The laborer aims a kick at the retreating back of the old woman but misses as she scuttles to safety. This so enrages the drunk that he grabs the metal pole in the center of the car and tries to wrench it out of its stanchion. I can see that one of his hands is cut and bleeding. The train lurches ahead, the passengers freeze up with fear. I get to my feet.

"I was young then, some twenty years ago, and in pretty good shape. I'd been putting in eight hours of aikido training nearly every day for the past three years. I liked to throw and grapple. I thought I was tough. Trouble was, my martial skill was untested in actual combat. As students of aikido, we were not allowed to fight.

"'Aikido,' my teacher had said again and again, 'is the art of reconciliation. Whoever has the mind to fight has broken his connection with the universe. If you try to dominate people, you are already defeated. We study how to resolve conflict, not how to start it.'

"I listened to his words. I tried hard. I even went so far as to cross the street to avoid the *chimpira*, the pinball punks who lounged around the train stations. My forbearance exalts me. I feel both tough and holy. In my heart, however, I want an absolutely legitimate opportunity whereby I might save the innocent by destroying the guilty.

"*This is it!* I say to myself, getting to my feet. People are in danger, and if I don't do something fast, they will probably get hurt. Seeing me stand up, the drunk recognizes a chance to focus his rage. 'Aha!' he roars. 'A foreigner! You need a lesson in Japanese manners!'

"I hold on lightly to the commuter strap overhead and give him a slow look of disgust and dismissal. I plan to take this turkey apart, but he has to make the first move. I want him mad, so I purse my lips and blow him an insolent kiss.

"'All right!' he hollers. 'You're gonna get a lesson.' He gathers himself for a rush at me.

"A split second before he can move, someone shouts 'Hey!' It's earsplitting. I remember the strangely joyous, lilting quality of it—as though you and a friend had been searching diligently for something, and he suddenly stumbled upon it. 'Hey!'

"I wheel to my left; the drunk spins to his right. We both stare down at a little old Japanese man. He must have been well into his seventies, this tiny gentleman, sitting there immaculate in his kimono. He takes no notice of me, but beams delightedly at the laborer, as though he has a most important, most welcome secret to share.

"'C'mere,' the old man says in an easy vernacular, beckoning to the drunk. 'C'mere and talk with me.' He waves his hand lightly.

"The big man follows, as if on a string. He plants his feet belligerently in front of the old gentleman, and roars above the clacking wheels, 'Why the hell should I talk to you?' The drunk now has his back to me. If his elbow moves so much as a millimeter, I'll drop him in his socks.

"The old man continues to beam at the laborer.

"'What'cha been drinkin'?' he asks, his eyes sparkling with interest.

"'I been drinkin' sake,' the laborer bellows back, 'and it's none of your business!' Flecks of spittle spatter the old man.

"'OK, that's wonderful,' the old man says. 'Absolutely wonderful! You see, I love sake too. Every night, me and my wife—she's seventy-six, you know—we warm up a little bottle of sake and take it out into the garden, and we sit on an old wooden bench. We watch the sun go down, and we look to see how our persimmon tree is doing. My great-grandfather planted that tree, and we worry about whether it will recover from those ice storms we had last winter. Our tree had done better than I expected, though especially when you consider the poor quality of the soil. It is gratifying to watch when we take our sake and go out to enjoy the evening—even when it rains!' He looked up at the laborer, eyes twinkling.

"As he struggles to follow the old man's conversation, the drunk's face begins to soften. His fists slowly unclench. 'Yeah,' he says, 'I love persimmons too. . . .' His voice trails off.

"'Yes,' says the old man, smiling, 'and I'm sure you have a wonderful wife.'

"'No,' replies the laborer. 'My wife died.' Very gently, swaying with the motion of the train, the big man begins to sob. 'I don't got no wife, I don't got no home, I don't got no job. I am so ashamed of myself.' Tears roll down his cheeks; a spasm of despair ripples through his body.

"Now it's my turn. Standing there in well-scrubbed youthful innocence, my make-this-world-safe-for-democracy righteousness, I suddenly feel dirtier than he is.

"Then the train arrives at my stop. As the doors open, I hear the old man cluck sympathetically. 'My, my,' he says, 'that is a difficult predicament, indeed. Sit down here and tell me about it.'

"I turn my head for one last look. The laborer's sprawled on the seat, his head in the old man's lap. The old man softly strokes the filthy, matted hair.

"As the train pulls away, I sit down on a bench. What I'd wanted to do with muscle has been accomplished with kind words. I had just seen aikido tried in combat, and the essence of it was love. I would have to practice the art with an entirely different spirit. It would be a long time before I could speak about the resolution of conflict."

Max stops talking and looks over the audience. After a moment, there's a smattering of applause, then chairs scrape as people amble out the door back to work. "Well," says the presenter, shaking his hand, "that was certainly novel." The event could be called a success, although after that, Bill gives up trying to make Max famous.

For the next month, Max traveled the state, teaching in one dojo after the other. His classes were packed, although not everyone appreciated his style. What some considered provocative and brilliant, others found narcissistic and bullying. He didn't seem to realize that he was cutting into the class time of the teachers who were generously hosting him, and that he was culling resentment. By the end of April, when he arrived full circle back in Marin, it became clear even to him that he'd worn out his welcome.

At five-thirty in the morning, Max sits at the kitchen table drinking bitter coffee, fingering the faded photo of his sullen preteen self laid out beside his half-eaten plate of fried eggs and toast, watching through the open window the reluctant dawn lighten the edges of the dense West Coast fog. He thinks of the fog as not born from the sea or air, but rather from his own body, carrying fearful dreams from the terrible night from which he's still trying to awake; dreams of himself as a lone soldier running from futile battles raging on distant mythic mountain tops, sometimes hiding, sometimes killed. If he were looking for a reason to get away from this coast, he thinks, refilling the cup and heading for the shower, the fog alone would suffice.

By the time he's out the door and hits the drizzly street, his thoughts shift to the day ahead of him, and he pulls down the brim of his old fedora and plants his fists in his leather jacket, lowers his head, and hurries—he's late to teach the morning class, a habit by now—through the thickening commuter crowd headed for downtown, turning left at the bottom of the residential hill.

Midway to the dojo, at the corner, he has to stop for breath. He puts a hand on the glass bay window of a coffee shop, crosses one foot over the other and wills himself to appear nonchalant, as if he's merely taking a moment to enjoy the urban landscape while, in effect, he's paralyzed by vertigo and his heart threatens to leap from his throat. He's distressed not only by the weakness in his body, but also by the irony of feeling so stricken, when only last year he had been introduced in an aikido demonstration at the UN as a legendary teacher of the art. He who had only half in jest warned his students to never miss a class, even if it meant dragging their iron lungs through the subway turnstile.

But that was back in New York when the streets were his, and this is Marin and how times have changed.

Thinking of New York, of the Bowery dojo he'd founded and led for so many years before the sirens of California lured him out with promises of fame and fortune—neither of which have materialized—reminds him that he's due shortly to return. Immediately, he feels better. He straightens his shoulders, wills his dizzy brain onward and upward, and soon finds himself breathily climbing the stairs toward the closed dojo door, a sign that the class has begun without him.

Which means, he grumbles to himself, his thick hand on the knob, that his gloss has worn thin and it's time to move on. *If I were truly legendary, class would wait for me, sitting on their hands if need be, impatient for my blessing.*

He changes in the empty dressing room, listening to the sounds of practice on the other side of the curtain. He puts on the worn *gi*, his name embroidered on the left sleeve by a former girlfriend, puts on the *hakima*, and when he's done carefully knotting the black belt, his bit of breakfast rebels, his stomach drools over his belt like a meringue. He gives it a smart rap and slips out on the deck with a joint in hand. He lights it, but as it heads for his mouth, he catches himself—do not get sloppy, do not teach stoned—and extinguishes it with a finger. Do not let on that you believe yourself to be the cobra in the bunny house, he warns himself, and with that, he opens the curtain and sails through.

Kevin is leading class in warm-ups. Max freezes him in place with a firm tap on the shoulder and Kevin turns long enough to fix his uncompromising gaze on Max before dissolving back into the class with a hollow bow.

Max bows deeply to the *kamiza*, the altar holding his teacher's photograph flanked by vases of purple irises; he bows to his class. The class bows to him; he claps three times. He scans his brain for an opener. Nothing. He starts shuffling toward the far side of the room, swinging the upper part of his body from left to right. Fifteen pairs of bare feet paddle behind him. Still nothing. Finally something comes to mind. He calls out, "*Irimi*, entering throw!" and practice begins: one person as *nage*, the attacker, the other as *uke*, the receiver of the attack.

He can't help but acknowledge this: how handsome and fluid these students are! The problem is, they know it. Except for the few genetic klutzes who hang out together on the far corners of the mat, everyone in the room acts as a star in his own Steven Seagal movie. He wants to rattle their reliance on good form by throwing them off point until they have no choice but to open up their instincts and work from their souls. To this end, he steps on their toes, grabs at crotches, rips shirts, and mocks narcissism, paws at egos, disdains old habits, questions all assumptions. It's his best teaching, this *crazy wisdom*, but not everyone can handle it, especially not Kevin who silently mocks him (he's sure) for allowing himself to get to so out of shape.

As he works the room, one particularly unbalanced pair—a large, white-belt guy in his forties working with a small wiry woman of higher rank—rankles him. The man is holding back; he thinks he has to pander to his partner's femininity. "Stop patronizing her," Max says, pushing him aside. "Here's what you look like." Exaggerating a wimpy attack, he flaps his hand on the woman's wrist. "This woman can destroy you, she can stand up to a tank—don't you condescend to her. Your job is to rise to the occasion. Give her your best so she can respond with her best."

He's noticed this girl in the unisex dressing room unwrapping her teen-boy body from a minidress he suspects she's made herself from a *Vogue* pattern. She's a pink-haired jackal capable of seriously damaging her insincere partner. He guesses she's been working on her strength because she's sick of feeling like prey. But maybe that's just him being novelistic.

"You want to know if it's like you see in the movies?" he says to her, folding his big fingers over her bony wrists.

"What do you mean?"

"I mean, you wonder if, when you meet an armed creep in a stair-well, this martial art can save your life?" The look she throws him is unmistakable. She's already met this creep. Feeling for her, he lowers his voice. "Your attacker wishes to hurt you. His desire defeats him from the get-go. Blend with his energy to drop him."

"Thank you Sensei," she says sarcastically. "You want I should lean into an attack while he has a knife in my throat? Maybe he'll ask me out for coffee?"

"No, you run like hell." With a quick twist, he brings her down to the mat, finishing what they'd begun. She jumps to her feet and bows.

"That's a terrible bow," he says to her, "and you know it. There's no room in a bow for irony. Bows must be utterly sincere. Now listen to me. This maniac thinks you are his meat, and so you learn to sense him before you stumble into his domain; you turn on your dime, and you disappear before he shows himself. That is what you train for. You train to transform violence, not to combat it. We are all bits of energy churning through space; we are all the same; we are all *ki*. You and I, we feel it through our flesh."

In a flash, he's behind her, covering her back with his body, lean-ing his chin on her shoulder, flooding her until—heaven help him—he images his *ki* burning right through her jog-bra. "Root yourself in the ground. Go ahead, you know about this. The *ki* is here, some place behind the belly button. Some people say they know the spot, that there is a real spot for *ki*. Gotta do something with that anger," he chides, poking her shoulder with an avuncular index finger. Then he spins around and claps his hands. The students turn to face him.

"Everyone wants to know if aikido works in the street. But don't try it.

"I had this kid once in New York, broke my heart," he says. "A fifth-*dan* black belt, the handsomest person you could imagine. He was an actor, and also he ran a street garage on 34th and Eighth, a little cubicle under the stairs in a tenement building where he kept his tools to repair trucks on the sidewalk. He had a world-class temper that he figured was under control after ten years of hard training in aikido. But he never counted on cornering a preteen gang rat robbing one of his trucks. It was the kid's gang initiation and his thirteenth birthday, and he wasn't going to fail, so when Tommy reached in the truck and tried to extract him by the hair, the kid planted a knife in his kidney. He died in the cab en route to the hospital.

"So forget about this street shit, leave that to *The Karate Kid*. Let's work on your spirit instead, so you learn how not to attract a teenager on the day he's being initiated into his gang. Now let us do—Wait. One more thing: when you ask about what self-defense means, ask yourself as well, what is this self we defend. Now work on that self."

The students resume, changing roles: the attacker becoming the attacked. Max prowls around, correcting moves, commenting, making sure to connect with everyone. "Well, don't you look exactly like a martial artist," he says to a black belt studiously executing perfect form. "Let us imagine you are on line for the movies, an 11:00 show in the Bronx. A kid slams into you demanding your wallet. Are you going make him wait while you assume your martial stance? No you are not. You will already be prepared to react. Preparedness is a mental state— don't advertise!" Neatly swiveling, he takes the student down, then jokingly puts a foot on his chest and preens. The kid laughingly tries to get up. Max mock-slaps him back down, then graciously extends a helping hand. "One of O-sensei's greatest lessons was to protect your enemy, for your enemy is your brother." The kid jumps up, bows, and says, "Thank you, sensei," with shining eyes.

Max claps and calls out, "Now, *kote gaeshi*, please, reversed wrist, you figure out what that means. Change partners, please. And again, forget that crap about the stronger upper body strength that men have over women, because we do not give a shit; our lower body strength is very similar, and where does our power come? Power comes from the waist down. We are grounded, people. If you are a big male and you think women are weaker, you are in for a surprise; and if you're a little woman, you are walling yourself into a room of helplessness."

Partners re-form. Cajoling, whirling, Max continues instructing. He demonstrates first with a white belt, then with a senior student. Students become looser, more enthralled, less self-conscious, time flies, they're about to go into overtime. Max realizes he should end the class right here on a high note. But there's something about the way this class has been trained to do *irimi nage* that bothers him. There's a more elegant way.

Slyly, he calls on Kevin to partner for a demonstration. Kevin rises to his feet, offers a perfunctory bow, and immediately attacks. Max looks unprepared: he's scratching his nose lethargically, but then, in a series of infinitesimal movements, he arches Kevin over his belly, one hand cupping his cheek while the other hand comes under his chin. A twist of his hips flips Kevin on the mat.

The class drops its collective jaw. The move was clearly dangerous: in lesser hands, it could have broken Kevin's neck. Max knows this. He says, "You have to be careful, make sure to cup the chin to control the motion of the head. Don't try that part yet. You can practice the first part, coming directly in with a twist of your hips."

"That was transcendent," someone says. "Not just the nose-scratching."

"I had moments with O-sensei, where he was simply magical. I'd stay up all night trying to figure out the gimmick. But of course, there wasn't any."

Kevin has remained lying at his feet on the mat. Max reaches down automatically, to give him a hand up. A phrase from some Japanese sensei—which he does not utter—flits across his mind, *I like making tall men small.* He should realize that, instead of feeling grateful for having been thrown hard by a superior in rank, Kevin feels humiliated. He should know that Kevin thinks of him as a slovenly, posturing East Coast bully—an inferior, in fact, despite the rank—and that's why he's lying there consumed with anger. And Max should deal with it, he should practice aikido to defuse what could be a dangerous situation—but instead he goes on pontificating about magical moments with his old teacher. If he had any idea how self-satisfied he sounded, he would have stuffed his ego back in its sack, for it's running amok and strutting in spades. The irony is that for two hours he's been on his students' backs about their inflated egos and now his own has blinded him.

Kevin suddenly shoots up, lunges, and punches him right in the heart. It takes all Max's strength to keep upright, but he does, he swirls into the attack and manages to ride Kevin's fury right back at him. With two slapping steps, he immobilizes him in his long thick arms, presses against his left ear and sticks two fingers in his mouth. Humping his belly sack in the hollow of Kevin's back, he twists them both around and lunges at the wall, stopping one hair's breadth from connecting Kevin's now terrified face with the exposed red brick. He

keeps him there long enough for the class to understand that no matter how well conditioned they are, how long they've trained, how
much younger and healthier they might be, he could smash any one
of them back to their molecular structure, because he is possibly insane.
Furthermore, he will never, ever do such a thing, because—he whispers this hoarsely, planting a kiss on the back of Kevin's head—"I
don't know why, but martial men are given to love."

That night there's a party. It's celebratory, but he's in a terrible mood.
That thing with Kevin never should have happened. It had ended in
injury—his chest was killing him, possibly that jerk had broken his
ribs. He'd come too close to seriously injuring a student. And worst,
most of the students were impressed. Shocked by the force of his violence, but impressed nonetheless. They'd be discussing his belly thrust
and practicing shoving their fingers into their attackers' mouths for
many classes to come, and that's the last thing he wants them to take
away from his teachings.

   In the parking lot, sitting cross-legged on the hood of his truck,
is the young woman he'd told to run like hell from danger. She's
there, he knows, because he's the danger now and she has no intention of running, she fucking likes it. Being sensei means he gets laid
a lot: many a woman has invited him to her chambers to discuss his
great big heart. He's up and down and around about the ethics of
sleeping with students, and currently he's on record as squarely against
the practice.

   So it's come to this, he thinks, putting a hand on her hip. That's
all right. You fuck up, you go down, you stay down for a while. And
then God willing, someone shines a little light down the well and

you think maybe it's possible to start climbing up. He reaches for her hand and says, "Go home. Please. And I will do the same."

"Esalen Institute" read the brochure, "promotes humanistic educa-tion for the harmonious development of the whole person." Surely one of the glory spots in the universe, and really, it didn't matter what you taught, as long as you were ayurvedic or swore to protect the planet, or, like Max, were privy to deep healing secrets from another culture.

Resplendent in his skirts, long gray hair caught in a ponytail, he stands on a cliff overlooking an incomparable swath of the Pacific Ocean with a bullwhip in his hands. His whip—the same one he used as a twelve-year-old to shred perch in Lake Champlain—is a replica of an Australian blacksnake whip, a present from his mother. It's flex-ible and shot-loaded, with a double-plaited underbelly, replaceable fall, and wrist loop. Over time, in his hands, the whip has come to be less of a food processor and more an extension of his own *ki*. In his hands, its sine curve illustrates the principles of aikido.

Smiling down at the nine professional yoga practitioners who sit at his feet, he bounces the coiled whip in his right hand, assessing its strength. His determined demeanor belies his internal question: has he not made a tactical error bringing such a fearful, snakelike, highly charged symbol of brutality into these halls of humanism? But that's precisely why the whip will be effective. The principles of energy are embodied in all of life, no matter how terrifying.

"I don't know why I brought this thing along," he says. "That's the trouble with tools. You bring them along, and you have to use them."

"Yeah, right on," someone says.

"A whip is the most useless artifact invented by the human being, don't you think?" He begins to pace in a circle, the still-coiled whip in his hand, making visual contact, taking his time, giving people a chance to relax with the whip, beaming benevolence as he acknowledges each participant in turn. "The whip has no purpose whatsoever. I mean, what do you do with it?" No one knows.

"OK, you can whip slaves," he goes on. "Not that any of you would have any slaves, but next time you come across a bunch, let me know and I'll come whip them. What else? Scare tigers. But you don't hit the tigers with the whip, you attack them with the noise." Releasing his grip, the whip slides slowly through his fingers along the floor. When it stops of its own volition, he says, "It is useful, however, in explaining aikido." With a twist of his wrist, he elegantly spirals his whip. "People, move back, please. Let us consider what's essential to the operation of a whip. I do hope we're all out of range here. OK." He brings it back behind him again and snaps it loudly.

"This thing works. Why?" He stops, brings the handle up to his eyes, and inspects it. "It doesn't work very well, because I keep getting the strings tangled on the handle, please forgive me." When he's loosened them, he starts snapping the whip back and forth. "It works because it's soft. When I wave my arm, you can see the energy move through it, it actually takes a shape. It cracks, so it's real. This is the real effect of energy passing through a soft and supple media. There are many movements in aikido that directly correlate with this movement of cracking the whip. In yoga as well—as I'm sure you've already seen for yourselves. Any rigidity in this whip, or in the handler, will hamper its ability to work right: which is to break air molecules, which is why you hear the sound."

"Breaking the sound barrier," says someone.

"Right. That too. I hope this is OK; I hope no one will be scared by this. Sometimes the sound can be kind of loud." With that, he brings it back with a full body twist and this time the sound is extremely loud, causing several quite-audible gasps. "OK?"

A nervous twitter, then silence.

"What you saw and heard was a circle of increasingly diminishing radius, until finally the tip moves fast enough to push the air molecules into each other and rend them, meaning—" He points to the same wise guy who'd caught him on the sound barrier.

"Sine curve," the guy laughs.

"Yeah, right, professor," says Max.

They now hear a bleating sound from above. The dinner horn calling them in.

"Thank you very much for coming," Max says, bowing his head, making a steeple with his fingers against his chest. Everyone gets up, mills around for a moment, expresses their appreciation and disappears, leaving him alone to pack up his things.

What just happened? He has no idea. Has a principle of aikido been transmitted? Sometimes Esalen feels like a New Age kindergarten party for grownups. Has knowledge flowed from him to one other human being? Oh, Lord, so busy are these people healing themselves and chanting *Om Shanti*, you could kill babies here and no one would care as long as you composted them.

He picks up his satchel and starts up the slope to the main hall. Inviting sounds of laughter and conversation drift through the fog. It's growing dark now, soft and damp and chilly.

As he reaches the step to the porch, something deep in his chest contracts hard, he shouts out and drops to his knees. His chest expands with pain, everything swells against his ribs, a great big sea rising against a fragile dam, his breath tangled in his throat, he cannot breathe. He starts crawling to the steps, fingers reaching for the conversation, the laughter, the doors softly opening and shutting, for the smells of coffee and wine. He cannot breathe! This must be it. His heart wants out any way it can get, it will smash around his ribs, slam down his anus, go flying out his nose and pummel him.

Dark falls, light breaks through, dark, light, dark, light, he's maybe twenty yards down the hill from the main house, hidden from the path.

The pain lessens. People are settling down on the porch that juts off to the left above him. He hears a guitar and then a smattering of drumbeats. Then the serious drumming begins. A voice rises above the beat. Other voices join in. A moment later, a most remarkable voice takes the lead: the voice of Krishna Das, deep and vast and unmistakable. Krishna Das has been leading a workshop in traditional Indian *Kirtan* chanting. A cellist has joined the group now, then the erotic hand-slap-drumming of tabla players.

Now he hears another male voice, exuberantly off-key: Ram Dass! The sound of the voice—so giddy in this temple of the sublime— thrills Max. He lies slumped against the bottom step looking wistfully up at the porch, but he can't move under the weight of death straddling his belly.

Oddly, he's not afraid. Death isn't angry at him: death sits on his skin like an obedient puppy waiting for a treat. If the wild *Kirtan* beat claimed his soul, why resist? Perhaps the chanting is just for him. *"Hare Krishna Hare Ram."* Oh, he'll just stay where he is. *"Om Namo*

Bhagavate Vaasudevaayaa. Hare Ram Ram Ram Sita Ram Ram Ram. In the Presence of the Lord."

The pain is terrible, everything they said it would be. Swirling lights, darkness, blinding lights, fading sound, the plump little brain cells drying up like stones, like raisins.

He slides back down in the wet Big Sur grass under the dribbling Big Sur sky. He hears his own voice pleading, "Please, God, don't let me drool."

Weeks later, Lena Zinelli flies in alone for a trade show at the Fort Mason Center on San Francisco Bay. The show's so expensive that Jocelyn feels he should stay home working on the orders they took in Baltimore. They leave it open: if the work's selling well enough to justify the added expense, he'll come down to help.

"That guy Max, Marianne's buddy?" Jocelyn says when she calls home after setting up the display. "He's in the hospital: the General. Dat man's accident prone. You could go visit him, if you get a free moment. He's likely all alone and deserves a glimpse of you."

"If I get a moment?" Lena's exhausted, worried about doing the show alone and feeling uneasy when she compares herself to the other artists in the show. The West Coast work is fresher, more lively, not so bound in tradition as it is back East, and she feels stodgy in comparison.

"You being hard on yourself. Stop dat," says Jocelyn. "I bet everyone's casting the work, that's how they come up with such free ideas. You holding yourself back by hand-building everything."

Jocelyn's come up with a plan. He's lobbying Lena to have some of her work cast. Between Baltimore and San Francisco, they'd taken in more orders than they can fill. He figures that if he were more active—more like a real partner instead of what he is now, a mere studio slave—they could make real money, and Lena could be more creative. If they mold her originals, then he can do the castings, as well as the sanding, firing, and packing, and she can pay attention to the marvelous glaze work she's become famous for. This way, they can turn out product—the word makes her wince—while keeping the prices down. She sees his point, but balks at sacrificing her hands in the clay, for this is the work she loves to do. And wasn't it that Persian poet Rumi who said, "Let the work you love be what you do"? Still, she's burned out, and Jocelyn has a point. Molding some of the work, sharing the labor, should free her to push new ideas.

"OK, take a few pieces to that Canadian master mold-maker Marianne talks about," she says, giving in. "But just two or three."

"Those spiral-shaped pieces, how about those? Maybe mold a couple of different spouts and handles. While we wait, test out some porcelain casting slips." Jocelyn sounds relieved, and she trusts Jocelyn, couldn't wish for a better partner. He's got the business mind she lacks; in fact that's why he's with her, he has earned a two-year grant to apprentice with a potter—with her—to gather skills to take back to Jamaica. Being lovers wasn't part of the agreement; that started when Julian began treating her poorly. It's a natural part of their working relationship now; lolling around in bed calculating glaze formulas.

"So go see dis guy in the hospital," he prods her.

"Why? I didn't think you especially liked him."

"Oh, I like him fine, he's a righteous man. Dis martial art of his, I wanna learn it. I went signed up for a class at his old dojo. People dere think he'll be coming back."

Lena promises at least to call him, if not to actually visit, and she goes so far as to get the hospital number from information after hanging up with Jocelyn. But then she feels too tired to open her mouth—talking with another human being seems like a gigantic task, it's hard enough to imagine dragging herself to the elevator, finding her room and passing out in front of the telly.

As it turns out, she needn't have worried: the West Coast loves Lena Zinelli and her vegetable-shaped semifunctional ware, so much so that Jocelyn flies out two days later and joins her in the booth, bringing with him containers of vegetable stew, baskets of fruit, and a blender for juice drinks.

That afternoon, she's deep in conversation with a gallery owner when she sees her husband walking toward her down the aisle. They've done so many shows together for so many years that the sight of him seems unfortunately normal. They haven't been living together since he walked out at Christmas, and now it's April. He's told her he's living alone in a shabby motel to the south of Burlington, but Lena knows that he's sharing a rental with his girlfriend on the waterfront. He still insists that he's in a temporary midlife fix and that Lena needs to be patient with him. And although Lena has no intention of ever living with him again, she hasn't yet found the magic words to finally break their passive alignment.

Maybe it's because he's still paying the bills and doesn't hold it against her.

He's wearing his Italian suit with a Hawaiian shirt and the Panama hat, carrying a slick attaché case purchased from a Sharper Image catalogue, and wearing high-top sneakers—the same color, she realizes with a jolt, as her own. While she finishes up with her customer, he slides his attaché case behind the curtain, picks up a roll of paper towels, and starts dusting the shelves.

"Greetings" says Jocelyn, from his chair on the aisle where he sits reading the *Wall Street Journal*. He's wearing his show outfit, a vintage tux that fits like Saran Wrap. He slowly folds his newspaper, puts his container of juice on the floor, and stands up. "Can I help you with somethin' or you just like cleaning shelves?"

"Excuse me?" Julian raises his eyebrows.

"Julian, just what the fuck," says Lena, her face flushing with anger.

"Oh, *Naa mek mi vex, mon!* [Don't piss me off!]" says Jocelyn, swishing off down the aisle.

Julian waits until he's out of range then asks Lena, "You think this island boy of yours is a good idea?"

"Oh, he's a great idea." Lena knows this, seeing as her audience is mainly middle-class, middle-aged white females.

"I would think this isn't the image—"

"I should market this image. We've done fantastically."

"You look beautiful." He makes a move toward her, then seems to change his mind.

"You look like shit," she says, picking a piece of tissue off his lapel. And he does look like hell, haggard and gray.

"I should have sent you flowers," he says.

"All right," she says, "All right."

"Congratulations on getting juried in here. It's probably the best show in America."

"Julian, I know that."

"You've lost weight," he says, picking up her wrist and turning it over in his hand as if inspecting a drumstick. "You could use a good meal."

He takes her to dinner at a very expensive French restaurant. They eat pâté and share a salad; she orders the duck, and he has the fish. The wine costs as much as the meal and tastes marvelous. She eats hungrily, making small talk, being smart and funny and cool. He's so lavish and attentive, you'd think he was buttering her up. But for what? She bides her time, holds her tongue, weighs her comments, and as he talks, telling her about the acts he's promoting, the new opportunities coming his way, she drains one glass after the other.

At the end of the meal, in a burst of verbiage, he finally comes out with it; he's in love with someone else. He says he's not the first person to fall out of love with his wife. It's embarrassing, he admits, she's so young. He's feeling a bit predictable. "There's nothing wrong with you, Lena, you're a beautiful woman. I never asked for this to happen. It just did." He takes her hand and empties what's left of their second bottle of wine in her glass.

Lena picks it up and waves it dangerously in front of her face, watching the precious liquid slosh around the expensive crystal until something occurs to her. He's jettisoned her because he's scared of growing old. Poor guy, she thinks. "Yeah, it happens, you meet someone on the plane, and before you know it you're fucking in the bathroom." She puts down her glass and sits upright, straightening her shirt. "Oh, let's get done with this. I want a divorce."

He takes her hand, looking startled, as if the idea hadn't occurred to him. "No, no no. We'll just wait it out. You'll see, I'll get over this."

"Oh, boring," she snaps. "I know what, let's get out of here." She folds her napkin and grabs her purse. "How about we go to your room?"

Not moving, Julian watches her, eyebrows twitching.

"No? Oh, I see, is the girlfriend in the room? Could it be that the dumpy little girl in the Mickey Mouse ears I saw you with over New Year's Eve is, even as we speak, lying on the bed watching maybe a *Dallas* rerun and ordering room service? Because you told her, what, you said maybe you were here on business?"

"Please Lena. This is painful for me too. She reminds me of you when you were her age."

"In that case, she'll be watching porn and ordering lobster in revenge for being used in this way. Girlfriend in one room, wife in the other, you bouncing in between dangling us both. You know what?" She's on her feet now, tugging at her skirt, balling up her napkin. "I owe you an apology. I've been so reluctant to break with you out of fear of having to make more production work to support myself alone. I had this idea that necessity would hold me back. I think you can follow this train of thought. And that's why I've bought into your, you know – that this is a bad patch, we'll wait it out—but hey, I just realized that being with you holds me back—and I'm not blaming you, I set it up for myself—and without you, the future is wide open. So thanks for ending it. I've got to get some sleep. Good-bye." And with a flourish—she thinks—she manages to convey herself out of the room, to the elevator and into her own room, where Jocelyn and his craft fair buddies are playing poker and eating vegetable stew.

The next morning before the show opens, she calls San Francisco General. A woman answers the phone. She hears muted conversation in the background, broken by laughter. She asks for Max, and is told he's off somewhere having X-rays. "He's had a cardiac event," the woman says. Lena feels shocked. She hadn't even thought to ask Jocelyn what kind of accident Max had had. "An event," says the woman. "Can you believe it? He's fine, though. Looking good."

Lena gives her name and asks her to tell Max she called and wishes him well. The woman then asks if she wants to speak to Max's wife, and Lena hangs up.

Jocelyn reminds her that only immediate family are allowed to visit a cardiac patient in the ICCU, so anyone in the room has had to pretended to be immediate family. There were probably a dozen "wives."

"True," she says. But why should Max's marital status concern her? Everyone's married, including her.

"Why you give that *pussy-clot* Julian all that slack," Jocelyn complains. "You in league with him, you act like bait. Yah got it all going for you, what you want mash it all up for?" He calls Julian *skenk, dat evilous dogheart,* and the one that makes her really happy to know him, *dat craven choke puppy.* "We do good, boss," he says. "Let's go home and get the act together."

3

Tonight, remove what remains.
Last night we lay listening to your one story,
of being in love. We lay around you,
stunned like the dead.

> —Jalal ad-Din Rumi, translated by Coleman Barks
> and John Moyne

Max says:

I got into an Ivy-ish school on a football scholarship but was quickly kicked out. After a year messing around Greenwich Village doing odd jobs, I joined the United States Marine Corps. I was way overweight, so they filtered me through the special "Fat Man's Platoon." I think I lost sixty pounds in three weeks. All day long you do push ups and get nothing to eat.

You know what the best thing is about the Marine Corps? It gives you a sense of solidarity with other people, and that's wonderful. The rest of it is ugly and insane. But there's a transcendent feeling that comes from belonging to a subclass of people who have no choice but to do what they are told.

I got assigned to an aircraft carrier preparing for combat and carrying nuclear arms. We spent three days loading ammunition in Norfolk without any sleep. My carrier was leading a battle group, and there were hundreds of boats.

I never got into actual combat, but standing on the ship watching the land go away, wondering if I'd ever come back, I got the feeling of going off to war. There were 3,000 more Marines on this carrier than was legal, and most of us slept head-to-toe on the hangar deck. I decided it would be crazy to try and sleep, even though we'd already been awake for three nights in a row, and right there I realized that war was hell.

When we finally got into the Mediterranean, the rumor spread that we were there to invade Beirut. Why, we had no idea. All we could see was a big crowded beach with Miami-style hotels. An advance recon was sent, followed by the regular grunts, and then us, the helicopter maintenance people. Through binoculars, we watched our Marines landing with drawn bayonets while all the people on the beach stood up and milled around trying to figure out what the fuck we were doing, which was absolutely nothing, and eventually all the Marines came back to the carrier.

We had a sergeant who was a real jerk. I'd made the mistake of using my full name when I'd joined up, and I tell you, a guy named Maxwell Norton Diebenkorn III from Park Avenue was going to absorb a certain amount of scorn. The sergeant caught me making fun of him behind his back—I was evincing some eighth-grade form of humor—and punished me by sentencing me to the ship's laundry so I couldn't invade Beirut.

It was August, and we were off of Africa; the laundry room was directly above the engine room, and it was 130 degrees or something. Because the heat was so intense, laundry room punishment was supposed to be limited to three days. When two weeks went by and no one came to get me, I went crazy thinking of my buddies lying on the beach with beautiful swarthy girls in their arms and their bayonets in the sand.

They put me on the sleeve machine. Now, a Navy officer's summer shirt has half sleeves. One guy presses the front and the back and then passes it to me, the sleeve guy. I slide the sleeve over two columns, press something, and it comes out with a nice crease. You have to be careful because if you push too far down, the seam will split.

By the time the third week was over, I felt desperate. What if that sergeant who hated me was trying to kill me and no one else knew I was down here? I felt I had to get someone's attention before it was too late, and to do this I started splitting the sleeves in the officer's newly laundered shirts and folding them so the split wouldn't show. And the cloth kind of glued itself together until all of a sudden these officers were saluting, and their shirts were flapping, and then they started yelling for the asshole responsible for their humiliation. Three officers came down and grabbed me off the sleeve machine and demanded I unfold one of the shirts. I shook it out enthusiastically and the shirtsleeve flapped.

So the officers said, "OK, before we shoot you, have you anything to say?"

"Yes sir," I said, and proceeded with my tale of woe. The upshot was they hauled me up in the fresh air. The reprimands went right up from that sadistic sergeant to the captain. As for me, I got a promotion to corporal.

North Hero, Vermont, 1985

Back from San Francisco, Lena and Jocelyn examine the molds made for them in Canada, and decide to go ahead full blast creating a line that's trippy, durable, funky, easy to mold, and utterly unique. On one of her trips to Montreal, with Zia in the back seat and a box of proto-types for the mold maker to look at in the trunk, Lena stops for gas at the general store in North Hero and runs into a woman she knows slightly, the director of the theater in Burlington. The woman launches into a description of a man she'd met last summer, whom Lena real-izes could be no one else but Max Diebenkorn. She keeps pumping gas while the woman gestures to where the road turns sharply to the left, and a narrow lane goes off to the right, and suggests that she check it out, if only for the turn-of-the-century nostalgia.

Lena backtracks a few hundred yards and takes the right turn, and immediately regrets it. The lane is deeply rutted and narrow, canopied by evergreens so thick it's like being sucked into a living tunnel: airless, dark, and almost silent, except for the whispery swooshing of branches scraping the sides, and though it's almost May there's still ice on the road and snow banks on the side, leaving barely enough room for a car. She can't even be sure she's on Max's road. What if someone else is living there, someone with a shotgun? There's no chance of turning around, no choice but to crawl forward and hope for a warning before she drives into the lake that she senses all around her. Agitated, Zia looms up, filling the back seat. She goes berserk, claws at the upholstery, causing the car to shake violently. Lena slams on the brake, yanks open the door, and Zia hurls herself out to vanish into the woods, then reappears in front of the car and lopes off with Lena inching behind, and vanishes again, appearing through gaps in the dense brush as a white blur as she canters along what must be a parallel utility road.

A fox darts out; two crows take off overhead. Lena's fear of nature begins running amok, she could be in a parallel universe operating on a different time zone, some place thicker and sunnier and teeming with dissatisfied spirits. Until suddenly, the oozing forest drops away and she emerges into a clearing. Here the road ends in a roundabout in front of a house beyond which glistens the expansive open lake ringed by mountains in the far distance all the way into New Hampshire. Golden late afternoon light streams through thick clouds. The sky vibrates with bird life: flocks of geese beating north, ducks in the water, terns on the rocks, gulls flashing light off their bellies. The lake sprawls at her feet, running turquoise under the ice and black where it breaks through. Jagged chunks of two-foot-thick ice still pile up in places at the shore. The air is wet and clean, joyful with all that birdsong and rustling wind. Lena gets out of the car and walks to the beach where Zia is picking her way gingerly over the rocks.

There comes from the water a low moan, a deep rumbling sound, and then a sharp crack. From the distance rings a faint tinkling sound of bells, swelling up and down the shore, then one bell sounds solid as church, followed by more rippling chords, and as the wind grows stronger the sound of millions of tiny crystals in cacophonous waves filling every molecule of air, space, and time.

It lasts for one exquisite, elongated moment; it was as if she'd been wandering through a silent cathedral where the chorus hid veiled in the corners picking through the notes of the universe to find the precise combination to touch her heart. It was a sacred concerto performed just for her. Then the sounds of the birds, the hiss of the wind, the moan of the lake beneath the ice starts up again, and the curtains part to reveal the ordinary loveliness of the cove, with the familiar red truck parked under a cottonwood tree. Max lives here, no doubt now.

It pleases her to see that the truck has been repaired and looks the way she imagines it would have before mating with that cow. Feeling suddenly shy, she grabs her dog and hurriedly drives away.

Weeks later, glazing pots for some gallery in Michigan she knows nothing about, thinking she hears the phone ring, she takes off her headphones just as the message machine clicks on. It's Max. He says he's been sick but he's OK now, and he's just booked a red-eye back home in early June.

"Do me a favor," he asks her. "You know where I live? Would you mind going up there, just to walk around and spread your vibes? Check things out?" She's so surprised and excited at the sound of his voice, it would embarrass her to actually talk to him. So she stops herself from picking up the phone. Anyway, what would she say? That she's already been there? Later that night, she runs the message back. She does it again before she goes to sleep.

He arrives by cab from the Burlington airport on the first of June. "Lucky guy, someone's mowed the lawn for you," the cabbie notes, letting Max out in front of his house. Sure enough, the big lawn has been mowed in militaristic swaths so close to the soil it looks scraped. A moving skin of cottonwood seed blows across it from the big female trees that loom along the edge of the lake behind the house. As the cab disappears he walks over to the newly scarified grass, where he first drops his luggage and then his clothes, piece by piece. Naked except for his boxers, he lifts up his arms, shuts his eyes, throws back his head, and starts to dance, turning in tight circles made with small *tenkan* steps. *Oh wind, wrap my body with your delicious lilac and dogwood and apple blossom. Oh wind, rid me of the disgusting stench of the hospital, of disease.* The wind carries on it the bonus smell of the fertilizer spread up and down the island. Tomorrow the shit tea may seep through the rocks and poison some fish and a few small dogs, but right now it fertilizes whatever dreams Max hopes to reignite here on the west coast of Vermont.

As he turns, he notices that rolling along with the feathery seed of hopeful pre-cottonwoods are balls of some thick white fur, the undercoat of a hairy being. *Ah*, he thinks, squatting to breathe in the smell, *Lena's been here with that wet white angel dog of hers, spreading her juju as I'd hoped. Bless her, wherever she is.* He stands still for a few moments relishing the pleasure of being back in his spot, as Castaneda would say, and then pulls on his clothes and goes off to find his scumbag cousins who are, he suspects, responsible for mowing his lawn. And why? Because they covet his little cove, which lies between their much grander spots. They mow his lawn to remind him he can't do it for himself.

Two of his cousins are leaning on a red tractor in his mother's former vegetable garden, watching him. One of their wives kneels on the newly plowed garden bed, placing tomato plants in holes cut in the black plastic. Max finds the plastic offensive and suburban, out of keeping with the pastoral landscape. When he was a kid, the old gardener worked every inch of the soil by hand, turning it into the most exquisite friable black gold, which is why his cousins are planting in his garden instead of plowing up gardens for themselves on their own properties. Their peas are already inching up a fence at the garden's edge.

Catching his eye, the cousins yell out "How the hell have you been, Max old boy?" and "How's the writing business, cuz?"

They've left him one flowerbed. Untended, it's on its way back to forest. Sumac, grapevines, wild raspberry, and burdock have taken over while everything else has been choked out. *Damn it,* he thinks, heading for the garden shed, he will bring this plot back by hand if he has to, pull out the tree stumps with pliers, and prune the cedars with his teeth. The shed has been cleaned out and filled with new red-handled tools hanging on hooks; his tools have been stuck in a cobwebbed corner. He grabs his old shovel and starts digging up the flowerbed. It's an easy task, for the soil is loose and dark and rich.

His cousins keep an eye on him as they work in the next plot. When he looks up, the oldest one, whom he has dubbed the Colonel, points meaningfully at the tractor, as if to say, *Hey, cuz, why don't you save yourself a broken back and borrow my beautiful tractor?* The Colonel would even offer to drive it himself, because in his eyes, Max is a lazy asshole, and that's why they've taken over his gardens. In the Colonel's opinion, Max should be grateful.

The cousins are from a distant branch of the family. They don't suffer with the Diebenkorn bellies and flat feet and bad teeth. They are both boyish men reaching their sixties with gravity-defying posture, mouths still filled with teeth, and wealthy second wives who collect good china and raise golden retrievers.

Here comes a golden retriever now to merrily sniff Max's toes. Max pats the long silken fur, saying "Hello, beautiful doggie," and accepts a mouthful of love in return. If the sweet animal has been warned to avoid him, it's rolled off her back. He wonders if she'll still lick his face when Queen Zia arrives and sets up new rules.

He laughs out loud now. For some reason, he's already living with Lena in his imagination. To hell with the cousins. Let them plow their skin off their bones. He'll throw them out when he's good and ready and he won't feel ashamed for not having turned out like them. And anyway, all their land is leased and not one of his family will ever own it, so why all the fuss.

Smiling, he shakes his head *No thank you for your beautiful tractor, fuck you.* He makes a temple of his fingers, and turns his back.

Leaning his shovel against a cedar, he goes off to look at the property, curious as to what else of his they've appropriated, for which he's supposed to feel grateful. For starters he finds that they've brushhogged his mother's old horse pasture, rolled his clay tennis court, stored their cars in his stable, started a deck on the gardener's old cabin, and tied their boats up at his dock.

His vision of his family has his roots deep in the murky, psychological past. These cousins who bullied him as a kid are bullying him now. They should have the decency to wait until his mother dies before squeezing him out like a bug in a trap.

Max's house squats atop a thirty-foot cliff gazing across Lake Champlain to the Green Mountains. At one time it was the splendid centerpiece of an Adirondack-style camp, built from vertical cedar logs taken from the land a hundred years ago, providing his Park Avenue family a summer residence of rustic opulence. The spaces between the logs were stuffed with horsehair; a great fireplace commanded the main room.

It's easy to imagine how it once had been, despite all the neglect and ruin.

He kicks open the waterlogged kitchen door. As soon as he steps inside, he's hit in the face by the stench of defrosted garbage. Everything is exactly the way he left it last December when he'd given up trying to make it through the winter and glided off into the frozen night to meet with his cow. Since there'd been no point heating the entire house, which was after all just a pile of logs with a rotten roof, he'd moved everything into the kitchen and shut it off from the rest of the house, tacked pink insulation over the logs, and built his sturdy bed platform above the enormous old Garland wood stove. Here he'd spent the dark hours burrowed under quilts, reading, nodding off, and studying the mice, squirrels, bats, and raccoons as they gently went about their business of reclaiming the house for their own. He'd begun thinking of himself as one of them, despite his flabby furless body and his great big brain.

And now he's back.

He takes a quick tour with a towel over his face, stirring up dust motes and bits of pink insulation. His kitchen is stocked with food, canned goods in cabinets, frozen Lean Cuisines and Tombstone Pizzas stuffed in two refrigerators. His shelves sag with books, with old favorites, classics, novels he's looked forward to reading. It's his home, he thinks, and feels a rush of joy. A line runs through his head: *Home is where you come to die*. He who finds that spot on time is a lucky man indeed. He exits through the porch and heads down the stone path that follows the lake, with a row of cabins on his right, and crosses a bit of lawn to the last cabin, set off by itself on a bluff. In it is his futon bed with two white down comforters and four new pillows protected by a plastic tarp. His books sit on their shelves, his clothes hang in his closet, and the bathroom lean-to looks like the men's room in a mill town bar, but it hasn't collapsed.

He spends a couple of hours pulling the plywood boards off the windows, sweeping and hauling up buckets of water from the lake to scrub the floors, working at a comfortable pace until dark, when he washes up as best as he can and drives to the lakeside restaurant down the road. Mike, the owner, greets him warmly and escorts him to a table by the big picture window. The pretty waitress brings him a stout—she remembers!—and asks all about California. He orders beer-batter shrimp and a house salad and lingers over coffee, leafing through a worn leather-bound volume of *The Green Mountain Boys*, written by an islander in 1911.

That night he dreams he's tucked in his bed drifting through the low-ering clouds gathering over Lake Champlain. Ice covers the lake, glis-tening fur on an animal's back. In the center, a river flows free toward Canada. His island looms on his left. The real Vermont, the one with the streams and the Green Mountains in the distance, stretches out to the right. He lies on his stomach wrapped in bed sheets, his chin hooked over the edge of the bed, staring down at the beach where a small figure struggles to pull a wooden platform over the rocks. A twist of his shoulder brings him down for a closer look.

The man below reaches the shore, falls, and begins to twirl on his spine, his legs in the air. With its rope trailing, the abandoned platform shoots down the ice like an escaped pet, disappears around a peninsula, reappears a moment later, and glides to a stop in front of the man, who is now back on his feet. A pole rises slowly through the boards. "This is my ship," Max declares, and begins to descend.

His sheets and blankets drop away on a gust of frozen wind. He hovers directly above the shore, casting a dark shadow over the man who is attempting to tie himself to the pole. Max dives off his bed, grabs the other's shoulders, somersaults, and enters through the head. It occurs to him that he's sliding through himself upside down. "No mean feet; I mean, feat," he says out loud, waking slightly. The dream recedes, he feels the cold, hears the groans and creaks of the wind outside, and pulls up the sleeping bag tangled at his feet.

"Hello," he says, returning to his dream. He passes through his own face, neck, shoulders, lungs, digestive system, elbowing his way down his ribs, righting himself along the way, fitting one leg then the other until he feels the edges of his toes. "Hello," he says back. "Hello."

Grounded in this body now, he wraps the rope through his belt loops, tying them off in a neat Flemish double-eight. He looks over the ice and determines to follow the open water in the middle of the lake north into Canada. He calculates the speed necessary to become airborne—the wind velocity, directional coordinates—the numbers clicking in his mind in loopy permutations that appear crucial but make no sense.

He's wearing a tattered bearskin coat that makes him feel like the original bear. When he lifts his arms it billows out and catches the wind that has angled up from the south. He winds the reins about his wrists and widens his stance as the chattering raft picks up speed. The farther out it travels over the rough ice, the harder it is to hang on. He pushes his cleats into the soft wet wood and throws back his head, stretching his skull deep into the thick fur. The stench of bear makes him gag. Thick leather gloves grow on his fingers, his coat sleeves bulge. *Wings up, right, throttle down, Roger. Liftoff.* The heaving ice turns translucent, offering a window through which he glimpses uplifted faces as he flies by. He sees piles of vehicles and a chamber filled with empty bleachers. Horses gallop through fields soft as pudding. The layered wreckage of his people.

He yanks at his rope. The raft drops away as he breaks through the clouds. The bearskin sail falls from his arms turned now to wings. He's a huge black bird beating through the joyous cumulus, screaming to the stars on his way to the stratosphere.

An abrupt buzzing noise blows it all away, fast. There's a cousin chain-sawing outside his window.

"Dreamus interruptus," he hears himself cry out. *Fuck.*

In the morning, after getting coffee and homemade apple cider dough-nuts at the general store and using the porta-potty round back, he comes home and walks across the lawn, inspecting the water pipeline he'd pulled up last fall, repairing leaks as best he can, making a parts list, and finally pulling the pump out of the shed where it was stored over the winter. Some of the fittings have burst, and he'd forgotten that the pump had seized at the end of last summer and needs a new motor. If he were smart, he'd replace the line with PVC pipe and bury it, but then he wouldn't have the dubious pleasure of jury-rigging a system that should have been discarded a decade ago.

There's only one road up and down the island, and so when he drives to the local hardware store, he retraces the route he took when he hit the cow. He never has been able to determine why he took the turn he did, the one that led him toward the lake and the field across from Lena Zinelli's house. It was a mistake, and he's curious to find out if it was an easy one to make.

It isn't. The turn is clearly marked; it's a sharp ninety degrees from the main road, which continues straight as an arrow. Even in a blind-ing rain in the dark, it would be hard to mistake. He would have had to completely stop at the corner to take that turn. So it seems that night his steering wheel possessed a brain and a strong desire to meet its fate.

At the counter in the hardware store, the owner looks up from his crossword puzzle and rags him, as he's been doing since Max was a kid, "If you had a brain it would be lonesome. Too cheap to buy a new pump, you throw away money on a piece of crap that's worthless as a hole in the snow." He shoots him a look with his turtle eyes that indi-cates yes, I mean the opposite, we both know there's a Zen in keeping machinery running that only seems to involve money, but still I'm compelled to try and sell you something you might not need.

Max smiles—yes, he fully comprehends—and heads back home holding his baggie of screws, batteries, and clamps on his lap, with the lumber and lengths of metal pipes he bought banging in the back.

When he reaches the fateful corner, he doesn't hesitate taking the turn into Yellow Barn Road. He parks in the cornfield, which seems washed of any memory of that night when he'd dented the apple tree with a cow on his hood about to end its sweet, dull life. He sits in his cab with the truck door open, appreciating the new corn poking through the ruts, and eventually climbs down to take a leak. He hangs on the door, pissing free-form while looking across the road at a long, tree-lined driveway, the shoulders neatly mowed. He can just see the edge of Lena Zinelli's roof. He shakes off, zips up, and slams the truck door—it hasn't worked right since the cow thing. At the noise, a furry white head pokes up from the middle of the driveway—Zia sleeping in the dust. She stretches her neck but doesn't get up.

"Hey Zia," he calls.

Curiously, Zia stays put in the drive, looking thoughtfully at him with her pink tongue over her teeth. Max walks toward her. Over her red leather collar she's wearing a second black nylon collar with two prongs and a small box flashing a red light.

So Lena has bought an invisible fence. The wild girl has been put in the zoo. He steps through the boundary, rubs her head, and speaks into her left ear. He says, "Don't fret, dear; Einstein said that the worst thing is to have too many choices. I'm paraphrasing here, but you know what I mean. Or it was maybe Freud." Her nametag reads ZIA and LENA ZINELLI followed by a phone number. Julian's name is still on the mailbox—ZINELLI/MOON, suggesting a pair of Sicilian astrologers—but Julian Moon does not own this dog.

Zia stands up, stretches, and leans against his side. He runs his hand over her spine, feels her skin ripple as clumps of fur fly off her pelt and roll over the grass. Her oval eyes glow with pleasure. His fingers move over her rib cage, over her eager dog heart, and circle her thin front leg. Pats of steam appear in her nostrils. Her nose, he sees, is slightly pink. There's an irregular streak of beige on her chest. "Take me to your mistress," he says, and walks down the road.

Lena's house sits in a straggly woodlot with ten acres of bog at its back. It's a decent-size seventies house, blandly anonymous, with angular spaces and a high cathedral ceiling bisected by a half balcony, a house begun with good intentions that must have fallen by the way when the builder ran out of money. The site is pleasant enough, Max decides, if suburban. Marianne's all-wheel Toyota is parked next to Lena's orange Peugeot. When no one greets him, he lights a cigarette and smokes it down, fact-checking the environment to deepen his knowledge of the occupant, noticing foundation cracks, cheap siding, warped jambs, flimsy hardware, hollow-core doors—and concludes that it's an unfortunate house no one has inhabited long enough to love.

The day feels sweet, sunlight licking at the back of his neck, a few bumblebees checking out his flip-flopped feet before buzzing off into the backwoods. If this were his house, how would he change it? Could he sassy it up enough to love it? A slate roof, teak deck, cedar shingles, French doors instead of sliders, a few more windows on the East, and an inviting entry sequence, for starters. He'd replace those ugly railroad ties holding up the bank with bluestone, round off the edge of the deck and step it down a couple of levels so it inhabits its site instead of sticking out like the top turd on a wheelbarrow. He'd add a tower for a writing room, with a view of the lake. Why bother living on an island if you can't even see the water?

A 1957 Chevy is parked near a side door. It's painted the green of an adolescent's dream; no dents, maybe needs a new bumper, white-wall tires, and a major paint job. Inside, gum wrappers and empty water bottles litter the floor; a grimy Rasta tam perches on a hundred-pound sack of plaster. Max runs his fingers over the curves, thinking it would be a crime if Jocelyn hauled this beauty over to Haiti or wher-ever he's going to start his ceramic village, and he'll probably be grate-ful for whatever he can get for it.

A burst of laughter comes from deep inside the house, and then the musical hiccups of someone flipping through the radio dials. A door slams, footprints slap on the gravel. He hastily grinds out his cig-arette. Zia appears around the corner followed by Lena with her arms around a large hunk of plaster. Zia trots up to him and does her little dance of pleasure.

"Oh hello," Lena says, setting the thing—a bust, head-shaped with a square opening the size of a small TV monitor instead of a face—on her feet, letting it lean on her legs. The plaster's left a damp swath on the short baggy blue *schmatta* she's wearing over black leggings. She pushes back her hair, and plaster dust falls on her shoulders.

"Marianne was talking about making a series of talking heads. Is this one of them?" He guesses she's gotten Lena to do most of the work, while she give orders.

"She's just leaving," Lena says, picking at the plaster on her dress.

Marianne appears, dragging a bucket. "Maxi, hello there. Meet the

Ronnie Reagan talking head," she says, pointing at the sculpture on Lena's feet. "It's going to sit on the Ronnie Reagan body. I'm taking it into town to fit it with a TV screen."

"I was thinking just that," says Max. "Perfect."

"Want to see the studio?" asks Lena.

"Would you help me put this thing in my car?" Marianne asks Max, who hoists it on his shoulder. It's heavier than he thought. Lena must be stronger than she looks.

"I'll be inside," says Lena, going off with Zia at her side.

"What are you doing here?" Marianne whispers when Lena's out of hearing range. "I didn't know you were seeing each other."

"Why are *you* here? We're not seeing each other. She invited me over, said she was stuck in the studio firing a kiln."

"Oh, she calls lots of people to keep her company."

"I'm different."

"That's true. I think I'll hang around and watch you two mate," says Marianne. She crosses her arms over her chest and smiles toothily.

"You have more important things to do," he says, heading off to the car. "Here's what you should show in this face. Go get the video footage of Hezbollah announcing they've kidnapped the CIA station chief in Beirut. Then I'll bet what happens next is that they'll wait a week or so to announce they're beheading him. It doesn't matter if it happens or not, the point is, that's your Reagan story. He's responsible for this stand-off. Don't let that brain-dead charmer off the hook. Now, drive safely, please." He puts the piece in her car and holds the door open, bowing for her to get into the car.

"Yes, boss," she says, not moving. "Buy me that Chevy and I'll go."

"Uh uh, that's mine."

"Actually it's Jocelyn's girlfriend's car."

"Girlfriend, girlfriend!" says Max sounding pleased. "Now, off you go."

The studio is a long, high-ceilinged room with a screened-in porch facing west, a basic converted garage with nice detailing—more love in this workspace than in the entire house—pine boards on the walls, skylights, track lighting, speakers in the rafters, built-in cabinetry, with an addition for the glaze room and two electric kilns and a covered walkway leading to a shed housing a gas kiln. Various configurations of worktables fill the center; shelves line the walls from top to bottom, all of them filled with works in progress. There's a big metal table with a platen for rolling slabs of clay, a large extruder, covered tubs labeled PORCELAIN, TERRA COTTA, STONEWARE, SLIP, and CRAP. On one side of the room, Jocelyn is standing in the U of three tables, holding a hose, pumping slip into plaster molds while Lena watches from a couch in the corner.

She beckons Max over with a finger and a smile.

"Great studio," he says, sitting down next to her. "I see you do an amazing array of different things here. I can relate to that. I write for myself and sell to the *Reader's Digest*. It's hard making a boundary between what you love and what you do."

"I'm glad you came," Lena says. "I didn't know if you got my message."

"Tell me, why did you call?"

"I'm not sure. You know, I think we're meant to be great friends, and I maybe wanted to get that started."

Later, they sit on his porch in the wicker swing in the waning afternoon sun, making small talk about her work and his trip to California while down the cliff the ducks drift in circles on the absolutely still water. He explains that these are dabbling ducks or diving ducks—he never can remember which—and soon the mother will lead her babies, as many as fourteen little ducks, out in the shallow water to teach them either dabbling or diving, and they can watch.

A breeze blows in smells of barbecue from a motor yacht anchored off the peninsula blaring rock music. Max opens a bottle of wine, fills two pewter goblets, and hands her one. "You taste it," he says. "Your dog has a more sophisticated palate that I do. You tell me if it's turned." He's liberated a case of it from his mother's wine cellar, where it's been stored for more than thirty years. It tastes, as it should, harsh and expensive and powerful, like Julian's Châteauneuf-du-Pape, only he'd never serve that in anything but glass. On the label are stamped the numerals 1-8-2.

"Dollars?" Lena asks, holding up the bottle, squinting.

"English pounds, more likely. I remember the chauffeur taking us kids to watch crates of things being lifted off cargo ships, and then driving them home in the Bentley. God, how pretentious. Please forgive me. In truth, I'd prefer a Dr. Pepper."

Lena smiles, Max smiles, as if they'd known each other since fourth grade and have learned that life is really just fourth grade going endlessly on and on. It's growing chilly now as the light dulls and the evening begins. Peepers come out, chipmunks chatter in the branches as they pick from a tray set up on a wicker table, a platter of Brie, grapes, and crackers with a pitcher of water.

"When I first came here?" Lena says, putting her feet up on the brown wicker ottoman, handing Zia—she's settled on a cushion at their feet—a bunch of green grapes. "I felt like I'd fallen into a fairy tale. It was quite eerie. I thought I heard people whispering, children laughing. But no one was there." Max pulls a brown quilt over her legs. "And then I heard the sound of tinkling all up and down the shore, like crystal chandeliers. Was I hallucinating?"

"So you got my message asking you to vibe the place?"

"I'm embarrassed about this, but actually I'd already been here. I'm so sorry, I just wanted to—I don't know. Curiosity."

"That's nice, I'm glad you did that. That sound of crystals? That's the ice breaking up: happens all the time. Only that doesn't diminish the magic of it, because when it happens it's only for a moment, and conditions have to be perfect. The ice has to be in the right place when the wind blows just so, and you have to be there to hear it, the biggest part of the equation. As for the whispering, those were my ancestors you heard in the trees. They don't come out for just anyone."

"Are we exchanging life stories? I'm half-Jewish, no ancestors in my trees."

"OK," he laughs. "My roots are seeped in war, alcohol, and money. For all her money, my mother was a miserable woman, an only child."

"My granny made jam in tin cans on our stove and took the BMT up to Times Square to hawk it. I'm also an only child."

"Her father used to say the only reason anyone would marry her was for her money, which came from Texas Cement. They put stocks in my name when I was in my twenties and told me to put it away for my future children. Whatever you do, they said, never sell your Texas Cement stocks. So I did; the sale kept me alive for years."

"What books do you read? Do you think John Irving writes like a woman?"

"I think he writes like a teenager. Really, the only novel worth reading is *Moby-Dick*. I'm going to spend the rest of my life reading it."

"All those blubber recipes?"

"You bet.

They drink more wine as the sun goes down. They smoke dope. Max brings out a baggie of pharmaceutical grade cocaine, but they leave it alone.

They learn their lives have crossed paths at several junctures. They could have met at any time, in any place, at any party. They're both in their forties, children of the sixties, married to other people. In 1974 they both lived in lofts near the Fulton Fish Market. They both spent Sundays at the Met, hate opera, love *Citizen Kane*, and admire to varying degrees Susan Sontag, Norman Mailer, Noam Chomsky, Robert Rauschenberg, Robert Pinsky, Virginia Woolf, Robert Bly, Joseph Campbell, James Hillman, Clement Greenberg, Harold Bloom, the Rolling Stones, Martin Scorsese, Wavy Gravy, Federico Fellini, Leonard Bernstein, Pete Hamill, Robert Moses, Leonard Cohen, Lawrence Ferlinghetti, Bruno Bettelheim, and John Waters.

"I'm sick of relationships," Lena suddenly blurts out.

"What do you mean? Everything's a relationship. You go for what you don't have." He slides his bare feet under the quilt and rubs her instep with his big toe.

Two minutes later she's in his lap with her dress around her hips. The swing creaks back and forth on its tracks. Candles flicker in the dark corners. On his sturdy body she feels light as the bat flying in and out of the unscreened window. She's in his hands, and he's making a cathedral out of her, and the pray-er and the penitent all in one. He doesn't let go of her for a moment; it's all for her. He watches intently, egging her on. In between kisses he pays homage to her collarbone, her shoulders, breasts, rib cage, navel, pelvis, and toes.

While she sleeps, he crawls quietly over to the couch where a big yellow moon hangs in the window, lights a cigarette, and picks up a book. He might as well be holding it upside down for all he's able to concentrate. "Thank you, moon," he whispers, closing the book. "Thank you for this marvelous gift." To drain a woman of her sorrow, especially a woman who appears not one iota sorrowful—is that not a lucky task designated by the gods? He leans back against the cushions and watches her sleep.

When she stretches and yawns, he throws her his robe. "Come on," he says, pulling her up, "I'll take you on a tour of the house. I want to show you what I'm up against."

As they move through the main room, a generous space with a ridge beam twenty feet from the floor, terrible lighting, and a crumbling fireplace, so crammed with furniture, extravagant leather sofas, hulking armoires, stacked chairs, side tables, and desks, Lena wonders what he means by *what he's up against*. Does he mean all this physical *stuff?* The mahogany banquet table with fourteen chairs? The warming dishes, divided for various vegetables, looking like utilitarian cafeteria ware except for having been crafted in Europe of real silver, with dented serving spoons and covers? The thirteen sets of sterling silverware, service for forty, every piece of which needs polishing? Or does he mean, look at all this historical baggage, this family, that's what I'm up against, the people at this dinner table, and those who shopped, cooked, served, and cleaned up for them? She can't imagine what it took to keep this place going; legions of maids and nannies and caretakers. She has no framework for a deeply American family like this with the chutzpah to slough off their wealth like roadkill, and after they die, taking up residence in the cedar tops where they'll forever remain glaring down at the living. She has no living history like this, no ancestors to steer her through life. Hers had been thoroughly eliminated, disappeared in European countries, victims of war, famine, plague, and Holocaust. At this moment, she felt bereft.

"Look at this stuff, can you believe it?" Opening a cabinet door, he shows her a shelf crammed with trophies and piles of medals with red, white, and blue ribbons. "Look, they rated themselves in ping pong, archery, English saddle riding, dog agility, golf, tennis, you name it. And look here." He opens a desk drawer. "Check receipts, invoices, shopping lists, and God, my report cards. Listen to this:

"Master Maxwell is a very bright boy but continues to have problems concentrating. I don't wish to lend humor to this situation, but perhaps we are boring him? He seems to have his anger better under control, but will fare much better once he understands there are better ways to express his superiority over his classmates than by bullying them."

"Which one of your family members was Bob?" she asks, handing him a dented second place for "Diving off the raft."

"Jesus, Bob was a dog. He's buried in the garden next to Austin and Flagel. Come here." He's standing in a room bigger than her bedroom divided into closets packed with waterlogged cardboard boxes, their contents spilling over the floor. "The cardboard box as we know and use it was invented in 1871 by an American named Albert Jones,"

Max says, handing her a garment from a Saks Fifth Avenue box. "My great-grandmother's bloomers, can you imagine? Beautiful silk, isn't it. All the boxes come from classy New York stores: Bonwit's, Lord & Taylor, Russek's Furs—Diane Arbus's family store. And the really good stuff is still in New York. Look at this. The ladies did a bit of tatting. Isn't that gorgeous?" He hands her a length of lace, then picks up a tiny pink booty made of the softest leather tied with a heavy silk cord.

"My booty," he says, handing it to her. "Stop laughing."

"You love this stuff. It's hopeless. I'm telling you, the only way out is to rent a dumpster."

"I'll frame the lace—wouldn't it look grand on a blue background—and give it to you as a present. Come see the ceramic collection. As a potter you'll have an eye for what's there." He leads her through the kitchen, a newer addition already pulling away from the main structure. New unpainted cabinets have been propped against one wall. A microwave, toaster, coffeemaker, and a half-filled box of cider doughnuts sit on a round oak table. There's no sign of the insulation he'd tacked up last winter.

They come to a hallway running the full length of the kitchen, with wide shelves on every wall crammed with appliances and china, hundreds of bowls, majolica pitchers, faience serving dishes, crystal glasses, porcelain platters, stainless-steel vegetable trays, silver warming trays, Tiffany salt and pepper shakers. He takes down an armful of plates. All of them have been broken or cracked, and all have been repaired. "So, what do you think?"

"Wow. Some of this stuff is priceless." She turns over a piece to check the watermark. "You've got the history of American ceramics here, all the famous production pottery, and what's this? A Clarice Cliff plate? You can give me a present of that!"

"It's yours. Take it away. Help me sort this crap out."

"Max, tell me, what are you doing here?"

"Maybe I've come home to die," he says, putting his thumb under her chin so she can't look away; but his words sound so ordinary they hardly register.

All night long they stay on the porch, talking, dozing, making love; and finally, while he seems to be asleep on the swing, she dresses hastily in the feeble, dawnish light, and whispers good night. "You can sleep here," he says, wide awake, reaching for her. "Your choice."

But she feels suddenly compelled to leave, his body—so pleasing to her only a moment ago—repels her now; it would be like bedding down with an animal who can't be trusted to wait until she falls asleep to begin chewing up her feet. She stands in the doorway wanting to flee, relating to those one-night stands in her past who tiptoed out the door before first light, but somehow she feels guilty, as if wanting to go sleep in her own bed is a cowardly act on her part. But she needn't worry, for he suddenly emits a huge snore, setting her free to dart through the door to her car.

Every day for the next month, Lena drives the twelve miles from her island to his, and every night before dawn she goes home to sleep in her own bed. Max no longer feels like a foreign species, but he snores like a pig—there's that—and she feels in her cells that as long as she wakes up alone with her dog, and doesn't share her coffee and oatmeal in the morning, she's safe from becoming entangled.

Or maybe it's because she really did hear him say he'd come home to die.

One morning she arrives home around dawn to find Marianne fumbling with the espresso machine in the studio.

"Honey," Marianne says, "thank god you got here. I can't figure this thing out, and I'm desperate for caffeine."

Showing her the ON switch, Lena goes over to the slop sink, washes her face with a paper towel, and flops down on the sofa. She's been away from the studio for so long it barely feels like hers. It's like she'd had a baby, set it down somewhere, and forgotten to feed it.

"What am I doing here?" she asks, mainly for her own benefit.

"I was about to ask you," Marianne says, spooning ground coffee into the basket. "All over the world women have gone berserk aching for a weekend with this man. He's fat and crazy and poor, but he would be on the cover of *People* magazine's 'World's Sexiest Men' issue, if they were told about him. All his old girlfriends will be stealing your sweaters and trying to find out your secret. Why don't you get a Mr. Coffee like everyone else? It takes forever to make a cup of coffee with this thing. I've got to be on the road. I'll stop at the diner on the way to the highway." She turns off the Gaggia and starts putting her things in a carton.

"He's just a guy." She stifles a yawn. "Where are you going?"

"Me? I'm cleaning up. I got awarded a residency at the Anderson Ranch for the summer. I'll pile the Ronnie in the corner for when I get back. By that time maybe someone will have hosed you guys off."

"Damn, I'm jealous. Where's Jocelyn?"

"It's me who's jealous. I'm serious. Max would make a fabulous life partner for you, just needs a bit of cleaning up. But then, so do you. Your studio associate is also in love. He's met this woman, Tonkey, you might know her, a singer in the Zone Out house band—I'm surprised you haven't run into her here."

"I haven't been here. I don't do anything. I wander around that flea market dreamland in someone else's life. I've lost my edge."

"Jocelyn's also acting like he's twelve years old. He's teaching Tonkey glazing. You ought to drop by some time and check out what they're doing in your name."

"Whatever they come up with, fine: I can't work, I have no ideas, I'm dried up. I'll just sign the pieces and collect the cash and lap up the applause. We'll be the School of Zinelli, like Rembrandt."

Marianne's right. Lena is smitten; she and Max have imprinted, spliced at the hips. They talk, talk, talk; they never shut up. Sometimes they take a break and read books, but in five minutes one of them starts commenting out loud or babbling on and on about the moon. When they're not talking, they're singing songs or fucking, and while they're fucking they team-write an ongoing pulp romance or babble about body parts. Max loves hypnagogic conversations at the edge of sleep, and Lena takes advantage of this to coax out information he would otherwise resist. Like how many women he's slept with. How many women he has asked to marry him. And do all vaginas look/act/smell/feel/behave/taste the same.

"You said you wanted a man who talks," says Max. "Beware of what you ask for."

On a glorious, pointillist July afternoon, with gulls darting around the one lone manatee-shaped cloud drifting off to the east, they leave Zia on shore and head out in an Old Town canoe toward the sailboats beating around St. Albans Bay, paddling through the onyx water hugging the shore. Lena's wearing a faded blue dress and a wide straw hat she found in the garden shed: his mother's hat, Max says, looking pleased. As soon as they round the peninsula and paddle into the shadow of the Colonel's big house up on the cliffs, his good mood darkens.

"There used to be an Adirondack-style log home there, just like mine. But after a mysterious fire, along comes this big prefab on a trailer. Then my cousin blasts for winter water without asking anyone. And the town doesn't even notice. If I try and wash my windows, I need a permit. There's a rumor going around that my cousin has brought a big Texas developer around to the old farmer, the last in the family that first leased this land to my grandparents." The house, set back and high on the cliff, is an A-frame structure with a deep deck and a huge American flag flapping on a pole off to the side.

"You obsess about these people," says Lena, shading her eyes and squinting up at the house. "What's with the giant flag up there?"

"You're obsessed with American flags."

"I know it. I hate flags, symbols of things that keep people apart, so we can keep killing each other." Lena comes from a deeply pacifist family; her father refused to stand up for the national anthem at Ebbets Field. In later years they could have been murdered for this, but Lena wasn't afraid—she just clung to her dad feeling revolutionary.

"Tell that to the Colonel. Look over there." Max paddles out a few yards until the other peninsula emerges, with an even bigger flag flying on an even higher pole.

"Well, that's offensive. I'm here in my canoe enjoying a beautiful day on the beautiful water. This is a billboard-free state. And what are these flags if not advertisements, incitements."

"I understand that, but you belong to a country—although it's OK to be subversive. As an artist, you're obliged to be, but be careful around the flag."

"While burning it?"

"You were one of those girls who welcomed soldiers back from Vietnam by spitting in their faces. Am I right?"

"I missed you?"

"What are we arguing about? One minute we're smack in the middle of a Seurat painting, and the next we're snarling at each other. What's going on?"

"I don't know. Maybe we've moved too fast. Maybe we need some time off."

"What are you really feeling?"

"I don't know."

Max parks his paddle on his knees and looks at her in silence. After a few minutes, he says, "You know I'm getting used to this. It's something you do: if you're feeling too close to me, you swing back the other way and come up with reasons to get away from me. I suppose everyone has their version of that, but I don't even think you know what you're doing. You're like those little black-and-white Scottie-dog novelty magnets: attract and repel."

"I'm sorry," she says. "But—"

"I'm sorry too."

"Max, are you dying?" she blurts out.

"Is that what's bothering you?"

At that moment, the weather suddenly shifts. A wave breaks at their bow, spinning them around like so much foam. "Better head straight in," Max yells, shoving his paddle in the water. "You work the other side. Head for that mess of rocks over there, we'll be better off in the lee of the island. We can leave the canoe wherever we land and come pick it up tomorrow." He starts paddling with long, even strokes, heading into a small cove where a number of boats bounce on their moorings. He steers around the tiny island, a wildlife sanctuary for nesting terns. *We're going to die*, Lena tells herself, as the wind tears at her hair. She's never been a boat person, is unfamiliar with the thrill of defying death by waves. "It'll be better on the other side," he shouts, but it isn't, here the wind smacks their faces and they can barely make headway. They wallow for a long, frightening moment in a deep trough, getting free of it by sliding sideways up a wave and taking on water. "Port!" Max suddenly yells, out, pulling on his paddle, sounding insanely joyful. "No, no, the other port!" Then, miraculously, they're deposited by the calmer shore current between the boats they'd seen from a distance, two antique Chris-Crafts, a little catamaran, a rubber dinghy, and a pretty red yawl, finally ending up wedged safely between big slabs of broken concrete jutting out from the beach—the remains of a boat dock that Max's grandfather built from Texas cement.

"Wow," Lena says, grabbing on to the rock. "We made it."

"But did you salute the flags on the boats as we went by? It's the family navy."

"Don't tease me. I said I'm sorry."

"I am too. You're right, we're doomed, everything's doomed, so we have nothing to do but march onward and upward. Now, look at this dock here: it's our personal Pompeii." He spreads his arms wide, taking in the stupendous mess his family hath wrought. "My grandfather comes in with his cement, right? Tons of cement. Cement has made him rich, and he thinks it's invincible. And he says, 'I'll build me a boat dock out of cement.' I showed you those pictures, right? My family's yacht drifting alongside the newly poured slabs for the boathouse, guests hanging off the sides holding champagne glasses, everyone partying compliments of Texas Cement. And the farmers laugh at him; they say, 'Oh, no, the ice will take it out when it thaws. After one winter it will be gone.' And guess what. The ice crushed it like cardboard. And what am I supposed to do with it? I say, turn it into an art piece. Don't fight it. Smithson's *Spiral Jetty* was a 1,500-foot coil consisting of 6,500 tons of rock. Now, let us consider the spiral; it's the same force you tap at the potter's wheel: it's universal."

He stops talking because Lena's looking at him in a fond manner usually reserved for family idiots. He pats her on the knee and says, "We weren't really in danger. The Colonel's somewhere on shore sharpening his lawnmower and watching us drown, just dying for the opportunity to tow poor pitiful us back to safety. But we didn't let him, did we. No, we did not."

4

This mood has nothing to do with you.

—Leonard Cohen, *Book of Longing*

Max says:

When I was discharged from the Marines, a contact of my mother's sponsored me for a private Peace Corps funded by the Episcopal Church in the Japanese Alps. Its goal was to help a rural community develop self-sufficiency. The Japanese assumed raising cattle in the mountains couldn't be done, but we Americans knew better, and so we were going to ship them some cows, and when the cow had a calf, it would go to another farmer, and so on. I'd work side-by-side with them, dig a trench, bring the cattle down, and fertilize the fields. All that was required was to be dumb and hungry and strong of back, which was just fine with me. At night I'd teach them English. There were nice-looking girls up there in those magnificent mountains, and I made friends with some of the young workers, but in general these people seemed to me like animated puppets.

One Sunday a guy took me to visit his family a couple of stations away. We sat in their living room, and they offered me tea, but I asked instead for a glass of water. Everyone fell silent. Now, my friend had warned me an American in the village would be a great curiosity, and sure enough, a crowd of maybe a hundred people had gathered and now stood outside, jostling each other to get a glimpse of me through the open shutters. A glass was set down at the table in front of me. I stared at it, knowing in my heart that my so-called friend had poisoned the water, and all these people had come to watch me die. And I knew that if I didn't drink the water, they might kill me anyway because it would be a sign of great disrespect. I took a sip. Everybody broke out in applause! They were yelling and screaming and jumping around. Amid general hilarity, they told me that the last American who had passed through had stopped and asked for a glass of water. That was fifteen years ago, when we believed the Japanese used human night soil to fertilize their crops, making the water unsafe to drink. This GI did as he always did, dropped in a pill that turned it piss green, and he drank the water, thanked them, and left. Ever since then they'd been betting each other that Americans would only drink water after they made it turn green, and when I showed up, it was their chance to settle their bets.

Japan was a very poor place in 1960, still reeling from World War II, suffering from shortages. The farmers could be very kind and sweet, but God, what an evil place underneath—really Thomas Hardy. Gargantuan agrarian cruelty is of course not confined to Japan, but it was there that I first came across it.

One day I walked into the farm office to find everyone congratulating themselves because the figures had just come out: they'd spread 100 tons of fertilizer that month. And I said, in English, "Gee, I did most of the spreading, and I'm sure it couldn't have been more then forty tons max." Obviously someone—it turned out to be the director himself—had been helping themselves to the fertilizer between delivery and the time I spread it on the fields. The director assumed that I was going to rat on him. He didn't dare fire me, but he sure could make me miserable enough to leave, and so he started a rumor that I was dying of syphilis and that my dishonored family had sent me to Japan to get rid of me, knowing full well that once the rumor spread, no one would want to have anything to do with me. And I was just bopping along, completely unaware, until I noticed that the guys I sat with at meals sort of slid away, and soon I was sitting alone at the movies and no one would even shake my hand. I was being ostracized, and I had no idea why. I begged people to tell me what I had done to offend them, but nobody said, "Hey, man, let's face it: you've got syphilis." Sometimes I could cry myself to sleep. Ostracism was the punishment the Greeks used to drive a person away: a terrible thing to do. I got to hate the place.

One day the workers discovered a nest of little baby field mice and were picking them up and ripping off their skin, laughing as the mice struggled until they died. When I protested, one of the guys picked up another mouse, held it up in front of my face, and slowly ripped its skin off. I picked up my pitchfork and said in English, "Do that again and I'll kill you." He put the creature down, and I found myself more hated than ever.

I started to think about suicide, and asked God whether I should live or die. I asked God to give me a sign, and soon enough, one day when I was working near the woods, He answered me. I heard a rustling sound, and a little old man jumped out, walked over to me, and started jabbering. Then he shoved a package at me and bowed his way back into the bushes. Later I learned that the man was a charcoal burner who had walked from his home a half-day journey away because he'd heard there was a young American working side-by-side with the Japanese in the fields, not as an overseer but as a laborer, and he thought this was so wonderful that he wanted to give me a gift. He brought me the most valuable possession he had. It happened that it was a Nambu semi-automatic pistol with a full magazine, his prized souvenir from World War II.

But I didn't know that, so when I went back to my room and opened this package and saw that this gift was a gun, I figured God had said, "OK, go kill yourself."

I felt extremely calm. There was no doubt now what I had to do. I field-stripped that gun, cleaned it, and put it back together again. The next Sunday I went deep into the mountains and tested its accuracy. When I got home, I set the gun in the crotch of an apple tree outside my room and put my thumb through the trigger bar. I was looking right down the barrel, getting ready to squeeze it off. I was just about to pull the trigger when something in my mind went, *Hey, wait a minute, here you are in Japan and you haven't been to Tokyo! What are you thinking?* So I put the gun away, figuring that I'd kill myself when I got back.

Still North Hero, still 1985

At the beginning of August, his brothers, deciding that Mother needs to leave this world of woe, call Max to New York. She's had another stroke, one that's left her hanging in the middle of here and there, and while the doctors agree that a few extra milligrams of Sister Morphine would gently tug her toward release, the family lawyer insists upon waiting for Max. If he wants a final word with her, he'd better book a flight.

In the waiting room, he finds his two wiry stepbrothers sitting on the one couch sharing the *Wall Street Journal* while his blood brother, the endomorphic Evans, hunches up in an inadequate armchair. All three wear double-breasted suits, red ties, and tasseled loafers. As if those identifiers aren't sufficient, Evans has the family crest monogrammed wherever it will fit: his jacket pocket, gold cuff links, handkerchief, and probably his custom shorts. Their eyes meet for a moment and then avert.

"Well," Max says, "it sure has been a long time. Five years since we've been together in one room. How you all doing. How're the wives and kids?" There are no free chairs and his stepbrothers show no inclination to move over for him, so he leans against the wall and crosses his feet for balance.

"Thanksgiving at my place in 1979," says the oldest stepbrother.

"Oh, yes." Max recalls a terrible evening in an obsessively renovated Vermont farmhouse, verging on violence, the stepbrothers smashed, the turkey dry, the kids out of control, and the wives about to explode. He'd predicted then that once Mother died, all three marriages would blow apart.

"We really should get together sometime soon," says a stepbrother.

"Go finish dividing up the booty while I have a word with Mother," says Max.

"Okey-doke," says Evans, reaching for his briefcase. "We'll be at the trattoria around the corner. Best Zuppa Inglese in the city, right Bro?"

Emily's private nurse sits at a desk doing paperwork with her patient's vital signs flickering greenly like marching ants over her starched white back. The family doctor pokes his head in the room, checks his watch, and says he'll be back in an hour.

Nodding, Max pulls up a chair. An hour is all he needs, for mother's been vanishing in parts over the last ten years. Sequentially: the part that walked and commanded, the part that argued, the part that ate, the part that chewed him to bits and swallowed him whole and convinced him it was all his fault; until all that remains is this bump in the hospital sheet the size of an eleven-year-old child. He's resigned to waging battle with her for all eternity, but still, he's going to give her a last chance for redemption. All she has to do is answer one question. It's the same one he'd been asking her all his life. He wants her to explain what happened to Dad.

When Max was four years old, his father vanished from the house. Every memory was therein expunged from the universe. His name was never again warmly mentioned. No one reminisced about him. There were no stories or jokes or comments. Nothing. Nada. When the kids nagged Mother for explanations, they were told he was a bad man and had to be sent away, and to prove it, she sent them with the chauffeur to a rundown building in a ratty neighborhood. They'd walked up three flights of stairs to find a drunk on the floor in the toilet—but Max might be making this up. Or maybe there was a drunk on the floor, but was this the father? That's what Max wants to find out. The rest he can embellish as he pleases. Surely no mother would deny a son the few words that might save him. She says an honest word about Dad, admits to some guilt around her relationship with her sons, and her reward is the subway token out of hell.

The official explanation is that Dad couldn't hold a job or his liquor and had scammed his way into Harvard Business School, but Max doesn't buy it, for there are so many drunks and corporate flops in the family one more clueless alcoholic dad would have blended right in. He thinks it was more likely that Dad left Mom. Had her father been right, that no man would ever love her except for her money? Was he, God forbid, gay?

So he puts his mouth to her ear and whispers a variation on the same question he's been asking since he was a little boy: "What happened to my father? I need to know, if I want to keep from killing myself. It's that urgent." The melodrama, he feels, is appropriate.

Emily smiles and says one word: "Son." Could he have heard that word? *Son?* She pulls him closer and garbles. He bends his ear to her lips. Then her voice rings out loud and clear: she says, "Annie Oakley was not a nice woman at all," and then hoots so loudly the nurse jumps up in confusion and rushes Max out of the room.

In the days that follow, as they wait for the reading of the will, Max books a room at the Gramercy Park Hotel. He intends avoiding his brothers, as the smell of their greed reminds him of his own desperate straits, something he doesn't want to think about, especially at this time, when he should be tending to his own grief. But is it grief he feels at all? Or is it the icy hand of his mother determined to pull him down with her to the pit of hell because he's always been her most challenging dinner conversationalist?

Whatever. He finds that he can't handle his lonely hotel room, and so he flips his Rolodex to N for New York and ends up inviting a different friend to dine with him in his hotel each night. First Sally, the former wife of a Buddhist friend; then Andrea, a cellist with the Brooklyn Symphony; and finally Sondra, a sociologist from Kentucky pursuing a doctorate at NYU. With each one, he enjoys good conversation, catches up on their lives, tells them all about his good fortune to have found true love this late in his life, and takes them to bed. Sally and Andrea leave playfully, fondly, and promise to keep in touch, but Sondra reminds him that he'd invited her up to Vermont over Labor Day weekend, and she's so looking forward to it, and although he can't remember inviting her, he somehow doesn't have the heart to dissuade her.

When the will is finally read, there's only one real surprise. As expected, his share of the estate goes to his wife and children, leaving him with only a small amount of money, but still, it's more than he's ever had in his entire life. The shock comes when he hears that Mother put Evans's name on the North Hero lease along with his own. It's a blow, because every time he's tried to do anything with his brother he gets screwed. Evans can't help it: he's genetically disposed to satisfy his hunger by stealing food, rather than working for it, and Mother called him a greedy, unscrupulous little creep, but—he'd forgotten this—she'd always counted on Max to protect him.

They're also bequeathed all the furniture in the apartment, some of it quite valuable. He imagines them negotiating the split piece by piece, like, *You want the china cabinet? I'll trade you for the clavichord*, and with that in mind—he believes—they arrange to meet at the apartment the next morning. But Evans has a different plan; he drives right uptown from the lawyers' office and hauls all the valuable stuff to Connecticut.

When Max arrives the next morning and sees only discards and junk scattered around the big dusty rooms, he pulls a dilapidated Queen Anne chair up to the window, lights a cigarette, and tells himself to chill out, it's their karmic connection, he should have anticipating being shafted once again by his very own brother. And isn't it more interesting being the junk man than the antiques thief, because any coward can steal beauty while it takes an artist to create beauty out of junk. Something he's been working on all his life.

As he smokes, mulling over old failed relationships with his family, he looks out the window at the building across the street that used to house the Soviet embassy. At least it did when he last lived here in 1960, before he'd left for Japan.

He'd just been discharged from the Marine Corps when Nikita Khrushchev went to the UN and started shrieking and bellowing, famously banging his shoe on the table to impress the world with Soviet power, but instead, in Max's opinion, as well as that of the Marine Corps, and of any true American, maybe even of God—for the world was deep in the Cold War back then—it showed Khrushchev for what he really was, a true primate. At the end of the spectacle, it was announced that the Soviets would convoy uptown to their embassy.

Max had been watching it all on television, from where he was now seated; he'd looked out his window, looked at the embassy, and realized that he'd be able to see Khrushchev get out of his car. Failing to find any binoculars, he took his mother's gun out of her bedroom and went back to his chair and begun fiddling with the scope. Sure enough, a crowd soon formed at the embassy, all the disgruntled Lithuanians, Ukrainians, and residents of the 'stans. Eventually the cavalcade pulled up, and guards leapt out to push back the crowd and hustle the president inside the building. A few minutes later Khrushchev appeared surrounded by bodyguards on a balcony that was two stories below Max, within direct viewing range of where he sat. He'd wanted to get a glimpse of Khrushchev, of course, if only to look into the eyes of the enemy. But he was also curious—was K. wearing only one shoe? Had he grabbed his shoe off his foot in a fit of passion, or was the gesture planned, and he'd carried a third shoe in his pocket?

So he'd trained his rifle on the biggest Soviet primate of all, first checking his feet, which were obscured by the flowerbeds, and then lifting his gun, and when he had Khrushchev's left earlobe in his crosshairs, placed his finger lightly on the trigger. He had a very clear image of himself, a twenty-three-year-old ex-Marine, unemployed and perhaps crazy, primed to assassinate the leader of the Soviet Union.

Why didn't he do it? Max stands up and repositions his armchair until he's satisfied he's looking down the same line of sight as he'd done fifteen years before. Of course it would have taken but a split second for the snipers surrounding Khrushchev to locate him, but he'd figured then—and substantiated it now—that he could have hit his target before himself being killed. And it would have been worth it, for he could have saved the world from the Red Menace and gone as deeply down in history as one can get. So what had stopped him?

Mother would have been pissed. Or would she?

Max takes the elevator to the lobby and speaks to the doorman, the very same Afro-American man about his own age who used to begrudgingly give in to young Master Max's curiosity about his race by inviting him to join the house servants who gathered in the back rooms of the vast apartments to smoke and socialize and rest themselves. Now he makes some phone calls to his buddies while Max goes off to rent a truck. When he arrives back at the apartment, he finds the loading zone reserved for him with a couple of guys waiting to help move the furniture out.

Lena's sitting on the porch in North Hero, wearing a heavy Icelandic sweater and pajama bottoms tucked in rubber boots, when he pulls up around 3:00 that morning. She's never spent a night in the cabin, and she'd thought to surprise him by conquering her phobias alone, but it hadn't worked out well. All night gangs of coy dogs had rampaged through the fields, mice screamed in the throats of owls, and raccoons lumbered through the barbecue as Zia tried tunneling under the floorboards.

"Thank you so much for being here," Max says, walking toward her. "But it looks like you didn't get much sleep."

"With all that wildlife trying to get through the door? How're you? You haven't taken amphetamines, have you? Listen, Max, I want you to tell me right here and now who you fucked in New York so I don't go making things up." Tucking herself into her sweater, she looks like a sullen child.

"What is the matter with you?" He sits down next to her, and she moves away.

"I wish I smoked," she says. "I was up here yesterday to do some gardening, and some one named Sondra called asking for directions. Ring a bell?"

"And you said?"

"I said, Max who? Wrong number." She watches him closely to see if he cares.

"I called up a couple of women in the city, and some went for it and some didn't," he says, taking her hand.

"OK." Lena puts three fingers on her pulse and counts. "Normal. I'm out of here."

"No, you're not." He pulls her up by her shoulders. "She's a friend." He almost said, "They are friends." "Look, I'm not going to try and dissemble or con you or anything, we're going to deal with truth here."

"You're not going to say that "Mummy died, and I needed comfort?"

"Man, you are being a bitch."

"I'm trying to walk away from you." She jumps up and spins around, holding her sweater close to her body. "So whatever it takes. I mean,

I don't need this. Who you sleep with has nothing to do with me. Fuck the sheep, if you feel the urge, if we had sheep."

"Of course it matters. Don't be stupid."

"Aren't you going to show me what more crap you lugged up here?" She saunters over to the truck, opens the tailgate and lets it drop with a loud bang. "You'll be thankful I wouldn't know Wedgwood from Bakelite."

He follows her, leans her against the truck and kisses her gratefully. "It would have broken my heart if you hadn't been here."

They sit on the tailgate drinking coffee and eating bagels he's brought from the city, watching the birds wake up and shoot off for worms. When they've finished they hook up a work light, and he starts hauling his stuff out. A long mahogany table with ornate legs emerges first. He drags it to a level spot on the lawn and regards it fondly. "I found it on the street, right by the police station on Mott and stored it in my old room See these initials? Look here, SS/ET 1981. I figure this is the table where Steven Spielberg worked on the *E.T.* script. Isn't that wonderful? Probably Evans couldn't figure how to get it out of the door." Next he brings out a lowboy with a missing drawer, then a set of six Chippendale chairs with ripped brocade upholstery, a leaf table with broken runners, a doorless curio cabinet, a map table painted green, and finally a Queen Anne desk that slips out of his hand and disintegrates on the grass.

"That's it for the furniture," he says, slapping his hands together. "Anything you want here, just say what, and I'll leave it at your place when I return the truck."

"No, you won't. Don't even think about putting anything in my basement. You look exhausted, Max. Why don't you get some sleep? Your eyes look like they stopped blinking somewhere back in the Bronx."

"Well, perhaps I'm running a bit of fever. From something on my leg, maybe I cut it. It's throbbing. Have a look? Bring that chair over here, would you?" He picks up his leg as though it were a log, rather than a personal body part, and lowers it down on the chair.

"What's the matter with it?" She bends down, pokes around his knee.

"Careful, please," he winces. "It started hurting around Albany. The skin on my shin is throbbing. Would you mind rolling my jeans up for me?" She gets on her knees, and he playfully tries to put a finger in her mouth, but she slaps him away. "I'm sorry you're still angry. Can't you roll the pant leg any farther up? Forget it, maybe I just need to move around. My leg probably swelled up from all that driving. I think I will get some sleep."

She follows him to the cabin, but then changes her mind and goes off for a swim.

Max takes off his jeans and sits down on the bed to look at his leg. He remembers vaguely banging his knee on the tailgate back in the city, but nothing to warrant such pain. He'll take care of it in the morning, he thinks, and climbs into bed.

When he wakes up around 8:00 a.m., he's alone. His leg looks and feels about the same, and it's painful to walk. He turns on the shower and carefully climbs in the tub and stands soaping himself until the hot water runs out. Then he kneels on his good leg and holds his throbbing knee under the cold water, and then decides that soaking in the lake—*mother-water heal me*—would be the best thing he could do. Fearful of falling on the rocks, he gets no farther than his deck, where he stands shivering as globular clouds wipe out the low-lying sun, scanning the beach for Lena. She's right there, maybe twenty yards from shore, lying on her stomach on a yellow plastic raft, reading. Zia, who has never taken to swimming, stands in the water up to her belly watching a sailboat tack out to the island. He decides to get dressed and finish unloading the truck, which has to be dropped off in Burlington by 6:00.

He makes himself coffee and hobbles over to the truck. Taking his time, he stacks the remaining cartons on the Steven Spielberg Memorial Writing Table, feeling only a little stupid. Then truth is, what he's doing is not about stuff, not really; it's as if buried in all this crap was some kind of message he needed to hear. And really, what was so terrible about caring about the past, about preservation, if that's all this turned out to be. So he sticks his bad leg into a bucket of icy water drawn from the garden hose and settles down to paw through his past.

By the time Lena comes back from her swim, empty boxes are scattered around the lawn, and Max sits at the table looking slightly stunned. She towels off and hands him a bottle of water and a box of trash bags and pulls up a chair.

"We're not throwing anything away yet." He takes the trash bag she's offering out of her hand.

"What do you mean?" Lena wrings out her hair with the towel. Obviously, she's had been looking forward to a massive green-up.

"This is not about hoarding too much stuff."

"What, then?"

"You know, everything you find out or remember about your past is in code. I'm in here, somewhere, and maybe I need to go shuffling through everything to—what? I hate this New Age idea of healing. Or maybe I shouldn't. If I'm sick"—both of them can't help but look at his leg still in the bucket—"I shouldn't be afraid of healing." He hands her a yellow pad of paper, crammed with peculiarly slanted words written in green ink. "In any case, some of this stuff is really fascinating. You get an interesting take on what a family like mine was like at the beginning of the century, not just visually, but in priceless documentation. You'll like this. It's an astrology reading for my mother's cousin, the one with the bloomers. I've read it; it's all about her being willful, strong, and daring. In short, unacceptable; who would want to marry her?"

"Strong as compared with?"

"The men in the family, who were all off in the bushes shooting at each other's assholes." Lena grins at him; she loves this image. "Yeah, sure," he goes on. "The girls all went to Bryn Mawr and were into Jung, Madame Blavatsky, and Gurdjieff. Populist spiritualism was a hot topic amongst the fems. Something like it is now."

"Really? I was getting an impression they were all kind of dour."

"Well, yeah, but they also had fun. After tennis, you'd find them in the gazebo with the Ouija board talking to their dead dogs. My mother had the complete works of Sherlock Holmes in the library. Did you know they were banned in Russia for occultism? Oh, look, I missed this note at the end. Read this to me, will you? I forgot my glasses."

She takes the scroll, and squinting over the handwriting, haltingly reads, ". . . the whole earth, and all the stars in the sky, are for Religion's sake."

"Walt Whitman," says Max.

"Listen, Max, you're right; you should preserve this stuff. I'm just saying, don't count on my basement for storage. I'm already seeing some strange cartons down there. It makes me wonder, are you stealthily moving in with me? Starting in the basement? Just noticing, Max, that's all."

"No, of course not. I'm thinking about moving *you* in with *me*." He laughs, with a dramatic sweep of his hand, taking in the collapsing cabins, the junk on the lawn, the stumps that serve as lawn furniture, the piles of dirt heaped up next to the trench he's been digging for the water lines. They both burst out laughing. They laugh and laugh, and carefully retrieve his leg—which looks almost normal—and make love. When he thinks she's asleep, he leans over to talk to her third eye, tickling it with its tongue to wake it up. He whispers to it, "Goddamn it, woman, winter is a-comin' in. 'Come, Winter, with thine angry howl, / And raging bend the naked tree; / Thy gloom will soothe my cheerless soul, / When nature all is sad like me!' That's Robert Burns. We need to get serious here."

"Then stop smoking." She rolls over on her side, awake.

"You think I won't."

"More or less."

"Give me marching orders. Command me. What would it take?"

She props herself up on one elbow and rubs her eyes. He can tell she's exasperated. What does she want that he's not giving her? "What's the matter? I'm telling you, we need to consider living together. This is neither weird nor horrible, nor unexpected, is it? How about we get married?" He stands up and pulls her to her feet. "Don't act as though I'm crazy. We love each other: we need to live together, to be married. So let's get hitched." When he locks his arms around her waist, she seizes up like a plank. He shakes her shoulders and pokes her body, then tightens his arms around her and anchors her with his belly for good measure and carefully stands on her feet. "You did say that; you said, 'Stop smoking'? Did I hear you right? You don't know what you're asking for. Smoke is my friend. It's something I count on. You can't imagine the depths of my despair, the misery I would inflict upon you, the wreckage I am capable of; my mood would be pure evil, I would poison your life, you might be in physical danger—did I say that?—I would wish to kill baby dolphins. Christ. I hope this won't be fatal."

Max now and then has stood on her feet to emphasize a point requiring she not leave the room, and she finds it somehow relaxing, standing belly to belly like two penguins discussing their mutual egg. She pokes a finger in his beard and says, "Furthermore, you have to decide to live. This is the real ultimatum." Once the finger's out of the dike, how the water does rush out.

"Do go on," he says, tightening his grip.

"You're like that little boy in the film of *Slaughterhouse-Five*, when his daddy tossed him into the pool to teach him to swim, to be a man. 'Ha-ha-ha-ha, sink or swim,' he told his kid and tossed him in. You see him peering down, a cigar in his face. And the camera followed the boy down underwater, and you saw that the kid wasn't even going to try to swim, that it was easier to sink, and down he goes the bottom. Boy, was his daddy pissed."

"Billy Pilgrim," he says. "Interesting. I'll make you a deal. You have to give up something just as difficult in return."

"The kid didn't even kick his little legs."

"You will have to give up Julian Moon."

"No contest," she says, looking away. "There's nothing to give up."

"I don't know why that jerk still has a hold on you, but he does. Now, about smoking, in due time, by methods unfathomable to me at the moment—it might be that someday I stop smoking. Maybe.

But as a condition for living together, I must say no. I'll smoke outside, though, you have my word for that."

"Well, then, no deal. And get off my toes." He doesn't move; she wiggles her toes and she's free. She's been free all along. She slides her feet from under his and leans against the U-Haul truck and starts to cry.

"Oh, God. Exactly how many women did you screw in New York, and what were their names, and what are we supposed to do with that?"

"So that's really the problem? Other women? Too many choices? We have no choice but to go ahead."

Lena wipes her eyes. The words of a stupid song enter her head:

> *In ancient Rome there was a poem*
> *About a dog who found two bones*
> *He picked at one, he licked the other*
> *He went in circles, he dropped dead*
> *Freedom of choice*
> *Is what you got*
> *Freedom from choice*
> *Is what you want*

"Well, that is succinct," Max laughs. "Who is it?"

"Devo."

"Never heard of him."

"Of course not; you're a Dolly Parton kind of guy, really. Which goes to show, we're not really compatible."

"More Carl Perkins, my dear. But let us leave all this for another day and do what we have to do, which is for me to drive this truck back to the rental place and you to follow. Then let's have dinner at the Thai restaurant and go to the movies, and when we come back we can carry on."

"Put your leg back in the bucket, OK?"

"No need, it's been cured by your love, my dear, by the little song about freedom from choice. I loved that. Maybe Pure Pop has the tape." The swelling has receded enough for his leg to bear some weight, but still he waits until she's turned her back to take a tentative step.

The day before Labor Day, Lena's parents call from Florida to discuss their annual September visit, which Lena dreads. Never a daughter to call her parents daily, or even monthly, she has yet to inform then about breaking up with Julian. She'd even thought to ask him if he'd pretend to be living at home. Although what to do with Max, she had no idea. Juggling two men wasn't her forte, though it had been her mother's idea of a good time, as evidenced by her serial affairs with family friends during her almost sixty years of marriage to her unsuspecting husband. No wonder Lena's got marriage issues.

So now, on the phone, Erica says they've decided to go on an Elderhostel trip to North Carolina instead of coming up to Vermont. She's going to paint while Marcos takes a class called "You Know Where Your Dog Puts His Mouth, and You Kiss Him on the Lips; Are You Nuts?"

"Great title, have a ball," says Lena, doing a little dance with her cordless phone.

She can't wait to tell Max.

He's cutting brush around the cabins, chainsawing away, piling up branches under the windows he's just washed, pulling out grapevines and scraping mold off the log walls. She follows him around, loath to distract him with the chain saw in his hands, until he puts it down and starts tossing the fallen branches into the wheelbarrow.

"Well, thank God my parents aren't coming up, they're taking a trip elsewhere," she tells him, putting her hands on his chest.

"That's good. If you're lucky, you'll never have to introduce us."

"So let's go to Quebec City over Labor Day."

Max props the wheelbarrow against a tree. "I can't do that," he says.

"Oh?" Curious, Lena leans closer. Max doesn't usually have problems meeting her eyes, but now he does.

"Before we got together, I invited a friend up for Labor Day."

"So maybe he'd like to come to Canada with us. Who is it?"

"My friend Sondra, from New York." Lena pops off his chest and grabs a branch from the top of the pile. She starts peeling off the bark, thinking hard. Is he telling her he's invited a woman up here? A woman? That woman who called? And here she was fretting about her mother and Julian and what to do with Max, and he's gone and invited a woman friend. To what, sleep in her bed? With them? Without her? She knows he has many friends, but it hasn't dawned on her until just this minute that he might still sleeping with one—with any—of them.

"So she can come with us." *Lame,* she thinks, *really lame.*

"Lena, ah, no. She doesn't—"

"Oh. I see. You haven't mentioned me. Well, this was before me, right? Before we were, uh, involved? So go tell her it won't work out, things have changed."

"It's not negotiable," says Max. He hasn't moved a muscle during this entire exchange, remaining propped against the cabin wall without ever once looking at her.

Oh fuck, she thinks, throwing down the branch. She walks off without a word. As she gets in her car, she hears the sound of the chain saw starting up again.

Max keeps on cutting brush until he hears her driving away, then he goes inside and calls Sondra with directions to the camp.

When Labor Day arrives, Lena stays home and starts cleaning. All day she cleans and cleans, ignoring the telephone, which rings hourly. Finally she shuts off the message machine so she can't hear Max sputtering. She scrubs the counters, floors, and the windows, gets on her knees with a toothbrush and attacks the floor tiles. In the studio, she takes down all the pots and scrubs the shelves with bleach and then puts everything back. Then she drags the sacks of dried-out clay on the deck, cuts them open, and breaks the clumps apart with a hammer. She sifts the particles into trash cans filled with water. Later, she drives into Burlington for a pint of Ben & Jerry's and eats it with a fork while watching a movie.

That night, she sleeps surprisingly well and wakes up early with an epiphany, that monogamy means war, and so monogamy needs to be avoided at all costs. She's back to her initial intuition—*don't get involved*—although she has no idea how to do that.

She stands in her kitchen halving oranges, until she remembers that the juicer is on the top shelf of his kitchen. Carefully, she squeezes an orange directly into her mouth. What she refuses to do is feel like a victim. It's her choice: make war on Max for what he's doing, or not, whatever "not" means. She doesn't like it, but doesn't have to retaliate. What she wants to do is paint her house. She wants her juicer back.

When the phone rings she picks it up without thinking, and as Max pleads for forgiveness—he loves her dearly; he misses her and can't wait to see her—she holds the phone away from her ear, from her mind, from her psyche, although she can't help but hear him groan "Just one more day," as if another twenty-four hours with a Ph.D. candidate sitting on his face was too much to bear.

Later, when she takes Zia for a walk, she finds an oversized bust of Elvis Presley propped against her mailbox. She and Max had wandered into a junk shop a while back and come across this atrocity, possibly the tackiest thing they'd ever seen, but she'd wanted it. And he's driven all the way back to that shop and bought it for her. It's made of painted plaster, and she knows if she leaves it and it starts raining—which it most likely will—it will disintegrate. She's smiling, but not all that much, so her first thought is to let it rot. By the time she gets back from Zia's walk, rain has begun falling. She runs into the studio for the garden cart and hauls the thing inside and goes about her day, washing the floors, scrubbing the bathtub, rearranging her sock drawer. Every time she passes Elvis, she recognizes a gift of laughter meant to lift her pain—and his too, if the misery in his voice is to be trusted.

Around noon, she decides to drive into town for groceries. On the way to the Co-op, she sees her husband, Julian, emerging from a jewelry store. She hastily crosses to the other side of the street, does her shopping, packs up her car, and goes back into the street thinking of lunch—but instead finds herself walking up three flights of dirty stairs to a gypsy fortune-teller.

Through the open door she sees a card table and two chairs, one of them holding a pile of folded laundry. At the back, printed curtains hang over a doorway, moving slightly in the breeze coming from the open window.

The curtains part and a small boy on a tricycle materializes, hugging the wall. His dirty little features are screwed up with concentration. He makes a few turns, keeping his eyes pinned to the floor as he maneuvers carefully around her before dipping back through the curtains.

A moment later, a short man appears. He's wearing a baggy suit of some shiny material over a T-shirt. His feet are bare and his long hair is wet, as though he'd just emerged from a shower. He's holding a deck of cards, which he places on the table. He sits down and motions her to take the opposite chair. "You have a big choice to make, now sit," and so she does.

Frowning, he tosses the deck on the table. Cards fall this way and that, half of them dropping to the floor. The deck is ordinary, shiny and stained. No medieval illustrations for this guy.

"How much? Fifteen dollars, twenty-five dollars, one hundred dollars?" He covers the deck with both hands, awaiting her reply.

"Twenty-five dollars." She has no idea.

He flicks a finger while she counts her cash, stopping when she places the money on the table. He regards her thoughtfully and pulls out a card.

The boy has come back and stands by his father, who reaches up absently to stroke his cheek.

"You are a pretty woman," he says. "I can tell you have confidence, you do important work, you have a house and friends, money, you live in the country, you are an artist, and you have two men." He shuffles the deck and throws it down, again spilling the cards. He lays out a hand of three, takes two more cards, places another, and then sweeps them all on the floor. "You need to choose between two men," he says, scooping up the cards.

"What?" She's not happy with this. *I'm turning into my mother? Two men? Anyway, they're doing the choosing, not me. I'm just reacting.*

"Yes, choose. You don't know that's an option, but it is." He hands the deck to the boy.

Smiling faintly, she asks, "That's it?"

"No. There's more. Listen to me." The gypsy leans over the deck and puts a finger to his mouth. "Shhm" he says, "shh," as if hushing up his own words. After a moment, they squeeze out in whispers, as if he means to add importance to their content. "Someone hates you. Someone has bought a piece of jewelry. It is a ring. I see it now, a blue ring. Not valuable, but pretty."

Lena nods, startled. *Julian coming out of the jewelry store.* A ring for the girl. *See,* she tells herself, *you have no choice, your husband's choosing someone else.*

"He gives it to someone who puts a spell on you," the gypsy goes on, seeing he has her attention. You are in great danger."

Oh, Lena thinks, *that's the setup. He's going to ask her for more money.* "And you're going to protect me, right?"

"If you wish. I go to a secret mountain in Canada, and there I light candles for you, one for each of your years, and they are exactly as tall as you. What are you, five-five? Five-six? While these candles burn, I pray for you. When it's over, the spell is over. One thousand dollars. If you don't do this, you die. You think about it. We are finished. Tell no one about what I said to you today; no one."

He takes his child by the hand and the two of them disappear behind the curtain.

Tuesday morning, Max comes barreling into the house so clearly delighted to see Lena that all her resentment vanishes, and she lets him hustle her into his truck and take her hastily to North Hero, with Zia between them towering over their heads.

He speeds along the road as fast as he dares, shouting over the ancient, straining motor. "Sondra left me a present—left us a present—some Ecstasy, you ever take it?" No, but she's heard about it. Adam, the love drug, everyone's into it these days. No side effects, no harm, only pure love. *It's the love drug.* She can feel his overheated thigh clamped against hers. She looks at his flushed, excited face and realizes why he's so eager to procure her—that's the word that comes to mind, not love or marry or enshrine—to procure, as in to acquire, especially with care and effort.

He wants to use her to change his life.

They drag air mattresses and sleeping bags, a case of Pellegrino water, candles, and pillows down to a little niche in the rocks just below the cabin. The sun is out, the lake is empty, and all the tourists have gone home: all in all, a great day to drop psychotropics.

"Look at the island over there. Isn't it lovely?" He pulls a vial of light blue pills from the pocket of his robe and hands her one, and they wash down their potents and face each other, smiling, each a little nervous, waiting to see what will happen if and when their hearts open up. Lena hopes it will be gentle.

After a few minutes, Max starts off with a "what if" scenario meant to set the tone of this uncharted journey. "What if we were ship-wrecked on that island over there," he supposes, placing his hand on her chest, "and there was nothing in the world except that island and all this water. What if we'd become resigned to the fact there's no food, and we will die, and just then, then a beautiful white gleam-ing yacht heaves to? We climb aboard. It has everything we ever wanted because *we have always wanted to be sailors*. Until this moment, we haven't known that. And somehow the reason we've been ship-wrecked is to give us this boat so we may be sailors and save our own lives. In the entire world, nothing exists except us and this yacht. There are so many nooks and crannies; it will take years to really know that vessel, much less the people on it. Our eyes are now bright from morning to night with discovery. We have found our home. Are you following this?"

She is and she isn't, but she nods nonetheless. Most of his words have dropped off on the way to her brain, which holds now only the image of the beautiful white boat. She says, "Do you know that the first time I came here I felt like it was coming home? I've never felt that, ever. Nor wanted to." The remark sounds so unlike her, she's not sure she said it. But then realizes she not only said it, she means it. Deeply.

He nods. "One of the landlord's sons—he wasn't allowed to play with the tenants, but he did, anyway—one day we were swimming in the mud hole behind the swamp. This kid, Louis, he couldn't swim. I'm feeling this drug a little bit and wish to sit down." He settles him-self on a rock by her feet and goes on. "So I thought, well, let's push him in so I can save him. So we did. I jumped in after him. When I went to grab him, he panicked and started climbing right up my body until he stood on my shoulders. And as he climbed, he was pushing me deeper into the mud. Finally, he had one foot on my shoulder and another on my head. I was sinking. You know how mud sucks you up; it grips you all over. I was underwater, and suddenly it occurred to me that if Louis was standing on me, maybe there was another guy under me and I was standing on him. I could hear Louis yelling, and I could feel him thrashing around. If I looked up, I could see the light. I felt totally peaceful. If I could only breathe, I could conceivably stay down here for a couple of years or so. Louis eventually floated off me, and I had to drop down and pull my legs out of the mud to get myself out of there."

"Oh, the jewel in the lotus thing," Lena says as her stomach turns over and she sits down so quickly, she falls in his lap.

"Robert Bly says we're not feeding our ancestors. Not paying attention to our myths. A myth, he says, takes 25,000 years to generate because it's a mass of detail. But with each of us joining in, the mass finally goes critical and becomes a myth. How do you feel?"

Lena brings her hand up to her eyes and says, "I can't even look at this thing without crying." Then she giggles.

"I've just thought of this—some of those stories from Grimm, you can go back and find little tiny references to them, but fragments of something, pre-stories or something. They didn't have Madison Avenue 25,000 years ago. Now we have guys who know how to evoke image and detail in everybody in thirty-second sound bytes. It's on TV, and pretty soon you are salivating. These guys are making myths. You see Golden Arches, you don't think of a birth canal, you think of McDonalds."

By this time, they've managed to get to their feet and move down the cliff where they now stand, again face to face, drilling into each other's eyes. His hand rests again over her heart. Below them the lake lifts and sighs, above them is infinity doing the same. Their minds shift and fold, open, drift, sink, swim. Their minds grow enormous. The world throbs gently, unspecific, inevitable. Every spoken word is the truth in a new, liquid language. His gray beard is trimmed, his fine gray hair fingering out on the breeze. His nostrils flare while words roll from his mouth into hers. He is wearing a long brown robe belted with a rope under his stomach. She wears nothing. He looks like King Lear. He looks like a wildebeest talking to the wind on its hind legs.

She knows exactly what she looks like to him: *Someone who could take him on.*

"I've come here to die," he says. "Come, let me show you how to do this."

Naked on the rocks, water moving about her knees like transparent oil. She's shivering. He urges her to dive in. Welcome it. But thunder rolls down the skyway and lighting plays high in the clouds, forking imperiously miles away over Camel's Hump. He dives in himself, see? *You lose nothing by dying.* "Too cold," she yells, prosaic mere mortal backing away. When he climbs out, she hunches her shoulders and flattens her breasts. She climbs on his back, mounts him like a buffalo. Her teeth chatter, her lips are blue. "This is not a good idea," she protests, then leaps up and shallow-dives into a breaking wave. It's he who takes fright—*she's going to crack her head open on the rocks*—and he dives after her, takes her in his arms and swims her, laughing and spitting water in his face, to where the ledge plunges and the lake is forty feet of glorious transparency. He tosses her over his shoulder.

She plummets away from everything she knows into feeling nothing, seeing nothing, hearing nothing, but there is nothing down there, so she twists and aims upward and comes out blind, she is poor little Pip out of *Moby-Dick,* a cork in all this vastness, no horizon, no sky, nothing to compare herself to, or she is as she was but it is the universe gone black: black hole, black sky, black ice, the anti-ness of matter, or else the whale has opened its mouth and taken her in. Oh, the whale has something to say to her.

She's on her stomach, her arms and legs dangling like tentacles, when her knee scrapes on rock. She's in three feet of water and Max is floating beside her, as he's been all along.

That night, when the air turns green and lightning cracks one, two, three, splitting a small maple tree on the lawn, Lena wakes up screaming. She's just seen Zia go through the screen door. This is real. They race out naked. Max drives the Peugeot, Lena stumbles along the paths. Zia plunges through the bushes to the parallel road; she runs barely touching the ground. Driving alongside her, Max marvels at her beauty, at her immensity, at her grace. She's gorgeous and mythical, but he's smarter, he knows where the roads converge and how to get there, and she does not. He slams on the accelerator and does a 180° just as the dog bursts from the woods.

It's all over now but the capture. Immobilized in the glare of his lights, Zia stands passively, letting Max grab her collar. She trots alongside him breathing heavily, climbs in the back seat, lies down, and meets his gaze.

He sits on the tailgate rubbing her ears. Maybe he's still tripping, or maybe X opens the door to the animal brain, either way he's right there in her little mind, so much smaller than his own, but filled with infinity rather than with the mounds of garbage clotting up the air space in his own vastly superior organ.

"So, who are you?" he asks her. "You owe me an apology. I have just saved you from becoming road kill. There is a sixteen-wheeler out there with your name on it. I tell you, my species is a stupid, cancerous, anthropomorphic stain on the earth, interested only in eradicating the wilderness in you, whatever it takes."

The dog turns her face away and burps.

"Be gone, oh human tick, is it?" says Max, pinching her neck. He swears she nods.

Lena grabs the dog and hurries her off to the cabin. When Max returns from securing the car, they're both on the floor, Lena propped up against the bed with Zia's head and front paws in her lap, crying—why, both of them are crying, he realizes, as he sits down on the bed, pulling off his clothes. The damnedest thing, the two of them gazing devotedly into each other's tears, how amazing is this. It's a moment he won't forget easily, but it is short; for Lena sits up, wipes her eyes and mutters, "Bitch."

"I thought she was a gossamer being in a dog suit," Max says. He turns out the bed light, lifts the covers, and says, "Come here."

5

Kokoro no kaze, *"my soul has come down with a cold."*

—Translation: Terry Dobson, as told to Lena

Max says:

On the train to Tokyo, I got a cinder in my eye and ended up in a hospital at 3:00 a.m. The ridiculousness of the situation was not lost on me—having planned to kill myself, why bother getting a cinder out of my eye? Waiting to be seen, I leafed through the *Tokyo Times,* where I saw an announcement for an aikido demonstration down in Yokohama. All I knew about aikido was that it was a martial art, and that's why I was in Japan, right? I thought maybe this aikido would give me a reason to hang around this planet.

There were about thirty Americans in the Bill Chickering Theater. These American bases are the pits, inhabited by American hillbillies living in Japan with Japanese hillbillies, their interest in martial arts being what to do when someone tries to kill them in a bar. The aikido people had sent down their best, and the star was Niyama, who was one of the most handsome men that Japan has ever produced. The poor guy was coming down from Tokyo to the base twice a week— and it's a long trip on a cold train—and he's teaching the art he loves to people squirming in their folding chairs because he's wearing a skirt. I sit down and immediately understand exactly what aikido is about. The moves are quick and filled with grace: two men face each other, become one, and are transformed. I was witnessing acts of heavenly transmission. What I saw shook my world so completely, my suicidal thoughts vanished. My understanding of aikido was as clear to me as it is now, and I knew without a doubt that the rest of my life would be in aikido. I'm completely starstruck, and Niyama takes notice.

We never really hit it off, Niyama and I, and I know that he wishes I had left this world a long time ago, but I have him to thank for turning me on to aikido—and as much as I dislike him, I love him for that.

After the demonstration, Niyama brought me to the dojo in Tokyo. We walked in just as O-sensei emerged from his room. Niyama took him aside and said, "Sensei, this foreigner is flipping out about aikido, what do I do?" I had no idea who O-sensei was, just that he was the main man. He must have smelled my desperation, for he turned and walked away without acknowledging me. Burning with shame, I vowed to do whatever I could for him to accept me. I bought the aikido book by Koichi Tohei and read it cover to cover on the train back to the mountains, and when I got home I threw out the gun.

Six months were left on my contract. I thought I could get through it, because now I had aikido. But I was ostracized, and no one would practice with me. And so I practiced on the branches of an apple tree— *shihonage, yokomen uchi, ikkyo.* I did this religiously.

On Sundays I took the train to the dojo—four hours from Kofu down to Tokyo—where I stood outside waiting for someone to let me in, and when no one did, I went back to the station.

As soon as I was free I moved to Tokyo. I'd arrive early in the morning and stay until someone threw me out. I was so bereft of anything else that I clung like a drowning man: soon O-sensei decided that I should be an *uchi deshi,* his live-in helper. Nobody else wanted a foreigner as *uchi deshi,* but of course they deferred to O-sensei.

He started taking me around to demonstrate aikido, often in these British men's clubs, with old curmudgeons sitting around on overstuffed chairs smoking cigars. I had to kneel by his side while he talked to these men about God for forty-five minutes. Then, when he felt like it, he made an invisible signal, which was supposed to tell me what move to make on him, and he'd start throwing me around between coffee tables. People would be sitting there holding out their cigars to keep this 200-pound American from landing in their laps. He would fire me up in the air and I'd end up between the outstretched legs of some vice president.

Obviously I was there just for show; I'm big and he's little. He would call for me to grab him, and he'd say, "Why do you grab my beard? I'm an old man." The first time he said it I was terribly embarrassed, because it was in front of a whole bunch of people. He said, "I don't have many hairs in my beard. If you grab them and you pull them out, I'll look terrible." Everybody laughed. About a week later, we went somewhere else. He called for me to attack him. This time I was very conscious, and I know I didn't touch his beard. But he said the same thing again. So I knew it was hype. It was a good joke; I was his joke, the big gorilla tossed around like a Frisbee.

But it wasn't only that. I'm sure he was taken by my devotion: as a teacher, you always notice the panting dogs, the ones who jump out the window for you. I was like that, an innocent with a beginner's mind, a dry sponge. Beginner's mind is the highest spiritual form of realization, and it's very seductive. People mistook my devotion for an understanding of their culture; complimenting my fine Japanese, encouraging me to feel I belonged. Every once in a while, I would come to my senses and say, *Hey, big boy, you are dreaming.*

The first time I went with him as his bag carrier on a trip, it was the blind leading the blind. Here we had our resident mystic talking to the persimmons, and I, who hardly spoke the language, was supposed to get him on the train to Osaka. When we got to the station, I paid the driver, jumped out of the car, and leapt over to his side of the cab to help him out. You have to keep in mind that he's four-foot-ten and eighty years old, but by the time I get over there, he's gone. It's high noon at the old Tokyo Station, and it's crowded. I charge off looking ferocious, swinging the bags to make us a path through the crowd. I must have hit at least forty people who were already trying to get out of my way: I'm trampling old ladies. Meanwhile, I see O-sensei way ahead of me, moving invisibly like a knife through butter! I get to the platform, drenched with sweat, and he's standing there completely cool, and he says, "Are you all right? I was afraid you were lost."

Whatever he needed, I would provide for him; sometimes in the morning I would hold his false teeth for him to brush, and while he's going on and on about life and death I'd be drifting off thinking about women.

One night we were making up his bath; the tub was pretty small. The one-up-from-me *deshi*—a sweet guy named Yoshi, I think—got the wood, chopped it up, and lit the fire underneath it. The rule is always that the sensei goes first, and that I, being the least-tenured *uchi deshi*, I go last. There are nineteen of us, so you can imagine how much anyone wanted the last bath. But I didn't care: I'd bathe in mud if that was the rule. But this time, O-sensei tells me to get in the bath. I shake my head no, but he insists. I look at Yoshi; he's glaring at me: clearly I've got to refuse at all costs. I remember wondering how come he hates me so much. What am I supposed to do? Bow out backward in obsequious terror?

O-sensei starts talking to me as if I were a little kid. He's smiling, he's purring—obviously, he's enjoying my suffering. He makes me take my clothes off, pour water over my head, and soap up. "Now, wash behind your ears, get in your ears, that's good," he says. Then he tells me to get in the tub and I say, "Sensei, please." I was so embarrassed. I could barely fit, but I get in the bath with my knees up to my chin. I think Yoshi came to hate me for that. All of them hated me. O-sensei's son's wife cooked lunch every day for the *uchi deshi,* all except me, the white guy, who didn't deserve to eat.

South Hero, Lena's house, 1986

Once winter arrives and Lena realizes that Max has moved into her house—at least his clothes hang in her closet and his wicker furniture fills her living room—she has to wonder, did his presence mean that she'd actually chosen between two men, as the gypsy had told her she must? Or was it more like one of them had slipped out of and the other slipped into her bed without her participation?

Had he really replaced Julian? In the sense there was someone to replace? Or was it only cosmetic? Max had spent his first few months repainting, rewiring, and otherwise infusing his personality on Julian's office by knocking out walls, installing a wood floor and wainscoting, and faux-painting a Pompeian orange with spray-painted Latinesque political slang—*pecunia non olet* ("money doesn't stink")—in short, turning it into a room Julian wouldn't care to enter. He'd installed the portraits of the two Daniels on opposite walls and stripped down the old curio cabinet from his mother's apartment and filled it with his reference books: thesaurus, Japanese dictionary, Bartlett's, a leather-bound set of the 1911 *Encyclopædia Britannica,* a new Webster's, half a dozen books on writing style, and a twenty-pound *New York Times Atlas,* his birthday present from Lena. On the Spielberg desk sits the red Selectric. Next to it is a $400 Tizio lamp. Above it all, he's bolted a platen and inserted a cylinder of continuous typing paper to feed into the typewriter like a roll of paper towels.

Lena likes to tell friends, "You know Max Diebenkorn? He's staying in the Kerouac suite."

"Not bad," Marianne observes, standing in the doorway with her coat on, holding a loaf of raisin bread. "Here, I baked it for you." She's been coming up for weekends since she got back from the residency full of ideas and she's dying to start working again in Lena's studio. In exchange, she's supposed to help organize the pottery, which now includes Jocelyn as a real partner and Tonkey as an intern. Lena's not convinced the arrangement will be workable with so many people in the house. Tonkey and Jocelyn have moved into the loft over the studio, Marianne's taken over the guest room, and she's got Max in her bed, along with Zia.

"That's so sweet of you." Lena takes the loaf and helps Marianne disengage from her arctic parka. "It's poetic, don't you think? A room for a poet?"

"Or Julian Schnabel, or maybe Beowulf. You have to admire Max's style. Old English plus city loft rat plus car mechanic. Tell me, what would have happened if you guys had just dated instead of plunging right down to the cellular subfloor on drugs? Do you have any idea what reality is?"

"Sure," says Lena, slipping an arm through her friend's. "It looks exactly like this."

February arrives and the only writing Max has managed to accomplish has been a letter to an editor at *Reader's Digest,* who'd expressed interest years back. He writes:

Mr. Don Layton, editor, The Reader's Digest

Dear Don,

How are you? Here is an outline for an article with the work-ing title of TACT—THE RIGHT MOVE AT THE RIGHT MOMENT, which the Reader's Digest expressed interest in several years ago.

He changes that to "in which your magazine once expressed interest" and sits back in his chair.

Tact. He has nothing to say about the subject, but still he plows on:

An Essay on Tact by Max Diebenkorn.

Tact, from the Latin word "Tactus"

Too didactic, he decides. With a roll of the paper, he begins again: "Here I am at a party, at the celery and Cheez Whiz dip, when some guy in a dashiki"—he crosses out *dashiki,* too racist, writes in *Hawai-ian shirt*—"comes up to me with one of those 'whaddya do if' ques-tions that refers to his desire to know if aikido really works in a real-life violent situation. 'What do you do if' some guy attacks you with a knife on Bond Street, will aikido work? How the fuck should I know, is what I want to reply, but in fact—"

Another roll of the platen. "Tact. In the sense of 'tactic.'" Another roll, and then, "The Latin word 'Tactus' is the root of Tact."

Jesus, he thinks, rocking back in his chair. He has nothing left to say about tact. He's written a book on tact, manuals on tact, and teach-ing guides on tact. But that's what the *Digest* wanted, yea those many years ago, and for all he knows, they may be longing still for his witty observations. Maybe he can find an old outline he can update instead of reinventing the wheel.

He slips a sheet of his embossed cream-colored letterhead over the platen and quickly types a cover letter, omitting the words *I have enclosed* and adding that the outline will be sent under separate cover. Then he signs his letter and puts it in an envelope. Holding it by the edge in one hand, he leans back in his chair, idly listening to his heart thumping on dully. *While my heart thumps on dully?*

He begins typing furiously again.

> It has been said that Tact is the intuition of the angels. Please God let me die before I type another first line of this drivel.

He rolls up the day's work, turns off the Selectric, and reaches for the index box of quotes for inspiration, picking one at random:

> "The sea had jeeringly kept his finite body up, but drowned the infinite of his soul."
> —p. 453, *Moby-Dick*.

Idly, he scratches his forearm.

Now that's real writing. But is it? A sea that jeers? Is this not lame? What's chilling is the up and down thing Melville understands so brilliantly. Ahab, looking down through the membrane for Moby-Dick, while the whale bursts upward searching for him. Fish and Man each imagining the other as agents of God: enough reason for insanity, hatred, and revenge. Why bother writing if you don't reach for that exalted level?

Thinking to get something to eat, he wanders into the kitchen, where he hears the booming baseline from The Clash's *Sandinista!*

tape bouncing through the studio door. It's shut, meaning he shouldn't go in. The crew is in high gear for the annual Baltimore trade show that's two weeks away, and he's the proverbial bull in the china shop.

He ends up on the living room couch in front of the TV watching the launch of the Soviet space station Mir. He goes through his pockets in search of a butt, finds only lint. He scratches his leg, scratches his forearms. Itching is his newest symptom of bodily distress, probably cigarette deprivation. Probably someone in the known universe has tried smoking lint. He could tell Lena he's going out for milk. He doesn't have to tell her anything. He should just get in his car and go to the store and buy one cigarette. Just one. He scratches his head. The itch relocates on his shoulder, on the wing, just out of reach. Is it spreading, or is it the same clump moving from place to place? The more he scratches the more he itches. He rolls up his sweater sleeves and inspects his forearm under a magnifying lens and sees a mass of tiny red bumps. Cancer. He stretches out his sweater collar and stares down his nose to his chest. He's riddled with whatever it is, swelling, pinpricks, contusions, rashes, cancer, pestilences, hives, *festerences*. Or else he's hallucinating; William Burroughs babbling on about bugs comes to mind, there's a tradition of feverish American writers he might fit in with.

He pads back to the office, where he pages through *Naked Lunch* looking for inspiration and finds this:

> "The Rube has a sincere little boy look, burns through him like blue neon. That one stepped right off a *Saturday Evening Post* cover with a string of bullheads, and preserved himself in junk."

You know this *Rube* inside out, don't you, no explanations needed. Burroughs wouldn't hesitate to smoke lint. He thinks he should call Sondra and see how she's doing. All this good behavior will kill him. He's itching now underneath his belt buckle; it's heading downward toward his own Bay of Pigs. Teeny tiny clusters of bright red bumps with black holes in the center the size of a pin.

Fleeing his room, he runs upstairs and jumps in the shower, turning the water as hot as possible on the theory that pain will scorch out the itch. It does. When he comes down, he finds the studio door open. It sounds normal in there, for the music has moved outside to the shed where, except for Lena, *El Rancho Bizarro*, as he's nicknamed the household, has gone to unload the big gas kiln.

He's not sure why these people must live with them, except that it's Lena's way of transitioning. In any case, each one of them seems to have something another one of them needs: Jocelyn's in love with clay the way Lena used to be; she wants that mud lust back and he wants her self-sufficiency. And Marianne needs to do real physical work while Lena needs to connect with her brain, imagination, and spirit. Quite Melvillean, actually, the synchronicity of desires, stretching up while what you long for is reaching down for you.

She's sitting by herself working on a four-foot-tall ceramic doll. It's made entirely of cast body parts of various animals. He's never seen anything quite like it. At this raw-clay stage, there's a totemic quality to it. Her face is hidden under a double cartridge respirator, her body under a heavy rubber apron. A cloud of dust drifts around her shoulders, making his nose stuff up and his mouth water and his eyes run. On the table a pile of dust masks lie under plastic. He grabs one and sits down beside her.

"I can't write about tact anymore," he says. "I think I need to write about my family. You get the family book out of your system, you know, then you can write fiction. I can't get started, baby. Finish up here and let's go to the movies. *Alien* is being revived in town. It's about a really interesting mother. Maybe it'll remind me of my own enough to get my juices flowing."

Lena continues sanding her sculpture, paying him no mind.

"Really," he goes on, "I think I need to write fiction. You heard about the people sucked out of the plane? What would that feel like? You write fiction hoping to create a better world than your reality. Your own country launches a space station, not its enemy."

He realizes now that Lena's wearing headphones and hasn't heard a word he's said. He taps her shoulder and she looks up and slips off her face mask and phones. She's got marks on her face, and her eyes are red.

"Come take a break," he tells her. "Let's go see Sigourney Weaver covered in slime. You'll identify with her." He cups her chin in his hand, dips a finger in her water glass, and traces a line through the clay on her face.

"Go away and write," she says, brushing him off with a smile.

"I can't. I'm lonely. I have a rash." He rolls up his sleeve and points to the infestation. She gives it a cursory inspection.

"Looks like fleas."

"More likely nicotine deficiency. Anyway, it's much more fun in here than in my gloomy prison; the good times roll in here. Mind if I hang out?" He backs up against the corner of a post, bends his legs and starts scratching his back against the pointed edge. "Oh, this feels wonderful. Oh, thank you, Lord." He closes his eyes in pleasure, lets his tongue loll from the corner of his lips. Max the bear grooming his pelt in bearish bliss, relieving his suffering so he may continue conducting meaningful artistic conversation. "Tell me, Goldilocks, what does this piece mean to you? Talk about its transformative, primordial power, how it evokes animalistic pre-goddess worship and is informed by—"

"Bullshit." She doesn't believe in interpretation. She thinks visual images trigger one part of the brain and words another. Labels in museums next to paintings give her headaches. But Max believes in logic and strategy and marching forward. He believes in articulation, clarification, and constant refinement. Only right now, all he can do is itch.

Jocelyn, Tonkey, and Marianne traipse in then, their faces red from the kiln heat and streaked with ash. "OK, OK, the firing turned out exactly *bonafide*," says Tonkey, wiping her face with a towel. She's a big girl in a tight T-shirt that says TOURISM SUCKS. "Yeah, sure. Some dripped pots, a stuck lid, but J. twisted it loose. Pretty cool. Here's the treasure." She shows Lena a small vase with a lovely celadon glaze dripping exactly right over some freewheeling calligraphy.

"There's got to be an easier way to do this," says Marianne, pulling up a stool. "We really have to take down the door each time brick by brick? Can't we just build a door? With hinges? Why don't you just use the electric kilns? And why not fire them at a lower temperature? And faster? This is so much work."

Jocelyn comes swooping in front of them, jumps up, and lands with his feet apart, knees open, ready to strike. "Max, man, yuh no dead yet? Hey, gimme your wrist."

"What's this? You been practicing aikido?"

"Yo, man. I been training at your old dojo. Looka me, I'm a martial man." He spins around, laughing.

"But have you learned how to swat flies yet?"

"What? What?"

"Come here." Max turns him around by the elbow to face him. "Come on, look at me. Don't laugh, this is serious. Ancient Japanese technique. One, two, three, swat," he says, lightly swatting Jocelyn on the forehead.

"Oh, swat fly," Jocelyn gets it. He growls, fixates Max with a ferocious stare, and swats back.

"Don't look me in the eye; look between my eyes. You don't want to be caught by the other person's beauty." He swats. Jocelyn misses. "Don't lose your concentration."

Tonkey, who has just begun training, says, "O-sensei swatted flies?"

"No, of course not. Come on, Jos, faster. That's it!" The two men are speeding up now, trading swats, until Max puts up a hand and backs off, wheezing. "I can't take any more, go easy on me." Lena gives him her chair and stands behind him, stroking his brow.

"You know," Max says, "there's a certain kind of American guy who thinks, 'Hey, going to the dojo two classes a week is too slow; I want to be really good really fast, so I'll practice twenty-four hours a day, and in a month I'll be a fifth *dan*.' Well it ain't gonna happen that way. Jocelyn, you're not an American boy. You don't have to fall for that shit, OK?"

"So," Tonkey says, "Sensei. Why aren't you teaching?"

When she says this, everyone looks at Max. It's the question they've all been sidestepping, the elephant in the corner they're afraid of tripping over. Behind his back, they discuss it: why isn't Max teaching, or at least practicing? But it takes someone who's never been told about the elephant to ask.

Tonkey looks from one to the other and says, "What?"

"It's OK," Max tells her. "You all figure it out and tell me about it."

"Puh-leez, this is an important question," says Marianne, who's been dying to ask him herself. She likes ragging Max, but in fact she's worried sick about him, can't imagine what was wrenching him from his life's passion.

"I don't teach because I don't know what to teach. You have to teach aikido from your soul, from where you stand in life at that moment. When I'm ready, I'll teach. Or not. I can show you how to roll, or deal with a particular attack, but so can what's-his-name, the guy you're training with now, at the dojo."

"Johnny Drumm," says Jocelyn. "He says you think he stole the dojo from you."

"Yes, of course he'd say that. Perhaps he did. But Johnny's not why I don't get on the mat. You may be too young to know this, but you spend the first part of your life racing toward something, and then with luck, *whoosh,* it's out of reach. Or it's no longer important. Or something else catches your attention. Or you can't run anymore. The truth is, whatever you think is the reason, isn't. You have no idea what's going on: or if you have any idea, it's wrong. So I figure I'd better sit down and stay put until I can figure out where life means for me to be. Maybe it's right here, in my chair, and I have to love the fate I get."

The phone rings then. Max mouths "Saved by the bell" and picks it up. "Hello Erica, hello Marcos," he says loudly, and hands Lena the cordless.

"Hi Mom," she says, turning her back.

Everyone can hear Erica yell, "Who is that man? Where's Julian?"

"Out. Dying his hair orange. Mom, where's your hearing aid?"

"How's the weather?" Marcos booms out. He's on the patio extension. "Just another day in paradise here! When are you coming down? Wish you were here, darling."

"The weather sucks. Just another day in hell here," says Lena, looking straight at Max.

Erica laughs suddenly. "You're funny. Good-bye." She hangs up.

"Dad? Are you still there?"

Lowering his voice, Marcos says, "Yesterday she heard something explode in her brain, dear. Not to worry. It'll all clear up. We just wanted to say hello. Our best to Julian. I'll call you in a few days. Kiss kiss," and now he hangs up.

"I love you too, Daddy." She puts down the phone Her friends have fallen silent. "My mother thinks her brain exploded. They're almost ninety years old and still living independently. My mother stores her shoes in the oven and swims straight out in the Gulf of Mexico after dark. It can't go on like this, but they won't think about it. At least not out loud. Certainly not to me."

"You haven't told them about me, have you?" says Max.

"Guess not."

"You've got to fly down there," says Marianne. She likes Lena's funny little parents, who she calls "Our Parents." She never had any of her own. She'd been raised in inner-city foster homes where she'd learned how to fake being a good surrogate daughter. She'd visit Our Parents herself, if she wasn't flying down to New York during the week, auditing a video class at NYU. Or if the idea of spoon-feeding toothless people didn't make her gag—one of her excuses for never having kids.

"You think it's every middle-aged kid's nightmare, but that it won't happen to you. I pay for a caterer down there to deliver meals. My mother spends hours studying the menu and then gets Dad to drive the food back. I don't know what they eat. The neighbors in the condo are getting sick of cooking them soup. And I'm sick of feeling guilty. I mean, I can't move them in here, can I?" She looks from one to the other. Her nicotine-deprived suitor shivering in his ragged bathrobe, two dreadlocked Jamaicans, and Marianne. "Well I can't."

"We got what, ten days to get this show together?" says Jocelyn.

"I'm due in the city tomorrow," says Marianne. "Grant interviews. Sorry."

"My mother's brain has 'exploded' four times so far," says Lena. "And Dad takes her to the ER or he calls 911. I think he doles out the wrong medicine for her, or overdoses or something, but he thinks he's doing a fine job. I saw him cutting her pills in little pieces. He has no idea what he's giving her. After her last hospitalization, I hired private nursing 24/7 after the Medicare nurses were through. Dad swore he was grateful. That he understood the situation. And when I called from back here to see how they were doing, Dad said, 'Oh, those nurses don't work here anymore.' If Medicare finds out, they'll turn me in for elder abuse. Florida has all this power. Short of hiring an airplane and kidnapping them, I don't know what to do."

"Hmm," says Max, looking thoughtful.

"Don't even think about it, I can't do that. Where would we put them?"

"Your mother doesn't want to burden you," says Tonkey. "I wish my mother felt the same. You a lucky girl."

"Yeah, but unfortunately the state feels Dad shouldn't be free to poison his wife or, God forbid, run over a kid. He can't even see above the steering wheel anymore."

"Come sit with me," says Max, reaching for her.

"You better get your ass down there," says Tonkey.

"So Tonkey and I will drive the truck to Baltimore," says Jocelyn, all business now. "We've got enough inventory as it is: we do fine without you. So you don't worry, dear, you go down dere and deal wit those crazy people."

Driving back from taking Lena to the airport, Max listens to the tape a friend sent him from Ram Dass's seminar on compassionate aging, looking for wisdom on how best to help Lena through this misery with her parents. But he's the one feeling old, as he climbs the few slippery steps to the front door clinging to the handrail. Inside he sits on the bench in the hallway removing his boots as Zia nails him with her big head in his lap. *El Rancho Bizarro* feels lonely with everyone gone. He's gotten use to all the bustle, all the fuss around work, the chatter, the music, wine, and cooking, the extended family of artist gypsies who turned up now and then in the hot tub. Tonkey and Jocelyn won't be back in Baltimore for two weeks, and Marianne is down in New York on her endless search for funding and who knows when Lena will return home.

In the kitchen, he turns on the tiny black-and-white television that Erica once acquired by opening a new bank account and then passed on to her daughter as an incentive to stay in the kitchen and cook for Julian. He microwaves one of the frozen soups Lena has prepared for her dog—soybeans and beef bones and rice—and pulls out a roast chicken, lettuce, mayonnaise, and bread for himself.

He feeds Zia, and sits down to watch yesterday's taped launch of the Soviet space station Mir. The phenomenon is breathtaking, he's completely dumbstruck by the magnitude of the accomplishment, but he can't help feeling resentful. It should be America's space station drifting around the galaxy like a giant Tinkertoy, it should be Americans hanging upside down inside the core. He imagines Lena watching it with her family, sitting between them, feeding them with a spoon from a bowl on her lap. He's guilty for not being with her in what must be a difficult time. He should be calling them "Our Parents," like Marianne does. What harm could it do? These frightened little people need all the love they can muster around them, even if they don't know it. How frightened they must be to think they can lock death out of their safe little condo. Who knows how anyone will deal with death once it arrives? Max will probably die before "Our Parents" do; a terrible thing to have a child predecease you, even if that child is a monstrous old guy you never liked but who's some how attached himself to your lovely only daughter.

This is how Max feels right now, monstrous and unlikable. He has no appetite: his stomach feels hard and gassy, his mouth filled with aftershave. He gives the rest of his sandwich to the patient dog and reaches for a bottle of spring water. Maybe it's the flu, or else it's the empty house making him sick. More likely, it's his old leg wound acting up. It had seemed to heal at the end of summer, but now it's back again, looking worse than ever. He gets up heavily, turns off the TV. Too tired to climb the stairs to his room, he carries a roll of fresh bandage to the office and sits down on the futon to change his dressing, something he tries to do without actually looking at his disgusting wound. When he's done, he takes Zia out for an express pee and goes to bed early.

During the next few days, while the black sky spits damp snow, he limps from sofa to bed, from television to a table piled with books, keeping track of the wound as it creeps up his shin and digs down through his tissues. The house is well heated, but he's never warm. He's thrown up several times; all he can keep down is water. Water, beautiful water; he upends gallons of Poland Spring water into his mouth and lets it run down his gullet without swallowing. He tells himself he'll go to the emergency room when the weather clears, in case there's another cow out there.

When Marianne returns from New York, she finds him too sick to get out of bed.

With her is a Tibetan man named Norbu Tendzen, whom she introduces to Max as a teaching assistant in her NYU video class. Immediately upon shaking his hand, Max feels his spirits lift. He likes him instantly; for the earmuffs spanning his bald head, for the good-humored heartbreak spilling from his unfathomable Tibetan eyes, for the way he drops his leather jacket on the floor and picks up Max's wrist to listen to his pulses.

Marianne says she's brought him home to help with the video she envisions playing in the head of her Ronnie Reagan puppet, but Max, in his growing delirium, knows Norbu has come for him. He believes Tibetans guard the spirit the way other cultures make money or war. He and Lena share a sense of awe concerning all things Tibetan, for Tibetans live closest to God, in their hearts and on their mountains, where they straddle the great rumbling belly driving every religion—the Chinese are taking a big risk fucking with it.

Bundled in a sweater, bathrobe, long johns, and a blanket, Max watches from the office window as Norbu and Marianne unload their minivan and traipse toward the house with cartons of computer and video editing equipment and groceries. Finally, a small brown dog— woeful face, silky fur down to the knees, paws the size of grapefruits, red bandana, name of Rufus—steps out of the rear and follows Norbu into the house.

That night, when Lena calls, Max describes Norbu to her as a man unbeaten by grief, the epitome of everything Tibetan. "I'm going to enjoy talking to him. He's a man of science and wonder." He says nothing about being sick, tries to keep his voice light. She has enough sickness to deal with.

She too is keeping things light, asking only, "Are they sleeping together?"

"You come back home and find out. Can we have phone sex now?"

She laughs and lowers her voice. "I'll have to ask Mom. We spent the day in the hammock together, we like to do this, have I ever told you? I know that I tend to describe her as the wicked witch, a terrible person. Which is true, but what's also true is that the witch adores me, even as she picks at me. We watch *Miami Vice* and bake cookies and she's kind of precious. She'd have phone sex with you. They're really happy to see me, Max. It's sweet."

"That's touching, sweetheart. I'm happy for you."

"Wait a minute." She muffles the receiver. "Mom just put dinner in the dishwasher. I'd better go before she turns it on. Take care of yourself, babe."

Days go by, he has no idea how many: maybe two, maybe a week. Norbu and Marianne shut themselves in the studio while also keeping watch over him, feeding him, even helping him bathe. Still trying to hide the severity of his wound, he insists upon changing the bandages himself. He hopes that rest will cure it. But it's hard to sleep, for he's running a fever—which he also hides—and he has to pee a lot. It embarrasses him to be heard dragging his misery back and forth from the toilet, so he sets up a bucket by his bedside and tosses his pee out the window.

A week goes by and his condition worsens, until one sleepless night around dawn, failing to locate any aspirin in the house, he decides to go find some elsewhere. It's way too early for the pharmacy, so he carefully dresses in layers of whatever clothing he can lay his hands on, gets in Lena's car, and drives to his cabin in North Hero. The gate is open. The lane has been plowed, and as the car crawls along, Max in his fevered state runs the loop of his cousins' perfidy, winter version. They've hired a stranger to plow this road without his permission: how stupid can they get, they've opened the lane to thieves, they'll all be wiped out, good thing he has nothing to lose. He scans the ground for footprints and sees only the spindly Y-shaped feet of birds and rabbit tracks. Along the back of the garden the snow has been trampled down by deer.

The closest cabin, Racketty-Packetty, lies only a few yards away, but the snow is deep and the effort exhausts him. He holds his left leg out like a club and hops on his right foot. By the time he's muscled open the flimsy door, bright spots dance on his retinas and his chest burns. What does he want here? He can't think. Papers, for one thing; he has an old manuscript somewhere. He needs to write about his family. For this he requires their letters, journals, and the genealogy chart. He stomps around, growing more bewildered. Sweat spills between his skin and clothing. He can't finish a thought; his feverish brain throws up obstacles. If he's writing fiction, why does he want documentation of his family? Would that not be autobiography? He's thumping angrily around the freezing cabin, looking for something, anything, when his eyes light on a small metal trunk sitting on the floor. It's shut but not locked. He grabs it by a handle and kicks open the door. The pain of doing so sends him to his knees in the snow bank. Half crawling, he manages to drag his trunk to the car and somehow to get it inside.

That night, Norbu brings him a bowl of soup with a plate of thick dumplings, a pitcher of water, and some bread. Max eats for the first time in days, and afterward he falls into a normal sleep. When he wakes hours later, his fever has broken. Norbu sits silhouetted by the window working a long set of Tibetan beads.

"Norbu, are you a saint? Are you a monk? What precious elixir was in the food you brought me?" he calls from his bed.

"Just food. Would you let me exam you?"

"Are you a doctor?"

"Yes. I trained in Tibetan medicine. I would only observe you, take your pulses, interview you, read your urine. Sickness is a matter of imbalance, as I'm sure you are aware. I would be honored. The medicine for me is my desire to help you."

"Ah. This reminds me of the story about a monk seen praying on a street corner in New York City. Every day, same time, same corner, this monk came out and sat on a cushion and ran mantras. One day someone says, 'Hey what are you doing this for? Are you praying to change the world? Don't you know it's hopeless?' The monk says, 'No, I am praying so that the world can't change me.'"

"Ah, that's a good one," Norbu laughs, putting down his beads. "I

don't know much about aikido, but I think its practitioners understand the movement of energy similar to the way Buddhists do. To us
it is the winds. To you it is *ki*."

Marianne opens the door and tiptoes in. She sits at the side of the
bed and puts her icy hand on Max's temple. "I want to show you something. It's so disgusting it'll make you rise from your sickbed like Jesus
and change the world. Can you walk? Can you make it downstairs?"

They help Max wash, lead him downstairs, and seat him on the
sofa across from the puppet propped against a pedestal. The doll sits
with its legs stretched out, and its arms bent, and its hands on the
floor. It wears an ill-fitting plaid jacket, a blue cowboy shirt, a red bow
tie, and a white cowboy hat. Its plaster feet are bare. Max's white scarf
hides the plaster neck. A TV monitor has been fitted into the rec-
tangle for its face. The electric cord extends down the back under the
jacket, along with three cables that hide under one of its legs, emerging at the foot and continuing the rest of the way to the computer
sitting on a table next to the sofa.

"Just a few minutes," says Norbu, sitting down at the computer.

"You run this by computer?" Max knows nothing about such things,
but he's fascinated.

"An IBM XT, 640 kilobytes of memory, a double disc drive, and a
word processing program," intones Norbu. He could be praying. "Someday we'll make our own videos on the computer; we will load in footage
and edit with the same sophistication we find today in a professional
studio, you wait."

"Never happen," says Marianne.

Norbu smiles to himself. "Just you wait. This is shot off the television; we've cleaned it up as much as possible."

The screen lights up, and goes to snow, then in the background, the engineers run their sound check. At the same time, the video snow morphs into rain. When it clears up a moment later, it becomes apparent that we're on a ship, the camera's on a high deck looking down at the bow. The sea is rough; what appeared to be rain turns out to be spray crashing over the deck in front of the camera lens. Several small groups of people stand motionless at the railings. A man holding a machine gun faces them. The camera pans along the deck, past an open doorway and down a flight of stairs, around a corner to a man in a wheelchair. One gunshot rings out, then another. The figure in the chair slumps. The frame then shifts to a second set of cameras shooting from a helicopter. The image is blurred but unmistakable: a man in a wheelchair falling from a great height into the ocean.

Then the chair jerks backward. As the side of the rail comes into view, it starts forward again. For the rest of the tape, the man in the wheelchair is jerked backward and forward. Gradually an audio track cuts in. It is the earnest voice of Ronald Reagan, the fortieth president of the United States.

He says, in his Howdy Doody voice: "In the thirty-eighth chapter of Ezekiel, it says that the land of Israel will come under attack by the armies of the ungodly nations, and it says that Libya will be among them. Do you understand the significance of that? Libya has now gone communist, and that is a sign that the day of Armageddon isn't far off."

Norbu shuts off the tape.

"Almost a thousand people on board, and they whack the crippled little Jew," says Marianne. "I'm really, really pissed. So what do you think?"

He cannot think, all he can do is hallucinate, and so he pulls his blanket around him, clears his throat, and addresses the blank screen: "Imagine you are a wolf out in the lonely forest. And one day you smell smoke, and find yourself at a campsite. Maybe there's room for you around this fire, and maybe not. If there is, you go and lie down. And soon as you do this, you're half asleep, and your fur is warm, and my God, someone is petting you, taking out the lice, and putting a spoon out near your face for you to lick. You lick. You sleep, you purr, you start to bring in the wood yourself, and that's it—you're inside the circle, and boy, that works out very well for you until you start having dreams again of racing around the forest, cold and hungry and free, smelling smoke from a distance."

Norbu and Marianne sit speechless.

Then Norbu realizes Max is about to collapse and rushes to him.

"Cut off my leg," Max begs him, clutching his arm. "My leg. Slice through my jeans directly. There are some shears in the left-hand kitchen drawer. I mean, cut off my pants. Please. Marianne. On the wall. My garden shears."

"He means we have to take a look at his leg," says Norbu, taking the shears from Marianne. "We cut through his pants and take a look." He starts cutting along the seam toward the knee and then stops. "You have every sign of a deep infection, my friend. Marianne, go downstairs and call for an ambulance."

"I can drive, fuck you," says Max through white lips, trembling with the effort of keeping still.

"I was born in Tibet," says Norbu, continuing to cut through the material. "My mother was an American whose first husband had been killed climbing in Nepal. Tell me if I'm hurting you. We went to

Lhasa, where my stepbrother lived in the monastery. I was eleven years old when we left. It was one year before His Holiness the Dalai Lama fled. We went first to Dharamsala, later to America, where my father went to medical school and became a Western doctor. After a few years he took us back to India. Tibetan medicine is the weirdest system you can imagine, very complex and crazy, based on memorizing a book that's a thousand years old. Marianne! Tell them this is a very virulent infection, maybe staph. Bring intravenous antibiotics. What can you expect from people who learn anatomy by cutting up their dead with chain saws and letting the birds peck clean their bones. We know the body inside and out. But if you were in Tibet right now, you would be dead in two hours. How lucky we are to be in America."

Marcos Zinelli sits in his office reading his daughter a letter he's writing to the governor explaining that someone posing as an advocate for the elderly is at this very moment convincing his wife to sign his rights away. He's referring to the slender woman wearing a beige pants suit sitting in the living room eating a cookie. She's asking Erica questions meant to determine her ability to live safely in her own home, checking the topics off on a clipboard resting on her lap. Lena sits on the guest room bed, straining to listen to both parents at the same time. She's conflicted between rooting for her mother's sanity and guiltily hoping the state will take her away. She hears Erica tell the social worker that her daughter—who's right there in the next room with her father—has arranged a catering service. If the social worker would only check out the fridge, Lena thinks, she'd see that the freezer's stuffed with half-eaten take-out.

While this is going on, her father's reading his letter out loud. He's progressed to the second paragraph. "As a member of the legal profession," he's saying, pointing a shaky index finger at her, "I know my rights."

Lena smiles indulgently. "Dad, you're a lawyer now?"

The phone rings then. Marcos doesn't hear it, so Lena picks up. It's Marianne, asking for her.

"It's me," says Lena, sliding down against the pillows and closing her eyes.

"You sound different. Like you're twelve years old."

"I am twelve years old. What's up?"

"You need to come home," says Marianne. "It's Max. He's in the hospital in critical condition. It's a staph infection in his leg, and there's danger of a total body infection. I got you a seat on the 3:30 Delta with a transfer in Newark."

Lena says nothing, her head begins to throb. She sits silently cradling the phone and watching her father shuffling about in circles penetrating the air with that lawyerly index finger. Marianne slowly repeats her message. *Strange*, Lena thinks, *I already know what she's saying; it's as if this has already happened*. "Yes, I can get to the plane. No, I don't need any help. Yes, pick me up at 7:00," she says, rings off, and goes to her father. "Dad, the governor doesn't give a shit about you." Holding on to his thin wrist, she gently brings him to the bed and sits down next to him. "Dad, can you give me your letter?"

"What do you think, doll?" he says, handing it to her and pulling off his glasses. "My eyes hurt so much; glaucoma, you know. Would you check it for spelling?"

"Of course, Dad." She holds it open in her lap, staring down at the page. She doesn't want to decipher her father's heartbreaking handwriting for fear of exposure to his demented world. *Dad*, she thinks, *Dad, what's going on inside that mind of yours?* "Are you putting in your drops?"

"Yes, I do. I put in my drops, but they burn my eyes. Do you think I should sign this without a notary?"

"That's fine, Daddy. You just sign it, and I'll take it with me to the airport." She walks him over to the desk, keeping her arms around him while he picks up his pen and scrawls his signature with a shaky hand, aiming for the paper but ending up signing the desk blotter.

"Airport?" he says, looking puzzled.

"You bet. I'll deliver it personally." She smooths her father's hair away from his cheek and holds him tight. He'd been a substantial man, over six feet tall, with a high, tight belly like a boxer. Now, she could almost lift him in her arms, he's so light. "Doll, take it in stride," he says, his voice cracking.

The doorbell rings then, and in comes the male nurse, Tim, who lives in with a gentleman down the hall who Lena has hired to help with her parents in her absence. He's large, and reassuring.

"Oh, daughter," says Erica, bobbing into the room behind the nurse. "Have you sent me this handsome man?" Everyone laughs. As her father tries to explain to his wife that their daughter is personally delivering his letter to the governor on her way back north, Lena manages a whispered conversation with Tim, arranging for meals, bathing, medicines. He'll wash Erica's hair and feed Marcos his Ensure, put them all to bed, and check in during the night. Money will be paid under the table. Tim lets the social worker out, reassuring her that the Zinellis will be safe under his care. He helps Lena pack while he calls her a cab; he tells her not to worry about a thing as he distracts her parents so she can slip out the door.

When Lena was fourteen, her grandmother Alice had a fatal heart attack during a wild night of gin rummy in a Miami motel. That night, alone in her Brooklyn bedroom while Erica flew to Florida, Lena felt Alice move into her body and settle down in her rib cage. She was exactly as she was in real life—long white braids wrapped around her head, black lace-up shoes, sup hose, and a faded black cotton dress. Lena's been carrying her around for over thirty years, along with a couple of lesser guardian angels acquired since childhood. Sitting on her plane now, squeezed between strangers, she thinks, *Granny, I'm being torn apart, my parents dying at my feet and my lover in the hospital. Who am I supposed to save first? Is this what's meant by middle age? Would you change places with me? Come back to this world and let me fly away?* Alice laughs in her particular way, with closed lips, glee spilling silently from her marvelous gray eyes. Lena can hear her voice: *Remember to keep your bloomers clean, for when you get run over by a car.* They both sleep then, waking only when the plane begins stretching down toward Newark. The moment before the wheels touch, Alice chides her, *I'm too busy watching over you to change places.*

Max has been put into an artificial coma in hopes of keeping the infection down. There's been talk of surgery and even amputation. Lena eases herself down beside him on the edge of the bed and instantly falls asleep, leaving Alice an opening to do what she can for him.

The morning nurse, seeing Lena in the bed, sends her away. At home Marianne appears in a cotton nightgown and brings her tea. They catch up in whispered voices, then Marianne hands her a Seconal. She sleeps for twenty-four hours, wakening once to use the bathroom, when she notices Norbu's dog curled up next to Zia—*Oh, yes, there's a Tibetan in the house; all will be well.*

While she sleeps, it snows. Around noon, Jocelyn and Tonkey pull up in the van, having driven through the storm from Baltimore. They head immediately to bed, At 3:30, Norbu and Marianne leave for an editing studio in South Burlington. By 5:00, Rufus and Zia nose Lena awake. She tries to coax them into her bed, but they're whining and hopping about. She puts on a robe, finds her slippers, and lets them out.

In the hall she stops in front of the chest and frowns. No doubt in her mind, this chest belongs to Max. It's dinged up and unadorned, with a domed lid and a broken padlock. The thing is, what's it doing in the hallway? And why is it unlocked? This is unlike Max, who likes his things locked up or bound up, lest they escape and go off to live on their own.

She makes a cup of coffee and brings it back to the hall, leaning on the trunk, absently watching the dogs play outside the window. After a while she puts down her cup and opens the trunk.

Max has talked, off and on, about owning weapons, but never in present time, and always casually, without seeming to fetishize them. To Lena, they'd seemed to be accessories to his stories: the gun Annie Oakley had given to his mother or the rifle he'd once sighted on Nikita Khrushchev, the whip used to illustrate the spiral qualities of aikido, the Japanese pistol handed to him by the charcoal man in the Alps.

But she'd been wrong. The weaponry of his stories is very real: she's staring right at them. The pistols and cutlery lie in full view on top of the burlap-wrapped rifles, which rest diagonally on an item at the bottom, bulky and heavy and wrapped in cloth. Her first impulse is to slam down the lid and run, but she's also fascinated. Max has touched these weapons, wiped them down, packed them away. She urges the knives halfway out of their fancy sheaths and notes that they're razor sharp and buffed to a mirrored perfection. She picks up the pistols by the barrels and sees they are clean and have been recently oiled. She handles them as if they were about to go off, as if they were coiled snakes, and lays each one down side-by-side on a towel. She picks up the rifles with two hands and places them on the floor still in their wrappings. She has no idea if the guns are loaded and has no intention of squinting down the mouth of a barrel to find out.

Only one item remains, big and bulky, wrapped in a faded kimono cloth. It's conceivable that this object might be a real treasure, an object of beauty a martial artist might be proud to collect and hang on his wall. Max has talked knowledgeably and longingly of medieval Japanese weaponry, noting similarities between these and the seventeenth-century dueling swords used in the West. She can't resist taking a look, so she sits down on the floor, puts the bundle on her lap, and carefully unravels the fragile old kimono cloth.

Underneath is a gruesome, utilitarian, and archaic hunting weapon: a double-stringed bow welded to a rifle stock painted in a cartoonish camouflage, with a scope and a trigger. It's like looking at the teeth of a corpse, the very essence of the killing-and-eating machine, when everything else has been wasted.

This is a shock of no small significance. It's a major reality reevaluation. A year into her relationship with Max Diebenkorn, she's learned about martial arts, warriorship, military honor, and life-and-death situations, all new concepts in her specialized existence as a trained-from-birth pacifist. Her abhorrence of guns and war is cellular. She didn't punch boys as a kid: never dated a football player, or incited a fight in a bar; has never been attracted to a bully, or been slapped around or even pushed. Rage she knows, but only repressed rage. Conflict she avoids. She has never yearned for an armed male. Oh, there was one, she remembers now, a guy named Wendell in Woodstock, New York, who liked wandering around at night naked with a bow and arrow, but only in season.

She stands up. Sliding off her lap, the crossbow bangs loudly on the tile floor. In the kitchen, she pours herself a glass of wine from the last bottle of Julian's stash and takes it out to the hot tub to think. The air feels raw, so she hunkers down in the steam. Definitely she's out of her league here. She feels disgusted and sick. She knows better, but right now she's going to compare her new lover with her old, wart for wart. Her ex might have been a refined jerk with repressed fury, but at least his passive-aggression made him avoid conflict at any cost. That's the way to behave in the twentieth century. Walk as though you are walking through water and no one will try to harm you, the current advice. Julian wouldn't have known what part was the trigger. Guns are not part of their conversation. People she knows don't get in their cars with crossbows. They don't walk down Church Street weighed down with quivers of arrows. They won't be found slithering along the back roads of small towns with foliage on their heads, and finding nothing to rip apart, go back to their trailers to abuse their wives in front of the TV, like the people he knows might; at least that's how she sees it.

Fifteen minutes later the wine hits the Seconal still in her system—
Lena has the kind of metabolism that downers wallow in for weeks—
and she slides down to that gentle spot where Alice keeps her safe.

Max, too, is thinking about his weapons. Lying in his hospital bed thirty
miles away from Lena, his mind finally free from fever, he thinks back
to the night of his delirium when he'd gone to North Hero and brought
those weapons, the worst part of his soul, into her house. He has always
looked into the ugly face of his own nature and taken on whatever it
shows him; violence or shame or greed or hunger, and at this time of
his life, weakness: failure mixed, he hopes, with redeeming love.

The martial arts teachers he admires use their own autobiography
to model the qualities suited to a contemporary warrior for their students. And they don't hide their violence, for the art of peace attracts
martial men, as the art of war attracts peacemakers. In this regard, he
has no apologies, although some might accuse him of indulgence. But
Lena isn't his student, and pistols aren't teaching tools. If she stumbles
upon his stash, she's bound to be repelled, as she should be. The trunk
is his Pandora's box, stuffed with paranoia, fear, and aggression, with
none of the love and compassion he's always mouthing off about. If
love's to be given a chance to soothe his demons, he needs to protect
Lena from this part of himself at all cost.

And there's more in her house she knows nothing about: the morphine that he takes traveling, and the oriental leather-sheathed *tanto*
dagger zipped into the pocket he'd slashed in her mattress. Not to
mention the Japanese *dadao* sword hanging in its ornamental sheath
over his office desk, and the wooden *jo* in the closet, harmless unless
you know how to use it—as he does.

But his real weapon of self-annihilation sits in full sight in her garage. It's the American way, death by automobile. He has already fallen out his truck door while driving on a curve; he's totaled a Chevy, a Datsun, and a lovely little Austin Healey; slid over a bank in a Toyota Land Cruiser, and hit a cow. Years ago, a psychic had told him to stay out of cars. She'd seen him dying in a vehicle parked on the side of the road. So if he wanted to kill himself, he would point his truck west to where the really big bridges bend over the really big rivers and let himself fall asleep at the wheel, something he fights all the time anyway, which is why Lena does the serious driving. He wouldn't trust being in a car with himself.

Of course he thinks of suicide, but only in spurts. If you're old or sick or dying, you keep your options open.

Lena's beyond furious. She goes to the hospital armed with an ultimatum; he either seeks therapy—he's obsessed with munitions, harbors a deeply ambivalent mother complex, is too ashamed to divorce a wife he hasn't lived with for nineteen years; he's never had a job or a owned a home; he drops his socks on the floor *next to* the hamper—or he's out. The clothes she wears reflect her determination: black.

He's lying on his back with his arms blotchy with bruises and his dreams running amok under his thin eyelids. She stands at the foot of his bed and picks up his chart and learns she's almost lost him.

She says, still holding the chart, "When I left Florida, my mother said, 'Promise to shoot me if I become a burden.'"

"And you said?" his eyes still closed, lips quivering. He's trembling at the sight of her.

"I said, 'How about I shoot you in advance?' And she said, 'That's my girl, be brave.'"

"You found the trunk." Max sighs. She has to wonder if he'd meant her to find it all along. But of course he had: the trunk filled up half her hallway. Of course she would look into it.

"Yeah." She puts the chart back in the folder and moves over to the window. Outside, snow falls lightly on the parking lot, melting as it hits the tops of the vapor lamps that turn on as she watches. Her resolve seems to soften as well, into something like sadness or a sense of inevitability.

"I'm glad you did. Seems I wanted you to." Max pushes himself to a sitting position and motions her over.

She sits down at his side and feels his forehead. He's hot, very hot, his skin spongy and lifeless. "You need help," she says, dryly.

"I do. I need your help."

"Not from me. Therapy. I mean it. Really. You have to do that."

"Sure. We'll find someone good. Lena, I want to tell you something. When I was twenty-four, and everything was new and fresh, I used to come up to the mountains near Nagano to train with a famous American martial artist. He was everything I imagined a real warrior to be. The mountain winters there are as harsh as in Vermont, with snow endlessly falling. It was much too cold to sleep in the barn where we'd been quartered. We were freezing and miserable. Then this sensei, this American guy, he must have been in his forties then, started telling jokes: really stupid, childish jokes. So ridiculous that soon we were squealing with laughter, and that's how we made it through the miserable night. The next day the sensei teased me, 'Should we go get some breakfast? Or should we be real warriors and not eat anything?'

'Breakfast! Breakfast!' I yelled out. 'I want some chocolate, I want some coffee, I want some ham!' That day we trained, and it was wonderful. There were horses there watching us from the stalls, and it was very natural; these animals seemed like a proper audience to perform for, idly standing there watching as the humans hooted and yelled and rolled in the heavy snow."

"Nice," she says, unsmiling. "You're avoiding the subject."

"So, you know any jokes?"

"No. None. I never know any jokes." But one comes to mind. It has nothing to do with anything, but there it is, a joke.

"Yeah, this is a really stupid dog joke. I'm thinking it's something Zia might tell when we're not around."

"Go for it."

"It's too stupid. One dog is telling another dog what happened at dinner that night. He says, 'There we were, sitting around the dinner table, knocking off a bottle of Côtes du Rhône and blathering about the Middle East—you've never heard such shallow, simplistic reasoning in your life—and one of them turns to me and says, "And what do you think, Barney? What do you think we should do?" And all I could come up with was, "Woof." I felt like such an ass.'"

6

You shouldn't be working on enlightenment,
you should be working on endarkenment.
You're not ready for enlightenment.

—James Hillman, quoted in *It's a lot like dancing...*

Max says:

If you're thinking about teaching wisdom, you need to have had a teacher yourself. I have in O-sensei a wonderful teacher. The man was real, and I have to be very careful about what I ascribe to him, to take great care to separate my fantasies about him from his reality. I feel very burdened by the need to present him honorably.

Here's the official history: O-sensei was tiny and sickly as a child. When he was ten years old he watched his father being beaten by a gang of thugs, and he resolved that nobody was ever going to push him around. He studied martial arts with every teacher he could find in Japan, Manchuria, China, and Korea, usually until he got a black belt—he had about sixty of them. He vowed to be the meanest son of a bitch in the valley, and by the age of fifty he had achieved his goal.

He was a prodigy with legendary strength. One day he was walking with one of his spiritual teachers past a rock; the teacher told him to move it, and he did. It took ten men to move it back.

But then he experienced a period of profound depression. He was the top dog, teaching the Japanese nobility, a man to be reckoned with, but he felt that his life had added up to zero. So he went back in the mountains to study. The question that haunted him was, *Is there a way to break through the duality of dominance or submission?*

In Japan, when a student wants to challenge a teacher it's a big deal, because if he wins, he leaves training and maybe takes students with him. One time a student challenged O-sensei by grabbing a wooden sword and attacking him. O-sensei responded by throwing away his own sword and dodging, instead of returning, the blows. Even without a sword he was unassailable, and finally the young man gave up.

Ueshiba went over to a well and pulled up a bucket of water and threw it over himself. As he did so a flood of golden light came over him. He speaks of this as his enlightenment, his understanding that the only victory to be won was over oneself. In that moment, aikido was born, and his hunger for power vanished. Until that time he'd been kicking ass and kissing ass, because in life, if you want your own dojo, you have to listen to some asshole admiral talk all night, hoping he will give you a check in the morning. His enlightenment freed him of all that.

O-sensei was not a moral policeman, and this is hard for us to understand, because Christian spiritual leaders like Billy Graham and Jerry Falwell have no compunction telling us what we ought to be doing. We know Jerry Falwell is out there fucking his brains out, but still we're attracted to him, maybe only because we want to learn how he gets away with his behavior.

I have no idea about O-sensei's private life, or if he had one. All I know is that he said not a word about my desire to screw bar waitresses on Saturday mornings. I'm sure that he saw in us *uchi deshi* massive moral failings. When, for example, he found out that one of his students had beat a dog to death, he didn't throw him out of the dojo: I wish he had thrown him out, but that's just me. The most proscriptive thing he ever said was, "Come to practice aikido." He'd say, "Oh, you are in practice. Wonderful."

One time, though, he really got mad at me and this Japanese guy— we just liked each other—we'd start fooling around by ourselves with the wooden swords after class. O-sensei came in and said, "Listen, *jo* training is too advanced for you, so put them away. OK?" We did, but the next morning we went at it again. He comes over and warns us again, talking to us like you'd talk to your kids, in a practical way, like,

"Don't do it, because you'll get hurt." We are not talking philosophy here. The next morning, we don't intend to—but pretty soon we do it again. And then he comes running in the room, screaming "Yee-e-e." And we were both full prostrate. It was terrifying.

I was lucky, in that by the time I came along he had worked through most of his trip and was less interested in power or recognition than the state of his kidneys. Notice that in most of his later pictures, his head is pointed upward; he was a man who talked primarily to God. I went on a four-day trip with him to Kyoto. Our rooms were next to each other, so I could hear every move he made. Night and day all he did was pray; he didn't go to the movies, date, or entertain, he just talked to God. That spoke more to me than anything he taught me in all my years with him.

O-sensei was not a warrior, in that sense of teaching war. He was teaching people how not to fight, but instead to learn a martial art of protection without violence. All this about warfare and warriors is just advertising, just salad, a hustle—like in ancient Greece, FOLLOW ME was written on the back of the hookers' sandals to get people into the temple. It's the same thing here, letting the word *warrior* intrigue people; it's the carrot to our temple.

He had immense hands for his size: gorgeous, wonderful hands, very strong and broad, but always gentle. I remember his hands much more than any other part of his body, except for his eyes. It felt a hundred different ways to be thrown by O-sensei. Some days I wasn't present, and my consciousness followed me like a small, disgruntled child.

Once in a while he would throw me with just a look, and I know there is some space or some realm that we are playing on, the threshold of something I can't possibly imagine or describe. You're supposed to hit this little guy, but you can't find him, he's not there. Then the little tiny guy gets in the middle of eight or nine other people, and they can't find him. He's invisible, unavailable. I don't know where he was. It's said that he liked to whiz around everyone's backs, so no one could see him, and maybe so—but still, we're talking cosmos here, touching energies that perhaps all things share.

It was like you met a Martian who unconsciously controlled you. When he was in the room, you knew he was in the room, and you knew exactly where he was in that room; you could look straight at him, and you never knew what you'd see. Maybe one day, I'd see "nice grandfather." Now, was that because he was in a grandfatherly mood? Or was I in a grandfather-accepting mood? Another time I'd look at him, and he'd be a fucking dragon with the fire of hell coming out of his eyes and you don't want to go near him.

There are many things he did that I can't explain, like the way in which he would hold his *bokken* straight up and ask people to push on it. Since he'd always ask the same people—Suginami, Harada, and Aihara—and he'd never include me, I'd think, *Oh, that son of a bitch.* So one day I slid in between Harada and Suginami and hit that *bokken* with everything I had; it was like hitting solid steel. Now, how did he do that? I have no idea. Let me demonstrate. I'm going to push on your chest. Don't let me throw you off balance. When I put my hands on you, you push me. Come on. Just a finger, very lightly. Just a little upward pressure. You see that you can stop me just by pressing back with two little fingers. Now you have gotten the same experience I had with that *bokken* with O-sensei.

People want to hear something fantastic when they ask me what it was like to be thrown by him. People relate to him as they do to the Virgin Mary or to Christ. Nobody's met Christ; nobody's met the Virgin Mary, and yet people feel deeply connected to them. So it is with O-sensei. They ask me this question, hoping that I might have something miraculous for them. And in fact, I do.

There was one time when he threw me, where I looked down over my shoulder and I saw the sea from a height of about 4,000 feet. I can see it with my mind as I saw it then. It wasn't a really sunny day, but there was a little light playing off the water, and given the glint, the angle of incidence on the water, I could tell it was morning. I don't know if I heard a seagull or saw one. This vision of the sea that I saw over my shoulder, looking down, was as real for me as sitting here. I'm going through the air and I have no worry. I looked down, and I had plenty of time. So much time that I felt I was totally unafraid, only curious about what it was I was seeing. I said to myself, *Shit, am I flying, or what? I mean, what's going to happen when I hit?* I started working out the details. Why was I looking at the ocean? All of those things went through my head in the split second it took to throw me down. It only happened that one time. But maybe those things were going on all the time, only I wasn't aware of it except that one time. Sometimes when I'm being thrown, I remember that. Even sitting at this table, there's a certain way my head will touch my shoulder, and that time comes back to me.

Burlington, Vermont, 1987

There's a pretty park behind Burlington's city hall where people come with their dogs and kids and bikes. Months from now, farm stalls and craft vendors will open up at the edges, attracting throngs of tourists and rollerbladers, but right now, on this uncannily warm morning in the middle of March, the park's a quiet place where office workers stroll and students read on benches eating lunch, while at times passing around mild narcotics under the mayor's second-story window.

A fine day—and a perfect audience, Marianne figures, for a Ronnie puppet test run. If it flies in Burlington, the next stop could be Boston, New York, who knows. So, early in the morning, she gathers the troops and the props and heads downtown with Norbu Tendzen in his electronically loaded van. Max follows in his truck with Lena, Ronnie, and the dogs.

By mid-morning, Marianne had firmed up an idea, gotten permits, and loaded the park with her people. Twenty-two men, women, and children, all wearing gray flannel suits, fedoras, mirrored sunglasses, white latex gloves, some of them carrying cameras and audio recording devices, sit on the benches, lean on trees, or recline on the grass. Another group of similarly clothed actors walk around with hats, offering fortune cookies to passersby.

Marianne's Ronnie Reagan doll is propped up on the bench closest to Cherry Street. The Klinghoffer videotape in its face runs on an infinite loop, with the low-level audio issuing from speakers in the trees. The doll has its back to the curb where the van has been parked. All its electronics lead through the open cargo door, where Norbu squats before a bank of computer screens.

A large box sits on a tripod next to the doll, facing the park. A sign on it reads ASK RONNIE. For a quarter, a thin sheet of paper posing a question pops out of a slot in the front of the box. After a moment, the answer to the question appears on the doll's screen, temporarily pausing the tape.

Lena and Marianne stand in the bushes recording the reactions of passers-by as they encounter Ronnie Reagan, digest the video, and interact with the ASK RONNIE box.

Max sits next to the doll, tucked under a blanket in a wheelchair, wearing a pair of mirrored wraparound sunglasses. Zia lies at his feet, next to a can with a sign asking for donations for the Klinghoffer family.

As the morning goes on, there are no interruptions from the authorities, for this is the-live-and-let-live Republic of Burlington. A State Police car now and then circles the block; in general, everything appears copasetic. Two selectmen, the head of the Arts Council, and the mayor's secretary have all come around, although the mayor himself, up for reelection, has sensibly remained in his office.

Later in the day a WCAX-TV truck pulls up behind the van. Norbu directs the crew to Marianne, who hands her camera to Max and goes off to be interviewed. Max pushes his dark glasses over his temples and looks through the camera, scanning for possible publicity shots. When his lens focuses on a group of Buddhist monks scrutinizing the ASK RONNIE box, he recognizes the American among them and calls out his name. "Russell, hey."

Russell, a compact man wearing a saffron robe under a down vest, is a meditation leader from the Shambhala Center in New York who is in town to help Norbu conduct a training program at the local meditation center on Riverside Avenue. He and Max know each other from the Bowery dojo and he greets his old friend with pleasure, coming over quickly and making room for himself on the bench. "So it's come to this," he exclaims in a teasing voice. "Max Diebenkorn, famous Park Avenue roustabout, transformed into a crippled, blind beggar wielding a thousand-dollar Hasselblad?"

Laughing, Max hands him the camera. "It's rented, and the wheelchair—that's just practice for later. I'm pretty good, thank you. What's with you and the sacred robes?"

"I'm an actual monk now, Max. Can you believe it?"

"Last I knew, you were an actual vice president of Gray Advertising. You're looking good, Russell. Really you are. Very clear." He focuses intently on his old friend's face and breaks into a warm smile. "Really, Monkdom does you good." Russell is touched, but he's also upset, because he can't in all honesty return the compliment. Max looks at him with sympathy. *Oh well,* he tells himself, *I'm a sick old man. Let us face this with good cheer.* He's about to ask about the workshop when Norbu emerges from the van. Russell gets up quickly and the two men hug. "This guy," Norbu says over his friend's shoulder, "was ordained by Trungpa Rinpoche himself. My teacher, you know. You've met Trungpa Rinpoche, Max?"

"I do know of him and we never did meet. I hear he's been very sick," says Max. It occurs to him that the Rinpoche is exactly his own age.

"My question to Ronnie Reagan was," says Russell, putting a hand on the puppet's head, "*What president said he'd make a good pope?* And he spit out the correct answer, *Richard Nixon.* So guys, tell me: What is it exactly that you all are doing here?"

"Educating the public about the Republican Party," says Max. "And also about international terrorism. A thankless task but noble, we think we're up to it."

"We're just slaves to Marianne Lubitsch, over there with the black hair and the clipboard. Her show," adds Norbu, gesturing.

"No flack from the powers that be?"

"This is a very permissive town," says Max. "You could run a talking bear for Chief of Police and he'd win as long as he carried his own pooper scooper."

"We have a permit for a theatrical event and no one's bothered to ask about its content," says Norbu.

"We hear you've been sick, my friend," Russell says to Max.

"Yeah, well, a little staph infection, a shot immune system—I catch stomach flu over the telephone. From what I hear, your Rinpoche's pretty sick. Injuries from that old car accident, is the official explanation. So what's wrong, really?" What else he hears is that Trungpa's half dead due to his own self abuse—the usual cocaine, sex, and alcohol—only no one in the community will admit it. Sure enough, Russell and Norbu stand there with their hands in their pockets staring past him into the cosmos, as if the answer to his question might lurk out there, billions of light years into the past. But Max really wants to know. He sloughs off his blanket and stands up. "How does he do that? I mean, the guy staggers onstage clutching a quart of Absolut, he's in bed screwing students, snorting poison through a straw, and still his popularity on the guru-meter is second only to His Holiness, the Dalai Lama." It's true that hordes of spiritual seekers are jumping ship from the Maharishi or Zazen or Sufism and glomming on to Trungpa despite his bad habits. But that's not what really irks him, for who is he to condemn the morals of another man. So what is it?

He shuffles around the wheelchair and grabs a bottle of water, stands drinking for a few moments catching up with his emotions, which are conflicted. On the one hand, he feels deep respect for anyone emerging through the gates of hell as an enlightened being, so called by others. But on the other hand . . . he doesn't quite get it yet.

What's bothering him has something to do with Trungpa's Shambhala being too easy. He's spoon-feeding Americans Buddha-lite. You can get the training in three easy sessions, when it should take practice all your life. He feels the same way about people who appropriate aikido principles without having devoted their lives to practice. He should ask outright, he decides, putting down the water bottle. "How come everyone I know is so smitten?"

"They're not," says Russell, dryly, pulling his gaze away from the cosmos. "For some, he's gone too far. It's not only the drugs, it's also his army of bodyguards, they're out of control and acting more like a militia."

"So tell me, is Trungpa a man of God with an alcohol problem? Or is he an alcoholic with a God problem?" asks Max, paraphrasing a witticism picked up from somewhere. Immediately he regrets repeating it—it's insulting, at least to Norbu, he can see that.

But Russell smiles benignly enough and says, "Trungpa pointed the way to the moon with his finger. Do we care if that finger had been stirring martinis? You have to look at him as a whole man. He drank, had sex with students, and chain-smoked. If you accused him of those things, he would have laughed with delight. Tibetans have a different morality, maybe. They have this *crazy guru* tradition. To label his drinking as "alcoholic" brands him as diseased. And Trungpa Rinpoche is anything but a diseased person. He is an enlightened being. All people have the right to be as they are. The trouble came when American students thought that because Trungpa drank, they too should get smashed. Unfortunately, they were not enlightened beings."

"Yeah, we Westerners understand disease. There's no money in *moxa* or leeches, as you well know, my dear Doctor Tendzen. These days I wouldn't mind being diagnosed with something a skilled surgeon might dig out of me."

"Be careful what you wish for," says Norbu, walking back to the van.

The next day, Max wakes up feeling as though he's swallowed a basketball. It's like a baby made of concrete that won't be born, his own little dollop of doom, a protrusion preventing him from tying his shoelaces. Some days it's smaller than others, but it's always there. Last week, he'd come out of the hospital supposedly free of infection, but maybe they didn't zap it all and now the staph has morphed into this lump in his belly where it sulks, biding its time.

In therapy—true to his word, he's seeing a psychologist, a commonsensical Ph.D. named Ostermeyer—Max has been exploring his core of identity and the list of grievances, physical and psychological, in residence there, the itching, swelling, sickness of heart, inability to commit, promiscuity, ego inflation, etc. In his mind, he's cleaning himself up so he can have a relationship with Lena, and he wonders if there may be some lesson to learn from Norbu's theories of disease. Accept it, for it's part of your wisdom. Your disease is here to teach you whatever it is you need to learn. But at the same time, don't let that stop you from seeing the best internist in town.

Dr. Marcus Meltzer is a small natty man with frizzy gray hair, a beak for a nose, and lambent eyes whose wife auctioned him off in the Vermont Public Radio fundraising waltz marathon, thereby launching him as *le docteur du jour* for the arty set. He's a cornucopia of mixed medical methodology, certified by the New England School of Acupuncture and licensed as a homeopathic practitioner, open to the

Alexander Technique, ayurvedic herbs, and shamanic psychic surgery. If you're lucky, he'll script Percocet for your ingrown toenail, but you might have to agree to colonic cleansing.

Meltzer spends an hour talking with Max about his lifestyle and the Red Sox before removing Max's bandage. "May I?" he asks, gently peeling it off. He stares at the oozing fissure for a long moment. "A terrible beauty," he says. "My poor boy." Then he adds with a sigh that there is a tradition in Western arts equating beauty with death. Then he bends down over it, as if he's about to kiss it.

Alarmed, Max tries to move his leg out of range. "Thoreau had TB," he says quickly. "He wrote that death and disease are 'often beautiful, like the hectic glow of consumption.'"

Meltzer beams. Lifting his face, he reaches for a new roll of bandages and carefully redresses the wound. They have established a common bond. He hands him a balloon and tells him to blow. Max tries, dissolves into a coughing fit and hands it back.

"OK, so it's what we know," says Meltzer, as he writes a few sentences in the record. "You have an oxygen debt. I just thought of something. You said you had a rash, right? Show me."

Max rolls up his sleeve. The two of them stare at the tiny red bumps with the black centers, big as the head of a pin. "I thought so," says Meltzer, pulling a magazine out of his file drawer. It's the most recent *The New England Journal of Medicine*, a pink sticky note marks an article entitled "Sarcoidosis, Diagnosis and Treatment."

"Take a look at this and tell me what you think," he says, handing it to Max.

Max reads:

> Sarcoidosis. From the Greek *sarkodes,* meaning "fleshy," and
> the suffix *osis*, meaning "condition." A fleshy condition, mul-
> tisystem, referring to peculiar lesions forming on various parts
> of the body, most notably the *erythema nodusum* that develop
> on the skin of the lower legs. Sarcoidosis is a disease of unknown
> etiology characterized by granuloma formation in a variety of
> organs. The resemblance to Tuberculosis has led to speculation
> that it might be an infectious disease. Although in many cases,
> the disease clears up on its own, it may lead to pulmonary hyper-
> tension. Once the lungs are involved in this manner, the con-
> dition grows chronic and usually worsens in time.

What does he think? It's disgusting, repugnant, the invasion of the body pods.

"You can't diagnose me from a magazine article and a Thoreau quote, Doc," he protests as he rolls down his sweater sleeve. His mind is racing, this disease is not what he expected, it's an unknown, fatal even. This quack has decided his body is filling up with scabs. Why isn't he ordering tests? On the other hand, he almost kissed the wound, he's a saint.

"Of course not," says Meltzer. "It's a place to start, a metaphor. Poetic."

"So send me for tests."

"There aren't any. Oh, we'll test your lung functions, see what shows up on the CAT scans. But what we'll see will be symptoms: enlarged heart, pulmonary hypertension. We'll have to rule out the possible causes one by one. We'll rule out allergies, heart disease, TB. Then we'll see what's left. Usually sarcoidosis is self-limiting, meaning that it resolves on its own. If we see signs of fibrosis, stiffening in the lungs, we'll treat. We'll attack with every weapon known to modern medicine."

"How about we find an article on a different disease?"

"Ha. Prednisone is the designated treatment." Meltzer reaches for the script pad. "You should feel relief quite quickly. We'll start you at a low dosage, then fiddle around until we come up with the right maintenance."

Lena holds the door open as Max lugs sacks of groceries in from the car. After seeing Meltzer, he took off on a shopping binge at the organic food co-op and the pharmacy. As he empties the bags on the kitchen counter, he gives a running commentary on how he loves this new Doc and how determined he is to change his life through good nutrition. He talks about the kiss with awe, as if it actually happened.

Never once in her year with Max has Lena actually seen him eat a vegetable; certainly, he's never brought one home. Helping him unpack, she marvels at his excitement. He's handing out carrots like they were wands. So many vegetables! She marvels at the squash, melons, carrots, lettuce. With pride, he shows her the low-sodium tamari and unfiltered oils. Hands out the ginger root, whole-wheat baguette, raw nuts, and apples, carefully folding the paper bags and piling them under the sink.

"He didn't really kiss your leg, Max, did he?" *Appalling*, she thinks, *disgusting*.

"It doesn't matter. Think of it as a metaphor. As a blessing. It's very Norbu-like, don't you think, accepting what's in the body?"

"But what's different is that after accepting it, Norbu wants to nourish it, but this guy, he wants to blast it out with toxic drugs." She's referring to the three-month supply of prednisone lying on the table heaped with the other stuff he'd pulled out from the bag from the pharmacy.

Skin cream, steroid nasal spray, the opiate Tussionex for cough, Lasix for water retention, something for his stomach, another something to stabilize his blood pressure, prednisone, Valium, and the new-generation sleeping pill Halcion.

Too much, Lena thinks, and sits down looking defeated.

Then Max shows her the article and gives her a lengthy explanation of sarcoidosis, keeping his tone light. "I know, I know what you're thinking. But really, it's not so bad, it could have been cancer or heart disease. My heart's strong, he says. And the steroids will work. Maybe it'll turn out to be something else—listen, he sent me down to radiology and I had a zillion tests—so we'll see." He decides not to mention Thoreau. "Steroids are hot, everyone's doing them."

But that's the problem, she's just seen a program on TV about a bodybuilder who took steroids and after a week put his ferret in the microwave. Side effects from prednisone were now so ubiquitous they were a syndrome all their own called, descriptively enough, "'Roid Rage." Max laughs when she tells him.

She puts up water for tea and stands leaning against the fridge, waiting for it to heat up. "This isn't funny," she says. But then goes on to tell him a story about how, when she was a kid, her dachshund tore a ligament in its leg and they gave it cortisone and it went off and deliberately jumped into the pond and drowned.

She puts the tea down and starts to cry. "Lena," he tells her, "dogs don't commit suicide. We're not in charge of our destiny. Maybe the dog just fell in. Come to bed. Tell you what, let's take this Halcion together, we could both use some sleep."

She nods, wipes her eyes. It's true, neither of them have been sleeping well.

They stay up for awhile, drinking their tea and arguing about the necessity of getting a second opinion. He's settled on his doctor, he needs to trust him, it would be impolite, a betrayal of the worst kind: oh no, he's not going to second-guess Meltzer. She keeps at him until at the end of an hour he agrees, and she goes up to bed. He waits until he hears the sound of the TV in their bedroom, then tiptoes upstairs and knocks softly on Norbu's door.

"This disease is of no importance," says Norbu, sounding as if these were the first words he'd spoken all day. Marianne's at a conference in Montreal and he's been puttering around the computers. "It is only a symptom. The basic theory of Tibetan medicine is to keep in balance the *Nyipa sum*—they are *rLung*, *mKhris-pa*, and *Bad-kan*. The long-term causative factors of *Nyipa sum* are the three poisons of desire, hatred, and delusion, which show how closely connected Tibetan medicine is with Buddhist philosophy."

Max blinks hard. His Halcion has started kicking in and already he doesn't understand a word.

"I know you don't want to hear this, Norb, but please cut to the chase, as my lungs are filling up with fibrous blobs as we speak." He looks around for somewhere to stretch out for a speed nap, but there's equipment on every surface.

But Norbu isn't into pontificating. He wants to get back to the computer program he's tweaking for the ANSWER BOX. "Tomorrow,

Max, we'll talk about your diet. Remember that the Medicine Buddha says that if the physician treats the patient according to the medical texts, the treatment will be beneficial. If the method of treatment fails, it is not the fault of the physician but the fault of the Medicine Buddha himself."

"Well, that lets you guys off the hook malpractice-wise," says Max, exiting quickly out the door.

That night, he sleeps well enough for a morning erection, something he barely recognizes, it has been so long. He hadn't mentioned his—face it—impotence to Meltzer, because he's frankly too embarrassed. "Cool drug, no?" he says, directing Lena's hand to the beautiful thing risen between his thighs. She doesn't move. Doesn't crack a smile. He leans over and tickles her nose. Nothing. Blows in her ear. Sings her a stanza of the morning song that usually pops her eyes right open:

> Today is Tuesday
> Today is Tuesday
> Tuesday's news day
> Tuesday's blues day
> All the little cubbies
> We wish the same to you.

Nothing. He says, loudly, "Oh, well, you're right. It's only a baby boner, but it's a start. Let us take this as a portent, an omen, and put myself into the priestly hands of dear Doctor Meltzer." He looks over for affirmation, but his partner's unconscious.

It's dark by the time Lena finally staggers to the table looking winsomely pathetic. He helps her to a chair and pushes a cup of cowboy coffee her way.

"What was I thinking?" she mutters, staring unseeingly at the cup. "I've had a sleeping pill only once. I slept for a week. I can't even take an aspirin. This must be what a lobotomy feels like." The next minute, she's conked out with her head on the table, where he has to leave her.

Only a year ago he would have easily carried her back to bed, but now he'd be hard pressed to bend over in order to pick up her boots.

Two weeks later, he finds himself sitting unhappily in Meltzer's office complaining that the prednisone isn't working. His itch has gotten even worse, the slightest physical effort takes his breath away, it's hard to climb a flight of stairs without stopping to rest on every other step. Furthermore, he adds, Halcion doesn't work; it puts him into an annoying state of being that's no way sleep, for it provides him no rest. It can't be sleep, because he doesn't really wake up.

Then there's the bloating. "Look at me," he says to Meltzer, "Humpty Dumpty too fat to fall off that bloody wall."

But Meltzer isn't concerned. He says that once Max comes off the prednisone, the bloat will go away, but meanwhile he's got to hunker down and bear the discomfort, for that's all it is. In fact, they might have to bump up the dosage if they want to get at the growths in his lungs. If Meltzer's theory is correct, Max's breathing will normalize as the visible rash disappears. "Think of the rash," he says, "as the little black shadow plane you see from your window seat. Where the visible shadow goes, so does the plane that you can't see because you're inside of it." From where Max sits, it's conceivable that Meltzer could be crazy.

"It looks like you're building resistance to the Halcion, so we'll add a little more of that as well. Don't worry about it, it's harmless, it's nothing like your mother's Valium."

Taking Halcion, Max says, makes his body feels like it's lying alone in the dugout while his mind goes off to root for a team in a different ballpark. He says that there's a noticeable change in his state of being that's not exactly sleep, but not normal waking consciousness either. Halcion induces a paralytic state, not particularly uncomfortable. He seems to be dreaming constantly, but the images don't emanate from his personal brain, they come from sleepers in other cultures that have entered with the drug. He says he doesn't exactly wake up; it's more accurate to say that he opens his eyes at a certain time, gets out of bed, and steps through a door where things wait to command his attention. At a certain point in time, he goes back to bed and from there to the dugout.

One evening Lena wakes up to find Max lying on his back, staring at the ceiling, his lips fluttering in the moonlight that drips along the window glass over his profile. Groggily, she leans on one elbow and asks what he's doing.

"Writing a novel," he says, and his lips keep moving.

"Haven't you slept?"

"I have no idea. I'm asleep now. The writing's going super, I tell you."

"Max, you're scaring me. Everyone has to sleep."

"I'm fine." He stares into deep space. "I know the name of the president. The year is 1987. In 1985 our country spent forty-seven billion military dollars in the Persian Gulf. Don't you worry about me."

On April 4th the Venerable Vajracharya Chögyam Mukpo, the eleventh Trungpa Rinpoche, is dead.

Lena gets the call from Russell in New York and runs up to North Hero, where Max is dealing with the water line. She thought she should tell him in person before he heard the news on the radio. She'd never met the man or knew any of his acolytes, but she thinks of herself as a naturally born Buddhist—"Isn't everyone?" Max would say— even though she's never practiced, meditated, or listened to the Dalai Lama talk. Often when she finds herself depressed or disheartened, she seeks out a Tibetan—a surprisingly easy find, as refugees from the Chinese occupation have begun resettling in Burlington—in her favorite Tibetan shop. A meditation group meets weekly over the shop, but she never thinks to join it.

It surprises no one that Norbu and she have become fast friends. Sometimes she thinks of him as her teacher, although he never does more than take her questions seriously and hand her books to read. Lately, she's been reading Trungpa's *Cutting Through Spiritual Materialism*.

She finds Max on the lawn trying to light a butane torch in the wind.

He says nothing for a long, long time. He sits on a log with his back absolutely straight, staring at the cottonwood tree. He's not surprised when she tells him they've taken the body to Nova Scotia to prepare it for cremation. It's at one of the meditation centers Trungpa founded, where he brought Tibetan Buddhism to the West. "I suppose they'll prepare the body there and the cremation ceremony will be in Tibet." He sighs and hands her the torch. "Here, hold this thing, will you? Open the valve really slowly and I'll look for my lighter."

"Actually, the cremation's being held here in Vermont, near the meditation center he founded in Barnet. That's what Norbu said."

"Can't be." says Max, looking puzzled. "Can't happen."

"Norbu says. He says that that a high Tibetan Lama's never been cremated outside of Tibet before. He says it might be in honor of the spread of Tibetan Buddhism to the West, or an insult to the Rinpoche." *But that can't be,* she thinks. *They wouldn't do that.*

"Oh Lord." Max takes the torch from her hand. "Let's go somewhere and be still. Come into my mother's old garden with me, my dear one, and let us feel the breath of an enlightened being as it prepares to leave this frightful plane of consciousness."

The day of the funeral starts out warm and sparkling. The night before, friends of Max's had flown down from Halifax, two animated women who've shaved their heads and traded their power suits for nun's garb. They'd brought an enormous cooler filled with small Nova Scotia lobsters which they'd cooked on the grill in North Hero and served on the beach before going back to Lena's for the night.

Lena drives with Max twisting around in the front seat exchanging Buddha gossip with the women in the back: what celebrity grew up a Dharma Brat; why Buddhism appeals to so many liberal Jews— Jewbu, the new word; who's been to Tibet this year; and who has been to China. They talk doctrine, Tibetan medicine. Lena mainly listens, for she has nothing to contribute to the conversation, as her own experience doesn't extend beyond the mystery and wonder; aside from Norbu, the only real Buddhist she feels she knows is Leonard Cohen, her one and only fantasy fuck, although the real possibility of meeting him is not the reason she's driving her sick lover and two nuns to the funeral of a Tibetan lama. Maybe it's her time for what the taller of the two nuns, whose name is Veronica, laughingly calls "Buddha-fication."

At the exit to Barnet, there are no signs to the funeral site, only a line of traffic extending as far as they can see down along Highway 5. After a few miles inching along, Max falls asleep, one hand trailing out the open window and the other on Lena's knee. Veronica taps Lena on the shoulder and whispers in her ear what a wonderful person Max is, says she's sorry he's sick, how brave Lena is to take it all on. Before Lena can answer, Max wakes up and starts talking about the rainbow.

"You know that when the 16th Karmapa was cremated, a giant rainbow ringed the sun even though the day was dry and clear? What remained of his heart rolled out of the pyre on the side facing Tibet and a small footprint appeared in the ashes in the same direction."

"A day like today," says Veronica. "Auspicious."

"Having a heart roll out in the direction of New Hampshire doesn't really do it for me," the other nun, Janie, laughs.

"And what do you all really think?" Lena asks. "About the rainbow?"

"Oh, it'll happen, you'll see," says Veronica, leaning back in the seat and clapping her hands joyfully.

Throngs of people carrying coolers, babies, and blankets, who have parked farther away, are now walking on the side of the road, slowing traffic to a crawl. The air is festival and casual, people talking and

laughing, dogs barking, children calling. Lena wonders where everyone's coming from, as there was no public announcement.

"Well, it goes to show what a far reach this stuff has," says Max.

"And how hungry people are," adds Janie. "Look, everyone's turning off now, there's a path up the mountain. Lena, you can park in
the lot across the road from the blue tent. Let Max off here." Without meaning to, she's identified the elephant in the car: Max is going
to require special handling. How on earth is he going to climb a
mountain?

"We'll get off here with Max and take all our stuff. I think the blue
tent has first aid, there probably are wheelchairs there, and I bet there's
water. Go park, and we'll meet you," says Veronica, quickly rescuing
the situation.

When Lena comes back from parking the car, she finds Max by
himself in a wheelchair. His friends are nowhere in sight. He has a
look on his face she's come to dread, tightness in his lips and a fierce
thrust of his chin. Illness is a shameful thing, isn't it? He's the teacher
who'd admonished his students to come to the dojo no matter what it
took. And now, he's humbled.

"I could walk. But then you wouldn't have a lap for all that stuff,"
he jokes, holding his hands out for the tote bag, water bottles, and
her camera equipment. She grabs the handles and pushes. It does not
budge.

As it turns out, the path they're on is the handicap access route.
It cuts around the base of the mountain and leads to the hospital
tent, which also serves for the press and second level VIPs, like may-
ors and film crews who are not part of the intimate community.
Young men and women are stationed along the path wearing brown

shirts with brown berets, one of them breaks away from his friends and takes over the wheelchair, muttering, *Ich spreche kein Englisch, traurig.*

Still, it's a beautiful, *auspicious* day. Sunlight flashes through the brightly colored flags flapping overhead in the sandalwood breeze. Groups of small buttery men in saffron, maroon, and chestnut robes pass them by, talking and laughing in different languages, many of them laying a hand on Max's shoulder in passing, a sweet gesture of solidarity. Soon they come upon another wheelchair being pushed by another brown-shirt, and then a group of Indians leaning on canes.

"It's alright, don't you think?" Max seems more cheerful. "We pilgrims, marching on to Lourdes?"

At the entrance to the press tent, their guard leaves them with a group of dark-suited Japanese gesturing excitedly at the sky. Lena pauses, curious as to what they see.

"They're insisting that no way can a rainbow form on such a clear day," Max translates for her.

"No, impossible," says one of the men in English. "No humidity."

Max answers in Japanese, pointing over his shoulder to Lena. The men stare at her, and then one of them bows. At that, they're all waved into the tent to join the milling crowd.

"I told them you were a famous rainbow maker," says Max, as the men vanish into the milling crowd. "And now they're taking bets."

In a moment, Norbu appears at their side. Taking over the wheelchair, he brings them to the table he's been holding for them. Lena unloads her stuff from Max's lap, reserves a chair for herself with her jacket, grabs her Nikon, and goes off to see how far the press pass provided by Norbu will get her.

From the sounds of chanting monks, she guesses where the entrance to the ceremonial city is, and that it's verboten. It's guarded by a couple of brown-shirts, so she stands unobtrusively off to the side, waiting for a chance to slip inside the forbidden zone.

Through the tent flap she can see the framework of what appears to be a large open atrium defined on all sides by layers of gauzy curtains. At the other end, there appear to be rooms opening into more rooms, and off to the side an enormous pile of logs in process of being assembled: robed monks and roadies file by pulling loaded carts. The other side of the plaza is densely packed with monks shoulder to shoulder on stadium risers, dirty feet sticking out from billowing robes. They're the source of the chanting she's been hearing since they started up the road, sounds growing louder as they'd climbed, rumbling here at the source as if ripped from the earth.

Here at the center of the din, she feels transported to the edge of a parallel universe unlike the one below. And yet the crowds milling around the central plaza, for all their odd clothes and multinational nuances, engage in recognizable discourse: meeting, greeting, laughing, crying. Light-haired women in flowing trousers and print dresses extend hands to the children darting between their legs, Asian men in good suits sway and smile with hands clasped behind their backs. Smaller, darker Asians in brown, black, saffron, and crimson robes walk about; the younger ones run and shout to one another. Western technicians with large color-coded nametags carry clipboards or equipment. Except for the funeral pyre in the center, you could be backstage at a Ravi Shankar concert.

Norbu slips past her inside the compound. With him is Marianne, holding a video camera. Norbu picks up her boom mike and steadies himself against a pole, holding the mike in front of the camera as Marianne films from her hip.

Lena hears a loud bang, it could be a cannon shot—it is a cannon shot—and she gets caught up in the lurching crowd, out the other side of the tent to the base of a wide field. Looking up, she sees thousands of people sitting on the grass as far up as the eye can see. Everyone's turning their heads to the top of the hill, where a solitary figure has just stepped out of the woods, a bagpiper marching smartly down the hill. Moments later, a covered litter borne by pallbearers emerges from the woods. On it sits, cross-legged, under a canopy made of loose silk cloth, the small, brown, buttered—it's hard to tell at this distance exactly what she's looking at—body of the Venerable Chögyam Trungpa Rinpoche, followed by a procession of monks, hands tucked behind their backs, bodies rocking side-to-side in their flat-footed monk lurch.

The entire ensemble—bagpiper, stretcher, Rinpoche, and monks— scrambles down the mountain between the crowd that's rising to its feet on either side and disappear into the city. As they vanish, a truly Tibetan cacophony lets loose, chanting, piping, horn blowing, drum beating—and the incongruous, ungainly bagpipes—the air vibrates with celebration. It's a feeling of being stuck in a drum roll forever.

On the hill, the onlookers are slowly being funneled down to the city, where they snake in single file around tables piled with silk scarves, which they bring to the pyre as an offering.

Lena notices that Rinpoche has been placed at the top of the funeral pyre. The sun is beginning to set, backlighting the tiny figure. She makes her way to the handicapped tent, where Max sits outside in his wheelchair surrounded by a group of Zen archers holding large wooden bows. Quivers with arrows are strapped to their backs. She walks up to him as one of the archers steps away to face the pyre. He lifts his bow, reaches behind his right shoulder for an arrow, lights the end of it, waits for the flame, inserts it, steadies his body, and takes aim. The other archers do the same. The moment elongates, elegant as a field of long grass waiting for a wind. At some hidden signal, twenty arms bend back and twenty flaming arrows soar through the air. As the first one hits, a tiny, bright, flicker licks out from deep inside the pyramid of logs. Another flare, and then it's like watching the stars emerge in a brilliantly black bright sky until fire finally punches through and everyone exhales. The little black sitting figure comes into view, then is lost in the thick black smoke, then revealed again, and then gone.

"Buttered toast," someone says, and it's over, except for the rainbow.

Later, when Marianne shows them the video, they will see the rainbow clearly. There is no mistaking it. The camera moves slowly up the flaming pyre to the apex with the lama silhouetted against the cloudless sky. It zooms in smoothly. Everything seems peaceful, almost playful; at one point a bird, perhaps a buzzard or a hawk, flies at a diagonal from top to bottom of the frame. The smoke drifts, spirals, dissolves, and finally spews across the body. A burst of brilliant flame, then another. The lens backs off quickly, pushing the fire back into the clear blue sky, then comes in again slowly and waits. A perfect cloudless sky, pierced by a plume of twisting black smoke carrying the essence of Buddha body, a sun-flecked haze rising from the will of the people. The camera records its dissolution and captures the moment of transformation into the rainbow.

One moment there is haze, and the next moment rainbow. The sky the palest of baby blue. Smoke drifts over the lens, it clears; the rainbow remains, for no reason at all.

Marianne kept the tape running. It shows people throwing up their arms and shouting, flinging themselves on the ground. The archers jettison their bows; the bodyguards toss their berets. Lena runs in pointing her camera at the sky. There is a splash of applause, and a shot of monks standing up on their chairs pumping their arms with open palms. The last shot is of Norbu Tendzen bending over Max, the two of them clapping with glee.

A week after the funeral, deciding to escape his decrepit cabins, Max drives down to Pete's RV out on the Williston Road and buys a seventeen-foot Terry Taurus trailer with a fifth wheel. He continues on to Shearer Chevrolet, where he pays cash for a brand-new all-wheel-drive pickup truck. He installs the trailer smack in the center of the old croquet court at the entrance to Mother's former rose garden, replacing the gazebo where the Bryn Mawr women used to sit with their watercolors, their journals, and astrologers. Every time he catches sight of its dull beige aluminum ugly self on its cinder-block feet, he feels a certain sense of pleasure knowing everyone in his family, living or dead, would find it offensive.

For Lena to accept it, he'll have to find a way to make it amusing, some kind of aesthetic/politic statement. He says to her, "OK, I'll give you the checkbook and carte blanche to redecorate." He tries to coax her to the junk shops piled up on either side of Route 2. He tries to make decorating his trailer funny and ironic and retro. How about covering it with dirt, she suggests: it would make a fine Chia Pet.

But the trailer suits him. He can sit in his swivel chair and reach everything he needs without getting up; he can open the refrigerator, turn on the stove, unhook a pot, and cook himself a hamburger. He can pull his clothes from his closet and put on his socks and piss in a coffee can. He can squeeze half his body into the shower stall, rinse off, turn around and do the other half, and go back to his chair. He eats his hamburgers and drinks his milk and swallows his prednisone and Halcion. If he's going crazy, he'll do it in this aluminum can. For it's here that he decides to finally buckle down and write a book.

Shortly after he settles in, he receives a letter from the editor at the *Reader's Digest* in response to the essay on tact he'd proposed a year ago.

> Dear Max,
>
> Great to hear you're back in the writing wars. I assume this means you forgive the *Reader's Digest* for being the *Reader's Digest* and are interested in giving us another chance. You might recall that I visited you at your campground (Vermont was it? Maine?) and you astonished me with an extremely intelligent and vocal tirade on the dumbing-down of the mass media. While we're always eager to consider new story ideas, I should remind you that you wrote that article on tact years ago, and unfortunately I rejected it. How about something new?
>
> Fondly,
>
> Don

He writes back immediately:

> Dear Don,
>
> Thank you for your candor (not to mention tact). I have an idea for a new book. It's the story of an American family, part Irish, part English, part Huguenot, that arrives with one of the

early flotillas, not exactly the Mayflower, but not too far off, and settles in St. Louis. It's a story that includes the Frontier, the settling of the American West, and moves from the earliest experiences of this great country—to the present, where the latest confused member of the family must come to terms with his warrior ancestry. This of course does not preclude an examination of "tact." Daniel Boone, a master of tact if there ever was one, figures strongly in the history. It would add to the interest of the story if the latest hero, a man now approaching his fifties, had spent a goodly part of his life in a foreign country, somewhere perhaps in Asia, to escape his heritage. But as we all know one can never escape one's heritage, especially one as glorious as ours. Do you think you might run this idea past your people and get back to me? I'd like to know what the chances might be for acceptance of such a story, before I go to the next step, one that is, as you know, extremely time-consuming and laborious, that of making a real plot outline.

And BTW, I am not averse to the idea of a condensed book.

He could roar with happiness. He won't wait for the *Digest* to respond.

The next day, he asks Lena to bring over the cartons of photographs and memorabilia he'd stored in her basement and asks her to stay while he unpacks the boxes and plows through the papers. Once everything's laid out on his table, spilling out all over the floor, he asks for her help sorting them out. He picks up and inspects every photo intently, for these people are the characters in his book. He can see them so clearly, they're coming alive in his head as he holds them in his trembling fingers. His mother in all her variations over the years. Her four girl cousins, with their smart-assed mouths and mocking eyes and a various assortment of suitors. The diminutive grandfather. His mother again holding a hoe, pretending to be planting the two-foot cedars that fifty years later will block all the sun from the garden, and yet again at her graduation defiantly swilling gin from the bottle. The dog, Bob, who one year won the diving trophy. By studying them carefully, he will recreate his family. The diaries, documents, letters, Valentines, and canceled checks, these will help him create the substance of his life.

After an hour of this, he seems confused. He picks photos up, only to put them down in the same place.

Lena wonders how much more he can take before he snaps. She's sure he's tripping on his drug cocktail, that this is his wild ride before the plunge down into despair. A part of her wants to call 911, but the other part of her is cheering him on and refuses to interfere. *Go, Max,* she urges silently, and fighting her urge to stay and protect him, finally leaves him to it.

When she's gone, he lies down on the bed and closes his eyes. Immediately, he has a sense of people arriving in the house that's formed in his brain. They take their luggage upstairs to their chosen rooms to comb their hair, put away their clothes, do whatever they usually do before joining the rest of the family across the kitchen table.

His Granny leans on the sink discussing dinner with the cook while the maid listens from the corner of the room where she sits sorting laundry. Uncles sleep in their chairs. The cousins look from one to the other. The girl who will grow up to be Max's mother is adjusting her hair. The last one down is the King of Cement. He brings over a bottle and fills all their glasses. They toast.

If this is a dream, it's a novelist's dream: Thank you, Halcion! All he has to do is take dictation. He can describe their outfits, analyze their body language, and take down the dialogue. Piece it all together and come out with his family's personal tale of the American dream, through the wars, the slaves, the industrial revolution, through Melville and Thoreau and Whitman and Carl Sandburg right up to June 9, 1937, when he himself is born. Here he is taking his first steps, and again being hoisted over the shoulder of a man who holds one hand under Max's chin so he won't drool on his suit.

Max turns on his side and begins to sob. "Dad," he calls out. "Father, I can see myself bumping along. Smell the damp wool of that suit. Feel the tickle of a bit of hair on my cheek. My round little mouth is open and wet. I can hear voices. People are laughing; I'm trying to twist around to see your face." As soon as he says this, his mind goes blank.

Days pass, weeks and then months. He has a standing appointment with Meltzer and dutifully takes his medicine without questioning. Sometimes he tries to get a grip on real time, making an effort to get outside, to do chores like raking leaves, helping Lena in the garden, now and then packing boxes in the studio. But mostly, he feels too sick to do more than sit on a stump polishing silver and watching his ducks. As the dark greens of summer go dry, he becomes fearful of driving, and goes no further than the store to get groceries, or to Lena's house. It gets chilly; he puts on a jacket and builds himself a fire. Days lead into other days. The solstice is reached; the moon grows full, the days grow shorter, and the moon wanes. None of this has any meaning to him.

By the time summer ends he's on twenty milligrams of prednisone a day. He's taking four Halcion pills just so his eyelids might close. Meltzer still refuses to quit; he's like a president who's declared a war he won't admit to losing until the last troop is dead. He's even called in other countries: he's added antihistamines and nasal sprays and a new drug called Prozac.

One day Max walks along the path and sees two men standing up to their knees in the water close to shore. Fucking survivalists, he decides, stealing his water.

"Hey," he yells. "Get out of my lake."

"In a minute," one of them, a tall dark guy wearing a colorful cap, answers. "We're almost done."

"You bet you're done; get out of my water." He should go inside and get a gun and shoot these suckers out of the water just the way his mother did so long ago with Annie Oakley's rifle. The next thing he knows, the two men are up on the lawn, holding lengths of water pipe. Max recognizes the black guy, Lena's friend, the Jamaican, what's his name. The other man he doesn't want to look at, for this is Johnny Drumm, the motherfucker who stole his dojo.

Knowing Max might try to pull his water line out himself—a terrible idea in his condition—Lena had called Johnny Drumm, the current director of the Burlington dojo, who also happened to be a plumber. Johnny Drumm was Max's first student in Burlington: they loved each other for years, but then one thing led to another until now they no longer speak. Johnny insists he's just a placeholder teacher for Max, keeping things together while Max was gone all these years, waiting for him to take over. Max is convinced that Johnny grabbed the dojo from under his feet. Lena has no idea who's right, nor does she much care.

Johnny's a small muscular bald man with the body Max jealously believes should have been reserved for him and who always seems to be looking over his shoulder, flashing what Max likes to call a deviant smile.

"Do you remember how you gave me my black belt?" Johnny says after a while.

"No."

"We were out here at the lake pulling out your water line, which you'd stupidly left in, and it was already snowing. The valve was stuck under a rock, so one of us had to get into the canoe and reach down under four feet of freezing, wild water to yank it out while the other one stayed on shore and pulled the pipe over the rocks. I'd been nagging you all summer to give me a black belt, but for some asshole reason, you refused to let me test. The wind was coming up, and neither one of us wanted to get into the fucking canoe. I was so frustrated with you, so fucking angry, that finally I just jumped in it and paddled like a madman against the wind. It was freezing and very dangerous. I would have gone hypothermic in ten minutes in that water. But I made it, I freed the valve, you pulled the pipe up, and when I banked that canoe you yelled, 'OK, Drumm, you are now a black belt!' Remember that?"

"No."

"Fuck you, you're going to hear this. You had your wife and kids up here, and you were trying to write in that icehouse. It's made of stone and has no windows, and it's about as big as a bathtub. Five minutes alone at your desk and you were crawling the walls. At the time, you were married and screwing around with someone named Mary, as well as someone else named Mary: Big and Little Mary. You were never home, and winter was around the corner, and you climbed the mountain looking for God.

"When you came back down, you said to me, 'I'm moving to New York City.' I said, 'You found God and that's what he told you? To move to New York?' You said, 'I have to do it.' I was devastated. Without you, I had nothing. You were the sensei, I was just a mechanic. But you didn't care about me or the dojo. You packed up the family and stashed them away somewhere while you hung out in New York City shacking up with one student, then another. You are also driving up here to Vermont, teaching and fucking with the Marys. You thought you could keep it all going, and somehow you did. One day you told me the sirens were calling to you from California, good-bye, good luck, and keep my side of the bed warm. More?"

"You wouldn't have passed the test for black belt," says Max, tossing a stone into the shallows and watching it ripple.

"Well, yeah. I knew that."

"I didn't climb that mountain looking for God."

"All right. Be picky about it. I'm listening." Johnny lobs off his own pebble. Max waits till it sinks before going on.

Max says, "In 1972, when I got back from Japan with my wife and kids, we had no prospects, no money, and winter was around the corner. You have to understand, I felt I had no options. I didn't know what to do, so I decided to go on what you now call a vision quest. Right? Well, that's what it was. I put on my *gi*, stuffed my heavy army ammo pack with food, a stove, and water, and lashed my eight-pound wooden *bokken* to the top—sixteen pounds of utter bullshit—and got my wife to drive me to the bottom of Mount Mansfield. It was pouring rain, and the steep climb was miserable, it was one solid bog of mud; two steps and you fell down, you had to pull yourself up by the shrubbery, so soon I'm crawling along like a bear, my pants filled with mud, and now I'm weighing 400 pounds at least."

"I remember you telling me about that. Go on."

"I slept in a cave for two nights. It was so small, my head was two inches from the ceiling. There was a little niche where I put my stove, and when I got hungry, I heated up everything all together: powdered coffee, oatmeal, granola, sugar, and ate until I was full. By the third day I ran out of food, and I figured that my conversation with God had been rained out."

"You went to talk to God, not find him. A picky distinction, but who's to argue with you?"

"Then the sun came out, and my spirits lifted, and I went on. I came to a place where the trail goes between two pine trees. The rain had washed the soil out from under the roots of these trees, and my big macho pack got caught in the pine branches. I am hung up. I am crucified, my weight hanging on the straps of my pack, my hands in the air, and my feet stuck in the roots. Pretty soon the sun gets hot, and I'm so wet I'm steaming. Then I see a sight that makes the hair stand up on the back of my neck: a crow flying across in front of my face. The crow looks at me with intelligence. It knows I cannot move. I realized that if this crow wanted to sit on my face and eat my eyes, there wasn't a goddamn thing I could do about it. I saw myself being pecked to death. I went fucking crazy, screaming, shrieking, twisting, until finally I busted free. Here's where God comes in. I begged God to help: 'Please help me. I need your help as to how to get out of this. Please tell me what to do.' And God said, 'Do it your-self. Fuck you.'"

"Ah, Max," says Johnny, putting his hands on his knees. "If only you could get your shit together and write. I know you're going around telling people I stole your dojo. If you really think that, I tell you I'll just leave town. Leave it, like that. It's all yours."

"I'm sick."

"I know that. Prednisone won't kill you, but it might make you do it yourself. What a shit way to go."

With Johnny's help, he packs up his things and closes up the trailer and moves back to Lena's house. The three of them go through the bath-rooms grabbing all the medicine bottles and flushing the pills down the toilet. Then Lena and Johnny help him to bed and undress him and cover him, and for the next few weeks watch over him like he's totally helpless, a baby, a foundling, a blubbering fool. They're pretty sure that quitting prednisone and Halcion cold turkey is a terrible idea, only Max isn't up for suggestions.

All he can do is lie still and watch TV. One day, he decides to mount the television on the wall. It doesn't occur to him to call for help, he's going to do it himself. He remembers having stashed a bracket and shelf in the closet for this very purpose, and now he pulls it out. Standing on the bed, he screws the pivoting arm into the wall. It doesn't occur to him to use Molly bolts. He hoists the television on the shelf and climbs back under the covers.

He watches *Good Morning America*, *As the World Turns*, and *General Hospital*. He watches *Miami Vice* and all the news about terrorists blowing up airplanes and Israeli raids. He watches movies where aliens attack, lesbians in prison hold food fights, and cute-looking dogs find missing kids.

During the commercials, his thoughts turn to suicide. How? He could get more Halcion and wash the pills down with a bottle of vodka. He could eat oysters, to which he is violently allergic. He could put a cinder block on his belly and drown in the hot tub. He could shoot himself or fall on the ornamental sword hanging over his desk in his office. He could slit his wrists in the hot tub. He could get in his truck and wait at the drawbridge for the warning light and gun the accelerator at exactly the right moment. The gong sounds, the barrier falls, the bridge begins to separate. If you start too soon, there won't be enough of a gap to fall through. If you wait too long, you won't be able to drive up the incline. Timing is everything, as always.

Lena's downstairs with Marianne, editing the cremation footage. They hear a loud crash from the second floor bedroom and race upstairs to find Max sitting calmly on the floor on top of his television.

"That's it, soldiers," he says, opening up his arms. "I thank you all for coming."

7

Take nothing but pictures.
Leave nothing but footprints.
Kill nothing but time.

—Motto of the Baltimore Grotto, a caving society

Max says:

All the time I was studying aikido, I always had some hustle going. Partially it was because I had no money—I believed hustling was the price for doing what I loved—but also because some crimp in my character gets high by hustling. Most Americans in Japan teach English on the side, but I hated it. If I had to ask Mr. Suzuki one more time, "What is your hobby?" and hear him answer, "Me hobbee is leading about Amelika," I would pop poor Mr. Suzuki: and I tell you this is not a great mindset for studying a martial art dedicated to peace and harmony.

When O-sensei got sick, I wasn't even around. I can't even be sure if I was in the last film they made of him. How much I would give to run that reel back. It's so ironic, the real feast of my life was at the Hombu Dojo, and everything I did kept me away from that table.

In 1964 I found myself crammed into a tiny apartment with a Japanese wife and a pet crow, and I didn't want to be home all that much. I'd married because that's what you were supposed to do and because I couldn't keep living in the dojo forever. Our wedding night was at one of those depressing honeymoon hotels guaranteed to drown romance. I knew immediately that I'd made a mistake, but one thing led to another, and soon we had two babies. My wife is a lovely woman, and she has made the best out of a bad deal, but we had nothing in common. I tell you I talked more to my pet crow than I did to my wife.

I missed the birth of both my children and so got on the wrong footing with them from the get-go. They were beautiful babies: bad luck to be born to me. This may sound insincere, but there's some pathetic truth in it: I couldn't bear being with them because I loved them so

213

much, and it broke my heart to keep coming up against what a terrible father I was; better to hide myself from them. I want no pity, but I do ask for compassion, and from my children, who have grown into exquisite creatures despite me, I ask forgiveness, absolution, redemption.

I'd convinced my wife that my career kept me on the road, although why it was so ill-paying was beyond my ability to explain. So she wrote to my mother for money, repeating my bullshit about my career, and Mother sent her what she asked for.

> Everything is very well, except we have no money. Max is so busy in his business he is never here. There is no food for the baby. Your son is an important man, please forgive me.

That's the kind of stuff she would be writing. And what's really horrible is that at the same time, unbeknownst to her, I was also writing Mother for money.

> My dear Mother, I trust you are well. I am about to embark on a very exciting business adventure with some friends here in high places in the government. For reasons of security, I am not at liberty to reveal their identities. All I require is a bit of an advance, which I will pay back immediately. Chiyo sends her love to you. I'll send pictures of the babies in my next letter.

My mother kept these letters. I found them when I cleaned out her apartment. I keep them because—who knows why I keep them. The same reason she did: narcissism, shame, historical necessity, stupidity, revenge. Or maybe just habit.

Marriage changed my lifestyle not a whit, except that I no longer lived in the dojo. I didn't bother to tell any of the other women whom I was seeing that I was no longer available. Each morning I would get up at 4:30 in the morning to make the first train to the dojo. All day long and well into the evening I'd be running in and out of classes, involved in an import business with other American friends, and getting laid in between appointments. When I quit teaching, I started working up one scam after another, literally racing around like a pimp— some of the foreign businessmen I met at hotels would want to get laid. I had so much wild energy I thought I could do it all. I did this for all the nine years I spent in Japan.

Mostly I was involved with a beautiful woman named Lin, who was only one definition away from prostitution. To keep her, I needed money and status, and for this I needed to network with the right people.

Networking meant being seen around town with the right people. In this case the Man was a Belgian Catholic priest, and my business partners and I spent $600 for the privilege of stepping out in his company. It worked: we were hired as spies in the fashion industry, I was sent on seven trips around the world in as many months, doing fashion research for Japanese department stores.

In the West, women were wearing dresses barely covering their crotches, but the Japanese thought their women believed that their legs were too fat for miniskirts. And of course they were all wrong. When the miniskirt finally came to Japan it was a huge success, but a lot of companies went out of business because they hadn't seen it coming. The whole world was turning upside down, and the Japanese didn't have a clue; when we were asked what we knew about fashion, we answered with a swagger that they'd come to the right people.

Of course, we knew nobody in the world of fashion. So I sat down and I wrote personal histories of fictional people. Like "Susanna is a twenty-two-year-old Swarthmore grad who then attended FIT, after which she worked for *WWD* in Paris, went on to Italian *Vogue,* and is now a departmental manager in the House of Dior," meaning to convince my potential bosses that I had access to Dior. As it turned out, my brother was getting married in New York. One of the bridesmaids was a woman who really did work for *Women's Wear Daily* in Paris, and she gave me a ticket to the Dior collections. I knew that if I took a Dior program back to Tokyo, I'd clinch our job.

On the way to the collection, I split the seam in my pants, a terrible thing, for you do not want to arrive at Dior with your crotch hanging, especially since to reach the collections, you had to climb a magnificent staircase with all those duchesses watching from below. What I did was, do *tenkans,* the basic aikido turning movement, all the way up the stairs. Very slow *tenkans.* One foot swiveling in front of the other, holding my split seam tight between my thighs, all the time looking up at the ceiling as if it was the most natural thing to walk up a staircase in the House of Dior with your thighs stuck together. But I made it, I got that program, and we got the job.

It didn't take long before our bosses figured out what frauds we were. Instead of just firing us, they tried to tear my partner and me apart by bad-mouthing each of us to the other. And when that failed, they decided to drive us crazy. They'd schedule a meeting in Kyoto for 9:00, and when we got there, they'd have changed it to Nagasaki, and this went on for nine months.

By that time, I had left my wife and kids; Lin had left me for a banker. O-sensei had died, his Japanese heirs had no use for me, and my company had convinced my partner I was acting like a crazy person who needed to be sent back to the States.

Jesus Christ himself could not have satisfied any of these people, so I figured I might as well go home.

Sarasota, Florida, 1988

While Max rehabs in Pennsylvania at the Pritikin Center on the advice of his new doctor, Lena and Marianne fly to Sarasota to check on "Our Parents," in spite of Lena's lobbying for Ibiza. She loves her parents, she really does, but she's been called down for so many emergencies, visiting when one or the other isn't falling down the stairs, or fainting in the supermarket, or getting nailed by the cops for driving the wrong way down I-75, seems beside the point. Once upon a time she'd enjoyed being with them, at least for the first few days, before Erica divulged her new sexual secrets—it's awesome how much trouble her mother manages to attract since her fantasy life took over—and Dad starts calling her by the name of their last dog, Speckles.

She's dying to fly somewhere with a two-piece bathing suit and flippers in her gym bag.

Marianne reminds her that Longboat Key is one beautiful white-sand beach stretching for twelve miles without interruption. Lena knows this. It's just that she'd forgotten that anyone ever went to Florida for pleasure.

"I'll take the aisle," Marianne says, as they board in Burlington. She dislikes leaving anything to chance, lest her immediate needs fail to be met. The good side of traveling with her: she spars with reservations clerks, cajoles stewardesses, puts in meal requests, knows tricks for successful couple-flying like requesting aisle and window seats in the section of the plane last to fill, where there's more chance of a vacant middle seat. On the other hand, she throws up from Atlanta to Tampa, which is why she needs to sit on the aisle.

Once they're safely above the soft, lumpy clouds, they dump the contents of their backpacks—mostly books and nutritional supplements: no clothes, as they intend to shop up a storm—on the seat between them and squeeze hands. Marianne lets go first to pull on a sweater and unbuckle her seatbelt.

"It's been one fucking hard year," says Lena, dabbing at her eyes. "Make me a deal. I tell you, after a week with parents"—she avoids the mutually possessive *Our*, she's their only kid, after all—"we'll need a vacation, as in truly vacating. How about we fly to southern Spain and play Eurotrash for a couple of years? What say? We'll come back, Max will be cured." Right. Max might be dead by then. That's the real fantasy, then, getting free of all these dying people so she can sail off on her own trip. But what if this *is* her trip? What if Max and her parents were her boatmates rather than burdens? As in, *we're all on the same boat?* If so, she'd be advised to improve her mood, if she wants to get through it.

"No, dear, we'll stay in America to sabotage our own culture before it destroys the planet." Marianne slips the black sleep mask, worn like a hat atop her thick hair, over her eyes and leans back, hoping to avoid a headache.

The key to Marianne's success, Lena decides, pulling down her window shade to save Marianne from glimpsing infinity through the porthole of their tin can whirling through space, is all about herself and her impact on her culture. Not much distracts her, not romance nor pleasure nor even water aerobics. She's free to concentrate on her image, the media, fundraising, and performance. But does she really think her art can make a difference? And what's the difference between what she does and propaganda? Max says that art has to transform its subject. You can yak the facts all you want, but to actually effect change, you need to transmit directly into another person.

"I always envied you, with your doting little parents," says Marianne. "Probably that's why you trust that everything's going to be all right, why you're so steady, why you just have to walk in the room while everyone else is doing the fandango to get Max's attention. You're such a free spirit."

Lena's taken aback. Free spirit? Maybe thirty years ago in San Francisco, at the Art Institute, with Janis Joplin in the courtyard, in the city of poetry, jazz, great drugs, and all-nighters, with the boys in the pot shop making abstract expressionist mayhem, and when their crazy pieces blew up, exhibiting the debris in art shows.

"You know," Marianne goes on, "Our mother told me how she used to paint in the attic, and you'd sit in the bathtub squeezing all the colors on the floor and that's how she knew you'd be an artist. I find that adorable."

"I found it manipulative."

It takes Lena a while to realize that Marianne is telling her that she's jealous of her. In her view, she's envied Marianne as far back as their University of Chicago days, when they were both philosophy majors, sharing a baroque attic room in the oldest dorm, trucking across the Midway to listen to the blues bands in the black ghetto behind the law school. She's envious of Marianne's wiry body, with how she balances her fragility with steely resolve, how she presents multiple personas to the public only to toss them away like so much wardrobe.

How she doesn't second-guess her motives, how she trusts the rightness of her ideas, no matter how outlandish. How she gets away with it all. When they were caught with hash balls their third year in college, it was Lena who passively accepted temporary suspension while Marianne disdainfully dropped out and moved to New York.

Marianne's looking pale, she leans back in her seat nervously fingering a vomit bag, "You're thinking I never liked Julian, and that's true. Maybe that's because I was the only one of your friends he didn't hit on."

"I hadn't been thinking about Julian," says Lena. But she had. Thinking of the past reminded her of the loft she and Marianne had shared on Canal Street, how Marianne had returned after a month in Paris as a gofer for Jean-Luc Godard to find Julian living there, which would have been OK had he not seemed, as Marianne had put it then, so blandly devious. She just didn't trust him, and Lena had known then she was making a mistake. If only she'd had more courage to maneuver her way in the world alone, like Marianne has, maybe she'd be a stronger person.

Just as the drink cart is about to arrive, Marianne pulls off her sleep mask and bolts for the bathroom. Lena asks for a bottle of mineral water, then changes her mind and orders a vodka and tonic. When Marianne limps back, she notices the two vodka bottles on Lena's tray table and raises her eyebrows. "*Oy vey*, I can't believe you can put that stuff in your mouth," she says, easing gently into her seat.

"I know, I don't drink," says Lena, offering up a roll of Wint-O-Green Life Savers. "I don't do Valium either. Only now, for our imminent descent down into the valley of pre-heaven, Valium and vodka are in order."

"Pre-heaven, I like that. 'Our Parents' take good care of themselves; they're going to live to be 100." Marianne wipes her lips daintily, removes a candy from the wrapper.

"But where will they live? You think they'll be bopping around that fancy apartment on the Gulf of Mexico at 100? Ten years to go, and they're already loopy. Mom asked me to shoot her if she becomes a burden."

"Let me do it for you. The three of you are in denial."

"I know that. Thank goodness Tim is there." At least he ought to be: she and the kids of another elderly tenant have rented him a condo in the building so he can caretake both sets of parents at the same time.

"Have you spoken with him?" Marianne sounds dubious.

"Not for a while. He's been out lately."

"Lena."

"I know. They probably fired him."

"You're so robust, Lena. Everything rolls right off you," says Marianne, pressing her hands over her closed lids as the plane points downward and the pilot crackles.

"That's because I never stick my neck out." Lena raises the shade. Below, blue-gray sea pinpricked with shrimp boats, yachts, cruise ships, and barges crisscrossing back and forth. She wishes she was on one of those ships, headed for somewhere without any parents.

"Lower that thing, will you? I hate landings. Being a studio potter is safe? You sound like you're a CPA."

"I might as well be. You know, the last couple of shows Jocelyn did were way down. Nothing's selling except the real high-end stuff, and the junk. Maybe it's a good time to drop the production. We're all getting old, even us."

"Nah, not me. But you need to do something else. Forget about money, it'll come." She knows Lena doesn't believe this, thinks that the sky will cave in if she's not working day and night for a dollar. "Hey, relax. Close down the candy store and make art, there's nothing to lose. Make lemonade out of, you know, a lemon."

"What, set Jocelyn loose? And Tonkey?"

"They'll go back to Jamaica, and market your designs as native and make more money than you've ever done."

"You're right, they'll be fine." And what, she wonders, will she do now? All these years setting her life up a certain way only to shut it down when things get tough? But what's wrong with that. Maybe she'll go for an MFA, there's that low residency program starting up at Vermont College. You pick a mentor to work with in your own studio and show up at campus twice a year. Marianne could be her mentor, now that would be a hoot. And Max would only encourage her: he's the great instigator, after all, as long as it's not for himself. "Max would dig that," she says, tugging up the shade.

"Dig what?" Marianne says. "I think we're going down."

"Descending, yup. Hang in there, cowgirl. He'd encourage me about art school. He's always egging us on, he's the Great Egger-oner. That's what he does. It's why we all love him. He pushes us into traffic like a crossing guard at the curb."

"I feel sick. Ninety percent of all crashes happen on night landings."

Resisting the impulse to laugh at her friend, Lena takes her hand and looks out the window. "Oh come on, relax. It's the middle of the day down here. I can see everything. We're parting the clouds and gliding like an eagle down to the gates of a beautiful Southern metropolis. I see a beltway of sun-dabbled white sand beaches half a mile wide. The little dots far below are people on beach chairs sipping incredibly intoxicating tropical cocktails. They're getting closer. I can just make out the parasols in their glasses. Offshore, I see schools of whales breeching turquoise sea. I see lifeguards."

Marianne whispers thanks, and Lena marvels at the bright lights of the city barreling through the black night toward her, drops the blind, and waits for the big bump.

Erica is limping and Dad's bent almost in half. Both are thin as nails, but still they vie for the luggage as the revolving door spits the four of them out of the baggage claim into the choking tropical evening. Luckily Dad has written down the parking lot aisle number on the back of his hand. When they find the car and Lena haltingly asks for the keys, he gives them over like an obedient child. "Thanks, doll," he says, using both hands to pull open the passenger door for his wife. "My eyes are burning hot right now."

They bump into Tim on the elevator landing and stop to talk. While Marcos and Erica drift off to weed the window planter, he tells them that Marcos changed the locks because a homeless person—that would be him, Tim—was sleeping in the den; at times he was so tired, he didn't bother going home. When he couldn't reach Lena, he'd contracted with a private day nurse to replace him.

"Such a sweet man," says Tim, looking fondly at Marcos, now curled up asleep against the potted palm.

So what, thinks Lena.

Each morning, while Marianne juices oranges with Erica in the kitchen, Lena and Marcos sit on the balcony five stories over the Gulf of Mexico, and Marcos says, "Welcome to paradise." Lena loves her father. He's the father she counts on to hate America every time it betrays the workingman, the father she trusts to hand her the entire Sunday *New York Times*, keeping only the sports section for himself, even though he wouldn't know the Red Sox from the New York Knickerbockers. But Dad no longer reads the *Times*, and he voted with the majority Republicans in the condo association to veto a sale to a homosexual Mexican sculptor. She keeps her eyes on the beach, watching the trucks dump sand dredged up from other parts of the coast—it boosts the real estate here on Longboat Key, Marcos explains. Lena thinks about the turtles being ground up in the dredger's maws, and how the ocean will soon sweep them all away.

Marcos and Erica have grown so old, they bob around like two little birds looking for food, taking tiny steps with their feet pointed out, passing gas. Marcos's hair has grown down to his shoulders and feels like it's been washed with Crisco. He asks about Julian each morning at seven, every two hours thereafter, and once again before they go to bed.

Erica, who always loved beautiful clothes and has a charge account at Lord & Taylor, refuses to go shopping with the girls, as she calls them, so they take Marcos's fifteen-year-old Peugeot to St. Armands Circle and loop through the beautiful shops and tacky souvenir joints. Lena spends two hundred dollars on Prada at the Sunglass Hut, they each buy bright-colored cocktail dresses, and Marianne picks up a polka-dotted bathing suit in a kid's shop. After spending an hour sitting on a bench in the shade eating ice cream and insulting the parade of art hags and tourists, they drive slowly home singing along with Marcos's Pavarotti tapes.

After a week of burned meals and clothes worn inside out and books read upside down, Lena's mother finally gives up the kitchen to the girls. They put on shorts, rev up the stereo, and start scrubbing. They throw out the hot dogs, margarine, and NutraSweet, and fill the fridge with organic produce. Lena hires a maid to sanitize the entire apartment while she takes her parents off to visit assisted-living homes. She replaces her mother's hearing aids, arranges for mail-order deliveries of their prescriptions, and gets new keys made for Tim. They consider selling the car and hiring a limo for shopping and doctor visits.

Between meals, when the parents aren't wandering around the house like penguins looking for the objects they hold in their hands, or sitting on the toilet, or playing Scrabble, they nap, and this is when Lena goes walking along the beach while Marianne wraps herself in bath sheets under the tiki hut and reads Margaret Atwood.

Since vast resources are going to be required to care for these nuggets—as Max calls them—through their nineties, Lena's lawyers advise her to wrest away their legal rights, take over their finances, pop them in a nursing home, and take a trip around the world. Some other daughter might do just that, she tells Marianne later, but she's not that daughter.

"Well I am," says Marianne. "When you're ready, let me know."

The last night, around 9:00 p.m., after tucking the nuggets in bed, they put on their new dresses and drive to the heavily Hemingwayesque Columbia Restaurant for Cuban *tapas*. The skimpy dresses get them a prime table around the dance floor in the rotunda, where they order *mejillones con chorizo*, *queso fundido*, *shrimp al ajillo*, stuffed red snapper, and sides of fried bananas.

After dinner, as they watch the band Omni setting up, they sip mojitos, ordered with double shots of Captain Morgan Spiced Rum, so relieved they are to feel among the young and vapid once again.

The band breaks into a raucous *son montuno*. The dance floor instantly fills up with stewardesses, Latino beach boys, Saudis, and middle-aged couples wearing matching pants suits. Lena can't help herself; she's dancing in her chair and quickly catches the eye of a dark-haired Saudi-prince type half her age, and off she goes without a thought to mamba the night away—at least for fifteen minutes before she slips back in her chair, breathing heavily.

"I think that's why I couldn't stand you in college. You always got the hottest guys," says Marianne, raising her mojito.

"Yeah, for an overnight." They tap glass and smile at each other.

"So, are you having any fun?" Lena looks at her, wondering what she means. Is she referring to fun now at this very moment or fun in the bigger sense of *is it fun being faithful to the sick guy who woke you up last week to discuss penile dysfunction?* She decides to address the bigger question.

She says, "You know, we've been together three years, three and a half if you count that cow. And I can't believe this, I've been totally faithful even without real sex; so yeah, we're having fun, I don't notice other men."

"Ah, the new faithful Lena. Are you drunk?"

"No, I mean it. Believe me."

"OK, I will. You're faithful, but is Max faithful? Wait, of course he's faithful, now that he can't do anything, right? Now that he's fucked up, he's faithful? You'll maybe hate me saying this, but all kinds of people truly captivate him, especially women. I've seen you leave the room and ten minutes later some girl's headed for his lap."

"Yeah, you can say it."

"They're on his lap revealing their most intimate secrets. How does he do that?"

"He gets them feeling they're the only one in the room. The more interesting question is, why does he do it?"

"But the minute you come back, he makes his brand-new friend move over and he only has eyes for you. In my humble option, because I have known him for a million years, I have never seen this happen before. In the past, before you, he would have simply kissed you good night and scooted off with his new fuck."

"Last week, he was off doing a workshop with the prison guards. Some girl called up, she told me she'd been waiting for Max for an hour in the rain and wanted to know if he remembered their dinner date. She thought maybe I was his sister? Or the wife that knew all about his dinner dates with other women? So I nailed him when he came home—"

"How?"

"I wrote down what she said word for word and went to bed. When he came upstairs, he swore he'd forgotten all about her. That's not the point, I told him. You collect women. You can't help seducing them. He insisted he wasn't seductive, she was only a student."

"Student? He's teaching?"

"A workshop at New U, one of those empowerment things he's been doing since the sarcoids disappeared. He'll teach what he calls *aikido lite*, but not aikido. His new doctor says he never had sarcoidosis."

"Jesus, you should sue that putz Meltzer. Did I tell you I saw him at the Iggy Pop concert at the Flynn? He was wearing—I swear—a vintage Chanel to die for, but with tacky mesh tights."

"I don't want to talk about Melzer."

"Why don't you sue him?"

"Max won't. Lawsuits are bad karma. So I said, 'The fact that she's a student doesn't get you off the hook. Students want to fuck you for knowledge, and you just can't resist now, can you?'"

"So he denied that?"

"Sure. I told him to go ask Ostermeyer how seducing students is good for our relationship."

"He's seeing Ostermeyer? The best there is. He loves bad actors. So?"

"So he came back from a session and said, 'Yeah, you're right, Ostermeyer says it's unconscious seduction, and so we're going to work on that.'"

"Wow, the new Lena, the new Max, I'll drink to that."

The next day, as they sit on their luggage by the curb, they each hold a parent and beg them personally to let Tim take care of them. Then they switch parents and beg again. "Tim is our friend," they say over and over. "If you shut him out and one of you gets carted off to the ER again, the state will take you away from me," says Lena. "Really daddy, they can do that in Florida."

Her father says, "Don't worry, darling. We are not juveniles. I know my rights."

"Shoot me," her mother says slyly, kissing her on the back of her hand.

"Costa del Sol, let's go," says Marianne with a wink, jumping up and waving down the limo.

Dr. Anne Simones, wearing an open lab coat over a plaid dress, sucking on a chunk of her thick shoulder-length hair, sits at her cluttered desk catching up on Max's medical file, now approaching the size of a Thomas Pynchon novel. There's a sorry-looking plant in the window, and a bunch of plastic kiddie toys on the floor next to a coffee table and floor-to-ceiling file cabinets. When she's finished, she hands the file to Max, who's lolling against Lena on the shabby brown sofa in the corner.

"So, let's forget the sarcoidosis. We can spend an hour venting about the suffering it caused you, or we can move on." She wants to put him in the hospital for a few tests to see what damage, if any, withdrawing cold turkey from prednisone and Halcion caused. She tells them it was a really, really, really stupid thing to do.

Max is resisting.

"Right," says Anne, removing her tortoiseshell glasses. "So let's talk instead about what's going on with you. We're not looking for a disease to strategize here. We're going to deal with your symptoms and medical history. You had phlebitis as a kid, right?"

"I did," says Max. "And it says that right here in the file; I threw a clot last month."

"I'm thinking you've been forming clots in your leg all along. You had a deep vein thrombus they were able to dissolve. I'm thinking you're throwing tiny clots as well, and these have been lodging in your lungs. Your lung scans show pulmonary hypertension. You can't get enough air, you accrue an oxygen debt, your heart enlarges as it tries to pump harder to make up for it, the strain causing arrhythmia and making you dizzy. That's what I think. The rash is puzzling. The idea that a rash on your arm indicates sarcoidosis is . . ." Her voice trails off, and she shakes her head.

"I'll just go check on your lab work," she says. "Be back in a few.

Happy reading, but don't panic. Much of what's written in those files is in code, illegible, or written by sleep-deprived idiots."

Lena and Max regard each other.

"Is this legal?" asks Max.

"Depends on who's watching," says Lena, reaching for the file.

In between the first record, dated July 2, 1985—faxed over from San Francisco General—and the most recent, dated a month ago, March 14, 1988, lies the story of An Obese White Gentleman in No Apparent Distress, the most poetic description among many of the patient (pt) Max Diebenkorn as he suffers, fattens, and sickens between the ages of forty-eight and almost fifty-one, as annotated by serial observers in the medical industry. From the very beginning, as questions arise about the underlying systemic disorder, clearly the pt is looked upon favorably by those entrusted with his examination, diagnosis, and consequential treatments. Dr. B. calls him an interesting gentleman. Dr. T. remarks on his good humor, intelligence, and curiosity. At the same time, it's remarked on the inability of the pt to comprehend the implications of his obesity. One frustrated intern remarks how difficult it is to examine him through all that belly fat. All in all, there are over a hundred entries, some consisting of a paragraph, others scrawled over pages, including forty-eight short paragraphs in Meltzer's flowery hand (mostly terse sentences summarizing the pt's complaints, along with copies of prescriptions written during two years of bimonthly visits), fourteen reports from radiologists, nine from various specialists referred by Meltzer—including one urology report describing how the Gentleman exhibited extreme nervousness about having his genitals examined—six emergency room visits for kidney stones, stitches, and one collapse in the snow in front of the university library, and a report suggesting apnea after a short hospitalization for a sleep study.

Nowhere is there any indication of the six-month reign and subsequent fall of the Egg Man, a.k.a. Max on Steroids. The Gentleman is, however, noted to be a martial artist (spelled "marshall artist" on several occasions), an author, a blacksmith, a teacher, in a satisfactory relationship with a local sculptor, as well as a dog, as noted by one A.D.

"Jesus," says Lena, dropping her head on her lover's obese white shoulder.

"Let that be my epitaph, no?"

"Right."

"Over a hundred entries, and I'm not even close to dead yet. Last week I figured I was passing yet another kidney stone and didn't want to wake you, so I snuck off in my truck. The road was so bumpy I blew the stone out somewhere between South Hero and Essex Junction."

"I didn't know your gall bladder was scanned. I didn't know you had gout. I can't believe you got in your truck instead of waking me up."

"Well, I threw that stone on my own. In the seventies I had surgery on my shoulder and was dumb enough to do an aikido demonstration before the bones had completely healed. Coming home on the subway, hanging onto a strap, I felt the pin—right there, you can feel it . . . come through the skin on my shoulder. I went to Roosevelt Hospital, where I'd had the surgery. I was told that the doctor who'd done my shoulder was unavailable. Some kid in the surgeon's practice looked me over and said, 'Oh, you'll have to wait until he gets back. I'm not going to touch this thing.' So I'm yelling at this kid, and he splits, and a nurse comes along and says to me, 'Go home, stop in a bar, have two shots of Jack Daniels. Then sterilize a knife and make a hole big enough for the tip of a pair of needle-nose pliers and pull the thing out. Save it and come back in the morning. Then they'll be forced by law to redo the surgery.'"

"And you did that? Your body isn't a VW, Max, you can't treat it like a truck."

"Better believe mechanics treat cars with more respect."

"They would have redone that surgery gratis," says Anne Simones, standing in the doorway with a cardboard tray and three Dunkin' Donuts coffees. "Big lawsuit potential, politics. It happens. Sugar? Fake milk?" She passes out the coffee and sits down. "Any questions? Translations needed?"

"Yeah," says Max, handing her the file. "What's with this 'Pt is an obese white gentleman in no apparent distress?' As I recall, at the time I was passing kidney stones, a distress-filled activity if ever there was one. I'd like to launch a rocket through this guy's urethra and see if he could come up with a more apt description."

"Oh, it just means that you're not dead yet, basically," says Anne, smiling. She'd told them it was all written in code.

"So you can understand why I took it upon myself to get in my truck and pass it the old-fashioned way, via potholes."

"I want you to take those tests. If you're worried about insurance, forget it. You don't own anything, right? We treat you, bill you, and you give us five bucks a month."

"No hospitalization," says Max. "I mean this. Once in Afghanistan, we were at the Hotel Kabul. I—"

Anne exchanges smiles with Lena. "Are you two married?"

"No," says Lena.

"Good. Then you're not liable for his bills. I need to know if you had any liver damage. Max. Your liver. Know anything?"

"Do you believe these smart bombs they have now can distinguish between hospitals and bunkers?" says Max.

Anne reaches for the record and starts leafing through. "I see you went down to the Pritikin Center. They could have done these tests at Pritikin, Too bad they couldn't work with you there." It wasn't his fault he'd failed the stress test. Since Lena was in Spain at the time, he'd decided to stay on for the health lectures, which he found interesting. There he'd met a bunch of mafioso guys, as he puts it, on their annual respite from the stress of their jobs compounded by too much *ossobuco alla milanese*. With them, he'd hung out in the card room playing gin rummy and ordering pizza. He'd arrived home feeling rested with a case of salt-free Pritikin chicken broth and a book of recipes, having gained ten pounds.

"Losing weight is crucial, actually," says Anne.

"You don't understand. Diets don't work for me. I can't do it. It's impossible. Ask Lena here. We did NutriSystem. The twenty pounds she lost went right on my hips. It's hopeless. I can defy any diet," says Max, but Anne's not listening; she's writing scripts one after the other and handing Lena informational sheets as if she expects that Lena feels like she's enough of a wife to take charge of Max's care and feeding.

"I don't exactly cook," Lena warns her.

"Try the Moosewood Restaurant vegetarian cookbook, it's really good," says Anne. She makes a deal with Max: no hospitalization as long as he agrees to outpatient tests starting next week.

It's not going to be easy. The trick is to control his heart rhythms while lowering his blood pressure and maintaining his kidney functions. He needs a blood thinner for his clots, one anti-inflammatory for his heart muscle and another for his gout. He needs decongestants, something for his apnea, and iron for his anemia. And he's got to figure a way to nourish himself while losing two pounds a week. He needs support hose for his veins and antacids for his stomach to neutralize all the shit he's going to be pouring through his system. And he's got to do all that without the side effects killing him, for as they all know, he's a sensitive guy. With luck, they'll hit on a regimen that will balance his system for a long period of time. Eventually, she thinks, this will happen, but until then they'll have to experiment. The worst of it will be coping with failure and having the courage to explore new combinations of drugs. Each time, it'll take several weeks to adjust, a few more to weigh damage against healing, and then a similar amount of time to wean him off a regimen, should it fail. The worst part may be a constant ricochet between hope and despair. And it'll be hard on his heart. There may be cardioversions and biopsies. He's at risk for stroke, cardiac arrest, diabetes, liver disease, kidney failure. He might be a candidate for something called a thromboendarterectomy, an experimental surgery, kind of a lung scrape, performed only at one hospital, by one surgical team at the present time, and if that's not an option, a heart-lung transplant.

The world *transplant* gets their attention.

Lena heads right to the psychics. The gypsy tells her she's going to come into a large sum of money but won't like the way it arrives, then he recites the candle motif so unconvincingly he lets her walk out in the middle of it. *Poor guy,* she thinks, *no one goes for this stuff.* A 400-pound woman in a little trailer flips open the Bible at random for guidance and tells her she's in a boat drifting in the reeds of a serene water garden. God be with her. Marianne's favorite, the Native American past-life person, tells her she was the son of a great teacher in Atlantis, and in this life their roles are reversed.

Done with the psychics, Lena helps him find a nutritionist, a masseur, and an acupuncturist. He signs up for ten weeks of Rolfing. He trots up steep steps to second-floor homeopaths, hypnotists, and allergists. He eats the Tibetan spoors in jars and mushrooms hanging off decomposing tree parts FedExed by his concerned fungally involved California friends.

This is the new Max. He diets. He stops smoking, for real. Never again. He buys a NordicTrack exercise machine and installs it in Lena's library next to a video player hooked up to an enormous TV screen.

He tries to double his Ostermeyer visits, but the shrink laughingly turns the request back on him: would he allow his students to double their practice so they could get a black belt faster? They're working on a lot of stuff, the psyche is a great big soup pot, time is on their side, he assures him. Go slow, do it right.

And eventually he's clear of his Meltzer drugs and has easily lost a bunch of weight, and although he's still itchy, he's breathing a little better. He decides to try teaching again. Dr. Anne agrees, intuiting that teaching will help him heal.

A medical administrator hires him as a management crisis consultant at a nun-run hospital recently purchased by a major HMO. Lena decides at the last minute to join him. She's curious about his subject, and so they fly to Minneapolis. The new management has warned the nuns that God has been replaced by a more materialistic CEO and wishes them to join the twentieth century. The challenge before both sides is how to satisfy Medicare regulations without compromising entry-level standards of compassion. Max sees his role as helping Catholic Charities vs. The Bottom Line to conceptualize some attainable common good. The pay is excellent, the aikido verbal only; he should be all right. From all he's been told, the nurses are every bit as rigid as the corporate vultures; this will be a struggle to the ideological death. Still, he'd like to help those kindly souls, who want above all to keep their jobs.

But on the airplane, his leg starts swelling, and when they land, the only way he can fit his foot back in its shoe is by taking off his sock and leaving the laces untied. By the time they get to the hotel, his foot is pounding. He has a problem: he has to shower, but he doesn't want to take off his shoe, he'll never get it back on—so he sponge-bathes in the sink. He naps with his leg elevated and then goes off to lecture sockless. He feels a little queasy, somewhat light-headed, as if he's coming down with a cold. But what better place to get sick, he tells himself, than in a hospital, surrounded by all those sisters of mercy and men of the bottom line.

The hospital is just as he imagined: a red brick campus and flowerbeds filled with plastic mulch. They're led down a badly lit corridor lined with men in bathrobes sitting on wooden benches, their bandaged heads resting on the peeling green walls, a corridor of despair. The few nurses they meet ignore them. "Maybe the nuns are the bad guys in this," he whispers to Lena. "Maybe this place is an argument for managed care."

"It's the fourteenth century," Lena whispers back. "Good luck with the spreadsheets."

"I'll leave that to my colleague here," he says, nodding at the administrator fiddling with a projector, the guy who hired him. "My job is to help them meet budget without losing sight of their humanity. This is not the first time in history business-school administrators insert themselves within church affairs."

He goes to the stage without notes and sits on a chair. He starts with some basic exercises, gets all the healers and administrators to stand up and wake up their *ki* by swinging their arms back and forth and by jumping up and down in place. When they're cooled off, he demonstrates—choosing a tiny nun in her sixties as a partner—how to ground oneself while being pushed. When they're back in their chairs, he makes the usual aikido suggestions of how both sides might give in to get their way, goes on to surprise everyone with an erudite history of the Crusades, which has nothing to do with the subject, but which holds everyone in thrall, and ends up turning the talk over to the conference organizer for the slide presentation, after which he returns to open the discussion to the floor.

The first one to put up her hand is a young nun wearing a starched white cape. Standing up, she looks pointedly at Max's feet and asks if he knows he's in heart failure.

"No I did not know that," he says, his eyes widening. "If I am, I'm in the right place at least. And sister, I have to tell you that what you just said excites me. I'm sure that what you say is true, for why else would you say it? I feel like you've given me a new way to look at my teaching, an epiphany really, rather than as a condemnation. I am in failure. The world is in failure. Your system has failed you. Now I see your problems exist not because one side of your conflict is right and the other is wrong, but because you're looking at each other as if you're in opposition. You are not. Neither of you has the answer. The hospital is in failure, the health system is in failure, and it's a mistake to think you can put a happy face around it. What you need to do is experience your misery so you can lift yourself up. Nature spirals in and out of failures, each one leading to the rebirth of something new. There's nothing final in failure, it moves into success, dark into the light and back again."

8

Don't forget nothing.

—Kenneth Roberts, *The Northwest Passage*

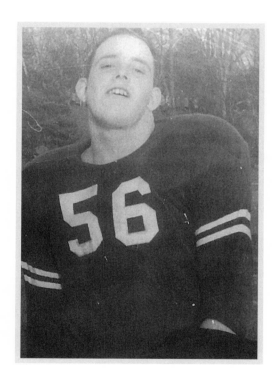

Max says:

When I got back to the States, Japanese teachers had already established dojos here. They weren't having an easy time of it. A martial arts teacher in Japan is like a fitness instructor, a back-door servant to the powerful. In Japan, martial arts were becoming revisionist, and O-sensei knew it. Only in the West would it would seem exotic. Out of the blue, these guys are flown on the big metal bird to the U.S., where they are lionized as emblems of a vast and ancient teaching. They find themselves feted, elevated, with prestige, sex, and whatever else they want. What would have happened if a basketball coach from Iowa was sent to Nepal and suddenly he finds himself a king in a little kingdom? Back home, he's just an asshole down in the park, and now in Nepal they give him a title. He becomes the repository of some ancient culture, he who can barely read. I can get really mean and bitchy about these guys. That's at my most compassionate. But on the flip side, I can see that they were handed something nobody could have dealt with.

By the time I got to New York in 1972, Niyama had been teaching there for six years. He was the Japanese lord of downtown aikido. Personally, he was a wreck: drinking, doing drugs, and carrying on. There were plenty of times he wouldn't show up for class at all. Since I was the next highest in rank, it would have been logical for me to take over for him when he was too blasted to teach, but he never asked me. I tried to follow the rules. If he wouldn't let me into his dojo, maybe he would let me start teaching at various colleges in New York. In that way, I could feed more serious students to his dojo and I could make a little money teaching the college kids. He wouldn't say no, but he wouldn't say yes. Which, of course, since he is Japanese, meant "no." Then I suggested starting a branch of his dojo in another part of town, with him as chief instructor and me as assistant instructor. He said, "Yeah, no, maybe, talk to me next week, I don't know." This went on and on until I gave up and started my own dojo with another American. Still acting out of respect, I asked Niyama to be the main demonstrator at our opening. I gave him a specific date, March 29. We put flyers all over New York, but he never showed up. I called him up and he said, "Oh, I'm sorry, I was sick." So I said well, "OK, sensei, let's reschedule for three weeks from now." He said OK, but he didn't show up the second time either, and after that we were in essential opposition.

He had a lot of money and could fly back to Japan and take the bigwigs out to dinner, and when those top dogs asked about me, he would say, "That son of a bitch, he's giving us a hard time." So it was no wonder that when these guys came to the States, they ignored me. I don't know what they thought in their hearts, but they had been eating his meals and drinking his sake, and naturally they swallowed what he wanted them to hear.

Now and then someone would invite me to teach at their dojo, and when Niyama found out, he would call them and say, "If you let Max teach, you're out." Even so, I have a spot of affection for Niyama, although it's not that big. He's been my enemy for so long that I'm used to him. He's the enemy I know. And since Niyama introduced me to O-sensei, I owe him my life, and it pisses me off no end.

I just remembered one more thing that soured me about these Japanese superstars. These New Age hotshots Kasper something-or-other and his wife Martha had a connection at the UN. They approached me with the idea of presenting aikido for the Emergency Forces, the guys who have to inner-position themselves between two warring parties. Out of respect, I suggested that a Japanese should do the demonstration, and so I asked this guy Suginami, who had started a dojo in Philadelphia.

Now, Suginami can't speak English; he speaks terrible English. He says "Ekorogy," and I say "No, it's 'Ecology.'" So I suggest that he doesn't give any big speech, and that he let what he does do the talking instead of his mouth.

He agrees, and then he gets up and starts giving this big speech about "Ekorogy." Nobody can understand a word he says, not even me, and I am his translator. So I hiss at him, "Do some aikido." He finally throws some people around, but then he starts talking about "Ekorogy" again and we're sunk. We had rented Japan House. We've got the ambassador from Mali, the second secretary from Trinidad, the defense minister from Finland. After the demo, which had finally come off quite well, we go backstage to change into street clothes. We're looking forward to eating with the audience and exchanging ideas. We've ordered nice little cakes, nice little sandwiches with the crusts cut off. But by the time we get back out, all the sandwiches and the little cakes are gone. The people are gone. It was the worst failure of my career. But if I show you my résumé, you'll be advised that we conducted a demonstration for forty-nine members of the United Nations.

Wait, it gets worse. Suginami has no money. Nobody has any money, certainly not me, and I'm getting bills for the announcements we sent out, phone bills, rent, all the little cakes. I go to see Kasper and Martha. They say, "Oh, you have all these bills. Thanks so much for coming. Good-bye." Are you getting the picture? I was having a hard time getting my star to shine in Manhattan. So when California calls for me, it's just in the nick of time. I go out there, five years, lots of hype, I do some good teaching, I do some bad. And then everything collapses and *bam, bang,* in the nick of time—Mother dies, I get a pittance, I get the land, and I come home. Like Arafat says, this is my homeland, ain't nobody can kick me out. I get sick. I fall in love. Can I turn my life around? Tune in next week.

The dojo, Burlington, Vermont, 1989

Very early one gray October morning in 1989, Max drives his new pickup truck to town. A gym bag holds a freshly washed uniform with his original, frayed white belt. Forgetting that the dojo has moved since he's last been there, he absentmindedly turns into the parking lot of the original building, realizes his mistake, and with a chuckle continues to the new dojo risen out of the ruins of an old meat packing plant on Flynn Avenue.

No one's there yet, but Johnny Drumm has tucked the key where he always has, taped to the back of the sign on the door. Max walks down a short hall decorated with photos: the most recent in full color, everyone staring down at the camera. At the end of the hall a black-and-white shows Max and Johnny in street clothes leaning against the walls of the old dojo with a group of Japanese friends.

The dojo he'd started and then left so many years ago had been a mean, cramped storefront. *How things have changed,* he tells himself, slipping off his shoes. The new space is harmonically square, with thirteen-foot ceilings, rows of industrial windows facing away from the street on three sides, brick walls, and a wide graceful altar, the *kamiza,* on the windowless side. Holding his shoes, he pads around the thick mat to the back of the room. Hardly a dust mote.

Other changes as well: separate dressing and bathrooms for each sex, a unisex toilet for the independents, a bank of lockers with real keys, a shower with hot water. He dresses quickly and stows his stuff in an open locker.

Max bows to the *kamiza*. When he lifts his eyes, he sees the old photo of O-sensei praying on his mountain, and next to it, the photo of himself, twenty-two years old, sitting across from the old man. O-sensei is working on his calligraphy and Max is helping him, both of them with bent heads, smiling, as if sharing a joke.

Max bows to the photo of his teacher and his younger, oh-so-serious self.

He takes several breaths and drops slowly to his knees, lowering his forehead to the floor. Uncurling his back, he attempts to sit on his heels. His thigh muscles contract, his stomach cramps. Pain shoots from knees to wrists, and he rocks forward, backward, then forward again. He used to be able to rock himself to a standing position this way, how long ago was that! Placing his hands on the floor, breathing deeply, he pushes himself up. This time he holds in his stomach when he bows to the *kamiza*. This time, his fingertips graze the floor.

In the east, the windows begin to glow. He closes his right nostril with his thumb and snorts a breath through his left nostril, then reverses the process, a yoga thing he's picked up from the Rolfer. Six times he does this. He bows again to the *kamiza*, swinging his arms to ease the pain in his shoulders. He tries again to sit on his heels; the vein in his forehead begins to throb. For an excruciating moment, he can't move at all, his calves tingle, his feet go numb, he grits his teeth. Once again he bows to the *kamiza*, concentrating on his breathing.

In-Breath. Out-Breath. Three more times, he bows to the *kamiza*. *Two more times,* he tells himself. This is his discipline now. He will breathe in and breathe out until, God willing, one day he will sit on his heels and properly bow to the *kamiza*. On that day he'll put on his black belt.

Johnny Drumm has been watching from the doorway for some time, looking as if he doesn't quite know what to do.

"I'm just here to watch class," Max says, panting. "I have no intention of teaching." He drops down to the nearest bench and wipes his face with his sleeve.

"You're kidding me, man. No one's going to let you get away with that white belt." Johnny comes into the room stripping off his leather jacket.

"They'll just have to adjust. I'm telling you, I've got to start from the beginning like any jerk right off the street."

"Save the humility," says Johnny, heading for the dressing room.

Sitting on a side bench, Max watches the students file in. There are a dozen people of various ages, half of whom used to train with him. Since he's come home, he'd run into a few of them—Linda and her partner Frankie, Leo and his son Sam, and Raoul, who must be in his seventies now—Raoul says people have been taking bets as to when he would show up at the dojo. Of the new people, he only knows Tonkey and Jocelyn. He's surprised to see them back in town, he'd thought they'd gone back to Jamaica when Lena stopped making functional pots. They both bow to Max, showing no surprise at seeing him there, and take their places on the mat.

Class starts: the usual, familiar warm-ups, the bowing, demonstrating, and practicing. Max watches, feeling happy just to be here, even though at times he finds Johnny's teaching too precious to bear, and he has to sit on his hands to keep himself from interfering.

The following Wednesday he feels ready to get on the mat. He thinks that if he wears his white belt, he'll be signifying he's no different than any other beginner who knows nothing about aikido and has everything to learn. He works mainly with Jocelyn at the back of the room, trying to follow the Kevin's instruction and deferring to Jocelyn. When class is over, they go to the Zone Out for coffee. The week after that other students join them, and by the following week, it's a ritual—eventually they commandeer a table of their own in the back room. Max is always the first one to arrive; by the time the regulars show up, the table's already crowded, and more often than not there's somebody new who listens to the conversation in a state of rapture and then follows them to class.

On one of those Wednesdays, Lena tiptoes in to sit at the back of the room. She's begun to take an interest in aikido, even though she has no thought of training herself, being athletically deficient and too old—her honest evaluation—but also because she knows she wouldn't be able to face Max on the mat. She'd either wither or play the fool. Let the aikido he teaches her flow through the principles of love between them, rather than be embedded in formalism. Let the aikido she practices be through her art in solitude. This is unspoken between them and unquestioned; it's worked for them so far.

That same Wednesday, in Sarasota, Marcos Zinelli sits on his patio in Longboat Key reading in the paper that the Boston Symphony Orchestra will be performing Schubert's *Trout* Piano Quintet at the

Van Wezel Performing Arts Hall. It's his favorite piece of music, he has fourteen tapes recorded off public radio stations over the years; he counts hearing it live at Carnegie Hall twenty years ago as one of the high points of his existence. The thought of experiencing it again in the famous—school of Frank Lloyd Wright—purple dome on the other side of Sarasota Bay sends a thrill down his spine.

The concert starts in a few hours, plenty of time to wash his car. Only it's not there in the parking lot. He stands in his empty space holding a big yellow sponge and a white bucket, feeling puzzled. After a while, he goes back upstairs and asks Erica if she knows anything. She's in the kitchen on the step stool reaching for something on the top shelf, and when she hears him come in, she starts to lose her balance, but she manages to catch herself on the edge of the counter. He helps her down. "Oh, shit," she says. "Oh shit shit shit. Oh, we need a new step stool." She puts a hand on his cheek, steadying them both. "Maybe one with legs."

"Do you know where we parked the car?" he asks.

She reminds him that he hasn't driven since ending up in the grassy median only inches from the oncoming traffic a year ago. *Poor Erica,* he thinks, *her mind is going.* He doesn't question his own mind. He decides to call his daughter and ask her to take them to the concert. It'll do her good, he's sure, considering all that rotten pop music she listens to. So he tries to call Lena, but forgets to dial the area code, and he keeps getting error messages and finally gives up.

He presses the "Play" button on the tape machine. In a moment, the wonderful goatlike darting strains of the *Trout* fill the room, as well as most of the fifth floor. The two old people sit across from each other nodding their almost identically white-capped heads and humming, Erica taking the part of the piano and Marcos echoing with the cello.

"Go call our daughter again," says Erica. *Where is that girl?*

"I just remembered something, doll," says Marcos. "I brought the car in for a tune-up." All he has to do is call the garage, and the nice young black man will deliver it.

As it happens, the car is in the garage, only Marcos hadn't brought it in, Tim had, months ago, under directions from Lena. She's wanted the cops to confiscate the car, but they said they had no authority and suggested she sell it. Not a bad idea—if only the car had been in her name, she would have done that. Instead, she had asked Tim to squirrel it away somewhere safe from Marcos, who has extra car keys secreted all over the house and believes that if he'd been a dangerous driver, the state of Florida wouldn't have renewed his license.

While Marcos is on the phone requesting the car—cannily identifying himself as his son-in-law, Julian—Tim brings over dinner from the caterers and keeps them company until the nurse arrives to take their blood pressure. She helps them wash up, buttons up their night-clothes, doles out their medication, and says good night. Soon after she leaves, the garage attendant calls from the lobby to say Julian's car is ready for him and the keys are in the ignition.

Marcos can barely see above the steering wheel. He tells himself it's like riding a bicycle, you never forget. He pulls forward slowly, stops at the end of the drive, looks right, looks left, and eases his old Peugeot into the slowly moving lane of cars down Gulf of Mexico Drive toward Sarasota Bay.

Max and Lena have just come in from class when the phone rings.

It's a detective from Sarasota.

"Your father," says Max, slowly putting down the phone and coming toward her, "apparently mistook the turn to the public boat dock for the Van Wezel parking lot and drove down the ramp right into the bay. A second elderly couple traveling closely behind in a late-model Buick followed suit, landed on top of the Peugeot, and then slid off. There were witnesses, the police arrived within fifteen minutes, but still there were no survivors. Lena, sit down. Did you hear me? Sweetheart, your parents are dead."

"So we're going to Sarasota," Lena says carefully. Marianne, who has heard everything, has already connected with Jocelyn to take care of Zia, and is already digging things out of her closet to throw into a bag.

"We are," says Max and leads her upstairs to pack.

So many questions running loops in her brain, Lena takes to her parents' bed the minute they enter her parents' apartment. It's never seemed so dirty, uncared for, or empty.

Were her parents depressed? Was this a suicide? If so, was it mutual? Would her father have acted by himself, making this a suicide/homicide? Was it premeditated from a desire to spare their only child the burdens of what might be a long, painful old age? Or was it a simple accident? Did he truly mistake the dirt road—not much more than a path, really—for the well-lit, paved double lanes leading to the concert hall? And what about the other couple? Did they know each other? Were they part of a suicide pact? Or had they tailgated innocently to their deaths? Lena sits mutely upright under the covers with the air conditioning full blast while Max and Marianne tend to the legalities, fend off the phone calls, and discuss the logistics of dealing with all the belongings. No one wants to touch anything; Lena says they should just throw everything away. But they can't help themselves, every few minutes some object calls to one of them—a porcelain candy jar, some old piece of Lena's with a broken handle, a photo album, a piece of Balinese cloth, an ivory figurine—asking mutely to be saved. *Look at me*, it says. *I'm all that's left of two lives; the footprints are gone, the nagging and lies and love. Remember me.*

They bring these things to Lena one by one, and she adds them to a growing pile beneath the covers.

When the ashes arrive, Max has them mixed into two of Lena's covered jars that her parents had sitting on the sideboard. "On the same shelf as the Picasso pitcher," says Marianne. "See how they put you on a pedestal."

At this, Lena finally breaks down. She lies on her back, cradled on the left by Marianne and by Max on the right. They hold her as she sobs, and when she stops for a while, they hand her tissues, bring her bottled water, try to get her to remember good things about her childhood. Max suggests there's a way to turn an enemy into a brother, or in this case, a narcissistic witch into a mother—repeat everything positive you'd ever heard said about this woman you're having difficulty with and soon your anger will dissipate. Lena sits up and thinks. Erica was a great fourth-grade teacher. She remembers how soothing it felt to be touched by her when she'd been sick, what a world-class pot roast she cooked, how she never served anything out of a can.

"We'll spread the ashes on the land," says Max. "When you're ready."

Marcos and Erica had few friends; many had died before them, so the service is short and not particularly wordy. And then, completely unforeseen, as people filed out of the condo chapel, a woman Lena had met only once before, who for her own sad agenda had latched on to Lena's parents, steps out from behind a column, grabs her by the hair, and accuses her of causing their deaths by neglect. Had Lena been a more attentive daughter, somehow she'd have been around to drive Marcos to hear the *Trout*. The woman has Lena backed up against a pillar while Max calls for security, and she's taken away. The accusation is ridiculous, of course. Erica had several times mentioned this woman and told Lena not to trust her. But the venom stings nevertheless—for doesn't every child feel in its soul somehow responsible for the death of a parent, if only by virtue of having been born?

Back in Vermont, Max and Lena now find their roles reversed. Max is strong, at least while his current pharmaceuticals hold his heart in rhythm—Anne's got him settled with a new beta blocker—while Lena is weak, the sleepless one, tumbling around in her bed with the weight of all the unanswered questions and implied responsibility and guilt and the simple fact of loss. She cries at night, keeping him up, sheltering herself in his arms. In the morning, unwilling to be alone, she rolls out of bed after him, with Zia after her, he can't move anywhere without them following. She shares his shower, wears his T-shirts as dresses belted at the waist.

Until enough time finally passes so that the reasons for the catastrophe no longer matter. Either explanation is acceptable: her father wanted to spare her, her father made a terrible mistake. In any case, her parents are dead.

But then she thinks of one more possibility.

A few months before, she'd been visiting, and it had gone relatively well; they'd been sitting on the sofa looking at old photos. Among these was a photo taken of her pretty mother standing with three children: Lena, who was two, another toddler, and an older boy, and with them was a man named Sander, their closest friend until he'd died several years back. The other two children were his.

Lena knows that Erica and Sander had had an affair for ten of those years, starting when she was four, until Erica had caught him in bed with one of her friends. She knows this because her mother had kept her informed, step by step. Herein lay the kernel of the distress between mother and daughter. It was this complicity, not the fact of the affair, that Lena blamed her mother for. Marcos didn't know, or didn't know he knew; or if he did, he didn't say.

So what if—she posits this scenario to Max one spring morning as they start to prepare the garden to be plowed—some forty years after her adultery, Erica suddenly decided she couldn't live with her guilt any longer and told Marcos that she'd slept with Sander?

No, she thinks, picking up a pair of snippers, people don't kill each other for things like this, not at ninety "I should have—" she starts to say. *But should have what?*

"There's nothing you should have done. Sweetheart, there's no way this is your fault. Just be with it. And don't just cut that grapevine, we need to dig up on either side of it and keep pulling to get its root." Max keeps on working. He's been feeling pretty good lately and it's marvelous to be outdoors. He's also delighted that Lena has finally taken an interest in the garden.

Lena picks up a shovel and slams it into the ground. "I should have assumed guardianship and put them in that nursing home where they would have been safe."

"Your father turned against you. His call."

"I should have given the car to the housekeeper."

"Right, you should have. Be careful not to slice the vine with the edge of that shovel."

"I could have said, 'Dad, remember Brooklyn?'" She's banging on either side of the vine now, working in toward the edge of the flowerbed, where the vine winds around a tree. "How do these things grow so long? I could have rented a plane and a pilot and kidnapped them."

"What I suggested in the first place. But you wouldn't do anything against Daddy's wishes."

"We could have drugged them and flown them away with a nurse at their side. There's a very nice nursing home outside Winooski. They would have forgotten all about Florida in a week." Exasperated at the vine, which still hasn't budged, Lena throws down the shovel, grabs it with both hands, and yanks hard.

"Lena, you have money now. Look at that. Think of what you want from it. If your parents hadn't wanted you to use it, they wouldn't have given it to you. Please, step aside there, little woman." He takes her place at the vine and begins working it patiently out of the ground.

The gypsy had been right, Lena thinks, watching him. She'd come into money and no, she didn't like the way it had come to her.

One evening Johnny arrives at the dojo with a tall, stocky man flanked by a small mixed-race entourage. This man is named Ichiro Rodrigo, he's a Japanese-Latino Max had trained with years ago in Hawaii.

Max is delighted to see him again, for Ichiro is a most decent man, a saint among all the thugs. The two men are the same age, but except for a slight hesitancy in his step, Ichiro looks ten years younger.

The minute he sees Max, he holds out his arms and laughingly points to the white belt. "Funny!" he exclaims, embracing him. To Max's surprise, when they hug Ichiro feels quite fragile. There's a suggestion of collapse at the shoulder, a quiver along his muscles. Perhaps he's sick or in recovery.

To draw him out, Max names his own condition, says he has heart failure. "I'm training to be an old, sick man, and in that sense, I'm a white belt. I'm a beginner in the old, sick man department."

Ichiro laughs, a big, full-throated *ha-ha*. "Oh, yes, me too. I wish I had thought of the white belt. I've got a herniated disc. I had a stroke last winter. I had to learn to walk all over again."

"What a bitch, this aging thing. But there's no good alternative. I'm looking forward to watching your teaching, Sensei," he says with a bow, and starts backing away.

"No, no, no, no," says Ichiro. *Onegaishimasu*—I welcome you to train with me."

Max considers this, but only for a moment, for to refuse would be an insult. And maybe they'll discover something interesting together. "My honor," he says, opening his mouth and pocketing his false teeth. And Ichiro does the same thing.

"So, please, go put on your *hakama*." Which Max does. When he comes out of the dressing room, Ichiro bows in the class, then the two men stand up to demonstrate, black belt to black belt.

Visions of O-sensei appear to Max. He sees himself at twenty-five, straining to understand as O-sensei throws people around without moving much himself. Younger, stronger men attack from various distances and fall every which way as O-sensei spins and swirls in place. What had impressed Max then and what he recalls now is how O-sensei had closed the distance between himself and his attacker, and how important this space—*ma'ai*, as it is called—is between *uke* and *nage*.

This is what he and Ichiro do instinctively. At first they seem awkward and stiff, but soon they begin moving as one, closing the space between them, so one man seems to slip along the side of the other, arm extended to slap the mat, rising instantaneously, repositioned along his own axis, rolling backward in a swirl of dark skirt.

"*Domo arigato gozaimashita*," says Max, finally, out of breath and clutching his heart. *Thank you very much.*

About this time, the first cycle of medications Dr. Anne has put him on fails.

She changes medicines. After an initial adjustment period of fatigue, vomiting, muscle pains, and insomnia, he gains strength. His heart stays in rhythm. His blood pressure is normal. For the next six months, he feels relatively good, at least as good as it gets—at least good enough to rise from his bed—and if he can keep his breakfast down, good enough to find his way to his writing chair, there to sit and daydream, to open a book and maybe read an entire paragraph, to speak with his daughter on the phone, lie in the sun with the beautiful dog or watch his beloved in her studio as she bends over a sculpture. Enough to borrow Jocelyn's dream machine when J. is in Jamaica and drive around visiting antique shops, dragging a bored Lena to the Saturday night auction in Alburg.

This cycle ends dramatically when he falls asleep at the wheel on the way to visit his son in Connecticut. He's not wearing a seatbelt, which saves his life, for he's down on the floor as the roof of the cab shears off under the overhanging boulders between Waitsfield and Montpelier.

He walks away from that accident and drives a rental car home. Three days later he begins his third drug cycle, which turns out to be the best one yet, the one with the Norpace and Vivactil and increased dosages of Coumadin.

Word races through the grapevine. Max is back on his feet. People begin showing up, detouring through Vermont en route elsewhere. Calls come in from strangers asking him to teach conflict resolution, to add an aikido element to seminars on politics, spiritual engagement, or conscious eating. It's wonderfully rewarding, being popular—almost enough to believe in the future—but he needs to keep in mind that he's at the mercy of uncertain chemistries, that it would be a miracle for his heart to repair itself, that all he has is this moment in time. He hesitates to commit, on the chance that he won't be able to fulfill. But then he thinks, *Fuck it, if I die at someone's lecturer's dais, won't that be a story to include on their résumé?* He's learned one helpful lesson: lowering one's expectations means you have less distance to fall when you fail.

So he starts accepting gigs. At first, only to places within driving distance, and only if Lena drives.

One time they drive to Ottawa, continue on to Toronto, stop in a couple of Midwestern dojos, and then cut back for a week in Montreal. Another time, he teaches in Pittsburgh, and again in Montreal, this time stopping in Buffalo. They make several trips to Boston and Connecticut. Gradually, he expands his field. They start flying. He teaches in Denver, gives a workshop in Oregon, and spends a week in Marin.

Everywhere he goes, he's treated with respect. He makes no attempt to hide his stiffness, or to pretend to feel better than he does. He jokes about his medication, he seems calm and relaxed, he's attained a kind of quiet wakefulness where nothing escapes his attention. Many people comment on how sweet he's become, how much more of a *mensch*, how he seems to have conquered his demons. When some student, male and in good physical shape, implies he should be sent out to pasture, Max feigns agreement before dumping him expertly on his ass.

Lena takes it all in, but tries to keep her distance from the adulation factory. It's not always easy; everyone's curious about the woman who, he insists, is the reason he's still on this planet. She's supposed to find this flattering, but instead feels like one of his teaching props. Here's the bullwhip to illustrate energy, the rag doll to teach the power of intention, the woman to show the miracle of love. The ex-girlfriends perch like crows looking her over for flaws. She learns to identify them in the welcoming committee, or at the first class, or the potluck supper afterward.

"He's so sweet with you, what happened?" one woman in Ottawa (blow jobs in the parking lot back in L.A. ten years ago, as Lena happens to know) asks outright.

Lena shrugs. The snap answer is that nothing happened: *He's sweet because he's dying, if you must know. Now go away.*

Another answer is that Max is sweet because he's in love with her. Dying or not, it made him happy just to be with her, look at her, watch her go about her day. *I had him when he was a puffed-up superstar*, the questioner seemed to be implying. *So of course it was more complicated.* Lena is not about to apologize for not having known him when he was a closet sociopath. So when she can't avoid the ex-girlfriends, she limits her conversation to wisecracks and homilies. When she's sick of it, she catches Max's eye and slips off by herself to explore whatever city she happens to be in, timing her reappearance just as he's about to wind up.

But sometimes, after class, when he's settled down like a king in the middle of his worshippers with a plate of food on his lap, Lena hangs around. No matter how often she's heard his stories, she's still mesmerized, for she lacks short-term memory—always has—and so she can listen as if for the very first time. She's his perfect audience. And when the story is familiar, she amuses herself comparing the versions, which may vary in form but never in message—find your own truth; kindness turneth away wrath; suicide is always an option; you can't find the light without the dark; God won't give a shit about you—and the characters remain constant: little bald old men, oafs from a different culture, venomous military men, powerful scumbags, hapless students seeking wisdom, flawed gentleman warriors.

But never, she notices, women. When she asks him, "What's that about? How come you never talk about your lovers? Why don't you talk about women?" he searches his soul but comes up with no answers. Never, she realizes, has she ever become a character in his imagination.

Lena flies to Jamaica with Jocelyn to look at a plantation he's discovered, a gorgeous old abandoned ruin that a consortium of local craftspeople, musicians, rich American artists, and officials have been eyeing to rebuild as a cultural learning center. Some people from an artist's retreat in Arizona are thinking of investing. The idea is to create a studio/retreat, kind of a creative spa, with studios for local artists who can also exchange them with American artisans for month-long residencies. The local studios would become productive eventually, selling their work in Jamaica as well as exporting internationally. It's a big vision demanding lots of capital and Lena fortunately is able to write a big check. She signs on as a board member before flying back home with the title to Jocelyn's Chevy in her purse.

At home, she immediately goes into the studio and starts drawing. She buys tons of giant pads, which she tacks on the wall and draws on from left to right without stopping. When she's come all the way around, she cuts out sections, delineating separate ideas. Most of the drawings are freehand charcoals of possible sculptures. Some are tiny pencil renderings of brick walls, brick by brick. When she's not drawing, she lays out slabs of clay and starts building, focusing intently upon the act of it, rather than any preconception or intent. Her hands move over clay with a new hunger to learn from it rather than to impose upon it something she already knows. It's an entirely new spirit, or the old spirit awakening, the one responsible for her falling in love with clay in the first place. Her first love, clay, taking her over in a way that men never could.

But now she's in love with a dying guy who's more alive than anyone she's ever known, demanding her attention and encouraging her engagement, not just with him, but with the universe.

If she can buckle down, so can he.

He enrolls in a two-week writing intensive at the university. He's the oldest guy in the class. The first night, he gets home at six, brings a bowl of cereal to his office, and stays up writing until after midnight. He wakes before dawn to fine-tune his piece, twelve pages of polished and, in his bent vision, truthful autobiography. The first poem he reads establishes him as the class star. That night he writes until first light, when he makes a Thermos of black coffee and heads into town to score doughnuts. He sits on a bench in the quad, ingesting sugar and caffeine, writing until the class starts.

Has he beaten the writer's block at last? If so, is it too late? Is the price too steep? Maybe. By the fourth day he loses his appetite, his arthritic thumb cramps, his eyes burn, and he can't imagine getting through until the weekend. His assignment for Monday is a synopsis of a fully developed short story with ten written pages. He produces four pages for a draft he calls *Spot Crude* and hands it over for critique:

> Max: I enjoyed this piece very much—there is a wonderful vividness to your descriptive passages, and the characterization of the cook as well as the passages of dialogue are especially well done, in fact as good as anything I've seen in the workshops over the course of some years. For these reasons I wish it were longer—it is extremely short, as you know. I look forward to seeing what you do with it this coming week.

But there is to be no coming week. The two-week intensive means eight hours of class with at least five hours writing every night, and his heart can't take it. He manages to finish twelve pages of *Spot Crude*, but then leaves it in midparagraph for an emergency ride to the hospital to be paddle-blasted.

Every year the teachers invite a student to a party to meet other writers and agents, and Max is the pick for this year. He feels like a fool, he tells Lena, for he will be networking—and that's what the party's about, isn't it?—he's won the beauty contest, but under false premises. He'll be the only one in the room who knows he has no literary future. He'd be a very bad investment. But he can't figure out how to convey this thought, so what the hell, he dresses carefully and goes off to the party alone. He comes home early and without a word takes off his suit, hangs it carefully in his closet, crawls back in bed, and calls Dr. Anne.

In an optimistic moment they'd booked a trip to London, just for fun, for shopping, and now they're uncertain if they should go. What if Max collapses in the plane—or worse, in front of the Turners at the Tate? Dr. Anne looks at his numbers and argues that the trip would help raise his spirits. And besides, they have doctors in London, it's not a third-rate medical system as it is here.

London will be fun, Max decides. Lena can shop all she wants at the sales, and she won't believe the amount of loot at the National Gallery. And he has old friends in London—of course he does, old friends turn up everywhere they go—and he thinks he might contact one or two of them.

They've only been out of the country—except for road trips to Canada, and a couple of trips to Jamaica—once, on a trip to Spain when they'd first met. In the interim both their passports have expired, so they take a quick flight to New York to renew them.

"We might as well get married. What do you think?" Max says, as they're landing at LaGuardia.

This is a loaded question indeed. It's been on Max's mind ever since they'd each divorced their former mates a year ago. It's not an unreasonable concept, marriage. They've been living together for years, they're living monogamously, they're committed to spending their lives together, they have a ball together, can't imagine being apart, and so on and so on. But Lena still thinks of marriage as a bad spell cast by whatever wicked witch presided at her parents' marriage. Whenever he brings it up, she runs to her gypsy psychic. "Remember the blue ring; someone wishes you evil," he repeats cryptically, when she asks about marriage. It may be entirely coincidental, but her mother's wedding band was made of light blue opals. And she'd learned from Julian that yes, indeed, he'd thought of purchasing a blue amethyst for his girlfriend, only she'd gone back to France before he could make up his mind to do so. It's all ridiculous, but still, gypsies count for something.

"Tess Gallagher married Raymond Carver, and he's dying of cancer," says Max, as they stand in line waiting for their passports.

"He probably had health insurance," says Lena. Max now has medical bills of almost $100,000, and rising, and Anne keeps reminding them not to jeopardize Lena's future.

Before they leave for England, cosseted in their cushy room at the Gramercy Park, he gives her a ring, a stone she'd admired set in gold. They talk about the vision he holds deep in his soul, of a man, a woman, a dog, the domestic hearth around which the uninvited wolves roam, howling their heads off with loneliness.

"I'll be with you for the rest of your life," she assures him. He knows he can't promise the same.

So they land in London, married in their fashion, on the first day Heathrow Airport is armed. Boys cradling Uzis prowl the passageways. Overhead, sharp voices bark orders, disseminate information.

They're funneled along narrow ramps ending in locked metal doors, down a grim corridor through a door into a large dark room and told to sit. After a long wait where nothing happens, a loudspeaker crackles and suddenly everyone leaves.

Ten hours ago, they had flown out of a peaceful airport bustling with commerce, where the only tension was Legal Sea Foods running out of clam chowder, and now they've landed in a war zone. Max, who'd slept through most of the flight and had to use a cane to maneuver the jetway, has suddenly come alert. Brandishing his cane, he presses against her, his eyes trolling for trouble.

"See those bag ladies over there by the loo? Brit spooks. Take a good look at your future, America. See those cameras up there? This is your former free world. Your pretty face has just been run through a database of every person who ever attended an IRA funeral."

Lena thinks he's being ridiculous. Then someone jumps out of the crowd, and she screams.

"Maxie, you fucking whore!" A giant of a man materializes, swoops Max up in his arms, engaging him in a jumping-up-and-down sort of melting-bear dance. The next moment they're ducking through a side door, waving identification at a guard, and emerging into the open air.

This huge guy—he's much bigger than Max—is his old friend Mack, a karate black belt and former pickpocket (circa 1975), in a thousand-dollar suit. They haven't seen each other in at least ten years. Max looks a bit sheepish: he hadn't mentioned arranging to network in London. "We were in the fashion espionage business together. The two Macks," says the stranger, scooping Max up in one arm, Lena in the other, then seeming to wish to squash them together under his chin. Lena's astonished: this is a man who makes Max look small.

He's a blockbuster, a monolith, with a flat reptilian gangster face and tiny canny eyes. He has that martial arts stance Lena now knows well: skewered down through the torso by an invisible pipe. He's more than exuberant; he is moved to tears, and his nose is running. "Yeah, Max, life isn't the same without you," he mumbles. "Come on, luv." Letting go of them, he grabs their bags and rushes them into a Mercedes parked at the curb, motor running and doors open.

"You can't leave a car at the curb," Max protests. "If we were in Israel, your Mercedes would be pulverized."

"Think of it this way, dearie," the big guy says as he squeals onto the A41, "Perhaps the spooks have given me a parking permit, ha-ha-ha."

That night, in the dismal B&B recommended by their Burlington travel agent ("Disgusting—we'll get you into the Mayfair tomorrow," promises Mack), after they've had a nap, and while Max is in the shower, the phone rings. Lena picks up. It's Mack demanding to know what's wrong with Max. "Let me have it straight, mate," he snaps. "He looks like shit; is it cancer? My heart breaks. How long have you known him?"

Lena bristles. Is he blaming her for something?

He doesn't wait for her to answer. "Last time he was in humongous shape, racing all over the fucking world, tarts here, tarts there. But you're too young to know anything about that." Lena clucks her tongue, cradles the phone on her shoulder, and starts to outline an eyebrow with a brown pencil. "I would have got the old crowd together; just as well I didn't. That's a sensitive man you've got there. Has he been looked at, for Christ's sake? Jesus, he looks like a dead man. Right. Now I'll send the car along in an hour and you get your bags packed and we'll get you out of this *shithole*."

Lena hangs up and gets into the narrow bed, pulls up the covers. "I'm staying in the *shithole* with my jet lag," she says to Max, when he comes out of the shower. "You *two* Mack trucks have fun reminiscing."

"No, Daphne, you have to come with me; that's an order." He pulls off the covers and sits her up. "That's a good girl. Thick upper lip, what? I think I saw a little shop down the street. Perhaps we can find you a nice short Nazi uniform to wear with those high-tops."

The night actually turns out quite magical. Mack drives them through the rain, pointing out sights completely obscured by the clouded windows. He's in a better mood, gentlemanly, almost kind. He says nothing to Max about his decrepitude, but keeps the conversation light, running inside jokes about the Queen and Diana—he seems to be an official photographer for the royals. In a restaurant so posh it opens on a nameless alley and has no sign, they sit at an L-shaped banquette in a curtained alcove. Food, unordered, begins to arrive almost immediately, tiny little courses of magnificent-tasting dishes. Around them, muffled conversation, tinkling crystal. At the bar sit two gowned women with lioness hairdos, their arms about each other's waists. There is no alcohol. Goblets filled with iced rose-flavored water appear the moment before they realize they are thirsty.

Flanked by the two meaty men, jet-lagged, her neck throbbing, Lena lets her presence be parenthetic between the two men, who are the real point of the conversation; men of the streets, sharing a past where controlled violence wrestled with beauty. Mack talks on, they listen. He's full of himself, very funny and generous, taking great pleasure including them in his perfectly marvelous life. He knows every-one: the royals, the Beatles, the paparazzi, the heads of state and the women they sleep with. Max slumps on her left, with his warm hand capping her knee, while on her right Mack shifts restlessly, pressing into her flesh perhaps more than he needs to. The minute Max goes to the men's room, Mack takes Lena's face in his hands, pins her thigh with his. "You are very sweet," he says. "Right. Not sweet. Steady then. Well, that's even better. Take care of him. I mean that. I adore your man." He gives her thigh an assessing squeeze and chatters on about the Turners at the National and Francis Bacon at the Tate. At the end of the evening, he sends for the car, tucks them in the back seat, and disappears with a wave into the ruddy, misty night.

Fighting sleep, Lena stretches out, feeling the cool leather against her bare leg, upon which it must be said the Brit photographer's touch still lingers—and leans against her lover's shoulder. "A divine con-versation. I wish we had that on tape," she whispers.

"Your wish is my command, Daphne," Max laughs, pulling the tiny tape recorder from his pocket. "Like Marianne says, 'A life not lived on tape is a life not worth living.'"

The rest of the trip is less dramatic. Big Mack has apparently dropped them, they never hear from him again. They're on their own, wandering the streets, sightseeing in buses and cabs, shopping at the sales, buying tribal rugs, taking tea at the Mayfair while the staff hangs out in front of the television mesmerized by a *Dallas* rerun. They go to the theater and eat pub food while commenting on the garrulous, crowded culture so like their own yet somehow more alive, seeming less tense, having more fun. Not as much fun as the Italians, but more than, say, in Minneapolis.

They watch a court case from the balcony in the Old Bailey. The kid in the docket has stolen a pair of jeans, and the prosecuting lawyer holds them up. "These are jeans?" he says, scowling, going for the easy shot. He might have been brandishing a sack of cow shit. Everyone howls; the judge bangs his gavel. "Not in America," says Max, when they're out in the street. "Here there are class distinctions. At home there is class war. Everything that is war in America here is discourse. The War on Drugs here is an actual conversation. The English at least have confidence they are assholes. They know they're racists. We're always pretending not to be. Listen to the language. Here there is language, real language! In America we are too protective of our individual opinions to dare debate them, lest we find them wanting, We are a nation of black and whites while the rest of the world knows everything is in shades of gray."

The afternoon they're due to leave, Lena wants to take one more trip to the Tate. Max declines, preferring to nap on the packed suitcases. So she cabs over and wanders around until she finds herself alone in a large room with Rothkos on three walls. As soon as she enters, she feels a definite vibration. She sits down on a bench across from a Caribbean guard who smiles and nods, as if to say it's alright, everyone gets dizzy in front of the Rothkos, seven of them in one room might be too much for the human brain. For almost an hour, she sits perfectly still staring at them while the guard nods off. The museum is crowded, people pass by, but no one ever comes in this room; she's in another dimension entirely. By the time she's due to meet Max downstairs, the entire room has begun levitating.

She was still on Planet Rothko when the cab let them off at the airport.

Boys with Uzis. Cameras pointed everywhere. FBI disguised as bag ladies. Max immediately jumps into super hero mode and drags her through the gate towards the jetway. As they arrive, a voice barks urgently over the speaker, "Get away from the gate, get away from the gate," without saying what gate it is to avoid or where they should go. The crowd mulls about, disorganized. Then the gate suddenly slams shut. "Get away from the gate," the voice keeps urging, but now there's nowhere to go. The empty jetway looms ominous in front of them, not even an employee at the boarding station.

It seems like a long while before a couple of policemen emerge from the plane holding dogs on leashes. They go off by themselves and light cigarettes. If these are bomb dogs—and a mangy lot they are, a couple of spotted mutts and a fucking Corgi—and there's a bomb on board and it goes off, they'll all be mincemeat. How inept it all seems.

Finally, a bus comes and takes them to their plane, which has been towed to the far end of the runway. It has started to rain and all their luggage sits outside the plane getting soaked. They have to identify each bag and hand-carry it themselves through an inspection point before it's put back in the cargo and they're allowed back on. "You can thank the IRA for this, mate," says their inspector, opening their duffel containing the three tribal rugs they bought, which are now double their weight with water.

Soon after they come back, Max collapses on the stairs. Lena drives him to the ER, where Anne meets them. As it turns out, his heart is out of rhythm and he's throwing another blood clot in his leg, This time he checks himself into the hospital without protest.

While he's there, Marianne, who's Zia-sitting at the house, forwards a message from an agent representing the poet Robert Bly, inviting him to teach at the Mendocino Men's Conference. Max loves Robert Bly; he's worked with him several times and is delighted to be invited back. He's not going to turn this down, no way, and tells Anne he's going no matter what.

Anne looks dubious. She takes his chart over to the door to read by the light in the hall. After a moment she looks up and asks when the conference is and, more to the point, what's Max going to do to get himself in shape.

"Four months. We got four months. They're paying me, which should make your people happy."

"My people," says Anne, shaking her head, going back to the chart.

"Seriously, will I make it?"

"Seriously, you are currently in heart failure with a giant blood clot maybe headed to your brain. If the clot dissolves, if the medication keeps your heart in rhythm, if you don't need surgery, if we're not in a nuclear war—"

"Oh, that," says Johnny, who's come into the room bearing an armful of flowers in one of the dojo vases. Throwing Max an air kiss, he goes over to the TV, which is buzzing with the news that Iraq has invaded Kuwait, and turns up the volume. He moves Max's feet out of the way and sits down. "We'll just take these rugheads out. Our bombs are so smart, not a stray dog will lose its tail. Piece of cake. I always thought Bly was an old windbag."

"You asshole," says Max. "I'm horrified, you consistently remind me of what a shallow person you are. Men like you are in terrible shape, you just don't grow up. I mean, look at you. Shorts, baseball cap, Red Sox T-shirt, Nikes. You're fifty years old and dress like a

Monkees fan. You are a *puer,* a fly-boy, you can't keep your feet on the ground," As he mouths off, his eyes keep drifting to the TV.

"Peter Pan, that's me. Your poet's a windbag because he wants to hold me down," says Johnny, sitting down on the bed. "Look at the telly, we're a nation of boys and these are our toys here; even you, o wise man, you can't keep your eyes off them, can you?"

"True. That's why we need men's work. We're so screwed up as a nation, we're about to have a television war. And we'll love it: no blood, no stench, no mess, no fuss. Whatever the networks want us to see is what we'll be seeing."

Lena comes into the room, shedding her jacket on the floor, looking for a place to sit. "So where's Kuwait?"

"Shh, wait. Motherfucker, we're really going to get into it. What do we care about Kuwait?" Johnny moves over and pats down the bed for her. She squeezes in.

"It's the Garden of Eden, that's what. Tell me this isn't a religious war," says Max.

"We're dropping bombs on Paradise? I thought it was in Iran," says Lena, reaching for his hand.

"Technically, yeah, or it's in Hawr al-Hawizeh, in Southern Iraq. For all we know, the garden could have been the entire Middle East. Hello, sweetheart. Get me out of here and I'll buy you a Rothko."

"Bomb, bomb away," says Johnny.

"Anne," says Max, seeing the doctor's still in the room, "why are you still hanging around here? I promise to keep my leg up. Go get some sleep."

"I want to talk to you about possible surgery. That's where we're headed."

"After I come back from Mendocino, we'll talk. How about we give the poets a real shot at curing me. Poets are closer to God than surgeons. Have you ever heard of a poet removing the wrong kidney? No, you haven't. You've got to help me get to this conference, you know you do."

"We can talk about it another time. Meanwhile, eat your Wheaties." She gets up, looks at her watch, and heads for the door.

"Wait up!" he calls. She turns around. "A little chat about lung scraping will be better than watching this shit. Sweetheart," he motions to Lena, "turn that thing off. Here's something to think about, Johnny. One reason this country goes to war so easily is because men want to get together in a way that affirms them. War is a very easy way to do it. Start a war, everybody gets together, and people help each other out. It's a wonderful feeling, a real expression of love. If our society offered more ways to affirm our love, we would not be so compelled to answer calls to war."

"That's ridiculous," says Lena, not moving. "With war waged on a screen, how can anyone bond?"

"Well maybe so. When I was in Spain I'd see, in the main squares of small Spanish towns, all these old men walking along, talking. I didn't know what they were talking about, and I don't think it matters. I could tell by the way they related to each other that there was honor there, respect, and camaraderie."

"Those guys are unemployed. They have nothing to do," Lena reminds him.

"Maybe so, but if there were more time for men to have real friendships, I don't think we would be so moved by the thought of going to war."

Johnny says, "So that's why Bly puts men together in the woods? So they can bond and be peaceful? So they won't make war?"

"Listen, don't diss Bly. He's the real article. The first time we worked together was at a small men's thing in Minnesota. He'd had just returned from a poetry conference in Russia organized by Yevtushenko. He and Bob Dylan were the two American writers invited by the Soviet government. On our way up to this in-the-woods thing, all the instructors were sitting in a restaurant in some Minnesota Norwegian town, and Bly was regaling us with stories. He starts talking about a character in Irish mythology called Thornbush Cockgiant. What he can't see is that behind him is this sea of ladies with rinsed heads. There's nobody in this town under seventy-five, and it's very cold, and it's very austere. The moment he says 'Thornbush Cockgiant' they all sort of dive for cover."

"Come on, we don't need mythology. We're going to war, goddamn it. The stupid bastards."

Anne barges back into the room now, looking stern. "Look, guys, I need to talk seriously. I just bumped into a visiting surgeon from San Diego lecturing in the medical school about this experimental surgery they're doing out there, and it's booked for a year. If we want to get you on the waiting list, we've got to do it now."

"OK," Max says, "sit down. What do I do?"

"You need to stay here for testing. We'll test everything, then I'll look the results over, with specialists if necessary, and then we'll write a letter to San Diego. First we need to know where the clots are. We have to have a firm diagnosis of thromboembolic pulmonary hypertension. It's almost always associated with lower-extremity deep-venous thrombosis, clotting: DVT. I'd say the disease is almost certain. But we have to document it. Add to that your unsuccessful history with drugs, that there's no curative role for medical management with this kind of hypertension—and you're relatively young, motivated, in good health otherwise—"

"So, what do I do?"

"Stay here for testing. Prove you're a viable candidate. They'll jump at the chance to have you, a strong young male with a great will to live. All that *ki*."

At this moment, an intern comes into the room carrying a black box about a foot wide and eight inches tall, with dials on the front and a valve on the top. He says hello, sits down next to Max, and looks up at Anne.

"Gotta go," says Johnny, quickly exiting.

"It's amazing he stayed so long." Max takes Lena's hand. "I should get him to go to Mendocino with me. I think he's starting to like me. So what's in the black box, doc?"

"Air. You have apnea. Maybe a physical obstruction or maybe not, it doesn't really matter at this point. So I ordered a breathing machine to help you oxygenate in your sleep."

"Jesus," says Max. "All right. Show me what to do."

The breathing machine is upsetting, but Max uses it diligently. With it, he can sleep through the night and wake up with a long-forgotten sense of refreshment. He can make love to Lena and follow Zia along her meanderings through the marshlands; he can swim and paddle his canoe out into the moonlight again. Food tastes almost palatable. Anne's got him on digitalis now. Weeks, months, then the entire summer without a sign of atrial flutter. All through September he reads and rereads everything he can get his hands on by the mythology mob: Joseph Campbell, Marie-Louise von Franz. He rereads Jung, Beowulf, whatever he can find of old Norse mythology. He stuffs himself with poets: Etheridge Knight, Mary Oliver, Yeats, Carol Frost, Donald Hall.

Meanwhile, Lena's been juried into a small group show at a prestigious Washington, D.C., gallery. The theme is war, and it fits into the question Lena's been obsessed with these last few months: is humankind genetically predisposed toward violence and war? Images arise in her mind, evoked by the questions she starts asking herself. She sees body parts growing out of and along with machine parts, all joined together by tiers of her red rectangular bricks. She's been building these pieces for months now. They're technically very difficult to make and subject to all sorts of calamities, collapsing when raw, falling apart when moved, blowing up in the kiln. Bringing the pieces to life has been painfully intense, but she's resolute, unstoppable. She has nine pieces ready now, all about four feet tall. A photographer friend of Max's photographed them professionally while he was in Vermont trying to interest Max to collaborate on a book. The opening's the same date Max is due to arrive back from Mendocino.

They make a plan: she'll fly to New York and meet his flight; they'll hit the city for a few days, then go on to D.C. for the opening. Everything's going to be fine.

"So what do you guys do out there?" Lena asks the evening before Max leaves. They've just watched *Murphy Brown* on TV, a segment with a send-up of Bly in the woods with the boys. It's evil and snarly and sarcastic.

"Do?" says Max, looking up from the suitcase he's been packing. "We have to do something?" He snarls, not at her but at Murphy Brown. "Why don't women like Bly?"

"Don't glare at me. They should be thanking Bly. Their men are a mess."

"So leave us alone in the woods to find our assholes."

"Ha."

"See, even you are pissed at us."

"Nah." She plants a kiss on his cheek and pulls off her shirt. She's gone shopping that day and feels suddenly anxious about her purchases. Probably she'll toss them all on the bottom of her closet and wear what she always wears to openings, black jeans, black tunic, silk shawl. With three-inch heels, if she can still stand in them.

"Women should want to get down on their knees and thank him." Max reaches up to fondle her right breast, then goes back to his packing. "A shamed, frightened, aggressive, bullshitting boy goes off in the woods and comes back a competent man. What's wrong with that? I'll tell you what's bothering women. Bly grabs the boys away from their mothers without their mittens. It's a wrenching away, taking a boy off the tit. Of course women are pissed on a biological, mythic level."

"I think it's more about who does the dishes."

"Don't nitpick. Wear that green velvet jacket I bought you, you look fabulous in it."

"Yeah, great, if I can find it." She walks to her closet and starts banging through the hangers. He continues, "I used to put down men's work, or what I thought was men's work. Women talking about men, that's natural, the kitchen talk. I couldn't imagine what men would talk about in the woods. They're supposed to shut up and get drunk and kill animals."

"Real men, that is," says Lena from the closet.

"I had the impression that Bly was some aging loony who had a lot of money or something. Then he offered me a gig and I thought, well why not, it paid the rent. I knew he was a poet, but after that gig I realized he was a real *Poet!* A person is a poet if he writes three lines in a notebook a year. But this guy is a serious poet: poetry is his life, he's passionate, he's read everything. In fact, Bly blew my mind. He's on the poetic end of psychology, or the psychic end of poetry. His knowledge of poetry is encyclopedic. I am happy to sit at his feet and listen. He says hundreds of things that I don't believe in, or agree with, and I don't care, he's so engaging, amusing, and interesting. He has the courage to be an asshole and say things that a child would know are not true. He won't try and convince you of what he's saying; he simply says what he thinks."

Lena comes out wearing the green jacket. It's velvet, fitted, with a mandarin collar. "What do you think?" She turns around and stops at the mirror, regarding herself anxiously.

"I think redheads should have their torsos painted green. You look fantastic. Wear it. Who knows what men's work is. Bly doesn't know." He looks up and she smiles fondly. It doesn't matter what she wears, she knows he thinks she's beautiful regardless.

"He runs the risk of becoming a symbol for men's work," she says, going back to the closet to check out the shoe situation. "No one will take him seriously as a poet. I'm getting fat, the buttons are pulling."

"Leave it open, it hangs better. He's gotten leveraged into this guru thing, but—well, maybe I'm looking for a mentor, a father maybe.

There's a difference between the two. A father might disagree with you, but he's got to love you. He's always testing you, and when you fail he withdraws that love. That's where it goes sour: men wind up shamed."

"Shamed?" Lena emerges holding a pair of orange wedgies. She sits down on a chair to try them on. She thinks, "I thought it was about his shaming mother."

"And a shamed man can't be a kind man."

"What about Mother?"

"We're talking here about men, Lena. Not about women. Men and their fathers. A mentor doesn't have to give a shit about you, so you can learn from him without the danger of being shamed. Somehow, men need to be initiated into man-ness. Without it, we are really stymied. To go into one's deeper feelings, into grief. We need to rec-ognize that we are both light and dark. Most of us WASP men need to reclaim some darkness. Some people have to get down in the shit and piss to do it; other's reclamation may be more elegant.

"There's this Yeats poem, 'The Wild Old Wicked Man.' There's one phrase: 'Girls down on the seashore / Who understand the dark.' It's very pregnant, very energetic. It's about a wild, old, wicked man who travels where God wills. Not to die on straw at home. And I'm paraphrasing Bly when I say that we need more kindness but less politeness. We've got plenty of cookie pushers, plenty of guys with creased pants. 'Shall I part my hair behind? Do I dare to eat a peach?' Got plenty of that shit. We need more hair. There's a difference between wildness and savagery. We've got enough savagery to last us till kingdom come. Dark is not necessarily evil. There's evil that's dark, but there's also dark that is not evil. Older men need to instruct younger men how to contain their darkness so it is of benefit to the tribe. And what paradoxically can reclaim us from that is wild old Bly. That kind of wildness is something we can't put into words because it's long before words, it's before we had the ability to talk."

"Therefore the drums." She stands up, holding onto the edge of the dresser, then tries unsuccessfully to walk a few steps. "I'm getting old," she says, kicking off the heels.

"Indeed. And we dance."

"You what?"

"We dance. Personally, I don't like it. But there is something to it. I've seen John Accountant transformed into some sort of prehistoric being." Seeing the look on Lena's face, he adds, "Sorry, you have to be there."

"That's what it was about when all the girls got mirrors and started looking up our vaginas. None of the men wanted to hear about it. You had to be there." She goes to the door, then walks back around the bed, sits down, gets up and finally stops to stare out the window.

"Are you really pissed off?" he asks, uncertain. "What's up?"

"Baby, have a ball. Go have a blast. I'm not at war with you. I'm just scared, that's all."

"You think something's going to happen to me?"

"No, not—it's just that things are going along so well. I'm not used to it. Something always..." her voice trails off, she doesn't want to spook anything by naming it. "It's just like here we are planning a normal thing. You're going away for a workshop, I've got a show in D.C., we're going to meet in New York. People do this all the time. I just don't want—"

"So I'll see you at LaGuardia. Babe, that's all we know."

Lena's been having a recurring dream. It takes place in the sleeping cabin in North Hero. She and Max lie on a mattress on the floor. Zia stretches out alongside them. An open fire burns in one corner; a storm rages outside. There's a knock on the door. A man comes in dressed for traveling in a trench coat, carrying a suitcase. He looks tired. He puts down his suitcase and approaches the mattress. "This is Jimmy," Max tells her, "I told you about him." His voice sounds strange, robotic. Another knock, a couple this time, a man bent under a heavy backpack and a woman holding a cat. They put their things down and stand for a moment rubbing their hands together. The woman's teeth chatter loudly. Max laughingly introduces them as Jane and Donald, from Wisconsin. People keep knocking on the door, walking in, putting down their suitcases. After Max introduces each new visitor to Lena, he or she crosses in front of the bed and goes out another door. Eventually, everyone's gone outside. Through the window, Lena can see them leaning against trees and smoking cigarettes in the rain.

It's a dream about saying good-bye.

She doesn't tell Max her dream. She doesn't want to jinx his trip, but she can't shake her uneasiness when she drops him off at the airport. She drives back trying to reconstruct the many times she's brought him to an airline gate. Each time, she tells herself, he's come home. This will be no different. She counts: four previous trips to Mendocino with Bly, at least twelve workshop trips, countless shuttles to New York and D.C., but she keeps losing track and has to start all over again. *He'll be all right,* she assures herself. *I'll ship my pieces to D.C. I'll buy new clothes for the opening. Ten days from now I'll drive myself to the airport. I'll take a shuttle to LaGuardia. He'll be there on the tarmac.*

Estragon: I can't go on like this.
Vladimir: That's what you think.

—Samuel Beckett, *Waiting for Godot*

Max says:

There's a line in a Robert Bly poem that comes into my mind. How strange it is to give up all ambition! How strange indeed to feel free of the drive to inspire my fellow man. I've gone as far as I can go, and I have to say it's a relief. Life is good, now that all hope is gone. Ye who enter abandon all, blah blah blah. My fellow man doesn't wish my inspiration, and that's fine by me. That said, I think I've got one more class to teach.

Here's what comes to mind: O-sensei said his enlightenment came in a golden wave, and he understood that the only victory was over oneself.

But ask yourself: "And then what? So you're enlightened, so what? Moses brought the tablets down from the mountain and says, here are the tablets, you guys read this shit. OK, so what did Moses do then? What did he do on the day after that?" He had to take his sandals in to get repaired. The ditch by his house got clogged up and he had to grab a hoe and dig it out. He went back to the daily round.

So, enlightened being that you might be, sooner or later, you've got to meet the road. Let's say that you really were enlightened, and you understood that what you had been vouchsafed by the universe was a very rare thing. And that the other people, although they could be profoundly moved by that, couldn't follow you into that space because they hadn't cleaned up their karma, or however you want to put it. They are just not going to do it.

You might get pushy and start saying, "Guys, here's the truth of the universe as I see it. I'm in a sacred space and you are not, so goddamn it, you'd better start living the truth as I see it." Well, who could stand being around you? If you had ten followers this afternoon, you would have two left by dinnertime. But it won't do you any good to lash these people with a whip; that's not how you bring people out of the karmic circle.

So what do you do with your knowledge? Maybe nothing; maybe you wander the earth with your begging bowl on the off chance that the universe will be a better place as long as you cause no harm. The other option is, you teach. But you have to be careful, because dealing with students is a little like walking down the beach looking for pretty pebbles. You know that there are millions of them there, and your attention flows to the most attractive, even though you know that lying next to it is a more homely pebble that in your hands could turn out magnificent.

Anyway, what do you teach? If you understand that the whip isn't an option, you eventually figure that your program starts by giving students the courage to find their own sacred place. You can offer a map, but you can't lead them there; they have to find out for themselves.

O-sensei used to make these shapes as he was demonstrating: circle, square, triangle. I never understood what they meant. I thought about it for maybe six years until one glorious spring day, while everybody in the dojo was tearing the place apart doing a spring cleaning, I found myself alone with O-sensei on this little veranda, and I grew bold and asked him, "Sensei, I notice when you teach, you frequently mention these symbols. Please explain." He looked at me really long. He looked down, he looked up, and he looked around. And I'm waiting, right? Then he said, "Go find out yourself." He got up and walked away. What a piss-off. But now I see that the question was really a high form of arrogance. Was I not asking for a shortcut to enlightenment?

So if, God willing, I'm given one more class to teach, it's not going to be a last shot at conveying the truth, because hey, what do I know? But what I can maybe do for whomever shows up—just maybe—is what O-sensei did for me: give them access to everything, don't hold anything back. In other words, let them in on what I'm looking at. O-sensei sat there talking to God. His kidneys were failing, he was tired, but he didn't stop teaching, he took us on even on his deathbed. Lying there, he showed us, without hiding anything, the real conflict between life and death. Look at me, I'm lying here, waiting to meet my maker.

All my life I've exhorted my students to be on point for this moment. But it's been only words; I never really got what that meant until right now. Now I see that meeting your maker isn't an abstract term, it's a real event for which you prepare all your life. I mean, I've known that, I've said it and taught it, but now I understand that this is the moment of a spiritual opening that is ours to access. It's the space O-sensei was in, Jesus was in—all the enlightened beings—and it is available to us all. Maybe I don't know how to get to that space. It's not like going to my garage. I can find my garage. I can find my asshole if I have a map and two hands. But I know that if you open yourselves to possibility, chances are that worlds you had no idea existed will open before you.

So, I'm thinking, I'll go ahead with their little surgery. I'll let them saw through my fat and muscles and bones and stop my heart and clean out my lungs and put it all back together again. They did it for Humpty fucking Dumpty, and they can do it for me.

New York, Chinatown, 1990

Lena lands at LaGuardia as his flight is deplaning. The last passengers have scattered by the time she reaches his gate, except for one old man who's moving very slowly. As the crew overtakes him, he flattens out against the wall.

Her heart sinks. She feels frozen. This morning on the phone he was laughing, filled with life and mischief, checking their schedules, babbling about his time in the woods with the men. He was made a member, he said, coughing—but only for a moment—of the White Moist Bear Clan, could you imagine that? They had laughed together. Didn't she see him more as one of the Agile Deer Clan, with a great rack? He had recited that marvelous poem from Yeats wearing a hair shirt and leaning on a staff, can you imagine?

Halfway down the ramp he trips, rights himself, then falls sideways, his duffel bag rolling to the side. She lunges, but the guard pushes her away, whips out a walkie-talkie, and runs toward the falling man. Max is up before the guard can reach him—she can feel the immense effort of it, can feel the walls shaking—and finally he sees her. He takes a deep breath and staggers four steps before hitting the floor for real. The guard coaxes him to his feet, looks back at her, mouthing that he's called for a medical team, then half-carries him to her.

"Hello, sweetheart," Max wheezes, twisting away from the guard. He takes her arm. "Move out of here," he whispers to her, then addresses the guard, "That airline food. Something in the creamed corn," placing a hand on his belly for emphasis. "My wife will help me from here on, thank you so kindly." Lena slides the duffel off his neck, takes hold of the strap, and puts her free arm around him.

"No doctor," he warns her. She can hear the panic in his voice, despite his attempt to cover up his condition. "It's always hard to with-draw after one of these workshops. You're in magic time where the air is different." As they walk down the corridor, he talks about hitting the Van Gogh megashow at MoMA, says he wants to eat Zuppa Inglese at the trattoria on Park Avenue and 53rd and sleep in an expensive hotel with her in his arms, telling her all about the forty wonderful men who were in the woods together, the marvelous ways the account-ants among them bloomed into poets. Marvelous. He can't keep away from the word. It was all marvelous. More than anything, he so wants not to disappoint her, or himself. "Food poisoning," he says, gripping her arm. "All the best people faint when they land."

He's trembling as they step on the escalator leading down to ground transportation. She can feel his belly pressed against her back.

When the automatic doors discharge them into the great swarm of the city, he seems revived by the toxic air. "We'll get us into town, park somewhere, and consider what to do."

"What's to consider, except where is the nearest emergency room?" If they'd let him fly, the best thing would be to catch the next flight to Burlington, where Anne could take charge.

"No hospital," he says, propelling her to the cab line.

Traffic is heavy on the BQE and almost unbearable across town. They head down Park, turn east again on 14th, and get as far as Lafayette and 13th, where they dead-end in front of a Dean & DeLuca truck unloading at the corner. Cursing, the cabbie signals left and tries edging around the truck. Max motions for him to pull over. He's feeling sick. He opens the door and scrambles out. Lena grabs their bags and waves a twenty at the driver, who shakes his head, signals to the right, and pulls in closer to the curb. He releases the door for her, says he'll wait. As Lena gets out, she catches his name on the license: Xinnong Cheng.

Max sprawls on a stoop, his face changing from gray to pink to gray to ash. Cheng calls out from the cab, do they want to go the hospital?

"No hospital," Max wheezes, coughing, squeezing words out through lips turning blue. "You see those guys?" He points a shaking finger at a group of men squatted over a refrigerator crate playing cards in front of a storefront. "Thugs," he hacks. "Are you afraid of them? I am, I'm scared shitless." He stops, can't go on, but Lena knows what he's thinking, he's feeling like bait left out for the piranha fish, and worse, he could not protect her should she be what they're after. He's talked about this, but only in the abstract: how he, who wrote a book on how not to be a victim; he, who was a fifth-degree black belt; he, who spent his life strategizing self-protection; he, who would laugh in the face of any thug—"You want to kill me? Let me help you"—has become one of the old and sick and crazy people who live as bait for a universe teeming with predators. He adjusts his jacket, runs a finger through his beard to catch his spittle, and wheezes, "I'm one of them now. Anyone can have me."

Lena jumps up and starts walking toward the card players.

"What the fuck are you doing?" Max says, grabbing her back.

"I'm asking them for directions to the nearest hospital!"

"No hospital." Max says, struggling to his feet. "Chinatown," he says to Cheng, who has come out of the cab to help him back inside.

Chinatown. They are jerking through the stinking streets inches from the bumper of the pissed-off cabbie in front of them, Max hanging out the window, squinting at the doorways. "46 Mott. Wait. No, not Mott—Mulberry. There's a gym over a market, west side of the street. Wei or Woo. Gym. Wrestling." He clutches his chest and gives out a high-pitched whistle. Lena knocks hard on the Plexiglas separating the driver and yells for him to take them to the nearest hospital.

"Woo, where the fuck are where you?" Max moans loudly.

Xinnong Cheng reaches over his shoulder and pushes the plexi open. He stares into his rearview and says loudly, "Wei Zhao boxer, not wrestler."

"How the fuck do you know?" Lena yells.

"This Chinatown, everyone know. Mister, you no look good. Maybe Wei see you, maybe not," and he yanks the wheel around a corner. He slams on his brakes in front of a glass storefront that's barely visible behind a staggering pile of garbage cans, with bloody food parts spilling from open lids.

Lena can only hope that this will turn out to be a nightmare, a shared hallucination. That all she has to do is whistle and she'll find herself in Bellevue.

"Wei Zhao is a boxer slash acupuncturist slash whatever you want," Max explains, condescendingly, as if any of this was reasonable. He slides out the door, pulling her out behind him. He's all business now, moving quickly toward the storefront. "Come on, the guy's a genius. You heard Cheng, everyone know who he is."

"Fourth Floor, Wei Zhao. Go fast, you have not much time," says Cheng, getting out of the car. He lights up a cigarette and leans on the cab with his hands in his pockets, watching them.

With Lena in tow, Max lurches toward the open door of the building through which they can see a staircase disappearing into the dauntingly vertical gloom. Cheng yells out, "No, no, go in market, elevator there, four floor," stabbing the air with his cigarette. "I stay here. Bags safe."

"Here, give him this," says Max, pressing bills into Lena's hand, but when she tries to hand them to Cheng, he shakes his head. "You come back, you pay. He dies, Wei pays."

Behind the market, which seems empty but for several large cloth bags of grains and a slab of some legless something swinging from the ceiling, they find a tiny elevator, door open, in which three Asian men stand pressed together staring at them. This is the final straw for Lena, blowing any lingering relationship to reality, and she digs in her heels—*we're not going in there*—shaking her head no, no. But Max is backing in, pulling her with him. A hand comes around them, pulls the elevator grill shut, and in a moment the cage groans and begins to rise, threateningly overloaded, inching upward, passing the closed-off second and third floors, coming to a groaning stop at the fourth, the door finally opening, discharging the ball of stuck-together passengers. The Japanese men push their way out gently, jabbering away and laughing. Max joins in, *ha-ha*. Then he says something in Japanese that makes everyone roar.

"Sweetheart," he wheezes into her ear as the Japanese jog away and disappear around a corner, "did you get that?" He starts propelling her forward by the neck. "The one with a Band-Aid under his ear—did you see that?"

"Where are we going?"

"Where they went. Listen to this. That guy was saying he came back from Malaysia with a big boil on his neck, and how Wei *needled* him and in the morning the boil exploded and out came this little frog."

"Shut the fuck up now," says Lena. She pulls away, determined to walk on her own.

The hallway leads to a big sunny room, empty except for a practice mat piled up in sections against a wall. They walk through the room and arrive at the far end, where there's another door and a small alcove where a man wearing black pants and a white shirt is bent over a sink washing his hands.

"Wei," says Max, grabbing Lena's elbow.

"You look like shit," says Wei, without looking up.

"Wei," whispers Max.

"I remember. Long time ago. Not good." He dries his hands on a towel and throws it on the floor. He looks up and stares at them. His chinless face is a scar with tiny eyes embedded in mushroom-colored flesh stretched taut over jutting cheekbones. He's almost as wide as he is tall, one ugly cube of a beat-up Chinese hoodlum. "Go somewhere," he says to Lena, waving her away. She doesn't move. He picks up Max's wrist, fingers the white flesh, listens to the pulses, and then shakes it off as he would a repugnant reptile. "You in bad shape. No pulses. You dead. Maybe you die here. Why don't you die in the street," Wei says. Then he turns Max around and shoves him through the door with Lena glued to his back

This room is large, white, and clean, undecorated except for an acupuncture poster on a wall and a carnivorous-looking spider plant spilling down over a pair of windows overlooking Canal Street. There's a pile of hospital gowns on a chair, a magazine rack, a shelf full of packaged herbs and disposable needles, and two narrow treatment tables covered with rumpled sheets under a fluorescent light. Wei grabs Max by the neck, pushes him down on one of the tables, unbuttons his shirt with one hand, extracts a huge needle from a drawer with the other hand, and plunges it into right into Max's heart.

Lena screams.

She comes to on the other table, lying in her underwear under a sheet, with needles sticking out of her toes. Wei stands holding her wrist while he's chatting with Max, who's sitting on a chair putting on his shoes. They are discussing the Red Sox, who happen to have made it to the playoffs this year.

Max smiles brightly at Lena. He says, "I'm flattered. You said you never fainted."

Wei pulls out Lena's needles and the two men leave her to dress. A woman comes in—she's old and extraordinarily beautiful, with ghost-white hair bunned up on her head and a skin taut as cream smoothed on over fine bones. "One for you and one for him," she says, handing her two paper bags, then adding, "Don't confuse. He very sick man."

The herbs may be different, but their effect is the same; neither of them have any recollection of the flight back to Vermont. They remember sitting with the cab driver Cheng at a cafeteria table, watching him pour hot water over herbs that smelled like boiled socks, and Max saying, "I'll have the shiitake mushrooms, please." The next thing they know, they're in Anne's car on the way to the hospital.

In January 1991, Anne writes this letter:

Dear Dr. M:

This is a letter to introduce you to Max Diebenkorn, a very pleasant fifty-three-year-old man who lives in Vermont. I am referring Max to your institution for consideration of a thromboembolectomy procedure. He has been significantly disabled by this respiratory status and has a variety of arrhythmias which we feel are secondary to his pulmonary hypertension. His most recent hospitalizations for these problems occurred in January 1991. When he presented with a recurrent thrombophlebitis his Coumadin became subtherapeutic. He began having increasing cardiac arrhythmias, and subsequent lung scan revealed more pulmonary emboli. He has not yet had an angiogram. Dr. K. of our pulmonary division felt this should be done at your institution, UC San Diego, if indeed you felt he was a candidate. Max is a bright, energetic man who is extremely frustrated by his situation and is willing to undergo any medical treatment that will improve his quality of life. Please let us know if you feel you can help us with this problem.

Anne Simones, Burlington, Vt.

Max returns from his surgery in a wheelchair, clutching his duffel bag. It holds only a change of underwear and his papers: his will and testament, his Rolodex, a new copy of *Moby-Dick,* one of the Rumi books translated by Robert Bly, and the twelve-page manuscript roll of *Spot Crude.* His surgeon had warned him he might come out of surgery temporarily insane. "Don't encourage him," Lena had begged. "He's suggestible." Indeed, he'd emerged raging and paranoid and coiled up on the windowsill, threatening the nurses if they stopped him from jumping.

He looks shrunken in his leather jacket, slumped forward to protect his rib cage, skinny legs lost in his jeans. "Thin at last," he jokes weakly. He looks like something pulled out of a lake, dead eyes flickering with phosphorescence from a former life. She'd set up a bedroom on the first floor. But he ignores it and rolls himself past it, heading for the stairs. Snorting and groaning, he pulls himself up. She has no choice but to help him do it.

He falls backward in their bed and sleeps for a week.

He smells like ground pepper and Vaseline, he smells of the slaughterhouse, like the New York she'd known when she'd lived over the meat markets; in fact he looks like meat, all dinged up from saws and hooks and picks. Lena can't help but imagine the purple gashes, spliced arteries, synthetic thread, the fractured bone, manhandled organs, scraped bronchia, the marks made by fingers trespassing in his chest cavity, their wedding rings bulging under the latex gloves. Flesh sticking to the bones, threaded fat, the purple arteries clamped with something similar to what she uses to hold back her hair. She unzips his jacket, unbuttons his shirt, slits his T-shirt very carefully with a razor blade. "Prepare yourself," he warns her, turning his cracked lips up, his roadkill smile. "But don't touch."

His body is back home, immobile in bed, with his breathing machine. He wants her to lie down with him, he wants to touch her, to feel her body, but his eyes drift toward a place behind the middle distance where their love affair waits at anchor.

That month, in late February, Zia requires knee surgery, one rear leg after the other. Then Lena pulls a muscle in her back. The household is thusly equalized: they are now a triad of three cripples all smelling of Tiger Balm. Each morning they limp out for the therapeutic walk down the center of the plowed road, holding the dog's leash and the breathing machine between them. Each day they travel a few more feet along the crunchy road. Breathing the frozen air makes it difficult to speak, so they trudge on in silence, with eyes fixed on the road, one step at a time.

They've tried to keep the surgery a secret, and failing that, a family affair, meaning between the two of them, their doctors, the nurses and social workers who come to help them, the kids, maybe the brother. But the family—she comes to understand this—goes way beyond these blood relations, and the secret passes quickly along all of Max's previous parade routes, relayed by poets, Buddha buddies, students, academics, girlfriends, filmmakers, hot tub companions, going all the way back to prep school and his old football buddies: even to the high school girlfriend, even John Denver, whom he never actually met, even to the stranger who turns up because she's sure her mother was once his governess. Max has left his footprints along many paths.

All this abundant outpouring is heartwarming. The messages of love and prayers for recovery feel poetic and sincere, the gifts arriving daily—a book, a basket of fruit, a couple of stones taken from the Colorado River, the pair of red lace panties with Wednesday embroidered on the crotch. Attached are sentimental notes wishing him good cheer. The thousands of dollars raised through dinners, appeals, benefit concerts, and readings help defray the enormous expenses.

Lena finds it all terribly moving—and she's appreciative—but at the same time it's annoyingly intrusive. The phone rings constantly. Finally, she adds another private line for the house and puts a message on the listed phone thanking everyone for their concern and promising to be in touch when Max recovers.

Max asks her to keep everyone at bay. He wants the A-list limited to Marianne, Norbu, Johnny (his close look at death has consolidated reconciliation), and Jocelyn. Marianne's already back in the guest room, Jocelyn soon arrives with Tonkey and they take over the first floor bedroom that Max still rejects.

Only Norbu is missing, he's been called to Tibet. His son, a medical resident in India, had snuck into Tibet to help out at a besieged monastery and had quickly been arrested at a demonstration in Lhasa. Officially, there had been no violence, but somehow the boy had been shot in the ankle with a Chinese bullet. Norbu had flown to Tibet as part of an international delegation to negotiate his son's release on medical grounds.

When he finally settles his son in New York with his wife and returns to Vermont, Max asks him to help get his stories down on tape.

Marianne, Lena, Norbu, and Max sit around the kitchen table with a microphone and a tape recorder. It's late April and chilly. A fire crackles in the Jøtul; a large pot of tofu stew simmers on the stove. The room smells of wood smoke, tomatoes, and wet dog. On the hearth sits a covered bowl filled with rising sourdough starter that Marianne brought on the plane from New York.

"Thank you," says Norbu. "I always feel welcome here." He's wearing a tattered kimono over his T-shirt, and to Lena, has the look of a weathered shepherd.

"I'm sorry we dragged you away from your son. But I needed you here," says Max.

"My son needs to be in New York with his mother, not me."

"Shall we?" says Marianne, anxious to begin. Max has agreed to this taping session, but only reluctantly. She's afraid he'll back out as soon as the tape starts rolling.

"I don't know where to start," says Max, closing his eyes.

"Wherever," says Norbu. "Just start."

"I had a terrible childhood," says Max, fiddling with his shirt. He's lost so much weight he keeps getting stuck in the folds of his clothing. "Should I start there?"

"It doesn't matter. We'll edit later." Norbu reaches around Max for a box of tissues and blows his nose. "Allergies," he says, apologetically. "I don't pay attention to my own medicine."

"Do you really think anyone wants to hear this shit?" Max looks dubious.

"What matters is that you want to hear this shit," says Norbu.

"I want to write a book," says Max. He pounds his fist on the table, laughing.

"Damn it. Let's do it."

"Wait," he calls out to Lena, who's heading to the kitchen. "I need you to be here. Don't worry about food, it'll happen. What about the Daniel Boone stories, does anyone care about Daniel Boone anymore?"

"Sure, we can include those," says Marianne, hooking up cables. "Whatever. Everything. Babble. Be free. It's what you do best. Put everything in; we can take it all out later."

"What about getting permission from the Federation?" He clears his throat. "Do we need that? Is that thing on? You know O-sensei treated his students just like these dogs here. You can put them outside, but you can't tell 'em to shit—that, each of them needs to figure out for itself...."

"Here we go," says Marianne, punching "Record."

By late afternoon they've used up the two cassettes Marianne had brought with her. Max is clearly exhausted, and it's a good time to take a break, so Marianne offers to drive to town for more tapes. Lena accompanies her outside with the dogs. They huddle for a moment working up a shopping list, then she drives away and Lena goes back inside.

Norbu is at the stove making tea. *He's always making tea*, Lena thinks, putting an arm around his thin shoulders. "What's with Tibetans and tea?" she asks.

"Do you think he's OK with this? Can you get him to drink tea?"

"No, I cannot. Just don't let him get too tired."

"I'm fine," says Max from the couch, where he now lies on his side with his arms around his oxygen machine.

"Listen to Norbu." Lena goes over to the couch to help adjust the CPAP mask. When she bends over, Max manages to slide a nipple in his mouth. "Go to sleep," she laughs, disengaging her body. By the time she's plugged in the machine, he's out cold.

She goes back to the table and sits down in front of the tape recorder. Norbu joins with the tea things and a bowl of crackers. He presses "Rewind," then stops the tape at random. They listen:

Max says:

The Japanese have a saying, *katsu hayabi*. It means, literally, "victory at the speed of sunlight." According to O-sensei, when one has achieved total self-mastery—*agatsu*—one will have the power of the entire universe at one's disposal, there no longer being any real difference between oneself and the universe. At this stage of spiritual advancement, the very intention of an attacker to perpetrate an act of violence breaks harmony with the fundamental principles of the universe—and no one can compete successfully against such principles. The expression of the fundamental principles of the universe in human life is love—*ai*—and according to the founder, has no enemies. Having no enemies, one has no need to fight, and thus always emerges victorious. When death comes, you will not resist, and your victory is instantaneous.

"What does that mean?" she asks Norbu, as he winds the recorder back. "He sounds like he's reading from the Bible. I hear two voices in this stuff: one's raunchy, irreverent, and smart, the other's academic, dry. Sometimes the voices merge, other times they clash. What do you think?"

Pouring the tea carefully, he weighs his words. "We should ask him what he thinks of the two voices. I've heard most of this before, some parts over and over. But each telling sounds subtly different. It's interesting; how does he do that? He reinvents himself, moment by moment."

"Let's make some rules. After two hours, he naps, ready or not. He uses the breathing machine, even if it makes his voice squeaky. If he says something's off the record, we shut down. He gets a walk and a hot tub twice a day. Even if he has no appetite, we cook. OK?"

That evening, after Marianne returns with more cassettes and groceries, while Max showers upstairs, they take turns playing back segments of the tape through headphones. Norbu takes notes. By the time Max is back down at the table, wearing a new striped shirt, fleece vest, and jeans Lena has bought to replace his old big-guy clothing, the bread's in the oven and the chili sits on the table with a big salad and bottles of Perrier.

While they eat, they discuss the dilemma of the two voices.

Max agrees that there is a dilemma. "As I see it, there's one voice like a good student memorizing his teacher, preachy and prissy—

'Oh, Sensei,'" he holds out his fork and mimics himself, "'Certain people insist there's no such thing as "No Touch," but I've seen you drop four men in a row without laying a hand upon them, please will you tell me how to do this?'" Everyone laughs, they know who he's referring to. He shakes his head in disbelief and takes up his fork. He put it down again, starts playing with his food.

"Take your time baby," says Lena. "We've got plenty of tape."

"Good. I had an epiphany in the shower; want to hear it?" He looks around the table. Of course they want to hear it, they want everything. "I realized, of course there are two voices, I'm a Gemini, there are two of me, and damn it, each one has something to say. Norbu, I know you think this is the story of some American warrior moving toward enlightenment. That's because you're a Tibetan, and you think along those lines. But I tell you, if we make that the story, it'll bore everyone to tears. And you know why? Because it'll all tie up in a neat little knot and that ain't the way life unfolds. The words will be dead if they come from the mouth of this quote-warrior-slash-spiritual-seeker-unquote, but if this guy also happens to be also a scumbag, we got some juice flowing here. Follow me?"

"So we have the bouncer story in there. Maybe it's next to the subway train story, for contrast." Norbu pushes his plate away and stretches. "Do you want some tea?"

Max looks at his barely touched plate. "Positioning the stories isn't enough. I'm proposing that we create a real character who starts off as a—well, what? Is he the Ginger Man? He's a real fictional character, and he does the talking, the experimenting, and the growing. And God willing, maybe he changes into someone more in tune with Norbu's perception of me by the end of the book. Fuck tea, I want an espresso. We've got to turn this narrator into an interesting fictional character himself who embodies the struggle instead of yakking on about it."

"Perhaps this segues into a discussion of your legendary writing block?" says Marianne, kicking Lena under the table.

"Oh, fuck my writer's block. It's true I haven't written anything in a long time. What I want to do feels like climbing Everest from the inside. I want to transform something that I did with O-sensei into an American language, and to do this I somehow have to turn my experience into fiction, while at the same time keeping O-sensei's spirit alive at my side."

"Are you scared of being criticized by the aikido community?" asks Norbu.

"Fuck, no. I've been plenty criticized. I have no students, I have no dojo; it's not that I have a real position to lose. But I have a perceived position, as an heir to a tradition."

"Well, you shouldn't have any trouble fictionalizing yourself," says Lena. "You've always done that." *A legend in your own mind,* she thinks, keeping the thought to herself. "It's what writers do," she hastens to add.

"Yeah, that's true. Thank you for that. Here's a hyperbole: say I'm a drunken painter and I'm out in the middle of nowhere. So far, everything I've painted is shit, and I'm drinking, and all of a sudden a sprite, an angel, a totally bizarre beautiful creature, sits down for its portrait. On the one hand, I'm overcome with awe. I cannot move toward the canvas. On the other hand, I have to move toward the canvas. On the third hand, can I spill paint on the floor? Can I make a mistake and change it later? So what I need to be encouraged to do is to go outside the boundaries, and be convinced that people with taste, people with aesthetics like yourselves, will know where I should draw the line."

"You make your own line."

"Are you telling us that this guy, the character in the book, needs to be somewhat shady, like you?" asks Marianne.

"Nap time," says Lena, looking around the table. As if on signal, the two dogs, who've been all this time nodding out underneath the table, start squirming their way out through the pairs of legs.

"One moment. Wait. One of the things about martial arts teachers, they're considered slightly less then gentlemen, not quite social equals, no matter what their rank in society—as if entering into that realm puts you slightly one down. In the English classical boarding school, the master next to the headmaster was the fencing master, also not quite a gentleman. Because he was interested in strategy, he was considered more than somewhat devious, and therefore feared. The fencing master teaches how to take life; instead of teaching the life-giving sword, he's teaching the death-dealing sword."

"I have no idea what this means," says Lena, reaching for Zia. "Oh, I'm getting stiff. How about we put these dogs out for a while and all of us take a nap." She's up now, walking to the hall, where their jackets hang on hooks.

"So what's the bouncer story?" asks Marianne, still in her seat, reaching for the plates.

"Oh, Christ," says Max.

"Now, come on. There's always tomorrow," says Lena. She's got her jacket on. Beside her the two dogs sit patiently.

Max waves her back in the room. "Maybe, maybe not. You got that thing on? You sure? OK. Here we go. I tell you, it's the last story for the night, OK? When I came back to the States in 1971 or 1972, I had nothing but a truck and credentials in a martial art no one had ever heard of. The sixties had been and gone without me, I thought in another language, I couldn't recognize Americans as 'my' people. But the Japanese certainly weren't my people either. And what about aikido? Maybe it worked in Samurai Land. How could I make it work in John Wayne Land?

"None of you were around here before the Zone Out got transformed into the cozy little hippy warren you like to frequent, when it was called Slades. It was a scumbag and biker haunt with sawdust on the floor like a medieval hall and twelve kinds of beer for food. I took a job there as the doorkeeper, selecting which of the peasants would be allowed to come in and get drunk and fall down in the sawdust. I figured it would be a good place to test out if aikido could be used to divert conflict in a situation where savagery erupted ten times a night as a matter of course.

"One night I arrived early. The only people there were the bartender setting things up and a great big guy passed out at end of the bar. The bartender was a bald biker guy. Yeah, you got it, that's our Johnny Drumm, it's how we met. To me, he looked like Billy Budd; beautiful and innocent, with features about to slide off his face, you know what I mean? Underneath the pretty package he was a true blackguard, just like Billy Budd. Johnny pointed to the drunk and told me to remove him. 'Sure,' I said. I poke around his shoulders and suggested in a reasonable manner that this bar was not a train station. After a few minutes, he blinked. I got him a cup of coffee and went off to check out the room, which by now was filling up. After a while, I looked back and fucking Drumm was handing him a beer. He introduced us, he said, 'Max, this is Doug. And Doug, Max is our doorman. So if anybody gives you a problem, talk to Max about it.' Well, it was all too complicated for me—he'd just asked me to eighty-six the guy—so I went back to carding kids at the door.

"An hour and a half went by. Doug wanted to use the men's room, but he couldn't get the door open because a kid had propped himself up against it; so what did Doug do but yank the kid up by the hair and serve him across the room like a tennis ball? I went over there, and I put a hand on his shoulder, which he took as a sign of my wishing to prevent him from taking a piss. I told him, 'No, no, please go to the men's room; feel welcome to use the facilities. As a matter of fact, I will stand outside and make sure nobody disturbs you.'

"At this point, I realized I was practicing aikido. Here was a fellow wishing to take a piss, and I was helping him do so. But Doug didn't know from aikido, he thought I was fucking around with him, and he started sliding his leather jacket down his arms, which meant he was making ready to blast me. So screw the aikido: I started hitting him as hard as I could, slamming him through the door and into the bathroom. Eventually he let go of his bladder. He really did have to piss. The force of his piss coming through his underwear and his trousers turned into the most beautiful nimbus, a golden light. The light was coming from behind him. I remember the observer part of me thinking that it was beautiful. We were in this toilet, where there was just shit and piss and beer and sawdust. And pink walls with graffiti, swastikas, and lines like 'Death to Faggots.' But to me it had become like the Grotto at Lourdes.

"I knew that O-sensei's enlightenment had been bathed in a golden mist. And here was my golden mist, just as as beautiful and significant. Apparently I was supposed to learn something in the men's toilet, and why not? You cannot see light unless it falls in a dark place. And what place would be darker than the room for our own excrement? If this was what my teacher had had in mind for me, I thought it behooved me to let go of Doug's throat. When I did, he gasped and dove right for the toilet, wrapping his arms around it, and when I pulled at him, he rose in the air and the toilet came along. Holding him with one arm— the toilet firm in his grasp—I kicked open the door. Outside, guys stood lining the hallway holding tankards of beer like in a Dutch painting. Like in the story about the lady and the tiger, no one knew who would be coming out that door. When they saw it was I, everyone clapped. Everyone but Johnny, that is. He said, 'Asshole, you broke my toilet.' And I realized this was the end of my bouncing career."

Lying in bed later that night, Max holds Lena and says, "Lena, to borrow a phrase, you are the reason I'm still in the world. You know how pissed off I get when Johnny reminds me that I'm responsible for him, because my teachings saved his life? Well, you saved mine, and now you are responsible for me. It's not fair, but we can't help these things."

"What are you saying?" Lena thinks she knows.

"That it's possible I won't be able to see this project through. You may have to take it over."

"You mean write your book for you? No chance, sorry. You'll have to do it yourself."

Eleven cassettes and eight days later, Max announces he's done talking, finished, milked dry, that's all there is, everyone please go home now, and he stands with his arms around Lena waving good-bye as they drive away, and then he pulls her back in the house, slamming the door, propelling her to the sofa, nothing weak about him. "Thank God that's over with," he says firmly. He sticks a foot under her knee, dropping her on her back on the sofa, his hands lowering her down slowly.

"Hey, watch your stitches," she warns him, holding him off with her hands.

He hoists his legs on either side of her and drops to his knees. "Now, listen up. "Jocelyn's due over here in a half hour, and he's taking me to town. We're going to stop at the hospital to get my blood tested and then over to the dojo because I want to watch class. When I'm gone," he starts unbuttoning her shirt, "I want you to get into the hot tub and take a long soak. You look exhausted. Babe, this week's been as hard on you as on me. You had to keep me propped up, fed, and sane while all I had to do was babble into a stick. Don't contradict me." He slides her shirtsleeves over her shoulders, takes hold of her skirt and panties and continues sliding until her clothes pile at his feet.

"Tell me you'll sit and watch class. That's all. Promise that."

"What, you think I'm dumb enough to practice?"

"I'm not sure. Let's see." She unbuttons his shirt and pulls it over his shoulders, exposing his scar. "You look like you've been sliced. Someone got in there and picked up your heart. Don't you dare get on the mat. Go get the Saran Wrap; we'll put you in the freezer until you're ready."

"Now, after the hot tub," he says, gently pushing her legs apart, "take a good long nap and then go into your studio and do whatever it is you've been postponing doing, and don't stop when I come home, don't cook me dinner, stay in there until you remember who you are again."

In this moment, Lena realizes later, Max took charge of his destiny. The last thing people required of him, that he required of himself—the taping of his stories—was now accomplished. He had nothing more to say. The medical profession was through with his body and had nothing more to offer. Although he never mentioned it, he suspected that the filter they'd inserted was no longer adequate to catch the clots, which were once again filling up his lungs.

Up until this moment, he'd been a fugue conducted by experts—doctors, friends, students, lovers, partner, kids—do this, do that, take these pills, exercise in this way, eat this food, think positive thoughts, breath through a tube, watch your weight, let us slice here, let us scrape a bit more on the left, swallow, strip, stoop, sleep. He'd been very patient.

Actually, he'd tried to escape earlier, when he was still deep in anesthesia, after his surgery. He remembers clearly weighing his options, to go back to his body or forward towards that proverbial light way off in the far horizon. He watched himself, a tiny figure in a great green field surrounded by gelatinous mountains picking off the leaves of a daisy: live, die. A stout dappled horse was standing by, waiting for his decision. The next thing he knew, he was on it, galloping furiously towards the light, one pain-free molecule sucked back to the source.

Then he'd heard voices behind him, faint at first but then growing louder. One of the voices was plaintive, childlike, and it begged him to turn back. "Daddy, Daddy, I love you," it called. At the sound of his daughter's voice, his horse disappeared below him and he was hurtling back to his body.

He took this as a sign he still had work to do. He needed to teach one last class.

After the taping, he shakes off all his handlers, stops taking his medication, and starts saying good-bye. He writes letters and leaves them in a pile to be mailed. He feels he's been given a certain amount of days, weeks, maybe even months, to go on with the project he came into this world with, but that's all.

Max seems calm. The calmer Max seems, the more frightened Lena becomes. Someone has switched reels in their movie. Max is now directing, and the film's in a language she doesn't really understand.

They eat and sleep, they go shopping, they take the dog to the vet, they cook meals, they laugh, they make love, curse at the television, joke around, play music, clean up the garden, but nothing feels real. They're just biding their time, dancing the last waltz as the credits fade away.

Of course he goes to the dojo. Of course he teaches.

Death calls him on the mat. *Irina nage, entering throw. Face your* uke *as you would your death.*

Our souls are like those orphans whose unwedded mothers die in bearing them: the secret of our paternity lies in their grave, and we must there to learn it.

—Herman Melville, *Moby-Dick*

Max says:
Nothing.

Vermont and California, 1992

Max rents a safe-deposit box and therein deposits safely the only existing copy of *Spot Crude*, the eleven audio tapes, a dozen signed blank checks, a thousand dollars in cash, and a sealed envelope containing his will, financial information, and another envelope addressed to each of his children. He brings Lena the key and tells her to open the box should something happen to him. As far as she knows, he never goes back to the box, never looks again at the manuscript, or listens to the tapes, or adds anything else. He brings her car in for a tune-up. He get Zia wormed. When summer comes, he puts the water lines in and arranges to have the garden plowed. He has the driveway repaved and the septic system pumped out. He hires workmen to repair Lena's leaky roof. He has the furnace checked. He takes Lena's hand and turns the triangular ring he gave her to face out to the world instead of inward to her own self. He buys her a wool coat, then a book on Matisse, an expensive easel, a Clarice Cliff platter, a load of compost for the garden. He would buy her anything she asks for, but she can't open her mouth. In July he has seven cords of wood delivered, split, and stacked.

In August, he tells her he's going to Mendocino with Bly and after that, he'll drive to San Francisco with some of the other teachers. He's going to teach one class, and then he'll come home. He calls it his last class, as if he were talking about retirement. He says the word "home" as if he means Vermont. He buys a round-trip ticket.

And then it's time to go.

In the car, he suddenly says there are three names she needs to know. The first is that of a Dagara shaman who'll be in Mendocino reenacting a ritual funeral. The second name is someone named Garret Hilton, whom she doesn't know yet, and the third is Norbu Tendzen. These three men will tell her everything she needs to know.

"I thought—"

"You thought we had time, didn't you?"

"I did. At least more time."

"Well, maybe we do. I'm teaching my last class. I promise. That's all I know. If I knew more I would tell you."

At the gate, he wraps his arms around her shoulders and holds her and looks at her with great kindness. It occurs to her that he's already gone and is only asking for her blessing.

"Don't forget—" she starts to say, and he interrupts.

"I won't, ever. There's nothing to forget. I am always with you."

She had meant to say, "Don't forget your breathing machine."

Lena remembers nothing of the next ten days.

It's 4:00 a.m. when the call comes and a stranger tells her that Max has suffered a cardiac arrest; he's in intensive care at San Francisco General Hospital in a coma. Jocelyn drives her to the airport, following the dawn as it rises out of the lake in the east, the sun's rays already shaking with an unseasonable heat. He waits until she boards. The flight across the country feels endless, excruciating—fog covers the entire continent, delaying flights from coast to coast. She's diverted from one airport to another. It is as though the coma he lies in spreads out over the country, halting every bit of motion. She feels she'll go crazy. She is already crazy. From the moment she'd picked up the phone she'd believed she could save him. Hadn't she always? Wasn't this her job? At every opportunity, she calls the hospital and tells whomever picks up to tell Max to hang on. Wait for her. She believes she can save him until the very moment she walks into his room.

The elevator opens to a corridor crowded with people. She stands uncertainly, wondering where to go. She hears her name called. Russell takes her bag and leads her through the crowd lining the corridor. Now and then, there's a familiar face, but mostly these are strangers.

Finally she stands next to his bed. Norbu Tendzen stretches over him, reading from the Tibetan Book of the Dead. Max lies on his side, one leg extended, the other bent at the knee, an arm across his chest, the other dangling over the side of the bed. The room is crowded, but no one speaks. Now and then someone comes up and hands her something. She collects a sheath of notes taken at his last class, Cormac McCarthy's *All the Pretty Horses*, a small bouquet of wildflowers.

Eventually, the nurses come in and shoo everyone out of the room. She puts everything in a tote bag and returns to the corridor. This time, the few people remaining know who she is and give her room to pass.

As she walks out of the house of death into the sullen night air, she suddenly is sure that, because of the difference in time, if she could get to the place where he'd collapsed the night before, she could catch the event before it happened and prevent his death. This is ridiculous, she knows that, but still she hails a taxi and rushes to the apartment where he'd been staying. Running up the stairs, she sees the scratches on the walls from the gurney. The door is open, the apartment is empty. Teacups are overturned on the coffee table, all the furniture has been pushed aside.

She wanders around dazed, trying to take it all in, the signs of struggle and the smells of calamity, of panic and haste and futility. Eventually she finds herself in his bedroom and notices his belongings neatly stacked in a pile, as if he'd been getting ready to pack for his early flight the next morning. A cordless phone lies on the covers, its battery is dead.

There is an open notebook lying on his pillow. She sits on the bed and picks it up. The handwriting does not belong to Max. It is a journal written by someone else.

She begins to read:

> The world of the Dagara includes the spirit world of the community ancestors, people who have left this plane of being but who continue to exist without their recognizable form. The dead are not dead, but alive in different ways. There is an energetic thread linking us through time to countless other souls. In the contemporary world outside indigenous cultures, our problems exist because we've stopped paying attention to this thread. Our conservative world does not recognize this kind of awakening—call it "spiritual" if you want—so when a person here finds his psyche expanding and his heart and soul taking over the job of thinking from his mind, he is thought to be truly weird. This kind of weird isn't a bad thing. According to Dagara wisdom, we become born because we have a project to carry out, one that is approved by our ancestors in our mother's womb. The project is not negotiable.

She puts the paper down and rubs her eyes. Her exhausted mind closes over an old recurring dream where she lay like this on a bed like this, and people lined up to bid Max good-bye. To shake it off, she forces herself to repeat the details of the last two days. She'd taken him to the airport. They'd sat in the car holding hands, and then he was gone. What happened to him after that, she can only know through the generosity of others.

Slowly, she learns that he'd spent ten days at the Bly conference devoted to a reenactment of a Dagara funeral. Then he'd been driven down to San Francisco to teach his last class. He'd taught it. After class, he'd come back to his apartment with friends and sat in the living room talking until he wasn't talking anymore. He had a cardiac arrest. He was in a coma. A student from Burlington attending the seminar had tracked her down.

She picks up the notes and continues reading.

> The shaman created a ritual to help the dead people reunite with their long dead ancestors. He created a funeral, and the American men at the Conference created a river, because in the ritual you crossed over from one side to the other, into the underworld, walking the thread lines that connect us with everyone who has come before, bringing with you messages written on pieces of paper. The shaman knew how to speak to our longing and fear of the spiritual plunge, and he cared deeply about curing our culture, not in the least because of the way Christianity was poisoning his own culture with its load of consumerism. Instill in Africans that success meant to own and have things, ensure that only Christians could obtain things: what better reason to convert? Pity poor Africa for its

pagan, uneducated ways: pity its poverty. How ironic for Africa to see itself as able, if not particularly willing, to save Christianity from spiritual death.

Now she gets up and empties out the half-packed duffel bag. She removes the clothes she's been wearing for two days and puts on one of his T-shirts. It smells just enough of him, milky and sweet. She holds his pillow tight between her legs. Now she reaches over to plug in the breathing machine that sits next to the mattress, next to the black case he would have used to carry it with him on the plane the next morning when he flew back home, to Burlington, to her. She puts the mask over her nostrils and lies there breathing for him. She tightens her knees against the pillow and goes back to her reading.

> Max Diebenkorn, the aikido teacher from Vermont, acted as though the ritual was just for him. He followed all the shaman's directions, criss-crossing the river from life to death, carrying message after message, as if expecting to encounter his death at any moment. There is a kind of radiance about him. Several times he collapsed; once on the lid of a casket. His enthusiasm was catching; the moaners were really moaning, the drummers pounding, the dancers frenzied. everyone walloping away to egg on spiritual evolution. Unless the spirit moves on, the community can't move forward. I felt this guy, whom I'd never met, was ready to sacrifice himself happily for my own well-being.

The full magnitude of his actions finally hit her. She lies still, marveling at the enormity of his will. Somehow his body had held up after he'd taught his last class so he could fulfill his mission project, as best he could. Somehow he had protected her from the minutiae of his dying by collapsing 3,000 miles away. And even then he'd managed to postpone his death, so she could be with him.

She puts down the notes, too stunned to cry. She falls asleep, but only for ten minutes. Her eyes open, she sees a tape recorder on the floor. She reaches for it and turns it on. It takes a moment to recognize the poetry of Jalal ad-Din Rumi, read by someone unfamiliar. *Let the lover be disgraceful, crazy, absentminded. Someone sober will worry about events going badly. Let the lover be.*

Her body folds itself in the same position she'd seen Max lying in, twisted on his side with one leg tucked under the other. She sees him clearly, on the other side of the city, on the seventh floor of San Francisco General Hospital, he is not her, but right now, she is him.

Lena throws the tape recorder across the room. She has to get back to the hospital. What if he's woken up? Of course he's woken up. He's waiting for her. She stands up and rips off the T-shirt, puts on her own dirty clothes, and leaves the apartment.

Namo amitabhaya

Samaya tistuam

Please accept drinking water, flowers, incense, light, perfume, food, and music.

I praise your magnificent wisdom and power.

Norbu Tendzen looks at her. She nods. *The Tibetans know about death. Follow their instructions.* A nun sits silently in the corner by the window working beads. Soon the room again fills with people, most gaining entrance by purporting to be a brother or sister or wife. So many wives.

What were the three names Max had urged her to remember?

The first name was Norbu. This name she knows well.

The second was that of the Dagara shaman. This name is familiar now.

The third was a name she'd never heard before, Garret Hilton.

Garret Hilton stands at the far side of the bed waiting to get her attention. He is the sensei of the dojo where Max taught his last class. When Lena looks up, he proposes they take Max out of the hospital and bring him to his home to die. For a moment, she hesitates, for she knows Max wishes to die in North Hero. For a few minutes, they debate whether or not this meant they'd have to find a pilot and fly him home, and decide that he probably wouldn't make it there. No, Lena decides, it doesn't matter where his soul releases. Her obligation is with the ashes.

Immediately, everyone gets into action, consulting, faxing documents, running after doctors; and soon permission is granted for a discharge. Heads are bowed in silence as the nurse slips Max away from his life support. He's on his own now, his soul flooding the room.

Norbu resumes chanting:

> You can liberate all sentient beings with one glance of your prajna *and* upaya.
>
> I request you to liberate the sentient beings who have passed and departed from their physical lives.
>
> May they be released from their samsaric fetters and attain liberation at once.

If not so, may they attain a good human birth, which is free and well-favored.

If that is not possible, may they be freed from the lower realms.

She must have fallen asleep, because the next thing she knows, she's in the chair by the window and the room is empty. She's been jolted awake by her pounding heart, nauseated stomach, throbbing head; and something else. Max lies on his side facing her with his eyes open. She has the distinct impression that he's shoving something into her brain, and it's not pleasant. She sees a letter, a giant three-dimensional block letter sliding in from the right and being pushed from behind by more letters. These spell out the name of his son. The voice of God roars through her cells, *Get Me My Son!* She leaps up and flies out of the room, staggers over to the nurses' station, and grabs the telephone. "He's loose," a nurse standing behind her says. "It happens all the time. We don't go in the room when they get loose." Lena nods. After speaking to his son, she walks shakily back to the room. The energy is normal now. A nurse stands over Max, adjusting the monitors. He lies in the same position, his eyes now shut. Again Lena sits in the chair, again she falls asleep, again she's awakened abruptly, again his eyes are open, again the air turns putrid. This time, an entire landscape pushes into her mind. There are mountains and a lake and thick white clouds racing through a stormy sky. Below them, water and whitecaps. It's the view seen through the windows of their cabin. In the second it takes her to process this information, the storm becomes violent and her head again threatens to explode. "Take it easy, big boy!" she calls out. Immediately, her mind empties. The room is normal. She knows what he wants. He insists she get him to North Hero. The question is, dead or alive? She asks him. Nothing. The room calms down. The clock resumes ticking, a nurse appears with a glass of water for her. It doesn't matter to him. She goes out and asks Garret Hilton to call for an ambulance.

Max takes his last breath in the ambulance en route to Garret Hilton's home high in the mountains above Tomales Bay. He'd been struggling for some time now, and the medic has orders to race to the nearest hospital unless he starts breathing on his own. Why? Because it's the law, and the law will supersede any directives she carries folded in her purse. Unbuckling her seat belt, she moves Max's head on her lap. The medic, Mike, tells her to put her belt back on, but she ignores him.

The driver, whose name is Freda, lets out a muffled curse because she's suddenly realized she's been reading the map Garret gave her turned upside-down. They've made a wrong turn off Sir Francis Drake and are climbing over to Stinson Beach instead of the heading the other way, to Point Reyes. Mike again tells Lena to put on her seat belt, this time it's an order. Again Lena refuses.

Max's daughter has taken her father's hand. For ten minutes everything's literally tossed up in the air. The law insisted that should the dying man appear to expire, he be rushed to the nearest hospital, while the document now in Lena's hand provides her with the authority to ensure that he not be resuscitated in any case. The medic, Mike, is well-trained and has his orders. Every time Max stops breathing, he jumps up and tries to insert the breathing tube. The gesture seems cruel, harsh, painful. Lena says, "Leave him be." She tells him to sit down. Her voice is calm and confident. He sits. He leaves Max be.

Freda whips the ambulance around on the scary incline and has them headed back toward Olema, where a throng of people await them. Lena's dreading the inevitable circus, the lack of privacy. After all, sharing his dying is all she has left of him. After this, his world can take over. She hooks eyes with Max's daughter and sees in them the same terrible plea, her daddy is dying, hers alone. So Lena turns her gaze on the medic and tells him to follow his heart. By this she means, to break the law for a larger law and let Max go. Do not subject him to another hospital.

He nods unhappily, resigning his authority, and sits back looking stunned. The two women move quickly and bow their bodies low over Max, taking him into their care.

Freda drives slowly up the long, winding driveway, parks off to the side of the house behind a small grove of fruit trees, and cuts the engine. At the house, a small group stands quietly next to an altar laid out on the deck while others mill around the wide lawn, or lie on the grass, or go off in the woods down the shaded paths. No one spots the ambulance. A long moment goes by.

Max takes one more breath, then stops. One more. Stops. Then his eyes open wide. Tears pool at his lids, then fall slowly down his skin. Then he gasps as if he has seen something amazing, and then he dies.

The ambulance starts up again and slowly turns and stops at the front door of the house. The doors slide open. Lena feels the gurney moving, feels Max sliding away, and she falls out of the ambulance into Norbu's arms.

She gives Max over then to the waiting drummers, the cooks, the archers, the poets, the men, the lovers, the dog, the singers; all his people. She finds a seat at the edge of the garden. It is so beautiful and peaceful here, she feels immensely grateful to his friends, even as she wills them all to disappear. She watches as he is brought out on the deck, laid out on a futon covered with blue sheets embroidered with little white moons and stars, as he's washed and prayed over and dressed in his *gi* and his *hakama*. There is a continual line of people arriving with flowers, kids, dogs, food, and gifts for the altar. When the time comes, close to evening, Norbu conducts a ceremony spoken in a language no one understands.

That evening, Lena lies down on her own mattress covered with blue sheets, her hair in the stars, her head on her dead lover's shoulder. He is so still, lying so clean and beautifully dressed, under the darkening sky. She feels she's guarding a bone, that's how thin he has become, one exquisitely gleaming bone. Above her the hawks plane on the wind currents in circles. Night comes on and she hears the house settle down. Every so often someone appears silhouetted in the moonlight looking down at the body. She hears fits of crying and laughter, she hears conversation and dogs barking, she smells flowers and cooking food and often the voice of a solitary singer swaying somewhere at the base of the woods. At some point she lifts her head and sees she's not the only sleeper on the deck; Max's son is there, curled up at his feet. His daughter lies across from her, her hand on her father's chest.

Nothing has changed, she knows this. Everything will go on. There will be seals and dolphins and songbirds, births, deaths, and boredom, hopes and failures and suffering. In the morning, someone will come and take what has become *the body* and bring her back a tin of warm ashes. In the afternoon, a procession will take the ashes to a site overlooking the delta where the ocean comes into the land, where they will join hundreds of other mourners and celebrants—they are one and the same out here in Tomales Bay, where the land is attached to the plate of Japan and moves with it away from the rest of North America.

They will mill around an ad hoc altar filling up with photographs, stones, feathers, bits of clothing, food, and lit candles, greeting each other, telling stories, and sharing anecdotes. Children will chase their dogs around the dunes and one will fall out of a tree and get up, unhurt. People will group and regroup, hug and converse, argue and weep. They will quote Rilke ("You must change your life!"), Yeats, Philip Larkin, Robert Bly, Nietzsche, Bertrand Russell, and Thich Nhat Hanh. Some will read their own poems, others will practice t'ai chi, a beautiful woman will open her arms and howl to the racing wind. Two more beautiful women will sing. The drummers will keep the rhythm on their three-foot drums, archers will flank the path. A famous calligrapher will create a scroll on the spot.

Many will tell stories of how once Max intimidated them, but how they came to love him. Several will say they became lesbians because of him. Three people will have already experienced visitations: one will have dreamed of handing him a map for his journey, another will have shot out of sleep when all the mirrors fell off her walls, and the third will speak of finding him standing on her deck looking through the sliding glass doors. At the end of the day, a lawyer from New York will stand up and suggest that if Max was listening to all this flattery, he'd be really pissed off. Everyone laughs. But so what, the guy goes on to say, we're going to do it anyway. At the end, they join in a spiral dance led by a dancer and in this way meet each other's eyes.

Namaste, they tell each other, safe journey.

She sees herself flying back to Vermont with the box on her lap. Jocelyn and Marianne will be there to drive her home. At home, too, a crowd has gathered, another ceremony has begun. Norbu will be with her, an altar will be rise under the Weeping Willow tree she'd given him as a birthday gift seven years ago. The East Coast students will stand in their *gis* to tell their stories. An old Episcopalian woman will spontaneously sing "Amazing Grace." And when night comes Zia will refuse to move from the altar, so Lena will spend the night beside her on the grass.

She sees herself, finally alone, lying in the cornfield across from her house, dreaming she and Max are flying together over Lake Champlain, swooping and planing in the wind currents, singing songs and having a fine old time. Max wears his big black bearskin coat, and she wears nothing at all. Ice covers the thick black lake. In the center a river flows free toward Canada.

"Dreamus interruptus," she hears him cry out. *"Perfect!"*

Acknowledgments

To my editors Barbara Mendes, Jane Pincus, Richard Marek, Philip Smith.

To all the aikido friends who shared their stories, especially Nancy Bertleson, Kini Collins, Shari Dyer, David Gamble, Sandy Jacobs, Ed Pincus, Rhiannon, David Rotman, Kaz Tanahashi, and Jan Watson.

To Robert Ostermeyer for everything.

To Michael Gruber, who thinks I'm Colette.

To Richard Grossinger and North Atlantic Books for crossing all these genres.

To Terry Dobson, for being the best cowriter one could wish for.

To Robert Bly, for being himself; and his tribe of poets, teachers, and healers.

Zia